SHADOWS OF THE DEEP

David Evans

LOUDHAILER BOOKS

This first edition published in 2024 by:

Loudhailer Books
13 Lyminster Avenue
Brighton
BN1 8JL

www.loudhailerbooks.com

contents

In the world of Robert Ford and Samantha Gooding, the contrasts between their backgrounds were not just a matter of wealth but also of experience. Robert, born into a family of affluence and privilege, had grown up surrounded by opulence. The Ford family estate was a sprawling mansion nestled amidst manicured gardens and rolling acres of land. It was a place where old money spoke volumes, and tradition was deeply ingrained.

From a young age, Robert had been groomed to take on the mantle of the Ford legacy. His father, Conrad Ford, had ensured that Robert received the finest education money could buy. He had attended prestigious schools and eventually Yale University, where he studied business and economics. But despite the privilege that came with his lineage, Robert had always yearned for a taste of adventure beyond the confines of boardrooms and corporate meetings.

Samantha, on the other hand, hailed from a world that was far removed from the polished halls of the Ford estate. Growing up in the bustling streets of Brooklyn, she had learned the value of hard work and determination from a young age. Her parents, both first-generation immigrants, had instilled in her the importance of education and the pursuit of her dreams.

After leaving college with a diploma in computer technology, Samantha had embarked on a career that seemed promising, but quickly proved unfulfilling. Her brief stint as a computer programmer in Hell's Kitchen had left her craving more than the monotony of office life.

Buoyed by her initial success, Samantha had cast a wider net, creating a women's support site that covered an array of topics. She had even ventured into the world of beauty and makeup, using her own experiences and learnings to create tutorials that resonated with her audience. In a few short years, Samantha had built an empire, employing a diverse team of talented individuals with varying levels of education, including a couple of PhDs.

It was Samantha's drive, determination, and unwavering belief in herself that had drawn the attention of the wealthy and charming Robert Ford. The two had crossed paths in the bustling city of Seattle, where Samantha had set up her headquarters. It was a city that symbolized her journey from humble beginnings to remarkable success.

Their love story had blossomed amidst the backdrop of the Pacific Northwest, where rugged landscapes met the vibrant energy of the city. Samantha's beauty, intelligence, and confidence had captivated Robert, who, despite his privileged background, found in her a sense of authenticity and adventure that had been missing from his life.

As they set sail on the Barracuda, their journey represented not only a voyage of exploration but also a merging of two worlds. Robert sought to share his world of luxury and tradition with Samantha, while Samantha, in turn, brought her entrepreneurial spirit and determination to the relationship. Little did they know that the adventure they had embarked upon would test their love and resilience in ways they could never have imagined.

Generations of Ford family members had upheld the legacy of Armitech, a name synonymous with weapons and arms. Conrad Ford's father had expanded the business to encompass cutting-edge research and development of new weaponry. Under Conrad's leadership, Armitech had soared to new heights, with substantial investments in weapon research and a global expansion of its market.

Conrad had taken a bold step to secure full ownership of the company by buying out the shareholders his father had relied on during expansion. For over two decades, Armitech had held a coveted position as one of the American government's preferred weapons and arms suppliers. However, Conrad faced a moral dilemma inherited from his great-great-grandfather: the inclination towards double-dealing. Regardless of creed, race, or political persuasion, Conrad was known as an equal-opportunity weapon supplier, selling arms to anyone who could afford to pay.

In contrast to the complexities of the arms industry, Robert Ford, at the tender age of twenty-three, enjoyed a life of privilege and affluence. Educated with a trust fund that dwarfed the lifetime earnings of most bankers, Robert had begrudgingly completed the exams and internships expected of him. He possessed ample wealth, allowing him the luxury of never having to lift a finger for financial gain. In his eyes, the years spent studying had seemed unnecessary, given that he could have secured a seat on the company's board regardless of his educational accomplishments.

Throughout Robert's life, his mother, Emilia Conrad, had resorted to gifts and promises as a means to manipulate him into following his father's wishes. For their engagement, Emilia had bestowed upon Robert and Samantha an extravagant gift—a five-star trip around the southern hemisphere. This voyage encompassed four months of sailing the world's oceans before Robert would assume his role on the company's board. However, there was a clandestine element to this journey, as Conrad Ford had entrusted Robert with a parcel that remained undeclared to Customs. Utilizing Armitech's private jet offered them a cloak of reduced scrutiny compared to commercial airlines. Before setting sail, Robert discreetly delivered this mysterious package to the captain of a small freight ship named Lotus Leaf, seamlessly blending business with pleasure.

Their journey thus far had been a wondrous exploration for the deeply enamoured couple. They had revelled in a few spirited evenings at Clarke Quay, explored the Singapore Zoo under the stars during a night-time safari, and sought thrills at Universal Studios on Sentosa Island. All of this was but a prelude to the grand adventure that awaited them.

Their voyage led them to the Indonesian islands, where they immersed themselves in the local culture and replenished their supplies of fuel. Yet the pinnacle of their journey was anchored in the archipelago of the Lesser Sunda Islands, where they beheld the awe-inspiring Komodo dragons in their natural habitat—an island named after these colossal lizards, the largest on Earth.

As the yacht sliced through the tranquil sea, Robert beckoned Samantha to join him. The spray of the sea breeze offered respite from the sun's warmth, and Samantha, adorned in a vibrant lime-green bikini, stood tall to witness a remarkable sight. A playful pod of dolphins frolicked in the wake of the boat, their sleek bodies dancing in the sea's embrace.

Curiosity piqued, Samantha turned to Robert and enquired about their current location. Amidst the spectacle of the dolphins, she couldn't help but wonder about their destination. Robert's response came amidst the intermittent noise of the yacht's motor, a reminder of their journey's soundtrack.

"We've just entered the Badung Strait, off the Indonesian island of Bali," Robert answered, a hint of excitement in his voice. "We'll anchor off the coast, as the maritime information advised against night-time docking in Bali's international marina."

Samantha's enthusiasm remained undiminished as she shouted back, "So, dinner on board again tonight?"

Robert grinned, his love for Samantha evident in his eyes. "Apologies, Sam," he called out over the motor's noise. "Tonight, it'll be my turn to play chef. I'll be cooking up some Aberdeen Angus steaks and lobster tails. The channel approach is tricky here, and those navigation lights aren't the brightest. We'll wait for a slack tide tomorrow when the waters are less turbulent."

As the sun cast its golden hues across the sea, painting a serene backdrop for their journey, Robert and Samantha eagerly anticipated their next adventure in a land of beauty and mystery. Unbeknownst to them, the tides of fate were about to turn, and their idyllic voyage would soon face challenges they could never have foreseen.

The turquoise waters of the Indian Ocean stretched out before them, glistening under the radiant sun, as Robert Ford and Samantha Gooding sailed deeper into their voyage. The journey aboard the Barracuda had been nothing short of enchanting, a tapestry of experiences woven with the threads of love, adventure, and the promise of the unknown.

The Barracuda, with its sleek, pure white hull adorned by a silver streak, was a vessel of luxury and elegance. Its three opulent cabins on the lower decks were a sanctuary of comfort and indulgence. Each cabin boasted double-sized beds swathed in sumptuous, sparkling white high-end cotton duvets and satin scatter cushions. Above the cabins lay an open-air leisure deck, a pristine haven featuring a curved, soft white leather couch and an ornate side table, reminiscent of a seven-star hotel. A veranda, positioned just outside the lounge, served as the barbecue and dining area, its stylish furniture harmonizing flawlessly with the vivid colour of the hull. From this vantage point, a mere eight steps led down to a gently curving platform that served as a springboard into the inviting warmth of the sea.

Robert, at the helm on the open-top deck, took in the breathtaking vista around him. A fridge nearby held his favourite Tiger beers, while bottles of eight-year-old French Chablis awaited Samantha's palate. The love they shared was palpable, and Robert was determined to make every moment of this journey memorable for the woman he adored.

Robert's connection to the sea ran deep, a respite from the responsibilities that came with his family's wealth and legacy. The Ford family had a long history dating back to the American Civil War when Robert's great-great-grandfather, Alfred Ford, had established himself as an arms manufacturer in 1861. The Fords had supplied weaponry to both the North and the South during those tumultuous times, selling repeating carbines and revolver pistols to the highest bidders. It was a legacy that had shaped Robert's life, leading him to attend Yale and ultimately secure a seat on the board of Armitech, the family-owned company.

Armitech had evolved over the generations. Conrad Ford, Robert's father, had expanded the business into research and development of cutting-edge weapons, catapulting it to new heights. Under Conrad's leadership, and beneath the veneer of success, there lingered a moral dilemma inherited from generations past— readiness to trade arms with any possessing the resources, irrespective of their belief system, ethnicity, or political connections.

In contrast to the weight of legacy that burdened Robert, Samantha was a beacon of fresh perspective. Hailing from Brooklyn, New York, her journey had been a testament to her determination and ingenuity.

Her entrepreneurial spirit had led her to create a unique niche in the digital landscape. Starting with an advisory website for pet rabbit owners, she had stumbled upon a thriving online business model. Samantha's innate talent for research, combined with her relentless drive, had resulted in monthly deposits of over $200,000 into her bank account. It was a taste of success that fuelled her ambitions.

She had expanded her digital empire further by creating a women's support site, offering guidance on a wide array of topics. Samantha's charisma and knack for teaching had prompted her to delve into the world of beauty, where she had taken makeup courses and shared her expertise through captivating tutorials. It was

Samantha's meteoric rise that had captured Robert's attention. Her beauty, intelligence, and entrepreneurial prowess had drawn him in, and their relationship had blossomed against the backdrop of Seattle, a city that symbolized Samantha's journey from humble beginnings to remarkable success.

As they ventured forth on their grand voyage, their shared experiences had become the fabric of their love story.

But the true magic had unfolded as they explored the Indonesian islands. Here, amidst the rich tapestry of cultures, they had gathered provisions and immersed themselves in the beauty of the archipelago of the Lesser Sunda Islands. It was here, in this remote and untamed paradise, that they had marvelled at the ancient giants of the animal kingdom—the Komodo dragons, massive creatures that had roamed the earth for centuries.

As they sailed further into the Badung Strait, the allure of Bali beckoned. Samantha, her lime-green bikini a vibrant contrast to the sun-kissed sea, stood tall on the yacht's deck. Her SPF 50 sunscreen ensured her fair skin remained untouched by the sun's harsh rays. With a pod of dolphins playing in the boat's wake, she couldn't contain her excitement.

"Where are we now, Robert?" Samantha asked, her eyes sparkling with wonder.

Robert, enjoying the sight of the dolphins, couldn't have been happier. "We've just entered the Badung Strait, off the Indonesian island of Bali," he replied, his voice carrying the thrill of anticipation. "We'll anchor off the coast, as the maritime information advised against night-time docking in Bali's international marina."

Their laughter and joy echoed across the sea as they continued their journey into the unknown. Samantha's question about dinner was met with a promise of culinary delights from Robert's capable hands. They sailed through the channel, guided by the dimly lit navigation markers. A tranquil sea beneath them, their love and excitement for the adventures ahead burned brighter than ever.

They had no clue. The trip had started as a perfect getaway, a chance to taste freedom and celebrate love, away from it all. But the world doesn't always go the way you want it. Instead of open skies and smooth sailing, what lay ahead was a detour into a nightmare.

Robert carefully examined the navigational charts, ensuring they were safely positioned away from any shipping or ferry lanes. Content with their location, he decided it was time to anchor the Barracuda. He finished the last of his beer, the bottle momentarily capturing the glint of the setting sun, and then released the anchor overboard, allowing the fluke to bite securely into the seabed. With the anchor set, the yacht would gently rotate around it, a peaceful dance in the tranquil waters.

"Break out the barbecue!" Samantha's voice carried an air of excitement as the day gracefully surrendered to the night. The shoreline's distant lights, mere pinpricks on the horizon, competed with the emerging stars above, casting a magical glow over the scene. Robert, always eager to indulge Samantha's wishes, retrieved the large gas barbecue and griddle from a storage locker on the deck. Meanwhile, Samantha descended into the galley, her mind set on selecting the perfect cuts of steak and lobster tails for their evening meal.

Within minutes, the fragrant scent of sizzling sirloins and paprika-infused lobster tails filled the air, an appetizing prelude to their feast. Samantha, her culinary skills as impressive as her beauty, prepared a refreshing salad while uncorking a bottle of fine red wine. As the deep ruby liquid flowed into a glass, her spirits soared, adding to the sense of joy that seemed to permeate every moment they spent together.

Robert manned the grill with precision, his attention dedicated to achieving the flawless medium-rare finish they loved on their steaks. Around him, the air filled with the hypnotic crackle and smoke, a sensory cloak that hid the silent encroachment of figures they hadn't anticipated. It was the sizzle, that comforting, familiar sound, that doomed them, allowing the intruders to infiltrate undetected until their presence became undeniable and impossible to ignore.

At first, Samantha assumed that Robert had accidentally knocked over the portable barbecue, a possibility she entertained as she heard a muted thud from the deck above the galley. Concerned about her dinner, she shouted up the narrow stairwell, "That had better not be my dinner on the deck!" When Robert's response didn't come, she worried that perhaps the sizzle of the steaks had drowned out her voice.

The soft melody of Samantha's humming was snatched away by the night wind as she emerged onto the deck, the salad bowl she carried now an afterthought. The scene before her yanked the comfort from under her feet. The serenity of the evening shattered, giving way to a pulse of fear that throbbed through the silence. Robert was gone, erased from the setting where he should've been, his absence a silent scream in her ears.

In his place, the deck had turned into a stage for an insidious pantomime. Four figures, shadow-drenched and dripping, were hunched in 'kambens', the traditional cloth sticking to their skins, betraying the contours of muscles and sinews underneath. The yacht's gentle lighting cast an ominous glow, highlighting the strangers' features in haunting clarity—local men, by their looks, but their eyes didn't carry the familiar warmth of island hospitality.

Samantha's heart pounded a brutal, frantic rhythm. The air was thick, charged with a foreboding that constricted her chest. The quiet surrounding them was deceptive, a predator lying in wait. These intruders, these harbingers of unknown intentions, had breached their haven of solitude.

There was no sign of struggle, no indication of where Robert might be, and the questions burned in her throat. But it was the not knowing, the haunting uncertainty, that had her blood running cold. Samantha knew the unspoken rules of this deadly game were about to unfold. Alone, cut off from the world on this drifting piece of steel and opulence, survival instincts kicked in. She held her breath, bracing for the storm of violence she felt certain was about to erupt.

Two of the intruders sat casually on the pristine white leather bench, helping themselves to Robert's stash of Tiger beer, while the other two held a rope over the side of the yacht, lifting and lowering it as if engaged in an odd form of fishing. Samantha's hands trembled, causing her to drop the salad bowl and utensils. Fear began to gnaw at her, its icy fingers wrapping around her heart.

"What do you want? Where is Robert?" Samantha's voice faltered, her voice a mixture of anger and fear as she confronted the inexplicable situation before her.

The four men fixated their gaze on her, their intentions as unclear as the dark waters surrounding the yacht. One of them, still gripping the rope, licked his lips hungrily, while another's gaze shamelessly travelled from her toes to her head, his eyes devouring every inch of her body. One of the seated men rose, his eyes locked onto Samantha's breasts, as he casually bent down to pick up a tomato from the scattered salad, consuming it with unsettling lasciviousness. The remaining intruder stayed seated, disturbingly occupied with the ritualistic handling of his own anatomy.

Samantha had experienced her fair share of leering glances from men throughout her life, but this situation was unlike anything she had ever encountered. She had always prepared herself mentally for the possibility of an attack, wondering if she would choose to fight or flee. Yet she had not anticipated the overwhelming terror that now gripped her, leaving her legs and hands trembling and her stomach churning with dread. Trapped between fear and the vast, unforgiving sea, Samantha found herself in a nightmare from which there seemed to be no escape.

The deck of the Barracuda was in disarray, with lettuce, cucumber, tomatoes, and dill scattered haphazardly across the pristine surface. Samantha's eyes darted wildly, searching for any sign of Robert, but he remained conspicuously absent.

Mang, seated next to the gang's leader, Mayan, continued to indulge in his perverse actions, a sinister grin playing on his face.

"Where… where is Robert?" Samantha's voice trembled, her fear intensifying with each passing moment as her mind conjured the worst possibilities.

Mayan, the menacing leader of this group, nonchalantly devoured a tomato, its seeds dribbling down his chin as he turned his attention to his two younger brothers positioned at the end of the rope.

"The bitch wants to see her man. Show her," Mayan ordered, his voice dripping with malevolence.

With a slow and deliberate effort, the two men at the end of the rope began to pull. Robert's lifeless body swayed precariously from side to side, droplets of water cascading down from his drenched form. With one final tug, they hoisted the catch at the end of the rope onto the deck of the opulent yacht. Mayan savoured the look of shock and terror that was etched across Samantha's face like a cruel masterpiece.

Samantha, her world unravelling before her eyes, staggered toward Robert's motionless body. Her legs betrayed her, buckling beneath the weight of her despair, and she felt the warmth of urine trickling down her trembling thighs. The dread that had gripped her from the moment of Robert's disappearance now intensified, leaving her disoriented and trembling. She clung to the handrail for support, feeling utterly helpless and vulnerable, caught in the hungry gaze of her attacker.

Robert lay before her, eyes wide and lifeless. Mang, one of Mayan's henchmen, shifted his attention from Robert's body to the rivulet of water forming as Samantha's fear-induced response mingled with the seawater dripping from Robert's form.

The cushions from the bench, where Samantha and Robert had made love just an hour earlier, were now strapped to Robert's legs with a tightly bound rope, rendering him completely immobile. Samantha, kneeling beside her boyfriend's lifeless body, found herself the target of Mang's lecherous gaze. His eyes never ventured above her neckline.

"Can't leave any marks, must look like he drowned," Mayan declared coldly, his piercing eyes locked onto Samantha, sending shivers down her spine.

Mayan, compact in stature but exuding an aura of menace, stood at just five foot four. His well-defined muscles were a tribute to his rigorous fitness regimen, and his brown, sun-kissed skin bore the creases of a life exposed to the elements. Mayan possessed a distinctive countenance, the kind that demanded a second look, but it was his eyes, cold and unrelenting as they bore into Samantha, that struck terror into her very soul.

Samantha felt herself spiralling into a dark abyss, her mind racing to comprehend the dire situation she found herself in. She convulsed, her body trembling uncontrollably, yet her mind remained sharp, calculating the perilous predicament she was trapped in. The menacing men began to circle her like vultures, their intentions all too clear.

She had seen what they had done to Robert, and their faces were etched in her memory. Escape from this yacht seemed impossible, and Samantha's intuition told her that death loomed. However, she was resolute—she would not allow herself to be abused and violated by these monsters.

Mayan and his two brothers seemed intent on using her body as their playground before condemning her to the depths of the ocean. In a fleeting moment of clarity, Samantha contemplated jumping overboard, but her legs refused to cooperate. She refused to become their helpless prisoner, their pawn in this nightmarish game. The same logical mind that had propelled her to success in the business world began to emerge from the shadow of fear, and Samantha resolved that if she was to meet her end, it would be on her terms.

"Can I go second after you?" pleaded Tut, the younger brother, to his older sibling, revealing the depths of their sinister intentions.

"You are third born, so you will take your turn accordingly. Once I have had my fill, if Mang can leave his balls alone, he will be next and you, Tut, can have the leftovers." Mayan's word was final.

"What about DNA?" Mang said.

"You are learning at last, brother. No penetration without a condom, and we will run her under the propeller when we are finished to disguise the odd tear she may suffer."

Samantha shuffled backward away from the pack of leering men. They assumed it was fright, but it was not. Samantha caught sight of the dropped steak knife near the galley hatch and edged toward it on her backside. She grabbed the serrated blade and waved the knife from side to side in Mayan's direction.

The three brothers laughed. Mayan spoke first.

"She wants to circumcise you, Tut. You'll have no dick left when she has finished," Mayan said.

Tut pulled out an Beretta 92 FS Brigadier pistol and pointed it at her.

"What are you going to do with that little piece of metal against this?" spat out Tut, hurt at his brother's comments.

"Take your pick, bitch. What do you want to do? Suck Mayan's cock or the pistol?" Mang said mockingly.

Samantha's heart raced as she clutched the knife, her mind racing for a way out of this nightmare. She knew she couldn't take them all on, but she refused to become a helpless victim. The yacht's deck seemed to shrink around her as the menacing men closed in, their cruel laughter echoing in her ears. She had to make a stand, fight for her life, and hope that somehow, she could escape this living nightmare.

"Spirit, I like spirit. See if you still have any left by the time Tut gets what's left over, bitch," Mayan responded, knowingly.

"You want to make this look like an accident, probably so you can steal the boat. You killed Robert to make it look like he drowned when the boat supposedly went down without a trace. You are going to do the same to me, aren't you?" Samantha's voice quivered with a mix of fear and defiance.

"Right on the nail, Mayan's voice was a serrated whisper, grating through the tension. "Your man? He slipped through easy. But you, sweetheart… You won't be that lucky." His eyes, cold slits of malice, stayed locked on hers as he closed the distance, each step a pronounced verdict of impending doom.

Samantha's hand trembled, the knife she wielded a scant shield against the darkness that rolled off him in waves. It was more than a threat; it was a guarantee of a nightmare yet to unfold, an unspoken promise that whatever had happened to Robert was mercy compared to the hell that awaited her.

In the electric silence, her heart was a riot, thrashing against her ribs, demanding escape from the inevitable. The blade in her hand might as well have been a toothpick against a tank, but it was all she had. As Mayan prowled closer, the air between them tightened, coiling with the intimacy of predator and prey locked in their final, fatal dance.

Then, in a surge of desperate reckoning, Samantha's survival instincts screamed into high gear. With a reflex as raw as it was ruthless, she jabbed the knife downward, embedding it into her own leg. Pain exploded, bright and blinding, a white-hot flare in the encroaching darkness. It was a wild card thrown onto the table, a drastic gamble to destabilize him, to inject uncertainty into his sadistic confidence.

In that shard of time, speared by her own blade, Samantha carved out an altogether different scenario than that Mayan had planned. Samantha had reached the breaking point, her survival instincts kicking into overdrive. With swift determination, she drew the serrated blade across the whole width of her thigh, just below the bottom of her bikini. Samantha severed her femoral artery instantly. The skin split and then peeled back, revealing a horrific scene beneath. Samantha's flawless white skin was now akin to a piece of meat on a butcher's slab, and her world was drenched in red. fluid, like a cheap 1970s nail varnish.

As she screamed and cried in pain, her life fluid burst out like an erupting volcano for the first minute. It was apparent she was fading fast. The red slick spread, staining the highly polished deck as it expanded like a sinister tableau of violence. Mayan and his two brothers, their sadistic intentions shattered, instinctively backed away from the gruesome spectacle. The sight and smell of blood filled the air, overwhelming their senses.

Then, as Samantha's severed artery contracted, the flow became sluggish and then decreased to a trickle. Her body went limp, and her eyes rolled to the back of their sockets, exposing only the white. Samantha made one last guttural sound, a haunting echo of her struggle, before passing from life into a piece of evidence on the yacht's once pristine deck.

"What about the bodies?" Mang enquired, without moving his eyes away from Samantha, the reality of their actions sinking in.

"Bitch!" Mayan muttered under his breath; his bravado now replaced by a chilling awareness of the consequences. "Clean this mess up, Tut, we have to deliver this boat by morning."

Mayan paused, his eyes fixated on Samantha's lifeless form, which edged ever closer to his white shoes. He knew they couldn't afford to leave any traces of their gruesome act behind. But even in the midst of this macabre situation, Mang's twisted desires remained intact.

"She's still warm," Mang said with a wicked grin. "Maybe we could still have some fun."

The words hung in the air like a sickening reminder that the horror was far from over.

chapter two
Twisted Path

A month had passed since they had cast Samantha and Robert overboard. Mayan felt a wave of unease wash over him as he observed the man he respectfully referred to as *Kepala*, which means 'boss' in Indonesian, on his closed-circuit television screen. Kasim Asfour, meticulously avoiding the marine equipment and scrap littered across the yard, made his way through the security gate into Mayan's boatyard. Asfour was resplendent in his Armani suit, determined not to let it come into contact with anything that might mar its perfection. Mayan, watching the screen, knew that his day had taken an unexpected and nerve-wracking turn.

Once inside the enclosed workshop, Mayan descended from his mezzanine office to greet Asfour. "Kepala, this is unexpected. If I had known, I would have had Tut meet you at the airport," Mayan admitted, his voice tinged with apprehension.

"Rahajeng semeng," Kasim Asfour replied in Balinese, a traditional Balinese greeting meaning 'Peace be with you.'

"Peace be with you," Mayan reciprocated, switching to English.

After the customary exchange of pleasantries and the acceptance of tea, Mayan and Kasim Asfour retreated to Mayan's office. As per the protocol for every visit from Asfour, Mayan took a moment to erase the CCTV recording of Asfour's entrance into the yard. He then closed the office door, muffling the sounds of the ongoing engineering work below.

Asfour, sitting in one of the office chairs, initiated the conversation. "Mayan, how long have you worked for me?"

Mayan's brow furrowed as he mentally counted the years. "Eh, three, no, four, or is it five years, Kepala?"

"You and your brothers have been compensated quite generously, Mayan. One of your primary responsibilities within my organization is to steal the yachts I instruct you to and ensure that any bodies associated with them vanish without a trace."

Mayan nodded, his apprehension deepening, sensing that he was about to face a stern reprimand.

"So tell me, why have Conrad Ford's son and his fiancée resurfaced, causing us unforeseen complications?" Asfour enquired, his tone measured and precise.

Mayan knew he had to explain, despite the sinking feeling in his gut. "A Japanese trawler, its nets go deep, scraping up anything from the ocean floor. The couple got entangled in the nets."

Asfour's response was stern and unforgiving. "That's no excuse, Mayan. You should have ensured that they were buried so deep in the sea that no net could ever reach them. You were aware that the Fords' son was a special case, and you should have taken extra precautions. To say I am disappointed would be an understatement."

Mayan felt himself squirming under Asfour's intense gaze as the silence hung heavy in the room. He knew, all too well, the gravity of his mistakes. Mayan had a vague understanding of the organization Kasim Asfour worked for—a terrorist organization, he suspected—but he knew nothing of Asfour's specific role within it.

His voice quivering, Mayan began to speak, "I'm sorry, Kepala. My brothers, they're not clever like you and me, and…"

Asfour raised a hand, abruptly cutting Mayan off mid-sentence. "Your apology is insufficient. This is your second blunder in the last six months. First, you accepted the shipment of arms from Armitech, and despite your assurances, we discovered that the new weapon promised to us was missing. We had to pay them twice for the same weapon. They, or rather Conrad Ford, swindled us, and it's your fault."

"Ampura," Mayan repeated his apology, this time in his native Balinese.

"My organization," the voice was as sharp as shards of glass, cold and calculating, "operates on the currency of trust. That's why you were chosen, Mayan. You were dispatched to intercept Conrad Ford's little pleasure cruise, to deliver a message he couldn't ignore. And the universe handed us a gift—his son, right there on that damned yacht."

A pause, heavy with menace, sliced through the room. "But Conrad Ford is now a man robbed of his lineage, mourning a son he'll never see again, all because he tried to play us. Because he thought he could pilfer money he didn't earn and wouldn't be missed."

The figure leaned forward, shadows clinging to his features, concealing a face accustomed to commanding fear and respect. "But revenge," he hissed, the word slithering into the space between them, "is an art. It's about finesse, not force. It's a whisper in the night, not a scream at high noon. It's the chill that settles in your bones, making you wish you could turn back the clock. But what it shouldn't be is a trail of crumbs leading right back to our doorstep."

His glare seared into Mayan; the threat unspoken but hanging in the air like a guillotine. "You turned finesse into folly. You made a spectacle where there should have been shadows. Now, that spectacle hangs around our necks like a noose. It's not just you in the crosshairs—it's me, it's all of us."

The silence that followed was a living entity, a coiled serpent ready to strike. In the game they played, mistakes were paid for in blood, and debts were settled with life. The figure's next words were a final warning, spoken quietly, yet carrying the weight of final judgment.

"You've led this debacle, Mayan, crashing through boundaries you should've tiptoed around. Now, you've got to clean up the mess, or it's not just Conrad Ford who'll be mourning. We don't leave loose ends. We can't afford to." The finality in his tone promised a reckoning, one that Mayan would be wise to heed if he valued his place among the living.

Desperate to make amends, Mayan asked, "What can I do to make it right, Kepala?"

Asfour's posture shifted, every muscle taut and ready. He leaned forward, the slow deliberate movement of a predator eyeing its prey. The indistinct light played shadows over his rugged face, amplifying the dangerous glint in his eyes. "Two things," he murmured, his voice low and raspy, each word dripping with menace.

"First, hand over the package," A pause, thick with tension, as his gaze never wavered, pinning the other man in place. "And second," he continued, his tone even but laden with a threat, "that yacht anchored below, it's the same one, isn't it? The one you took from those American kids., three months ago."

Each word in the air was razor-edged, dangerous, and coiled like a spring ready to unleash. The room was a minefield, electric with the kind of tension that made the air feel heavy, almost liquid. In the scant space between breaths, entire lifetimes of lesser men could be lived and lost. This was no parlour game; this was the high-stakes table, and the currency was survival.

Asfour's eyes didn't flicker, didn't shift from Mayan's face, didn't do anything but bore into him, seeing through the facade to the desperate calculations happening behind the eyes of a cornered man. There was a beat, almost imperceptible, where everything seemed to hang in the balance.

Then, with resignation edged with defiance, Mayan reached under the desk, the slight strain of his muscles the only betrayal of his inner turmoil. The package emerged, deceptively mundane for something so coveted, drenched in Samantha's dried blood.

"Here's the cargo," Mayan grunted, the lines around his mouth hardening. He was not used to be spoken to like this.

The package landed with a soft thud between them, a punctuation in their deadly dialogue. Asfour's eyes, those scrutinizing windows, flickered just once toward the package and then resettled on Mayan, a silent, brooding judgment.

"And the yacht," Asfour's voice scraped the room, a grating reminder of the thin ice beneath Mayan's feet, "that's the Trenches' yacht under new management, am I right?"

A flicker of something, perhaps annoyance, perhaps fear, passed through Mayan's eyes. "Yeah," he spat out, begrudging every syllable, "it's the Trench yacht."

"You will receive no payment for it," Asfour declared, leaving Mayan in no doubt about the consequences of his failures.

"Have you resolved the issue with the security team Conrad Ford sent, as I instructed you to do last week?" Asfour enquired, shifting to another pressing matter.

"Yes, Kepala, we have settled it. We left them dead, deep in the jungle. I have paid off the police superintendent who provided us with information about them," Mayan replied.

Asfour warned with a stern tone, "It's fortunate for you that they disappeared without a trace. Any comeback, and my other sources on the island will bury you and your brothers right alongside them, Mayan."

Mayan, understanding the gravity of the situation, spoke softly, "They will never be found, and the police superintendent has assured us that their disappearance won't be investigated."

Silence descended like a guillotine, sharp and final, severing the tension-filled dialogue as Asfour rose from his chair. In the void of sound, Mayan's errors were almost palpable entities, crowding the air, whispering of betrayals and miscalculations. They clung to him, invisible shackles that were all too heavy for the eye to see but as real as the danger that prowled in Asfour's shadow.

Turning, Asfour moved towards the exit, each step measured and resonant, a countdown to an unspoken ultimatum. He didn't glance back; he didn't need to. His presence had already filled the room, a lingering aura of threat that didn't dissipate with distance.

"Erase the CCTV footage," he commanded without turning, his voice low, the kind of sound you felt in your bones, a dark caress that held within it the icy grip of the grave. "All of it. Without a trace."

He paused at the threshold. "And Mayan," he said, the name a curse, a promise. "Don't disappoint me again. Ford's security detail will seem like naïve schoolboys compared to the hell I'll bring to your doorstep. They'll seem like mercy incarnate."

It wasn't a threat. It was a law of nature, as certain as gravity, as unforgiving as time. With those final words, Asfour stepped into the engulfing darkness beyond the door, leaving behind a cold, treacherous silence that promised nothing but a storm on the horizon. Mayan, alone amidst the echoing quiet, felt the weight of that promise settle in his stomach, a seed of ice that wouldn't thaw, precursor of a reckoning that lurked just out of sight.

****

Kasim Asfour, an imposing figure with an athletic build and the ability to blend in effortlessly, maintained a year-round suntan to aid his shape-shifting persona. Two days after his meeting with Mayan, Asfour arrived in Amman, Jordan, using a Kuwaiti passport under an assumed name. The bustling city of Amman, the fifth most visited Arab city in the world, provided the perfect backdrop for Asfour's veiled activities. Dressed in a traditional ankle-length white cotton shirt called a thawb, he conversed fluently in Arabic with the immigration officials. With a few days' worth of black stubble on his face, he blended seamlessly into the surroundings, appearing as just another Arab businessperson.

Across the street from the Grand Hyatt hotel, Umair Aziz sat in a café with a clear view of the hotel's entrance. Umair Aziz, once known as Richard Hussein, had been born in Snow Hill, Birmingham, United Kingdom. His school years had been marked by bullying and isolation, leaving him with few friends and a deep sense of being an outcast. However, in his final year of school, he had excelled in technology and computer science, achieving two As and demonstrating fluency in French and Spanish. Despite these talents, Aziz struggled with low self-esteem and saw himself as a lone wolf rather than the friendless introvert he had been.

Aziz's life took a dramatic turn when he began attending his local mosque, where guest lecturers often espoused Islamic fundamentalism. Drawn to the rigid ideology and intolerance of opposing views, he finally found companionship among like-minded individuals. For the first time in his life, he formed bonds with others, united by their disdain for Western values. Aziz soon found himself radicalized, and his transformation was complete. The identity of Richard Hussein was left behind, and he embraced his new persona as Umair Aziz, with a new family who shared his extremist beliefs.

Between 2008 and 2010, Aziz underwent training in Al-Qaeda camps in Yemen and Afghanistan. His proficiency in computers and languages quickly set him apart from his peers. Unfortunately, most of the friends who had travelled with him from Britain had perished in raids in Iraq and Afghanistan.

2011, Baghdad, a city that never really slept, always one open eye, wary. Aziz knew it all too well. The dust, the chaos, the uncertainty hanging in the air like the city's ever-present, never-settling smog. But it was on these very streets, amidst the cacophony of survival, that Aziz found his calling. Al-Qaeda saw it in him before he recognized it himself—the keen edge of his charisma, the persuasive poison in his pen. They didn't need to look twice; they knew a natural when they saw one.

They pulled him from anonymity, away from the grunt work on the ground. Aziz wasn't just another foot soldier; he was a weaver of words, a craftsman of conviction. So they set him up with a screen and a keyboard instead of an AK-47, and he understood right then—the keyboard was a trigger, too, in its own sinister way.

From the confines of nondescript rooms that could have been in any city in the world, Aziz started to build an empire of influence. His blogs, his reports, they weren't just texts; they were seductive whispers in the night to those who felt they had no place. Europe's lost, disaffected Muslim youth became his target, a generation teetering on the edge of identity, seeking purpose, belonging, vengeance—whatever fit the hollow spaces inside them.

Aziz didn't sell them war; he sold them significance. He sold them a narrative drenched in the perfume of purpose and brotherhood. And they bought it—every line, every word, every promise of a 'noble' fight.

Then the world's stage shifted. ISIS rose, rabid and brutal, casting a shadow vast and dark across the land. Savage, even in the eyes of the savage. And Aziz adapted, like he always did. With the landscape altered, his orders came anew: Al-Qaeda needed a new mask, a softer guise, a 'moderate' cloak to the uninitiated eye compared to the ISIS butchers.

So Aziz wove that narrative, threading each word with calculated care through his websites, his podcasts—digital sermons consumed voraciously by those hungry for a cause. He didn't just paint Al-Qaeda in softer shades; he swathed them in the very colours of resistance and righteousness, masterfully contrasting them against the stark, bloodied tableau of ISIS.

For years, he played puppeteer to a shadow audience, his screen aglow with the reflection of a war not only fought with drones, bullets, and barbarity—but with stories, promises, and lies. A different kind of battlefield, invisible, intangible, and just as deadly.

Now, Umair Aziz found himself in a privileged position. He was about to meet Kasim Asfour, a high-ranking figure in Al-Qaeda, and discuss a critical matter concerning a Somalian pirate and Al-Shabaab sympathizer he had been in contact with through the dark web. Al-Shabaab, an affiliate of Al-Qaeda, courted ISIS, and Aziz had been tasked with cultivating this contact.

Asfour arrived at suite 119, where two Al-Qaeda security operatives had already conducted a thorough sweep for listening devices. They set up a counter-surveillance device to ensure the utmost secrecy. Aziz arrived a short while later and was subjected to security checks before being escorted into the suite.

"Salam," Aziz greeted Asfour with reverence.

"As-salamu alaykum. Please sit; we have much to discuss. We will converse in your native language to avoid misunderstandings. Although your Arabic is commendable, it is not perfect," Asfour replied.

"As you wish," Aziz agreed, his Birmingham accent revealing his origins. To Asfour, his accent seemed like a blend of various northern English dialects, making it challenging to pinpoint his exact location of origin.

Asfour retrieved a file from his briefcase and opened it. The first document displayed a picture of Aziz in his English school uniform. The following pages contained detailed information, and Asfour perused them in silence for several minutes.

The room was still, almost breathless. Asfour's presence seemed to suck all the air out of it, a vacuum of anticipation. His eyes, hard and unyielding, fixed on Aziz, who sat opposite him, tension running through his veins like poison.

"I and the other leaders have been watching you, Aziz," Asfour began, his voice low, almost a whisper, but it carried through the silence like a gunshot in the night. "Watched you climb the rungs, one bloody step at a time." There was a dangerous kind of pride in his tone, like a general admiring a soldier, not for his humanity, but for the precise way he snuffed it out. "You've got a sharp mind, loyal to the bone. That's rarer than you'd think."

A flicker of recognition ignited something deep within Aziz, a slow burn of pride that expanded, filling the hollow spaces of his existence with a purpose he'd always craved. Asfour. The name wasn't just known; it was legendary. A name whispered in hushed tones in the hidden corners where the disenchanted sought dangerous solace.

Aziz felt the weight of the moment settle on his shoulders, heavy and daunting, but not unwelcome. This was the crucible he'd been seeking, the fire that would either forge him into something fearsome or reduce him to ashes. The air between them crackled, charged with an energy that was almost sacred, a current that bound him to Asfour in a tapestry of unseen threads.

He was aware of whom Asfour meant — those ghostly entities that lingered on the fringes of their movement, the untouchable echelons that orchestrated their symphony of disruption from behind impenetrable curtains. To be a cog in their machine wasn't just an honour; it was a sanctification, a blessing dressed in the vestments of a holy war.

His chest swelled, and in that breath, he tasted the metallic tang of destiny, sharp and undeniable. Aziz knew, with the clarity that comes from fanatical dedication, that he was exactly where he was meant to be. He was no longer just a man. He was a mission, a message, a martyr in waiting. And in that sacred space, under Asfour's penetrating gaze, Aziz was reenergised.

"Now, you're standing on the precipice of something much bigger than you or me. This mission," he paused, the weight of his gaze anchoring Aziz to the spot, "it's not just another mark on the scoreboard. It's the legacy you're going to leave behind. Screw it up, and that's all that you will be known for. Nail it, and you're looking at eternity in paradise."

Every word was a tightly coiled spring, the room charged with an atmosphere of volatile danger. The stakes were clear, and in this deadly game, the wrong move could mean everything.

Asfour leaned in, his voice a hushed growl. "I need your wizardry, Aziz. The digital frontier is where you'll wage this war."

A flicker of fierce determination flashed in Aziz's eyes, a flame ignited by years of unshakable faith and unquestionable allegiance. "I am the blade in your hand," he responded, voice unwavering. "Point me in the direction, and I'll cut through hell, if need be, even if it means carving my way there personally."

Asfour handed Aziz a brown envelope, from which Aziz retrieved two photographs. The first was of a naval merchant officer named Gareth Cummings, and the second depicted Dan Williams, a third officer from the same ship. Aziz glanced at Asfour, waiting for further instructions.

"The first photograph is of Gareth Cummings, the communications officer from the Reef Explorer. The second is Dan Williams, the third officer on the same vessel. The Reef Explorer is scheduled to dock in Sharm El Sheikh in four days. According to my source on the ground, both of these men frequently visits the local market for supplies for the officer's mess. Asfour instructed, sliding the images back into the envelope.

"Next Tuesday, I want one of these men taken from the market," Asfour continued, outlining the mission.

Aziz raised a practical concern, "How do you suggest I carry out such an operation in the midst of a bustling market?"

The air was thick with menace, and Asfour's words sliced through the heavy silence with surgical precision. "You don't," he said, calm in his voice. "I have a man, Kamal, in Sharm El Sheikh. That's your next stop."

He slid a passport across the metal table, the gentle brush of paper on steel, the whisper of conspiracy. "Kilcoyne Hall," Asfour said, his eyes steely flint. "You're British now. Clean yourself up. Lose the edge. You're a tourist. Keep it convincing."

Aziz flipped open the passport, the face of another man staring back at him, a challenge issued in biometric form. His life was now a borrowed story, and he had to tell it convincingly or not at all.

"The Egyptians," Asfour continued, a smirk twisting half his mouth, "are still playing catch-up. No facial recognition to worry about. Just don't give them a reason to look too closely."

Asfour's hand moved to a small cardboard box, his movements deliberate, almost reverent. He set out two vials, one ominously dark, the other as clear as the lie Aziz now had to live. "Cobra venom," he explained, no room for doubt in his tone. "And the only thing standing between your target and a one-way trip into the dark."

Aziz's gaze fixed on the vial of venom, and a cold shiver slithered down his spine, a primal echo from darker, more primitive times. His fear of snakes wasn't just an inconvenience; it was a tangible entity in the room with them, a silent third participant in their grim collusion.

Snakes. Even the thought sent old, reptilian impulses skittering along the edges of his mind, raw and unbidden. They were stealth and sinew, lethal grace wrapped in silence. They didn't announce death with a bang; they brought it whispering, a secret between predator and prey.

The vial seemed to throb with a life of its own, dark and viscous, a coiled killer waiting to strike. It was a distillation of every nightmare that had ever quickened his pulse, the embodiment of a deep-seated dread that had nestled in his chest since childhood.

But this fear—it wasn't going to steer him. Aziz could feel the weight of Asfour's scrutiny, heavy and expectant. This was the test, then. Not the planning, not the new identity, not even the target. It was about harnessing the terror, riding it until he was the one holding the reins.

With a hand he willed steady, Aziz reached for the vial. His fingertips brushed the cool glass, and for a heart-stopping moment, he felt the ghost of a serpent's sleek scales instead. It would have been so easy to recoil, to let the revulsion dictate his movements.

But he didn't.

He wrapped his fingers around the vial, and in that clench, he felt a shift within himself, steel sliding into the core of his resolve. Fear would not be his master. He was more than the sum of his phobias. He was a weapon, and this venom was just another bullet in his chamber.

"Just a whisper of this," Asfour's voice cut through the room, low and steady as he motioned to the ominous vial on the table, "and he's yours. He won't even see you coming."

"You get Hamid to administer this," Asfour continued, placing the second vial firmly in Aziz's other hand, "and he comes back from the dead. But make no mistake, he'll be on a razor's edge between life and death, but the promise of more antidote will get Hamid all the information we need."

The implication hung in the air like a charged storm cloud, laden with inevitable violence. They weren't in the business of saving lives; they were engaged in the precarious trade of prolonging death for information, for leverage, for whatever suited their needs in the shadowy world of warfare.

"What follows," Asfour said, a dark implication in his tone, "is when the sailor will truly know fear. You'll make him wish he hadn't come back."

Aziz examined the vials carefully before returning them to the box. "What is the plan once Hamid has one of them?"

Asfour unrolled a small map on the table, highlighting a specific grid. "There is a derelict building located here, near the market but concealed from the main thoroughfare. He should have ample time to extract the information I seek."

Aziz committed the grid reference to memory, while Asfour refilled their cups with herbal tea. "Your mission also includes gathering data on the Reef Explorer's systems, access points, camera coverage, itinerary changes, vulnerabilities, emergency procedures, crew and passenger counts, and any other pertinent information."

"Would you like the ship's layout as well?" Aziz enquired.

"The ship's schematics and layout are provided in the box. Study them thoroughly," Asfour directed, concluding their discussion for the time being.

"What should be done with the officer once we obtain the information?" Aziz enquired.

"You're aware of what I expect, Aziz—no traces left. You stay away from the operation until it's completed, get the information from Hamid and get a flight to Hurghada," Asfour ordered.

"Understood. And once there?"

"You will meet your team. Passports and the location of a safe haven are all contained in this package," Asfour indicated the cardboard box. "There's also an encrypted Phone; we'll exclusively communicate through the secure line after this meeting."

"And what about the funds for this operation?" Aziz queried, reverting to his Birmingham slang.

"I presume you're referring to finances, Aziz. The tickets are covered, and once you reach the designated location, there will be finances and weaponry at your disposal."

"Are our objectives centred on seizing control of the ship, causing its destruction, or kidnapping someone from it?" Aziz sought clarification.

"All will be revealed upon reaching Hurghada. I have four marine specialists who will rendezvous with you there. You will serve as the team leader, and they, along with your team, will report to you, with you answering to me," Asfour explained.

"So I'll receive the full details in Hurghada, then?" Aziz probed further.

"That's correct," Asfour affirmed. "You know a Somalian called Awaale. I understand you're close to him and have used him on several occasions. Please provide some insights about him."

"Yes, once in Mogadishu, near Marka, his hometown in Somalia, and once in Kenya. It's quite unsettling when you first meet him. He was affected by leprosy as a child, which has left him scarred," Aziz said.

Aziz paused to sip his tea before elaborating further. "Over the past decade, Awaale has been involved in hijackings of commercial ships, sometimes for us, most often for survival. Although he's been paid well, he hasn't managed to amass the wealth that the group's leaders have. They've invested their capital in beachfront properties in Kenya and built portfolios filled with shares and gold bars, thanks to the hefty fees collected from shipowners and maritime insurance companies."

Asfour nodded thoughtfully. "He's more like a follower than a leader," he remarked.

"Awaale is a Muslim, but not devout, he operates on the fringes of the Somalian terrorist group and is aligned to them for economic and survival purposes, rather than a fervent admirer. He is married with four children aged between six months and twelve years old. He has links with Al-Shabaab, an affiliate organisation of Al–Qaeda.

Asfour leaned back, his expression tinged with a hint of amusement. "Seems like Awaale is driven by money, but he tends to squander it recklessly."

Aziz chuckled softly. "Indeed, as they say: 'A fool and his money are soon parted.'

Asfour replied "A couple of weeks ago, I used some of my connections to help Kenyan police officers raid his property, and they made off with his possessions and ill-gotten gains."

"Took his possessions, why?" Aziz's voice was barely more than a whisper, a husky notes in the quiet, laced with an edge Awaale's eyes widened with understanding. "So you have a clever plan?"

"We need him," Asfour declared, his voice cutting through the room's stillness like a knife through the dense fabric of tension. "And not just him—his entire crew. Also, I have a cargo shop in the Port of Mogadishu next Friday, I want him and his men on it"

Aziz felt the shift in the air, the tightening of an invisible noose. Asfour wasn't asking. This was a directive, the kind that came with heavy consequences. The kind you didn't refuse.

"Reach out to him," Asfour continued, each word dropping like a stone into the dark well of their conspiracy. "Let him know there's a contract on the table. More money than he's seen in his life. Enough to make a man forget his morals."

The silence stretched between them, taut and expectant. Aziz understood the gravity of the task.

"And one more thing," Asfour's voice cut through the silence, sharp as a blade in the cold air. His eyes, those calculating slits of scrutiny, turned to steel. Not the kind that folded, but the kind that sliced through bone and marrow. "He's not an outsider on this. He's in the trenches with your men. Shoulder to shoulder. Blood to blood."

He paused, letting the weight of allegiance hang heavy in the room. "Front them ten grand each. A gesture," he said, the corner of his mouth twisting in what could pass for a smile in another world. "On survival—their survival—two million each."

Asfour understood the language of motivation, the raw rhythm of greed. It was a song of loyalty bought not earned, of fealty sworn on the altar of survival, not honour.

He slid a pre-loaded card across the table, its innocuous plastic sheen belying the weight of the promise it held—$100,000. Just numbers on a screen, but life and death in the real world. "This takes care of the home front. Expenses. Consolation for the families," he added, his tone devoid of genuine sympathy. "Chances are they're walking into a black hole. But that's not for their ears."

The cash was just a fragment, a sliver of the vast wealth Asfour had accrued from the criminal organisation he had set in motion years before. Yachts, gleaming symbols of opulence and excess, snatched from the embrace of the Indian Ocean, and beyond. Each vessel a hefty deposit in his swelling account, a game of maritime chess played from the dark corners of the world. Human lives were the stakes, owners who vanished into the night, whispers on the water, their fates as lost as the ships they once commanded. The luxury vessels were repainted, rechristened, and sold into new hands, the perfect crime hidden beneath layers of fresh lacquer and falsified documents.

The nod was imperceptible, nothing more than a brief conceding dip of the head, but in the language of men like them, it was a covenant etched in steel. In that scant motion, Aziz sealed an unvoiced pact.

Asfour's next move was unexpected. He leaned forward, closing the distance, and took both of Aziz's hands in his own. The contact was not one of warmth; it was a transfer of resolve, a tactile reinforcement of their alliance.

"Allah be praised," Asfour intoned, his voice a low rumble, not of religious fervour, but of invoking a higher witness to their earthly machinations. It was less a prayer and more a call to arms, an invocation of divine oversight.

Releasing Aziz's hands, Asfour rose in one fluid motion, the embodiment of lethal grace. There was no further reassurance, no camaraderie. Without another word, Asfour turned and departed. Alone now, Aziz felt the weight of the coming maelstrom.

Aziz navigated the dark web of his contacts, his fingers moving swiftly over the phone's surface. Awaale's name glowed in the digital darkness. With a few keystrokes, he dispatched a message—not a request, but a directive, edged with the sharpness of authority.

"Join the encrypted video chat. Now."

This was no ordinary call. As Aziz initiated the connection, digital echoes began to scatter across the cyber void. The signal, cloaked in layers of encryption, fractured into a hundred pieces, shooting through the arteries of the internet, bouncing from server to server, continent to continent. Every leap was a ghost's step, a whisper in the chaos, leaving no trace, no scent for the hounds on their trail. This was communication in the underworld, a game of hide and seek played with stakes as high as the men were deep underground.

Twenty minutes ticked by—twenty minutes of coiled tension, of watching the seconds jab like a boxer, relentless and sharp. And then, connection.

Awaale's face erupted onto the screen, scars etched across his dark skin like a roadmap of past violence, each one a tale of survival, of battles fought. His eyes, hard as they met Aziz's, didn't just see; they pierced, looking through the digital space as if capable of discerning lies from truth in the pixels themselves.

No pleasantries were exchanged. They were beyond that.

"I need you and your team Awaale. More money than you have ever seen before," Aziz said.

"A lot of money has passed before my eyes," Awaale responded.

"$10,000 sent to your men's family before you leave, and up to two million dollars when you succeed," Aziz said.

"I'm listening," Awaale said.

Aziz nodded. "We're going to seize a massive treasure, and we need someone with your reputation and skills to make it work."

Awaale leaned forward, intrigued. "Tell me more."

Aziz surveyed the hotel suite, a luxurious expanse that now felt too open, too exposed. His gaze, sharp and methodical, raked over every shadow, every potential hiding spot. The place was empty, silent except for the distant, muffled sounds of the city beyond the walls. But in this business, solitude was an illusion, safety a mirage.

He leaned closer to the screen, his voice dropping to a conspiratorial whisper. "We're going after the high seas' grand prize, Awaale. A cruise liner, swelling with the savings and excesses of the rich." His eyes, hard with resolve, didn't waver. "We'll seize it, hold the elite, and demand a king's ransom for their pampered lives."

The room was still, but for the flickering of his screen. On the other side, Awaale's eyes came alive, a dangerous glint of greed and trepidation playing within them. They were the eyes of a man who'd walked through hell and still flirted with the fire.

"That's a bold move," Awaale responded, the slow grin of a seasoned predator stretching across his face. "But you've got my attention. Where do I come in?"

Aziz replied, "We need you, Awaale, to lend your notoriety to our cause. Your reputation as a pirate figurehead will strike fear into the hearts of the passengers and their families. It will ensure that our demands are met swiftly."

Awaale considered the proposition, weighing the risks and rewards. "What do you need from me now?"

Aziz slowly waved the credit card across the screen camera rough. "Each of your men gets $10,000. Today. Right now. But here's the rub: you're boarding a cargo ship by Friday. Where it's headed, you don't need to know right now. But it's a maximum five-day journey."

Awaale's dark eyes studied the card for a moment, then shifted to Aziz's, probing for a hint, a clue, any sign of deception. "Five days at, let's say, twenty knots. That's around thirteen to fifteen hundred nautical miles. North puts us around Egypt, Israel, maybe Jordan. We head south or east, and we hit dead water—

nothing worth our time. And let me be clear, Aziz," his voice low and gruff with a hint of warning, "we don't want anything to do with operations involving Israel."

Aziz's smile was a predator's grin, sharp and calculating. "No dealings with Israel, that's a promise. So what's it going to be, Awaale?"

Awaale's silence stretched between them, heavy with calculation. "Transfer $10,000 per man today, $90,000 in total and you've got yourself a deal," he said, his mind already deducting the $5,000 each he'd give to his men's families—small fortunes in this part of the world.

"Excellent," Aziz purred, the word slithering into the tension-thick air. "The vessel docks in Port Mogadishu five days from now. Gather your crew at pier 12, come 7 in the morning. One of my associates will be there to receive you."

Awaale's eyes, glinting with a hard, desperate light, didn't stray from Aziz. "Since Covid, it's been nothing but bones for us. This couldn't be timelier."

Aziz leaned forward, his voice dropping to a dangerous whisper. "This pact is sacred, Awaale. Betrayal would open a rift that no time could heal. It would rain misfortune on you and your men."

"I'm a man of my word, Aziz. It's ironclad," Awaale responded, his tone brooking no argument.

"Good," Aziz replied, his gaze like steel. "And remember, secrets spilled to the wind can't be blamed when the trees hear them."

Awaale nodded, a solemn vow passing in his silence.

"Fi Amanullah," Awaale intoned, the customary words acknowledging the dangerous path they'd tread together.

<h1 style="text-align:right">chapter three
Breakfast in the Everglades</h1>

Cheryl Ross knew the drill, every gritty detail of it. Breakfast was more than a meal; it was a strategy. In the silent dawn of Everglade City—a place too small, too damn honest to be called a "city"—she moved with purpose. The population barely scratched 400, all crammed in the kind of place where secrets were luxuries no one could afford.

MIDAS agents were coming. Not the type to shuffle in sleepy-eyed clutching coffee, but the kind who had seen things that kept you up at night. They were her guests, and Cheryl was the fortress they didn't know they were seeking refuge in.

Her kitchen was a tactical operation by sunrise, dishes orchestrated like chess moves. The home she shared with Esme— her kid, her anchor—and Tuck, the unexpected wildcard in her life's hand, filled with the scent of a promise. A promise of a day when you could almost forget there were monsters wearing human faces outside the sanctuary of Collier County, Florida. Max Cutler, the co-founder of MIDAS (Marine Investigations for Death at Sea), had readily agreed with Cheryl's choice to establish the company's headquarters in the heart of the Everglades. The ease of access to the sprawling marshlands had its own allure for Cutler, who frequently spent his free time on his recently acquired airboat, fostering a deeper connection with nature. Additionally, the region was tailor-made for his love of parachuting, with several nearby facilities offering excellent jumping opportunities. The proximity to Miami, a short drive away, allowed him to indulge in the company of women and savor a few beers when the mood struck.

Cutler was a man who played chess on a global board, pieces poised in silent threat, always thinking three moves ahead. Geneva was more than a city to him; it was a fortress, a place where American fingers couldn't pry, or so he believed. MIDAS needed that—Geneva's neutrality, its grey zones, its bank-vault silence.

Everglade City was a different animal, swampland and gator-grit, more about survival training and paper-pushing than the high-octane adrenaline that fuelled fieldwork. It was the muscle behind the mind, the grounded reality that supported the abstract intelligence to hunt the killers out across oceans.

But in Geneva, on Rue des Pâquis, MIDAS wasn't just another discreet plaque on a door. It was a nerve centre, veins of information pulsing in and out, hidden in plain sight amidst the postcard perfection of Lake Lucerne nearby. Here, in the heart of everything and away from prying eyes, was Fabienne. Not just an analyst, but a guardian of secrets, a weaver of invisible threads.

The Swiss operation was airtight, a vault. Doors with biometric locks, cameras peering through shadows, and data streams ciphered into obscurity. It was a bubble of the future nestled in the ancient city, a place where whispers materialized on screens, where lives and nations could teeter on the brink, pivoting on the fragment of a sentence in a decrypted message.

Preparing breakfast for the diverse group of employees had required meticulous planning. Cutler, Tuck, and Colton were the easy ones to cater for, enjoying an all-American breakfast comprising crispy streaky bacon, over-easy eggs, fluffy pancakes drenched in rich maple syrup, all washed down with freshly blended Florida orange juice. In contrast, Matt Rice, who was affectionately known as Basmati, was a vegetarian and savoured a fresh compote and muesli combination.

To accommodate the international palette of their team, a variety of options were available. For Shultz, a native of Germany, there was a selection of salami, cold cuts, and Bavarian frankfurters. Ghislaine, hailing from Palestine, had her choice of hummus and falafels. Fabienne, the team's versatile epicurean, devoured everything with gusto, paying little heed to national sensitivities. Esme, Cheryl's daughter, had already left for school after enjoying a hearty breakfast of French toast and strawberry yogurt.

Breakfast was a distant memory, the last crumbs disappearing beneath Fabienne's precise fingertips. Cutler didn't need to speak; his very stance was a clarion call, a silent command that it was time to move. They left the warmth of the gathering behind, stepping out into the world that was Everglade City, a microcosm nestled in the Florida wilderness.

Their walk wasn't long, but it was transformative, a brief journey from domesticity to the front lines of intelligence. The MIDAS building was close, yet in those hundreds of yards, everything changed. They passed the old church, its white walls a silent prayer, a beacon of something timeless and hopeful, its simplicity underscored by the guardian-like palms at its sides. It was a hallmark of the past, a symbol that not all was lost to the relentless march of time.

The motor museum sat quietly, a gentle nod to yesteryears with its prized possession, a 1904 Ford Model A, basking in the reverence of history enthusiasts. It was a touch of class, a whisper of the golden days of church followed by key lime pie. But not everything in this scene spoke of respectful preservation.

Cutler's jaw tightened, a flicker of irritation in his eyes as they brushed over the incongruous sight of the newly erected mobile towers. They stood defiantly in the main square, steel giants uncaring of the aesthetic sacrilege they committed, overshadowing the quaint church, marring the skyline. They were an affront, a bureaucratic decision void of community spirit, a reminder that progress could sometimes strangle even as it promised to nurture.

With each step, Cutler felt the shift, the mental gears moving from the tranquillity of their communal breakfast to the high-stakes reality that awaited in the MIDAS headquarters. They were leaving behind a world where history was revered, stepping into one where history was made.

Turning left past the Everglades Hotel, they couldn't help but notice a group of pelicans clacking away on picket fences overlooking the serene river. Soon, they arrived at the offices, a two-story structure elevated on sturdy wooden supports, providing ample space underneath for the storage of multiple 4x4 vehicles and the Zodiac Craft that Tuck used for navigating the local waterways. MIDAS owned the entire building, and they had no intention of subletting to other businesses.

From the exterior, the structure appeared to be constructed mainly of wood, much like the other commercial properties in the area. However, this was merely a façade. In truth, the building was reinforced with steel and boasted eight-inch-thick concrete panels. These panels and the decking were lined with steel plates, with insulation and plasterboard concealing the formidable structure. Closed-circuit television cameras were strategically placed on every side of the building, while a high-tech security system covered the entire premises, ensuring that any unauthorized access would be promptly detected.

The first level of the building housed six separate rooms, each accessible via a key code entry system. Swipe cards were required to access the corridors leading to the offices, ensuring that only MIDAS employees and authorized guests could enter. The security measures were so stringent that Cheryl, during the last hour of the workday, would personally clean the offices if they had been in use.

The first office belonged to Max Cutler and was sparsely furnished, featuring a desk with a central computer screen, a telephone, and a pristine white leather sofa. Cheryl's office, the second one, was notably different, equipped with multiple computers, including two screens built into the walls.

Rooms three and four served as forensic laboratories, furnished with a wide array of state-of-the-art equipment. They boasted analysers, DNA testing equipment, microscopes, centrifuges, computerized systems for chemical and air analysis, and an assortment of other technical tools stored in cupboards and beneath the sturdy workbenches.

Room five was dedicated to the rugged military server, responsible for managing the multitude of computers within MIDAS. It also hosted the backup systems for MIDAS' software and data, which were situated in Geneva. The room was equipped with an efficient air-cooling system independent of the building's air conditioning, complete with battery backup to safeguard against electrical failures. Its military-grade firewall provided robust protection, making it as close to impenetrable as possible with the available technology.

The final room, room six, contained locked steel cabinets that reached from floor to ceiling. These cabinets housed the extensive collection of firearms and ammunition used by the team, ranging from standard firearms to non-lethal weapons such as tasers and pepper spray aerosols. The arsenal was a reflection of the diverse skills and needs of the MIDAS team, ready for any situation they might encounter on their investigations.

The operations room at MIDAS wasn't made for comfort. It was a place of shadows, of half-light, where the glow of screens didn't quite reach the corners. It was a place for secrets, for decisions that weren't to be weighed lightly. This was where Max Cutler thrived.

He stood, a natural stillness about him, not needing to command silence. It fell automatically, a shared breath held amongst the team, the elite, each one a story of prowess in their own right. They were his chess pieces, carefully selected for their skills, their nerve, their willingness to stride into the grey where others faltered. They waited, watching him, the man who had brought them all together.

Cutler's presence filled the room, not just his height but the breadth of him, the raw solidity that made people step aside, listen, and follow. His blue eyes were the kind that missed nothing, taking in the expectant faces, the straight spines, the hands silently at rest, ready to leap into action.

There was no need for theatrics with Cutler. No grand speeches. He was all about the job—the mission at hand. His hair, black and closely shorn, his jawline, like it was carved from bedrock, spoke of a man who had no time for superfluous details. His ruggedness wasn't the kind found on magazine covers; it was born from the field, from quick decisions and the kind of work that didn't pause for doubt.

He began to speak, his voice not loud but reaching every corner, every ear. It was the sound of certainty, of a road map drawn in clear, bold lines, no room for detours. They were there to do a job. To make real the plans meticulously crafted and known only to the shadow-filled room of MIDAS. And as Cutler talked, in the world of threat levels and international chess, his team knew one thing—they were the players who would change the game.

"Welcome all," Cutler began, his voice carrying an air of authority. "It's been some time since we last had a meeting like this. For those who haven't had the pleasure of meeting our newest operative, this is Nathan Colton." Cutler's gaze shifted toward the towering figure in the room. Colton, a former Drug Enforcement agent, was an imposing presence, standing at a formidable six feet six inches. His muscular frame was reminiscent of a professional wrestler, and he brought a wealth of investigative experience to the team.

Cutler continued the introductions, gesturing towards various members of the team. "That's Tuck over there, alongside Basmati. To their left is Ghislaine. The gentleman with the eye patch is Stahmer, and on his right is Shultz. Fabienne is our tech expert, and of course, you all know Cheryl. Unfortunately, one of our agents, Philip Cortez, is currently on leave," Cutler added.

Tuck Walters, a former SAS operative and MIDAS' lead investigator, greeted Colton in his native Maori language, "Kia Ora." Tuck was a Maori, distinguished by his olive skin, square jaw, and black hair. He possessed a powerful, V-shaped physique, and his combat skills were formidable. Despite his warrior-like exterior, Tuck had shown a softer side since falling in love with Cheryl and her young daughter, Esme. His calloused hands, which once ended lives during his SAS service, more used to tenderly stroking Esme's blonde hair.

"For Colton's benefit, I'll provide a brief overview of the company and the reasons behind its establishment," Cutler began, taking a sip of water before continuing. "Cheryl lost her husband five years ago when he was brutally beaten to death by drunken youths on the Big Pink Boat off the coast of the Bahamas. My sister was killed by a serial killer on a cruise ship anchored in Auke Bay, Alaska, four years ago."

"The bastard is dead now, thanks to Stahmer, but not before Stahmer lost an eye to him," Tuck added, his voice carrying a tinge of bitterness. Robert Stahmer, an ex-British military intelligence investigator, was MIDAS' resident Sherlock Holmes, known for his exceptional deductive skills. At 45 years old, Stahmer was the oldest and wisest member of the team.

"Thank you for the vivid description, Tuck," Stahmer commented dryly, absently touching the black eye patch that concealed his missing eye. His years of experience had made him an indispensable asset to the team.

"What Cheryl and I discovered was the complete lack of a cohesive strategy to investigate, let alone apprehend and bring these killers to justice. The seas were lawless, without borders, and too often an invitation for random acts of violence," Cutler emphasized.

"Not anymore," Cheryl chimed in with determination, her resolve unwavering.

"That's the primary function of MIDAS," Cutler continued. "We investigate where no one else dares to venture—at sea, where there are no borders, and where crime scenes can vanish with the ebb and flow of the tides. This is why Cheryl and I joined forces, why each of you was carefully recruited, and why we welcome Colton into our ranks."

"Hey, glad to be here, boss-man," Colton responded with a boisterous laugh, his soft Caribbean accent adding warmth to his words.

"Please, call me Cutler, Colton," Cutler insisted, stressing the informality of their operation.

"I prefer Max," Ghislaine Lyman giggled, her presence commanding the attention of everyone in the room. Ghislaine, of Palestinian descent and born on the Gaza Strip, possessed the striking beauty of a supermodel. Her jet-black hair cascaded like silken curtains, her olive skin radiated youth, and her tall frame, accentuated by high heels, made her appear even taller than her five feet nine inches. A linguistic prodigy, Ghislaine had mastered five languages by the age of fourteen. Her journey from university to a career with Interpol had brought her into Cutler's orbit, thanks to her linguistic prowess and her ability to remain composed in the field.

"You'd prefer him naked, Ghislaine," Fabienne Asper remarked in her raspy Swiss-accented voice. Fabienne, a robust, muscular brunette, was the opposite of Ghislaine in terms of appearance. Her broad shoulders and masculine features made her seem more like a weightlifter than a field agent. Yet none of that mattered, as Fabienne possessed a unique skill set that made her indispensable to the team.

"And wouldn't you?" Ghislaine retorted, her remark causing a faint blush to colour Cutler's cheeks.

Cutler rapped his pen against his glass, signalling for the banter to cease. "Let's focus, if you please. Currently, we have eight separate investigations in progress. Five of these will be placed on the back burner as long-term projects. The remaining three are of utmost priority and will require the attention of everyone in this room. Oceanic Enterprises from Hamburg operates cruise ships in the Mediterranean and the Red Sea. They've reported a missing senior officer who disappeared during a shore visit at Sharm El Sheikh last week."

Cheryl Ross, the co-head of MIDAS, took the floor to address the team. As she began, the room filled with hushed anticipation.

"Gareth Cummings, communications officer of the cruise ship Reef Explorer, visited a market on the outskirts of Sharm El Sheikh, outside the tourist protection area, last Thursday. He's known as a reliable officer and a family man. However, there's been no word on his whereabouts since then, and his company wants to reassure his family by confirming that his disappearance is being thoroughly investigated," Cheryl explained, her voice carrying a sense of urgency. "Our mission is to uncover what happened to

Gareth Cummings and report our findings. While it could be a simple accident or medical emergency, we cannot rule out more sinister possibilities, such as a Western or religiously motivated abduction."

As Cheryl spoke, Cutler glanced around at his team. A faint smile tugged at the corners of his lips as he observed Fabienne Asper's rapt attention. Fabienne, a Swiss-born tech expert, had a remarkable capacity for absorbing every detail, and Cutler had lured her away from MI5 for her exceptional skills. While her interpersonal skills were not her strong suit, her brilliance more than made up for it.

"Max?" Cheryl prompted, drawing Cutler's attention away from his thoughts. She was the only one allowed to address him by his first name.

Cutler rose to his feet, addressing the group with his characteristic authority. "While this is distressing for Mr. Cummings' family and concerning for Oceanic Enterprises, it currently appears to be a low-level and low-risk situation. As such, I'm assigning a small team to investigate. Stahmer will lead the team, with Ghislaine accompanying him as an interpreter due to potential language barriers. For added security, Shultz will join to provide protection."

Shultz, a trusted operative with a personal vendetta, had become a valuable asset to the team. His wife had been a victim of a horrific crime, and Shultz had pursued her murderer relentlessly. Cutler knew that Shultz's methods were unorthodox but effective, having partnered with him during a dollar-counterfeiting investigation in Bavaria.

"I've briefed Stahmer in advance, and he has formulated a plan that he'll share with us shortly," Cutler continued.

Stahmer, rose to his feet, his posture rigid and impeccable.

"Our strategy involves tracing Gareth Cummings' last known movements, interviewing locals and law enforcement, and conducting a thorough investigation of the area. Cheryl has compiled a detailed file on radical groups and criminal organizations operating in the region, which will serve as our reference. Additionally, we aim to board the Reef Explorer when it arrives in Hurghada, Egypt, ten days from now, to speak with the crew and gather further information," Stahmer explained.

Cheryl interjected, "Thank you, Robert. Now, moving on to the second investigation. I'm sure most of you are familiar with Conrad Ford?"

All heads nodded in recognition, except for Nathan Colton's.

Silence gripped the room, a living entity, thick, almost palpable. In that vacuum of quiet, Basmati found his moment. He wasn't the usual operative muscle you'd picture, no. The man was a maestro of forensic science, and when it came to drones, he flew them as if they were extensions of his own sharp, agile mind. He was the kind of talent that made the impossible look lazy. And he'd jumped ship from a yawning career of forensic pathology, chasing something with more pulse, more heat. All before the world had turned him twenty-eight.

The dimmed briefing room was suddenly dominated by an image on the screen: Conrad Ford's face, larger than life. Those in the room could feel the weight of his gaze, even through the pixels. There was an arrogance in his eyes, a confidence that seemed to permeate the room. His steely grey hair, sharp features, and a look that seemed to challenge anyone who dared to cross him. The room's temperature seemed to drop a degree or two as the picture held everyone's attention. It wasn't just a briefing anymore; it was personal.

"Conrad Ford," Basmati broke the silence, the name hitting the room's four walls before anyone had a chance to process it. "Guy was top of the food chain. Big league. Schmoozing with the likes of ex-President Nash, even had the current VP in his pocket. But Ford got hungry, bit off more than he could chew with shady deals nobody wanted to see."

He paused, letting it sink in, his eyes scanning the room, not quite looking at anyone. "Old regime? They didn't care. Or maybe they did but chose to keep it hush-hush. Then the shift in power, new president, new rules. Suddenly, Ford's out in the freeze. VP tried to cover for him, made a case more than once. No dice."

Basmati leaned forward, hands flat on the table, every line and muscle in his body rigid. "Now Ford's out in the wild. Scrambling, dealing with any Tom, Dick, or Harry with cash in hand, doesn't matter who. He's desperate, selling firepower to anyone, anywhere. And my sources? They say he doesn't give a damn who's buying."

Basmati paused, letting the information sink in, in that room of sharp minds and restless energy. His fingers, always moving, were still for once.

"Correct," Fabienne affirmed. "Despite his legal troubles, Ford still has influential connections as Basmati said in the White House, particularly with the vice president."

"Conrad Ford maintains a weapons manufacturing division in Malaysia and a research and development division in the United

States, indicating that he's still active in the arms trade," Fabienne added.

Cheryl took the floor, her voice calm but carrying a sharpness that demanded every ear in the room. "Ford's downfall isn't just tucked away in the political shadows. It's hit home. Hard," she said, the weight of her words virtually palpable in the air. "His son, his future daughter-in-law, gone. Indonesian waters off Bali." She paused, a beat allowing the gravity to sink in before continuing, "A Japanese trawler sweeping the seabed hauled up a catch that'll haunt them to their graves. Identified the bodies—Robert Ford and Samantha Gooding."

The screen transitioned, the stark features of Conrad Ford dissolving into the last known moments of Robert Ford and Samantha Gooding. The backdrop was a starlit night, the kind where the sky competes with the sea for darkness, their yacht a small oasis of light. They were encapsulated in a bubble of luxury, their smiles wide as they clinked glasses, oblivious to the impending doom.

In the poorly lit briefing room, the team watched the couple frozen in time. There was a stark contrast between this image and the previous one of Conrad; here, there was life, joy, and no hint of the terror that would unfold.

The room was silent, each operative lost in the scene's tragic beauty, knowing all too well the darkness lurking just beyond that camera's frame. The image underscored the high stakes of their mission—it wasn't just about strategy or intelligence; it was about real lives that had met a premature end, and a darkness that needed to be dragged into the light.

She caught a breath, steeling herself before laying out the harsh facts. "The autopsies tell a grim tale. Robert? Looks like he drowned, but his body wore marks that screamed restraint, maybe ropes. Samantha?" Cheryl's voice hitched, just a fraction. "It's a scene straight from a nightmare. Those lacerations, self-inflicted in a frenzy. And the violation of her body happened when she was beyond feeling anything."

The room felt colder, the air thicker. "Jim Fitch, stationed in Jakarta, doesn't see this as random. Says it's a yacht hijacking that spiralled into hell." Her gaze met each of theirs, ensuring the severity of the situation was understood, the dark narrative hanging between them, an unspoken vow for justice igniting in the dim room.

The mood darkened further as the screen shifted again. This time, it wasn't the carefree laughter or the deceptive tranquillity of a starry night. It was something colder, something that made the air in the room feel heavy, like a wet cloth over their faces.

Images filled the screen, clinical and harsh in the brightness of their exposure. They were stolen shots, courtesy of Fabienne's digital prowling—a hack into the Indonesian pathologist's database that no one there had yet realised.

Two faces stared back at the MIDAS team, white, not with the pallor of death, but with the unmistakable freeze of fear that had set in just before life had been cruelly snatched away. The eyes were the most haunting, the terror within them had been captured in stunning clarity, a moment of pure human dread, encapsulated forever in pixels.

Nobody in the room dared breathe, as if their breaths could fog the frozen moment displayed before them. These were more than victims; they were a message, a stark reminder that this was what they were up against.

It wasn't just the depravity of violence or the greed of ransom. It was the kind of evil that could freeze blood, that moment when hope was gone, and all that remained was the innate, primitive fear of something going horribly wrong.

The images seared themselves into the minds of everyone present, a fuel for the long, sleepless nights that undoubtedly lay ahead in their search for justice. This wasn't just a mission anymore. It was personal.

"There's a special breed of evil fuckers out there," Tuck growled, the shadows in the room seeming to lean in towards him. His knuckles whitened, the urge for action turning each word into a snarl. "Just a few minutes. That's all I'd need with these bastards."

The air in the room charged with his fury, an electric current of raw, undiluted rage that begged for an outlet. There was no jest in his tone, no hyperbole. Just a bone-deep promise of retribution, waiting to be unleashed.

Cutler leaned forward, elbows on the table, his eyes sharp and intense. "Think back, team. The Trench siblings, remember? Their yacht vanished, like smoke in the wind. Over six months now. And all signs pointed to the waters near Bali." He paused, letting the weight of his words sink in.

"We didn't dig deep at first, we did a desktop investigation. Mrs. Trench, she's not rolling in cash. Her son had the money, but with him gone and no body to prove it, his fortunes in limbo. But now?" He tapped his fingers on the tabletop. "With everything that's happening, it's time to connect the dots. We might be looking at the same predator."

Fabienne cut in, her voice calm but carrying an urgency that drew all eyes to her. "The Trench case wasn't an outlier. It was a signal." She looked around the room, ensuring she had everyone's undivided attention.

"After the Trench duo disappeared, I kept my eyes peeled on that stretch of water. The result? Disturbing. Three more yachts, gone, just like that—and with them, their owners, or lessees. Vanished into thin air. All within the same territory." She took a moment, allowing the gravity of her words to settle on everyone present.

"Bali, Nusa Penida, Nusa Lembongan, Nusa Cenningan," Cutler began, his voice cutting through the room, sharp as a tack. "This isn't happenstance. It's a damn blueprint. Disappearances, all huddled together within a hundred-mile hot zone. Two years rolling, and it's like everyone's been blind." There was an edge to his tone, the spark of someone who lives for the hunt. His gaze hardened, the blue in his eyes icy with resolve. "Not anymore.

Cheryl looked up, her gaze sweeping across the team, ensuring she had each of their attentions. "Someone's hunting in those waters. And they're not just after yachts. They're erasing everything. No traces. No bodies. We're dealing with a ghost, and it's our job to hunt it down."

Basmati chimed in again, "So, what's our primary objective? Are we investigating the disappearance of Ford's son and his fiancée alone, or are we also including the case of the missing couple from Florida?"

"Our main objective is to identify and apprehend the individuals responsible for the murder of Robert Ford," Cheryl clarified.

Tuck Walters, the team's former SAS operative, added his perspective, "It's likely that these cases are connected. I can't imagine multiple criminal gangs operating in such a localized area."

"It sounds to me like an organized network, with operations spanning across the region," Cutler mused. "Whoever they are, they won't take kindly to our interference. We also need to be prepared for potential clashes with corrupt local law enforcement, as some of the police in the area are known to be on the take. It's a way of life over there. We might encounter challenges on that front. As a precaution, we need to formulate an emergency escape plan."

Tuck voiced a cynical perspective, "If the cops are corrupt, what's the point of catching these bastards? Pay them off in pesos, dollars, or whatever currency they prefer, and they'll be partying within a week."

"Valid point, Tuck," Cheryl conceded. "And that's precisely why Conrad Ford wants the culprits delivered to his security team at an undisclosed aerodrome, a detail we've yet to receive."

Fabienne, spoke up, "Cheryl asked me to research the gang culture in Bali and gather intelligence. I'm still compiling reports, but I've already uncovered some intriguing information. The photograph I'm about to share was taken at Bali airport just two weeks ago. It features three individuals who all work for Conrad Ford."

Tuck raised an eyebrow and enquired, "His security team?"

Fabienne confirmed, "Yes, it appears they were attempting to track the gang responsible. I intercepted some chatter and emails exchanged between them and Julie Birch, Ford's head of security."

Colton seemed puzzled by Fabienne's capabilities. "You can access Ford's communications?"

"Fabienne worked for MI5 before joining us," Cheryl explained. "It's best not to ask how she obtains her information, Nathan."

Tuck chimed in with a grin, "She's a spook, Colton, probably knows more about you than you do."

Cutler concluded, "Rest assured, Colton, you've passed her scrutiny."

Fabienne took the floor, her expertise in full display as she continued her briefing.

"If I may continue, gentlemen. I've identified that the security team had been staying at the Villa Lotus by Seminyak Square. They paid for a one-week stay upfront and had to, as customary, surrender their passports. The problem is, they haven't been seen since the fifth day of their stay. The hotel notified the local police three days after their expected checkout date when the passports remained uncollected," Fabienne provided the details.

"So Ford sends out his A-team, they vanish—kidnapped or worse—and then he hires us," Tuck summarized, his tone reflecting a mix of intrigue and readiness for action.

Cutler remained composed; his focus fixed on the mission at hand. "It's as much news to me as it is to you, Tuck. But it doesn't change the mission. There's a risk in everything we do; this is just another one to be aware of and manage."

Unperturbed, Cutler continued with the mission briefing. "

"I have to go to Robert Ford's funeral in two days. Ford want us on-side, but there are a few things I need to iron out with him. The outline plan assuming all goes well with Conrad Ford is we fly out in six days to Bali; Ford has given us a private flight into Bali. Two teams: team one, Basmati, will be working with me, and we'll go by the codename Alpha One. We'll pose as divers, and Basmati will create Professional Association of Diving Instructors (PADI) certificates for himself, most of you know Tuck and I have the genuine article."

Basmati, however, seemed concerned. "I've never dived before."

Cutler's voice was steady, a calm in the storm of planning. "You won't actually be diving. You can handle the boat. They're small crafts, nothing complicated," he said. He shifted in his seat, eyes sharp.

"Tuck, Colton, you're heading to Bali. Port of Benoa. It's the nerve centre, right on the island's southern edge, a stone's throw from Denpasar. That place doesn't just deal with cargo; it's a thoroughfare, alive with fishermen and tourists, cruise ships docking in."

He leaned forward, the light catching the hard lines of his face. "That's where you'll sniff around. Something tells me that's where you'll find information on the gangs and traffickers, They'll be there, blending with the legitimate. We'll split accommodations, keep it casual. No need to parade like we're a military squad on a beach holiday."

There was a pause, weighty and significant. "We don't repeat mistakes here, especially not the kind that Ford's security detail made. We're ghosts, gentlemen. We're there, and yet, we're not." His gaze held theirs, a silent command passing between them, understood, and acknowledged.

Colton chimed in, offering unexpected expertise. "If there's diving involved, I don't have a certificate, but I've been diving since I was a kid."

Cutler, equipped with Fabienne's research, added a surprising titbit. "You do have a caution from the Cook Island police when you were fourteen, though, for removing and not reporting gold coins and other treasure from a shipwreck. Considering it was 60 meters deep, I figured you knew your way around underwater."

Colton's eyes widened, and he turned to Fabienne for confirmation. She nodded, her knowledge once again revealing hidden details.

Tuck brought up an important question. "Can we trust Conrad Ford?"

Cutler's response was measured, reflecting his pragmatic approach. "No, but it's a job like any other. A man's lost his kid and the woman he was going to marry. That's the long and short of it." He paused, letting the room absorb the finality of his words. "Now, let's get on with it." There was no room for sentiment in his tone, just the hard edge of a man used to putting emotions aside and focusing on the task at hand."

Ghislaine, curious about their upcoming tasks, asked, "What are we going to do for the next few days while you're at the funeral?"

Cutler explained their immediate plans. "Tuck is heading to do some more wingsuit training."

Tuck seemed disappointed about the change in plans. "I'll need a wingman, Cutler. It's no fun alone."

Cutler shot a look at Colton, his mind turning over the facts like a seasoned poker player. "Colton," he said, a decision snapping into place, "you're clocking over a hundred HALO jumps. You're with Tuck on this." Colton's eyebrows shot up, a rare break in his usual cool facade.

"Wingsuits?" Ghislaine chimed in, her tone a mix of confusion and curiosity.

Cutler leaned back; his explanation as concise as a bullet. "You jump off a cliff or out of an aircraft. You're wearing these suits, see, with fabric stretched between the limbs. Makes you sort of like a human hawk. You soar, you dive, you navigate. Then you pull the chute when you're close enough to land that you don't give the game away."

Ghislaine's expression was one of disbelief mingled with a hint of amusement. "That's insanity. You two need to get out more."

Cheryl couldn't resist a jab, her eyes sparkling with mischief. "Well, I can't speak for Cutler, but Tuck here doesn't need any more social encouragement, trust me!"

The room filled with a brief round of chuckles, a momentary lapse in the room's usual high-tension atmosphere. In their world, where danger was the currency, these brief flashes of camaraderie were like finding water in the desert.

Basmati's upcoming assignment was of particular interest. Cutler addressed him directly. "Basmati, you're off to Key West for a couple of days. An ex-US Air Force general down there runs a drone training school, said to be the best in the country. Be cautious; the drones you'll be working with are top-notch and don't come cheap."

Stahmer piped up, an edge of eagerness in his seasoned voice, "I wouldn't mind shadowing Basmati on this one."

Cutler's reply was immediate, the words delivered with the kind of finality that didn't invite argument. "Those drones," he began, his gaze steady, "are an $85,000 ticket each. No way I'm letting a one-eyed man take the sticks. Your job is back at base. Kick back, keep the beer cold and the mosquitoes angry."

His tone wasn't mocking, but there was a hard kind of practicality to it. In this line of work, there was no room for sentiment, no space for ego. Everyone had their part, and every role was crucial. Stahmer, caught between the impulse to protest and the understanding of his own limitations, simply nodded.

The comment sparked laughter throughout the room. Ghislaine added her perspective, "So Tuck and Colton are soaring above the Everglades, Basmati gets to play with their drones, Stahmer can put his feet up and I'm stuck in an office learning Indonesian?"

Tuck couldn't resist joining in the playful banter. "That's right. Ghislaine, while you're at it, help Cheryl wash the mountains of dishes left from this morning's feast."

Ghislaine shot back, "You're a misogynist bastard Tuck."

Laughter filled the room as the team embraced the camaraderie that came with their high-stakes missions.

chapter four
A Pact Sealed in Grief

It had been over a month since the news of Robert and Samantha's disappearance, and time had dragged on agonizingly slowly for Conrad Ford. Emilia had been kept under constant sedation, a blessing in her state of grief and shock. Two weeks prior, the American ambassador in Jakarta had delivered devastating news. The Akuma, aptly named 'demon,' was a monstrous ship that roamed the seas off the coast of Indonesia, decimating the fish stocks, thanks to substantial donations made to several high-ranking Indonesian government officials.

Robert Ford and Samantha Gooding's lifeless bodies were reported to the Balinese authorities. Akuma's massive nets had inadvertently ensnared the weighted, bound bodies from the seabed, alongside a live catshark and various scavengers that had been feasting on the remains. The Balinese coastguard had made a grim trip out to the trawler to recover the bodies.

Conrad Ford dreaded the moment when he would have to bring Emilia out of her medicated stupor for the joint funerals of their son and fiancée. Ford had used his considerable influence, ensuring the bodies were transported back by a US Air Force C-17 Globemaster III to Anderson Air Force Base. From there, Conrad had hired a Learjet 45XR jet for his deceased son and fiancée's final journey back to Seattle.

During the day, Ford occupied himself with the grim details and oversaw his staff, maintaining the routine that had been his solace for years. He entrusted his head of security, Julie Birch, with the task of finding outside contractors to investigate on his behalf. Having already lost three of his men, Ford could not afford any more casualties.

Birch presented two possibilities: T4G, a security company known for its operations in war zones, offering services like bodyguards and investigations. The second option was MIDAS, and after careful consideration and thorough research, MIDAS appeared to possess the skills and knowledge base more suited to Ford's specific needs.

In Seattle, the autumn day unfolded typically. The once-green leaves of deciduous trees had transitioned to shades of tan, swirling in eddies across the cemetery grounds. The cherry trees, which had once adorned the graveyard with beautifully detailed white blossoms, were now a distant memory. Dressed in conifers and pines, the cemetery emanated the scent of wet grass and decaying leaves. Mourners, their footsteps crushing the dying foliage beneath their feet, gathered on the sodden turf of Lake View Cemetery.

Lake View Cemetery, steeped in history and nestled on a gentle slope, boasted a verdant landscape and sweeping vistas that set the perfect stage for this sad gathering. Its elevated location allowed visitors to enjoy unobstructed views of the vast Pacific Ocean, making it an ideal spot for reflection and contemplation. Originally known as the Seattle Masonic Cemetery, it earned its new name due to the breathtaking panorama it offered, with Lake Washington stretching gracefully to the east.

Rows of white chairs surrounded the burial plot, some twenty rows deep, an indication to the expected turnout for the funeral. The grave had been prepared the previous day and was now concealed beneath rolls of synthetic grass, with no earth in sight.

Pallbearers, their hands gripping the brass handles of the straight-grained, highly polished white coffins, lifted the caskets from the hearse. They gently smoothed the stars and stripes flags of the United States that adorned the coffins. Slowly, they began their descent down a slight incline toward the open grave. There, they carefully positioned the two coffins, each draped in an American flag, side by side on a hydraulic lift.

A crisp breeze swept down from the north, demanding jackets and coats from the mourners gathered at Lake View Cemetery. The sky above painted a brilliant blue canvas, adorned with sporadic stratus clouds that occasionally diffused the sun's rays. The soft rustling of swirling leaves in the background merged with the heartfelt sobs of Emilia and a multitude of young friends who had come to bid farewell to the departed souls. To these friends, Robert and Samantha were more than just names on a tombstone; they were confidants and sources of inspiration, their lives tragically cut short. The elder guests adhered to the tradition of wearing mourning attire in black, while the younger group, consisting of Robert and Samantha's friends, chose to don a variety of vibrant, colourful outfits—a poignant tribute to the youthful lives that had been tragically cut short.

Conrad Ford had always taken his and Emilia's security with utmost seriousness. His regular team consisted of six ex-Secret

Service operatives who served as his dedicated bodyguards. However, for this solemn occasion, he had bolstered security with three retired Navy SEALs, strategically positioned in the cemetery. Their designated meeting point was located about 120 yards up the hill from the burial site.

Robert and Samantha were to be laid to rest side by side; a request Emilia had made with unwavering determination. In her grief-stricken heart, she clung to the belief that Samantha would continue to watch over Robert in the afterlife. Conrad, for once, remained silent on the matter, understanding that any small comfort for Emilia during these trying times was a precious gift.

The security detail operated with precision; each member tasked with specific duties. Two guards closely protected Emilia and Conrad, ensuring their safety. Two more vigilantly observed the visitors to the cemetery, discreetly checking them for concealed weapons, a breach of local by-laws. The final pair was stationed near one of the cemetery's main attractions, the final resting place of martial arts legend and actor Bruce Lee. Bruce's grave continued to draw admirers, and beside it stood a black memorial gravestone honouring his son, Brandon Lee, tragically killed during the filming of "The Crow" when a blank bullet ejected a live round already in the chamber. This site held special significance for fans of the Lee family.

Among the admirers and curious onlookers, Cutler immediately recognized the security detail. They stood as monuments of strength, radiating the unmistakable aura of military discipline.

Cutler studied their eyes, steely and unyielding, a testament to the unimaginable horrors they had witnessed.

Joe Redman, a SEAL veteran of over a decade before retirement, was stationed at the entry point. He swiftly identified Cutler as someone warranting a thorough inspection. His years of experience had honed his instincts to detect those with an air of danger.

"What's going on, Joe? Don't you recognize a brother in arms?" Steve Reagan, another member of the detail, asked the first bodyguard.

"How are you, Cutler? It's been a while," Reagan enquired with a broad grin.

"Not long enough. The last time we crossed paths was in San Diego; I had a hangover that lasted three days," Cutler replied.

"Yeah, I remember, right after little Jeanie was born," Reagan reminisced.

"How's the little troublemaker? She must be seven or eight years old by now," Cutler enquired.

"Eight going on twenty-eight. Like her mom—just uses me as an ATM. Anyway, enough of the reminiscing, the boss has given me instructions to let you pass. Are you carrying?" Cutler questioned the security personnel who stood before him, arms folded, their expressions hardened by years of service.

"Out of my cold, dead hands," Cutler mimicked Charlton Heston's famous phrase from the National Rifle Association speech, a hint of dry humour in his voice.

"Will have to take it, Cutler. There's several Secret Service around guarding the vice president and if we don't take it, they will."

"I was just tugging at your strings, Reagan," Cutler replied with a half-smile, as he handed over his SIG-Sauer P229 pistol. Cutler rarely left what he called his 'baby' behind, a standard sidearm for all special agents, which had been his preferred weapon since his days at the Secret Service.

Cutler lingered at the rear of the crowd; his gaze fixed on the proceedings. The Catholic priest, a stranger to both the deceased, lamented over the young lives cut tragically short. Several prayers later, the American flags were removed, signifying the sombre transition from ceremony to internment. The priest's assistant pressed a console button, and the two white coffins were lowered into the graves, side by side, to the sound of The Star-Spangled Banner.

Emilia wept loudly throughout the funeral, her grief pouring out in unrestrained sobs. Nearby, Samantha's mother, Janet, rocked back and forth, her tear-stained face a reflection of unbearable loss. She had turned to alcohol to numb the pain of the past month. Sitting between them was Vice President Richard Treisman, flanked by Conrad Ford. The dedications and farewells from friends and family continued for some time, each person paying their respects in their own way.

Conrad Ford wanted the ordeal over, his stoic demeanour masking the profound sorrow within. Emilia was supported by her physician, who sat beside her and occasionally offered a small tablet and a flask of undetermined liquid to ease her suffering.

As the mourners began to disperse, Ford escorted Emilia to their waiting car, planting a gentle kiss on her forehead before leaving her in the care of the attending doctor. He then turned back, his eyes scanning the area until they locked onto Cutler's familiar face amidst the crowd. With purposeful strides, he made his way toward the former Secret Service agent, his head slightly bowed under the weight of the occasion.

"Walk with me, Cutler," Ford ordered, the urgency in his voice betraying the gravity of the matter at hand.

They strolled up the grassy incline, veering south of Bruce Lee's grave to avoid a small gathering of people paying their respects. Two security personnel followed them at a discreet distance, their vigilant eyes trained on the surroundings.

Cutler waited for Ford to speak, knowing that pleasantries were the last thing either of them needed on this solemn day.

"We are pretty sure it's Bali," Ford replied, his voice laced with a tinge of frustration and urgency.

Cutler arched an eyebrow, probing further, "Was that confirmed before your security team went missing?"

"You have been doing your homework, Cutler," Ford acknowledged with a weary nod. "My security went missing because they were getting close."

Cutler's reply was blunt, "They're probably dead."

"You don't have to state the obvious to me, Cutler," Ford retorted, the weight of his son's death etched in his eyes. "Are you going to take the job, or do I need to be speaking to your competition?"

"As you are no doubt aware, we have no competition in this area of investigation. We will leave tomorrow," Cutler affirmed, his tone resolute. "Your scoping contract means that if we track the killers down and hand them over to the police, with enough money, they will buy their way out. You've already spent for a short-term gain in sending your own men in; this will not be completed in a week, just so you know."

"I am paying you the same, whether it's a week or a month, so it's in your interest to get this done as soon as possible. You will get half of the cost upfront and the half when you hand them over to my security, Cutler," Ford stated, his impatience showing.

"And as I told your head of security, Julie Birch, last week, we will defend ourselves vigorously, but we are not assassins. If that is what you are looking for, well, you have the wrong company," Cutler declared firmly.

"Yes, I have been thoroughly briefed on what you will and will not do. If I wanted them dead, I would be sending a team of mercenaries. I want you and your team to locate them, and then I want you to deliver them to my security team, who will give them to me," Ford pronounced with a chilling determination.

Cutler reiterated, "The same terms and conditions apply, we won't convey them to your security team to dispose of them, it's the same outcome. We will not be implicit in their murder."

"There are far worse places around the world than Guantanamo Bay, Cutler. I don't want these scum dead, that's too easy. Did you look around you today?" Ford gestured subtly to the mourners dispersing around them. "The vice president was one of the least influential persons here. I have power and influence and a whole lot of favours I can pull in at any time. You can be assured these 'pirates,' as you have tagged them, will be alive for a very long time, living every day in some hellhole. Give it a year, they will be begging to be put out of their misery," he declared with chilling resolve.

"As an individual and as head of MIDAS, I don't have a problem with that, but I will want written assurances as to their safe transport and imprisonment. Just as important, I want your word," Cutler stated firmly, his unwavering commitment to justice evident.

"You have my word. I will have my attorney draw up the contract and your terms and conditions," Ford assured him. He extended his hand, and Cutler reciprocated with a firm handshake. "My son lies dead in that cold grave over there, my wife is distraught, and for the first time in my life, I don't know how to fix the problem. Like you, Cutler, I need to find a resolution."

Cutler offered a sombre nod, understanding the depths of Ford's despair. "You can't trust your mind when your emotions are so raw. Are you sure you want to go ahead with this?" he enquired, a glimmer of concern in his eyes.

Conrad Ford shook Cutler's hand, his expression a mix of gratitude and anguish. With a heavy heart, he turned and began his slow, solitary journey back to his son's grave.

"Keep me informed," Ford requested, his usual air of authority momentarily replaced by the weight of grief. "You are welcome at the wake," he added.

Cutler had other plans. Ford would never suspect that the sanctity of his grief would be intruded upon. Cutler knew this was the perfect time to penetrate Ford's inner sanctum.

Under the cloak of night, leveraging years of experience from countless discreet operations, Cutler made his approach. The Ford residence, a fortress in its own right, was equipped with state-of-the-art security technology. However, no electronic system was infallible against Cutler, whose meticulous planning accounted for every patrol pattern and surveillance blind spot.

Infiltrating the house required a blend of cyber skill and physical stealth. First, a diversion was created by triggering a false alarm at a nearby outhouse, pulling away the bulk of the security detail. Then, Cutler bypassed the electronic locks and security system, temporarily disabling motion sensors and cameras with a device Fabienne had custom-built.

Once inside, he moved with purpose, his form barely more than a whisper against the luxurious décor of the Ford mansion. The bugs he placed weren't the standard fare used by intelligence agencies. These were cutting-edge, virtually undetectable devices that utilized a range of technologies, from quantum encryption to signal dispersal, making them invisible to even the most sophisticated sweeps. They were so advanced that they could capture not just audio but video, digital information, and electronic communications, transmitting them back to Cutler's team using a mesh of randomized signals to avoid interception.

Placing them strategically throughout the house—in Conrad's private study, the meeting room, and various points of communication like phones and computers—was a task that required precision. Each bug was no larger than a speck of dust, adhering to surfaces on a molecular level, making them impossible to detect and remove without specialized knowledge and equipment.

With the task completed, Cutler exfiltrated the premises just before the security systems came back online, erasing his digital footprints and leaving no physical trace of his intrusion. As he disappeared into the darkness, the house remained silent and unaware, now a wellspring of information that would flow directly to Cutler and his team.

chapter five
Desert Showdown

The jet lag weighed heavily on Stahmer, despite the luxuries of business class travel. The long and gruelling journey from Miami to London Heathrow, followed by a brief layover, and then another flight to Sharm El Sheikh, had taken its toll. Meanwhile, Ghislaine, significantly younger than Stahmer, settled into the luxurious Occidental Hotel, located as close to the Red Sea as one could get. Stahmer, however, headed straight to his room to recuperate.

In the hotel bar, Shultz pulled out his adapted Microsoft Surface Pro from his backpack. He powered it up and connected to the complimentary Wi-Fi, though he ignored the passcode on the key card, knowing that the network was not secure. Instead, he used the encrypted MIDAS dongle issued to each member of their team.

Ghislaine, dressed in white shorts and a sleeveless white cotton blouse that accentuated her ever-tanned skin, joined him. Her striking beauty didn't go unnoticed, and an Egyptian cocktail waiter couldn't resist stealing glances. Shultz, protective by nature, quickly discouraged the waiter's advances, though Ghislaine was more than capable of handling such situations herself. She was accustomed to the attention, but she appreciated Shultz's protective instincts.

Over complimentary Wi-Fi, Shultz received emails from Cheryl, containing instructions and an updated report on Gareth Cummings' disappearance. They diligently reviewed the reports, highlighting critical points for their upcoming meeting with Stahmer the following morning. As they sipped margaritas and analysed the information, Ghislaine, feeling the exhaustion of the long journey, eventually excused herself.

In the morning, Stahmer, donned in a cream-colored suit and a Panama hat, and Shultz, dressed in khaki shorts, joined Ghislaine, who wore a white linen suit. Together, they blended in with the other tourists in the hotel's breakfast hall.

Exiting the hotel, they sought shelter from the scorching sun under the entrance canopy where taxis waited. The heat hit them immediately, and they donned their sunglasses before crossing the lawn to a wooden jetty overlooking the Red Sea. The calm, warm waters glistened in the sunlight, creating a mesmerizing view.

As they waited for a hotel chef to finish his cigarette break, they marvelled at the marine life visible in the clear waters. Puffer fish, scorpions, clownfish, and tiddlers swam by, providing a brief distraction from their mission.

Shultz had thoroughly reviewed the briefing documents the night before and shared the details with his colleagues. He informed them about their scheduled meetings and the attached investigative document Fabienne was working on. After the briefing, they exchanged thoughts and quotes, and Stahmer quoted Mark Twain, saying, "The secret of getting ahead is getting started."

Their meeting with Chief of Police Omar Ahmed was scheduled at the hotel, as he preferred to avoid the chaotic atmosphere of his police station. Ahmed arrived late, displaying an arrogant attitude and a bearing that instantly rubbed Ghislaine the wrong way. Despite his tardiness, Ahmed offered no apology and seemed disinterested in assisting with their investigation. Stahmer introduced himself and his colleagues and acknowledged that the police report contained limited information about Gareth Cummings' disappearance.

"It's a rather unusual case, with scanty facts, you'll understand," Ahmed responded, his words somewhat rushed.

Stahmer pressed further, enquiring about Inspector Shariff's possible insights. Ahmed's response was curt. "Inspector Shariff is unavailable."

Stahmer didn't mince words in expressing his disappointment. "We have been assured of your complete cooperation, sir. This does not appear to be the assistance we were told you would provide."

Omar Ahmed squirmed in his chair, caught between his obligations and the reality of the situation. The recent downturn in tourism due to terrorism had put pressure on local authorities, and Oceanic Enterprises' continued support was something Chief of Police Omar Ahmed couldn't ignore, especially after a call from the tourism minister.

"Inspector Shariff has been missing for two days. He is one of our most reliable officers, and at the moment, we have no explanation for his disappearance. We have no reason to believe it has any connection with your investigation, I might add," Chief of Police Omar Ahmed said, trying to assert control.

Shultz, however, wasn't ready to let this slide. He pointed out the bizarre circumstances. "You have a missing marine officer from a cruise ship; now the police officer who is investigating the disappearance has himself gone missing. Do you not find that strange?"

The chief of police's patience was wearing thin. He wasn't accustomed to being questioned, especially by foreigners. Yet he couldn't afford to let a formal complaint reach the ministry.

"Inspector Shariff had quite a workload, and while I can see why you want to link the two disappearances together, it may be unrelated and to do with one of his other cases. It may well be he has decided to go away for a few days," Chief of Police Omar Ahmed retorted, though unconvincingly.

Stahmer pushed further. "By your own words, the officer is reliable. How many tourists, mariners, or police officers have disappeared this year or last year?"

Ahmed's curt reply was telling. "None."

Stahmer emphasized the glaring need for a thorough investigation. "Well, by the very fact that you have two men vanishing who are linked and no satisfactory explanation for either, we can assume, at the very least, there may be a connection and it should be investigated as such."

Ghislaine, despite understanding the customs in the region, couldn't hold back any longer. She questioned Chief of Police Omar Ahmed about the police's efforts and the lack of real-time information in the briefing document. Her questions further infuriated the police chief.

Stahmer, ever the diplomat, thanked the chief and assured him they would keep him updated on their findings.

After Ahmed left, Ghislaine expressed her frustration. Stahmer reminded her of the delicate balance they needed to maintain on this unfamiliar turf, especially considering Chief of Police Omar Ahmed 's influence.

With limited information, they decided to start with Gareth Cummings' last known whereabouts—heading to the market outside Sharm El Sheikh to buy supplies for the officers' mess. Their investigation was about to hit the road.

Shultz arranged for a rental car, and soon they were driving in a weathered Jeep Cherokee. As they approached a checkpoint controlling access to the area, they were stopped to show their passports. Upon clearing the checkpoint, they were trailed by a brand-new police car, adding a new layer of intrigue to their journey.

Stahmer couldn't shake the feeling that the police unit tailing them was more of an annoyance than assistance, but he understood Ahmed's likely motives. The police chief had already faced an affront to his pride earlier in the day and didn't want the foreigners to laugh at the local patrol car.

They parked in an area across from the market, which served as a makeshift parking lot. The space was cluttered with old, battered vehicles and tethered carts and donkeys. Shultz parked the Jeep Cherokee next to a weathered Volkswagen Beetle, while the police car parked nearby, effectively blocking two more decrepit vehicles.

The marketplace was a bustling hub, with a prominent statue of a pharaoh, a lone security guard, and a triple-tiered mosque under renovation. The central square was filled with vendors offering fresh produce, meat, trinkets, and even a snake charmer. Tourists outnumbered the local population by a considerable margin.

Sergeant Yacoub introduced himself and his team, pledging their assistance. After exchanging greetings, Stahmer divided tasks among them. He instructed two police officers to interview stallholders, particularly focusing on any unusual incidents on the day Cummings went missing. Ghislaine, who was fluent in Egyptian, accompanied them to ensure accurate reporting, given her suspicions about Chief of Police Omar Ahmed 's potential influence.

Shultz was tasked with speaking to local residents along the perimeter. Some locals spoke English, which could prove helpful. Stahmer asked Sergeant Yacoub for the best café in the area and invited the sergeant to join him for coffee. They walked to the western perimeter, where they found a number of tables with ancient wooden chairs. After a brief exchange, two men vacated a table for Stahmer and the sergeant to occupy.

The scorching heat persisted, with a swirling sandstorm occasionally passing through the market. Tourists sought refuge by washing sand from their eyes using the manufactured waterfall, while others improvised by donning traditional Arab scarves. Some locals used umbrellas to shield themselves from the relentless sun and abrasive sand particles.

Stahmer opted for tea with lemon, a cautious choice due to water quality concerns, hoping the lemon would sterilize any impurities. Sergeant Yacoub surprised him by ordering Nescafe with condensed milk.

Stahmer, still sipping his tea, continued to question Sergeant Yacoub about Inspector Shariff's disappearance. The sergeant's English, with its distinct American twang, was surprisingly good, learned from old Western movies and further honed through a Rosetta Stone self-study course.

Sergeant Yacoub had nothing but praise for Inspector Shariff, describing him as a family man of integrity and honesty. He expressed genuine concern for his missing friend and assured Stahmer of his willingness to assist in any way possible, even if it meant going against the chief's orders.

The sergeant revealed that Inspector Shariff had gone missing two days ago after spending the morning reviewing CCTV tapes. These cameras had been strategically placed along the main highway between points twelve and sixteen by an English security company, following the bombing of a Russian jet. These points were used for monitoring security and preventing terrorist threats, though they had yet to catch any terrorists. The sergeant speculated that Inspector Shariff might have been investigating something at one of these points.

Stahmer expressed his gratitude and accepted a map the sergeant offered, which marked the area where Inspector Shariff might have gone. He also enquired about the format of the CCTV tapes, which the sergeant believed were stored on a hard drive.

Back at the hotel, Stahmer arranged a debriefing for the officers and provided them with a hearty meal. During the debriefing, one of the officers reported a piece of valuable information—a fruit seller had witnessed a foreigner being bitten by a cobra and taken to the hospital by two men, one of whom had a peculiar walk and was exceptionally large.

After the officers left, Stahmer, Ghislaine, and Shultz discussed their findings. Stahmer suspected that they had stumbled upon some luck, as the local police seemed motivated to catch whoever had taken Inspector Shariff. However, he cautioned that their trust in the local officers should only extend so far.

Shultz reported no significant progress from his discussions with locals along the perimeter, but he was unaware that one of the vendors, Hamid, was an informant paid to keep Aziz informed. Hamid promptly called Aziz, who in turn contacted Kamal, Asfour's man in the region. Kamal, in possession of damning information about Deputy Chief Officer Saleh, had manipulated Saleh into serving their interests, using his fear and desperation as leverage.

Saleh, burdened by guilt and living in constant fear of exposure, had tampered with Inspector Shariff's case files, erasing vital evidence. Chief of Police Omar Ahmed, though aware of the tampering, was unable to confront Saleh due to his own compromising access to his officers' activities. The situation grew increasingly complex, with layers of deception and vulnerability.

Saleh, a man trapped in the clutches of guilt, lived in perpetual fear of his dark secrets coming to light. His restless nights were haunted by the knowledge that he had manipulated Inspector Shariff's case files, methodically erasing vital evidence like a surgeon removing a malignant tumour. This act of sabotage weighed heavily on his conscience, shackling him to a life of relentless anxiety.

Chief of Police Omar Ahmed, though privy to Saleh's treacherous deeds, found himself in a precarious position. His own access to his officers' activities had become a double-edged sword, rendering him powerless to confront Saleh's betrayal. The situation grew increasingly convoluted, like an intricate puzzle with pieces that refused to fit together. Layers of deception and vulnerability enveloped them all, like a suffocating shroud.

The impending threat of exposure loomed over Chief of Police Omar Ahmed like a sword of Damocles. If the truth were to surface during the Cummings investigation, he would be held accountable for the web of deceit that had taken root under his watchful eye. Worse yet, if this tangled web were connected to the missing cruise line officer, the repercussions could reach the highest echelons of power, implicating the tourist minister. Chief of Police Omar Ahmed stood to lose not only his position but also the privileges that came with it. Despite his distaste for the situation, he yearned for this mess to disappear like a mirage in the desert.

In the aftermath of the discovery, he took the precautionary step of reinstating password controls on the police computers. It was a small price to pay to avoid another potential security risk, even if it meant enduring the complaints and grumbles of his officers over restricted internet access.

Later that evening, amidst the backdrop of an upscale restaurant, where surf and turf graced their plates and imported wines flowed freely, Stahmer's pager emitted a barely audible buzz. It pierced the ambient melody of a pianist playing mellow tunes in the background. They hastily concluded their meal and regrouped in Stahmer's suite on the eighth floor of the hotel.

Ghislaine had been equipped with a specially adapted Surface Pro; a technological marvel forged by Fabienne's expertise to rival the impenetrable vaults of Fort Knox. With practiced ease, Ghislaine unlocked the tablet by entering a complex alphanumeric code. A second screen materialized, and Ghislaine underwent a retinal scan, her face briefly illuminated by the device's scanning beam. Once the rigorous security checks had been satisfied, a secure link was established, revealing Cheryl's cheerful countenance.

"Hi, everyone. I hope you're all basking in the sun and enjoying your expense account," Cheryl greeted them, her tone radiating warmth.

Ghislaine couldn't resist a playful quip, "You could fry an egg on the patio, and the wine tastes like it's been filtered through a swimming pool."

Chuckling, Cheryl continued, "Well, while you've been enduring those hardships, I've been hard at work processing the requests you sent earlier today. Satellite imagery of the area will be sent after our little video conference. Now, as for hacking into the inspector's computer, I hit a solid brick wall; that firewall was way above my pay grade. However, Fabienne has graciously dedicated some of her time from the Bali mission to assist you. I'll transfer you to her in Geneva now. Enjoy."

The screen blinked, and Fabienne appeared, somewhat dishevelled, as she devoured what appeared to be an oversized chocolate éclair.

"Apologies for that, I thought Cheryl would be available a bit longer," Fabienne said, wiping her mouth with a paper serviette.

Eagerly, Ghislaine enquired, "What do you have for us?"

Fabienne flashed a confident grin and replied, "Oh, I have quite the treasure trove of information for you. You see, I wasn't surprised that Cheryl encountered a roadblock; the moment she began accessing the site, I knew we were dealing with a formidable firewall. And here's the twist: I happen to be intimately familiar with it, having written the code myself during my tenure at GCHQ, working for British intelligence."

Stahmer, standing alongside Ghislaine, confessed, "I'm not quite following. Are you suggesting that a rogue software company has access to the British government's resources?"

Fabienne clarified, "No, it's the British government itself that's behind this ingenious operation. Still not connecting the dots, I see."

Stahmer, joined by Shultz, pressed further, "So you mean to say that GCHQ is running the software and computers for an Egyptian police force? And for what purpose?"

Fabienne elaborated, "Precisely. GCHQ is directly involved; instead, they've set up localized police stations near tourist hotspots like Sharm El Sheikh, Hurghada, the Valley of the Kings and Queens, and even the police force on the Giza Plateau, where the pyramids are situated. Essentially, anywhere the Egyptian authorities are concerned about potential tourist attacks."

Shultz, catching on, summarized, "They're outsourcing top-notch security services at a discounted rate, effectively gaining access to invaluable intelligence."

Fabienne nodded with approval, "Exactly! They've been burned by a series of bombing attacks in the Middle East and Africa due to intelligence gaps. After the Russian commercial aircraft incident, it appears they decided to take matters into their own hands. The supposed security company provides them with advice and assistance to reduce the risk of attacks. Moreover, they can monitor every keystroke made on the computers they've supplied as part of their deal. What's more, every time someone enters information, a photograph of the user is captured and sent back to GCHQ, along with their telephone data."

Stahmer, though visibly uneasy, allowed Fabienne to continue, "It seems they're particularly concerned about the security personnel as well. They're pushing for facial recognition to match names to users. This way, if someone within the police force collaborates with terrorists and uses these computers, GCHQ is instantly alerted."

"So, Fabienne, how does this all help us?" Ghislaine enquired with a hint of curiosity; her eyes focused on the computer screen.

Fabienne leaned back in her chair, a smug grin crossing her face as she adjusted her glasses. "Well, my dear Ghislaine, you may think the CCTV footage was deleted, but in the digital world, nothing truly disappears. I've not only recovered the deleted footage, but I've also identified the person responsible. I'm about to send you some attachments—one is the recording, and the other is Inspector Shariff's notes."

The trio gathered around the computer screen, anticipation building. Fabienne continued, "Now, according to Inspector Shariff's notes, the missing inspector had a conversation with a local stallholder. This stallholder recalled a tourist who was supposedly bitten by a cobra during a snake charmer's performance. Oddly enough, the stallholder had never seen that snake charmer before and insisted that when the tourist collapsed, he was nowhere near the charmer."

Stahmer nodded, absorbing the information. "That aligns with what we've learned so far."

Fabienne's fingers danced across the keyboard as she explained further, "But there's more to the story. The same stallholder witnessed the collapsed tourist being carried away by two men in Arab attire. Now, here's where it gets interesting—when you watch the recording, you'll see one of those men, and he's quite the imposing figure, easily over seven feet tall. Inspector Shariff studied the CCTV images and noticed that the same white Fiat van appeared at various checkpoints along the highway. What's puzzling is that it took an unusually long time for the van to pass through checkpoints thirteen and fourteen. Two hours instead of the expected thirty minutes."

Ghislaine couldn't help but be impressed. "Fabienne, you're amazing. Is there anything else?"

Fabienne grinned, unable to conceal her pride. "Oh, absolutely. I've extracted images of the two Arabs who abducted Gareth Cummings from the CCTV footage. I ran them through my facial recognition software—the one I built myself. The larger man didn't match any records, but the smaller one did."

Stahmer leaned in, his interest piqued. "Tell us about this smaller man."

Fabienne continued, "He was born Richard Hussain in Birmingham, England. He became radicalized and started as a foot soldier for Al-Qaeda, eventually moving up to their technical recruitment team. He was captured by the Americans but released during an insurgent attack on the Al Ghraib prison. He now goes by the name Umar Aziz."

Shultz couldn't contain his enthusiasm. "Fabienne, you're a true rock star!"

Fabienne laughed, basking in the compliments. "Well, I may be a rock star, but remember, without all of you out there in the field, I'd just be a custodian of knowledge."

Stahmer interjected, his tone serious. "Checkpoints thirteen and fourteen seem crucial to our investigation. But we need to be cautious. Going directly to thirteen might expose our intelligence. Trust, but don't trust too far."

The team exited the comfort of the air-conditioned hotel into the scorching midday heat. They spotted Sergeant Yacoub and his officers sitting in the shade beneath a lone palm tree in the hotel's parking lot, nodding at them in acknowledgment.

As they continued down the highway, Ghislaine's iPhone rang, playing the familiar tune of *Yellow Submarine*. It was Fabienne's emergency signal, prompting an immediate call. Stahmer pulled the jeep to the side of the road, the police car parking beside them.

Fabienne's voice crackled through the phone, "I've intercepted some chatter. I programmed my software with keywords like 'Cummings' and the missing inspector's name, and…"

Stahmer interrupted, his urgency apparent. "Get to the point, Fabienne."

Fabienne continued, "Deputy Chief of Police Omar Ahmed's right-hand man, Saleh, made a call on a disposable phone—a burner. He's the same guy who wiped Inspector Shariff's hard drive. The keyword that alerted me was 'Inspector Shariff'. Saleh called someone named Kamal and mentioned that you and your team were in the area, asking questions. The conversation is about two hours old, so be cautious—you might have company."

Stahmer thanked her and then asked, "Anything else, Fabienne?"

"One more thing," she added, "I've been studying satellite images of the area you suspect Cummings might have been taken to. Based on your GPS coordinates, if you continue on the main road for another six and a quarter miles, just before checkpoint thirteen, you'll see a left turn. It appears to be a track leading nowhere, but if you pass a fishing village and continue for two more miles, the track forks. Take the right fork, and there's an old building at the end of it. Local records show it's been uninhabited for over a decade. This could be an ideal location for a kidnapper."

Stahmer disconnected the call and approached Sergeant Yacoub, leading him a bit further into the stony desert for a private conversation. A few moments later, Shultz swapped attire with a policeman, switching places with him in the vehicles and the police car sped away, leaving Stahmer and his team to continue their journey without a police escort. They knew that checkpoints thirteen and fourteen held crucial information, but they needed to tread carefully in this high-stakes game of cat and mouse.

Stahmer's decision to deviate from their original plan and head towards checkpoint thirteen was a calculated risk, driven by a pressing need for answers. As the jeep rumbled onward, the open desert surroundings made normal conversation impossible due to the noise generated by the tyres on the stony ground.

Ghislaine, her face shielded from the sun by a scarf, clung to the back of the jeep's seat as they bumped and jolted along the uneven terrain. The wind whipped through her hair, carrying with it the gritty embrace of the desert. She scanned the horizon, searching for any signs of the elusive checkpoint.

It was Ghislaine who first spotted the faint traces of tyre tracks veering off the beaten path. She had to shout at Stahmer to be heard over the howling wind. The going was slow, the old fishing road now reduced to a rugged trail that sloped down to a secluded bay before disappearing into the desolate desert landscape. They had to rely on subtle clues like flattened stones, occasional oil stains, and rare tyre tracks to navigate their way to their destination.

Fabienne's information from the emergency call had pinpointed this location as the primary site, a fact Stahmer and Sergeant Yacoub agreed to act upon. Searching for this site was a gamble, one that came with potential consequences they couldn't predict. But in their line of work, taking risks was an inherent part of the job.

As they disembarked from the jeep and surveyed their surroundings, an unsettling feeling washed over Stahmer. There was no audible sound other than the desert wind, but he sensed a subtle change in the atmosphere. It was a sixth sense he had honed over years of fieldwork, and it had never led him astray. In a swift and instinctive move, he pulled Ghislaine from her seat across to where he had been sitting a moment ago, hoping he had chosen the right side.

The Egyptian desert stretched out around them, an unbroken sea of golden sand dunes that seemed to go on forever. The relentless sun hung overhead, casting a harsh and unforgiving light that shimmered in the dry desert air. The heat was oppressive, a relentless force that pressed down upon them, making each step a struggle.

Stahmer couldn't shake the feeling that they were stepping into a Pandora's box of trouble, but he had little choice. The information from Fabienne's emergency call had pointed them here, and the risk was one they had to take. He knew that their presence in this unforgiving desert held both peril and promise.

As they finally dismounted the jeep, the subtle change in the air caught Stahmer's attention. It was a sixth sense, an instinct that had saved his life more than once. He grabbed Ghislaine and pulled her down just as the unmistakable sound of a bullet whizzed past them, striking the police officer in the rear of the jeep.

In the back of the jeep, the police officer, who had swapped clothes with Shultz, was in the process of climbing out when the world around them erupted in chaos. He was blown clear of the vehicle, catching the top of the wheel as he tumbled. Stahmer quickly scrambled alongside the injured officer, taking cover behind the bulk of the vehicle. A glance told him the police officer was alive but bleeding heavily from a shoulder wound.

The desert was no longer their ally but a merciless battlefield. The sniper had them pinned down, and their only chance lay in the distant gunfire they could hear, a signal of hope from Sergeant Yacoub and Shultz, racing to their aid.

Stahmer swiftly pulled the injured officer behind the rear wheel, exposing him to further injuries from the rocky ground. Ghislaine, using two fingers, worked to staunch the bleeding from the officer's shoulder. The ping of a second bullet hitting the roll bar above their heads reinforced the fact that they were under attack.

Back at Saleh's end, he had been informed that an investigation with outside agencies was underway. He was in deep trouble and had no choice but to call Kamal with the information that foreign investigators had zeroed in on an area of interest. Kamal, using Snapchat, passed this critical information to Aziz, who instructed Kamal to go to the primary site and eliminate any threats that might surface.

Kamal preferred night-time operations; his sharp eyes more reliable in the evening light than the harsh daytime sun. Most snipers operated in two-man teams, but Kamal had no spotter. Aziz had taken the rest of the team to Hurghada, leaving Kamal to handle all tasks alone. The challenge was that the environmental parameters he had checked could change rapidly—and they did. Kamal had his sights trained on the most prominent target, the person standing at the rear of the jeep. His aim was on the chest region, ensuring a kill shot even if he missed the heart. But in the seconds between assessing wind direction and squeezing the trigger, a slight shift could mean the difference between hitting vital organs or mere bone and muscle.

Amidst the frantic chaos that followed the shooting, Ghislaine, crouched behind the front wheel with her fingers buried in the injured officer's wound, dialled Shultz's number on her mobile with her free hand. The urgency in her voice was palpable as she spoke, "Police officer down, we're under fire! I've sent you our coordinates directly to your phone. How far away are you?"

Shultz replied, "About ten minutes away. We've circled around from the back. The sergeant knows these off-road tracks like the back of his hand. From which direction did the shot come from? He's asking."

Ghislaine responded, "From the west, maybe north-northwest, can't be sure, but that's the general direction."

Shultz relayed the information, "If you're near the old building, the sergeant thinks north-northwest is likely, as there's no cover directly west. There are some large boulders in that area, the only concealment for a sniper, given the flat terrain. Hang in there, Ghislaine. We'll be there as fast as we can."

Ghislaine's voice was tense as she replied, "Hurry, Shultz. He's systematically targeting the jeep's tyres one by one, hoping for a better shot." Another bullet struck the tyre she was using for cover, emphasizing the urgency of their situation.

"Copy that," Shultz replied urgently. "The sergeant is asking about his officer."

"Alive for now," Ghislaine conveyed with a sense of gravity. "It's up to you guys whether we get out of this."

Kamal found himself in a dilemma. Should he stay in his current position or attempt to flank his targets for a clear shot? Flanking would take time and expose him momentarily, which was a risk he couldn't ignore. Saleh had mentioned a police guard, but none was in sight at the moment. They might have abandoned the foreign investigators, taken a break, or were positioned at the head of the road to prevent any vehicles from approaching from behind. Kamal couldn't ascertain whether the foreigners were armed, and he had a crucial decision to make.

Aziz had instructed him that the bodies could not be discovered for three days. After that, it wouldn't matter. If he retreated now, the place would be swarming with police and regional intelligence officers within hours. Kamal chose not to remain in his position, taking advantage of the approaching darkness as cover.

The once pristine police car now bore chip marks from the flying stones kicked up by the terrain. Sergeant Yacoub had abandoned caution due to the wounded officer. He gauged that the sniper had a fixed view on his kill zone and wouldn't anticipate the approaching dust cloud from the opposite direction.

Sergeant Yacoub retrieved two shotguns from the car's trunk, handing one to his officer and keeping one for himself. He also handed a pistol to Shultz, retrieved from a small holster strapped to his thigh above his boot, instructing, "For defence only." They parked the car about a quarter of a mile from their suspected sniper position. The relatively silent engine noise of their new vehicle allowed them to get closer than a standard police car would have.

The three of them spread out, maintaining a distance of 100 yards between each other, as they began a cautious trot across the scorching desert towards three large boulders in the distance. Their available weapons had limited range compared to the snipers, so their plan was to get as close as possible without alerting the shooter to their presence. It wasn't the ideal plan, but with one officer down and two MIDAS operatives pinned down, it was their only option.

As the daylight rapidly faded, the boulders ahead took on a candy-apple-red hue for a brief moment. What was conspicuously missing, however, was any sign of a human presence. The sniper might be lying low, but an experienced sharpshooter would have utilized the elevated vantage point provided by the boulders to maximize their view of the kill zone.

Navigating through the boulders, it became evident to Shultz, Sergeant Yacoub, and the young police officer that the sniper was no longer present. Shultz scanned the area, detecting signs of disturbance and a lone piece of chewed gum stuck to a rock. He deduced that the sniper chewed gum. It was also apparent that the sniper had not considered the endgame; no professional assassin would leave such a blatant piece of DNA evidence behind.

After running another 70 yards, Shultz spotted a dark object on the harsh desert floor. Something about it seemed out of place. Perhaps a dead animal had recognized the approaching swarm of flies for what it was. Shultz dashed over the rugged terrain to the darkened object. The cloud of flies hovered above it, waiting their turn to land and lay eggs to feed on the necrotic flesh. Accompanying the flies were parasites and several scorpions, all-consuming the exposed flesh. Swatting them away, Shultz swiftly moved his arm just above the body, regretting it immediately as the flies invaded his mouth and swarmed around him.

Clearing his mouth of the bitter taste of several insects he had unwittingly swallowed, Shultz knelt to inspect what remained of the body. Judging by its size, it was almost certainly a man, and the tattered clothing resembled a uniform. From the digital records Fabienne had provided, Shultz knew that Gareth Cummings had a distinctive scar from a harelip, which he typically concealed with a moustache. Shultz scrutinized the head, swatting away the persistent insects. The eyes were gone, replaced by writhing maggots in empty sockets. Above the missing lips, facial hair remained, and there was evidence of scar tissue running up to what remained of the nose. Shultz was convinced that they had found Gareth Cummings.

With no time to lose, Shultz started making his way back toward the ramshackle building, leaving the swarming insects to continue their grisly feast on Cummings' body.

Meanwhile, Kamal had begun a deliberate approach, walking half a mile toward his intended targets. He veered to the right of their line of sight and periodically fired a round into the jeep to keep them pinned down. Seeking cover in a dry creek, he aimed at the front side of the jeep's body before advancing once more.

Shultz was the first to spot the sniper, though he remained some distance away. Positioned about 50 yards in front and 150 yards to the right of the vehicle, the sniper was a formidable figure. At that moment, Shultz realized that they wouldn't reach their colleagues in time.

The darkness they had come to rely on descended quickly. Once the twilight steadied, Kamal reached for the night scope in his backpack, kneeling for a few seconds to attach it before advancing for the final time.

Shultz raised his pistol into the air and began firing wildly. Sergeant Yacoub, bewildered by the sudden turn of events, quickly assessed the situation. They had arrived too late. He squeezed the trigger of his shotgun, and the deafening noise echoed through the silent desert night.

Stahmer was the first to react. Though the distant gunfire was too far away to be of immediate help, it served as a clear warning and would distract the sniper momentarily. He prodded Ghislaine in the arm, scooped up the injured police officer, and together, they sprinted as fast as they could across the short distance to the dilapidated structure's broken frame.

Ghislaine, being the first to enter the building, stumbled over an object on the floor. Stahmer followed with the injured officer, his weight resting heavily on his shoulders. As their senses adjusted to the dim light inside, the grim reality of their surroundings slowly revealed itself.

The first sense to be assaulted was their sense of smell—an overwhelming, putrid, sweet, and rotten odour permeated the air, unmistakably the smell of death. The second sense was touch as they swatted away a multitude of flies that had been feasting on a grotesque stockpile of food. Lastly, their night vision stabilized, revealing a horrifying scene.

There was no recognizable face on the body; the bullet had entered through the back of the head, obliterating all identifying features on its exit. This was the site where the majority of flies had been indulging in a macabre banquet. The key identifier, however, lay in the blood-stained clothing—distinctly a uniform, though not the type worn by cruise ship staff. It was unmistakably the attire of an Egyptian police inspector. Ghislaine had inadvertently stumbled upon the lifeless body of Inspector Shariff.

Kamal crouched in the darkness, his heart pounding in his chest. The distant gunfire was a stark reminder of the police closing in on him. He cursed himself for disabling the jeep's tyres, leaving his Kawasaki motorbike a mile away in a hidden recess. The decision to shoot out the tyres had bought him time, but now he needed to find cover and eliminate the occupants of the building.

His night scope revealed at least three figures approaching him with purpose, zigzagging to make themselves harder targets. In the dim light, he took three precise shots, and one of the pursuers fell, but the others pressed on. Bullets zipped past him, kicking up puffs of sand, growing louder with each shot.

Kamal knew he had to reach the safety of the dilapidated building ahead. It was a race against time, and he had little cover in the open desert. Shultz watched Kamal's movements, relaying updates to Ghislaine via the satellite phone. He knew that Kamal's entry into the building would be a crucial moment.

As Kamal reached the window, his rifle poised and his night sight engaged, the red laser spot danced erratically in the empty room. He straddled the window frame to enter but found himself in an ungainly and vulnerable position, with his feet off the ground and the window's brickwork between his legs.

Stahmer, anticipating Kamal's actions, moved in the shadows. Barefoot and armed with the wounded officer's gun, he positioned himself behind Kamal, his weapon aimed at the assassin's head. With a swift click of the gun's safety, Stahmer had the upper hand.

The nape of Kamal's neck felt the cold steel of the gun. Stahmer spoke with a steely resolve, warning Kamal not to make any sudden moves. Kamal pleaded for his life, knowing the consequences if the police found Inspector Shariff's body inside the building.

But Stahmer had a different plan. He lifted the gun's butt and delivered a brutal blow to the back of Kamal's head. Kamal slumped forward, unconscious, his cheekbone colliding with a rusty nail, causing an unintended injury.

Shultz arrived at the scene just in time to witness Stahmer's decisive action. Panting with exhaustion, he couldn't help but crack a joke, acknowledging Stahmer's resourcefulness.

With Kamal securely bound and gagged, they waited for the backup police car to arrive. Sergeant Yacoub retrieved his injured officer from the desert, and Ghislaine attended to the wounded policeman from the vehicle. Stahmer took a moment to speak with the sergeant in private, revealing a startling revelation about Deputy Chief Officer Saleh's involvement in the betrayal of Inspector Shariff.

"Saleh won't see the sunrise; that, I can promise you," Sergeant Yacoub declared with grim certainty.

chapter six
Man Down

utler had handpicked Nathan Colton for this mission, knowing that he was a man of few words but immense action. Colton's background as a former Marine and his subsequent service with the DEA had made him a highly capable operative. His adaptability to new technology and quick thinking were qualities that Cutler valued greatly. As the two teams had arrived in Bali, Cutler had every confidence in Colton's ability to handle the mission alongside Tuck Walters.

Colton's physical presence was imposing—he was a large man with ebony skin, an imposing figure that commanded respect. It was his bravery and resourcefulness that had earned him a senior non-commissioned officer position in the Marines, and those same qualities made him an asset to the team.

After their arrival in Bali and a transfer to the Indonesian Pearl Hotel in Denpasar, Colton and Tuck had adopted a cover as a rowdy stag party. They donned colourful shirts and shorts, blending in with the crowd of revellers at local bars. Their imposing physiques deterred any unwanted attention, Fabienne had pointed them towards a well know criminal, Adi Budiman.

Adi Budiaman, a Jakarta native with a violent history, had risen through the criminal ranks with brutality and ruthlessness. His tactics included extorting money from local businesses under the pretence of providing security, using car battery acid on those who refused to pay. However, Adi's downfall came when he targeted the wrong person, leading to a gang war and his eventual capture by a rival gang.

Adi's gang had drugged him and intended to bury him alive in an abandoned coffee plantation on the outskirts of Jakarta. But Adi's resilience, fuelled by his drug tolerance, allowed him to survive the sedation. He managed to retrieve a small Beretta Pico pistol concealed in his boot and used it to turn the tables on his would-be assassins.

After eliminating his attackers and escaping the grave, Adi had decided to leave Jakarta and build a new criminal empire in Bali. Over the years, he had become a prominent figure in the drug and counterfeit goods trade on the island and was on Fabienne's watch list.

As Tuck and Colton began their surveillance of Adi, they frequented local bars to gather information. Adi had a notorious reputation, and his presence was known to many. However, there was no information linking him to yacht theft. Tuck's innocuous questions over a pint had alerted him to their presence, it wasn't the question but how he and his friend looked. Military types stand in a certain way, look through you rather than at you; these two guys were after something.

The night was thick with menace, the air a heady mix of danger and the sour stench of fear. In a dive bar, where the walls sweated and the floor stuck to your boots, Tuck and Colton had been nursing their pints, their eyes and ears open, searching for whispers, for rumours about Adi—a name that was spoken in hushed tones, one that lips would only dare utter behind a protective hand, and even then, only for a crisp hundred-dollar bill.

Tuck's seemingly harmless enquiries, casually posed over a pint, had inadvertently tipped off their quarry. It wasn't the content of the questions that raised alarms but rather their gate and presence. Men from military backgrounds carry a distinctive posture, a penetrating gaze that seems to scan past you, delving beyond the immediate. It was clear to Adi these two weren't just friendly patrons; they were on a hunt for something far more significant. He'd been here before in Jakarta.

The shanty bar spilled them out like afterthoughts into the murky street, where the light feared to tread. Tuck's sixth sense, homed in hostile terrains from the sandy deserts of Afghanistan to the urban jungles of the Balkans, prickled at the back of his neck. Danger was near, as palpable as the grime under his fingernails.

Colton, a human fortress, caught the shift in Tuck's stance. No words were needed between men.

From the shadows, where despair and lawlessness lingered, the night birthed five figures. These were not ordinary men, but hardened embodiments of life's merciless grind, their histories carved deep into their grim expressions and the confident, menacing grip on their blades. They wielded their knives with the casual expertise of those well-acquainted with violence.

The scant urban light glinted off the steel, casting sinister shadows as the men encircled Tuck and Colton. The air grew thick with tension, almost electric as past and present sins seemed to charge it with an unseen but palpably dangerous energy. Every sound became a backdrop to this deadly attraction, where each breath could be the sharp inhale before a fatal plunge.

In this precarious position, the unspoken understanding passed between Tuck and Colton—professionals amidst predators. The urban jungle around them stood still, as if watching, waiting for the bloodshed to seep. The standoff wasn't just a confrontation; it was a collision of wills, a test of survival, where the slightest twitch could mean the difference between living and becoming another forgotten stain on the sidewalk.

Tuck felt the hint of a smile tug at his lips, the thrill of the game with danger quickening his pulse. "Looks like we've got ourselves a fucking reception committee," he murmured, the darkness in his voice more a welcome than a warning. "You're up for a bit of fun with the ones on the left, Colton."

Their backs together, a force to be reckoned with, they waited, the electric charge of the impending clash filling the spaces between their steady breaths.

"Who sent you to ask questions about Adi?" The gang leader, more scar than man, stepped forward, his blade catching a stray beam of moonlight, his voice a gravelly menace.

Tuck, fearless, the history of his countless skirmishes reflected in the cold glint of his eyes, grinned. It was the grin of a man who had not known fear. "My mate here," he nodded at Colton, brute force barely contained in human form, "reckons you're as thick as a brick and half as useful. Says he's about to rearrange your face with a single hit."

Colton couldn't help but interject, "I don't believe 'low profile' meant picking fights in dark alleys, Tuck."

The gang leader, his face a map of anger, vowed that he would make Tuck and Colton bleed. The circle tightened as the five men, sensing blood, moved in like a pack of wolves who had cornered their prey. He let his men attack first, he would end them when they were down.

Colton reacted with the lethal grace of a striking panther. He dodged the leading thug's frenzied stab, twisted his arm with a sickening crack of fracturing bone, and wrenched the knife away, leaving the man crumpled in a heap, howling in agony.

Simultaneously, Tuck sprang into action. He was a storm personified, his moves a blur of deadly elegance. The nearest attacker lunged, blade glinting. Yet, in a breathtaking display of speed and control, Tuck unleashed a ferocious kick, connecting with the knife's hilt. The weapon spun out of the assailant's grasp, turning end over end, and whistling through the dense, charged air.

Without missing a beat, Tuck surged forward, locking his adversary in a crushing embrace. With a violent twist and shove, he repurposed human flesh and bone into a living projectile, hurtling the disoriented thug into an oncoming assailant. The collision was brutal, a mess of limbs and surprised pain as they tumbled to the ground, momentarily stunned and useless in the dirt.

Then, with the fallen knife now in his possession, Colton became a figure of sheer terror. The blade moved as an extension of his own will, a silver flash of death in the dim light. It was a dance with the devil, each step measured, each stroke promising oblivion. The remaining assailants, witnessing the swift downfall of their comrades, were gripped by a primal fear that eclipsed their lust for violence.

Their courage shattered, a raw, instinctive need to survive overtook them. It screamed through their veins louder than any battle cry, urging them to flee. As if sharing a single terrified thought, they backed away before turning to run, their bravado abandoned, leaving behind only the echo of their footfalls against the cold, uncaring concrete.

Their frantic retreat echoed through the dimly lit alleyway as they scrambled away from Colton's deadly presence. Though Colton held his blade steady, prepared to defend himself against any sudden turn of events, it soon became evident that the assailants had seen enough. The only sounds that remained in the alley were the soft groans of the incapacitated gang members, as silence descended once more, punctuated only by the distant sounds of the city beyond.

Tuck, still holding the gang leader in a vice-like grip, demanded information about Adi's whereabouts. With a knife dangerously close to the man's face, he threatened to gouge his eye.

In a desperate plea for mercy, the gang leader revealed Adi's location, but Tuck remained sceptical. He twisted the man's arm, snapping it, to ensure they wouldn't be followed.

Colton, observing the wounded man and the pooling blood, offered him his shirt as a makeshift bandage. "Wrap it tight; we don't want the roaches getting a free meal."

"Fuck him!"

Tuck pulled harder on the arm, and the man finally screamed out Adi's address.

Tuck realised the information they had received was accurate, leading them to the seventh house with minimal security. Overpowering the lone guard, they made their way inside.

Adi, fuelled by drugs, initially proved difficult to subdue. Even after Tuck fractured his leg with a sweeping kick, Adi continued to resist Colton's formidable grip. With resourcefulness, they bound and subdued him, eventually forcing him to the ground.

Tuck, catching his breath, mused about the effects of cocaine, acknowledging its ability to grant seemingly superhuman strength.

He retrieved sodas from the fridge, sharing one with Colton. "Mother fucker had some fight in him, be the drugs"

Colton couldn't help but comment on Tuck's frequent use of expletives. "Ever complete a sentence without the 'F' word?"

Tuck, shaking his head, responded defensively, "I don't curse in front of Esme, my adopted daughter."

Their focus shifted back to Adi, realizing they needed to find his vulnerability to extract information about the yacht heists. Colton, examining the room, discovered hidden stashes of drugs and a significant amount of cash.

"Let's move him to the kitchen, Tuck," Colton suggested, positioning Adi where he could witness the disposal of his narcotics.

As Colton flushed the drugs down the drain, Adi's desperation grew. Threats of violence filled the room as the remaining narcotics met a watery demise.

"Once this is all gone, your stash is next," Tuck warned. "Now, who has the means to hijack and move yachts around Bali?"

Adi, fearing the loss of his illicit fortune, began to spill the information they sought. "Mayan, he's the only one with a boatyard."

With instructions to stay with Adi, Colton watched over their captive while Tuck relayed the newfound lead to Fabienne. The pieces of the puzzle were slowly coming together, and their pursuit of the yacht thieves was gaining momentum.

Tuck's conversation with Fabienne had shed some light on their situation. He relayed the information to Colton, who stood a safe distance from Adi, primarily due to the overpowering halitosis emanating from the captured gangster.

"Colton, no record of a boatyard, but the satellite images show what appears to be a boat repair yard, complete with a channel and docking stage suitable for sizable ships," Tuck informed him. "And there's something else, a gang in Jakarta that seems mightily interested in getting their hands on our friend Adi."

"Thanks for the update, Fabienne," Tuck said as he closed his phone.

Colton remained vigilant over Adi, keeping a cautious distance. The question now was what to do with Adi to ensure he remained silent about their involvement. Tuck contemplated their options aloud.

"It seems we have two choices," Tuck began. "We could burn the fucker, but then we're left with his stash, which is a death sentence in these parts if we get caught. Or we could relieve him of his cash or both. What's your take on this, Adi?" Colton nudged him lightly with the toe of his boot.

Adi's response was laced with bitterness. "You're both as good as dead."

A sly smile formed on Tuck's face. "Funny you should say that, Adi. You get to keep your precious Charlie and your greenbacks. However, there are conditions. If you so much as breathe a word to this Mayan character, someone will be more than happy to make a phone call to that Jakarta gang, providing them with your exact whereabouts."

Adi's eyes widened in a mixture of disbelief and terror as Tuck laid out the terms of their agreement. "Just don't tell Mayan it was me who fingered him."

****

Cutler and Basmati manoeuvred through the marina, a blend of opulent multi-million-dollar yachts and more modest hundred-thousand-dollar vessels. At the end of a mooring pier, they discovered a stone shed, its frontage cluttered with yellow, black, and grey aqualung tanks, and wet and dry suits hanging from metal rails. Cutler took his time, investing thirty minutes in selecting their diving gear, and settled the bill in local currency. He also ordered additional tanks and masks for Tuck and Colton, knowing they'd return to collect the gear once they secured a boat.

The morning proved fruitful at the marina's bar-restaurant, but Cutler wasn't interested in hiring from the affluent patrons; he was on the hunt for someone down on their luck. He needed both a boat and information, and he wasn't inclined to break the bank for either. Cutler had employed this tactic before, knowing that individuals who had fallen on hard times often proved more willing to share information. Most yacht owners had a penchant for talking about themselves and their vessels.

Sipping his fourth pot of green tea, Basmati noticed Cutler's attention shift to a dishevelled older man entering the bar. The man donned faded blue corduroy jeans and a well-worn fisherman's khaki waistcoat. He carefully counted coins before ordering coffee. Cutler took notice and approached the man, placing three 10,000 rupiah notes on the counter to cover the cost.

"This one's on me," Cutler offered.

"Appreciate it. Times are tough right now, sir," Old Joe replied.

"Let me guess, British? Ex-Royal or Merchant Navy?" Cutler enquired.

"Ex-Royal Navy—Chief Petty Officer Joe Allen. I've been called Old Joe since my hair turned from jet black to grey overnight after a rough day in the Falklands conflict."

"How long have you been in Bali?" Cutler asked.

"Two months. It'll be another three before I can scrape together enough to afford the fuel for a voyage to Perth."

"Cutler," he introduced himself. "So you served in the Falklands. Must have been quite an experience?"

"What are you getting at, Mr. Cutler? You buy me coffee, and I'm sure you don't want to listen to an old man's war stories," Old Joe replied.

"Fair enough. I'm in search of a boat to rent, one large enough for four of us," Cutler said.

Old Joe's eyes gleamed with a glimmer of hope at the prospect of some unexpected income. He leaned in closer to Cutler, his voice a little more enthusiastic now.

"I do have a cat ketch," he began, "it's an old-timer, almost 30 years old, but let me tell you, she's as solid as they come. The engine purrs like a kitten, and I've taken good care of her."

Cutler nodded, pleased with the response. "That's what we're looking for, Old Joe. Solid and reliable?"

Old Joe's weathered face broke into a grin. "Absolutely, Mr. Cutler. You won't be disappointed. She's not the fanciest vessel in the marina, but she's got character and heart. I've named her 'The Sea Serpent,' and she's taken me on some memorable journeys. What do you want her for?"

"We're planning some diving trips, so we need a boat we can trust. Can you show it to us?"

"My arse," Old Joe remarked, nodding toward Basmati. "He looks like a geek. You're a little too beefy. You're either military or ex-military."

"Listen, let's be frank with each other," Cutler began. "We are ex-military, now working as insurance investigators. We're searching for a yacht that disappeared a little over a month ago. We have two young people dead and two people missing. We need a boat, and we need information." Cutler decided that a partial truth would be enough to gain the old sailor's trust.

Old Joe's discomfort was evident. His eyes darted nervously, and Cutler could sense he was concealing something. The subject of the missing yachts had struck a chord, evident from the old man's body language—his dry mouth, his hand clutching at his chest, and his shifting gaze hinted at concealed secrets.

Cutler had always prided himself on his ability to read people. It was a skill he had honed during his time in the Secret Service, and it had served him well in various concealed operations. He believed that all sane human beings exhibited the six classical emotions, and over time, he had trained himself to detect even the subtlest of emotions: satisfaction, regret, distaste, irritation, confusion and anxiety. These emotions, he knew, often provoked distinct physical responses that could reveal much about a person's thoughts and feelings.

As he sat across from Old Joe in the dimly lit marina bar, Cutler couldn't help but notice the old sailor's body language. The news of two dead bodies from the Ford Yacht and two others missing from the Trench's yacht had visibly shaken him. His heart rate had increased, and his blood pressure seemed to be on the rise. Old Joe appeared shocked, and he fidgeted in his seat, rubbing his eyes as if they were suddenly irritated. Cutler knew he had struck a chord with the mention of the missing children.

"You, okay? You look like a ghost just walked over your grave," Cutler remarked, his trained eyes assessing every nuance of Old Joe's reaction.

"Two dead kids and two missing, you say?" Old Joe replied, his voice trembling slightly. His emotions were on full display, and Cutler could see regret etched across his face. Old Joe's sudden hyperactivity was likely the result of an adrenaline rush.

"Afraid so, maybe more," Cutler confirmed, keeping a close watch on Old Joe's reactions.

Cutler's next question was calculated. "Can we pay you to use your boat?"

Old Joe hesitated for a moment, his eyes darting around nervously. Finally, he responded, "Sure, 5,000 dollars deposit, 300 bucks a day and fuel. Just leave her with a full tank of fuel."

Without hesitation, Cutler counted out fifty-one-hundred-dollar bills and handed them to Old Joe, sealing the deal. He knew that money talked, and it often spoke louder than words.

As Cutler left the bar, he couldn't help but feel that Old Joe held more information than he was letting on. Something about the missing yachts and children had touched a nerve, and Cutler was determined to uncover the truth. Their journey had only just begun, and the mystery surrounding Mayan and his operations was deepening with each passing moment.

Cutler and his team had arrived at Tanjung Benoa Beach, one of the primary hubs for watersports and recreational activities on the island of Bali. The beach was a bustling, chaotic scene, filled with tourists and locals alike, all seeking their share of sun, sea, and adrenaline.

Tanjung Benoa Beach, bathed in the golden glow of the tropical sun, was a lively tableau of sun, sea, and exhilaration. Nestled on the southern coast of Bali, this vibrant shoreline was a haven for tourists seeking aquatic adventures and thrill-seekers craving a taste of adrenaline. As the team of investigators arrived at this aquatic playground, they were immediately swept up in the frenzy of activity that defined Tanjung Benoa.

The beach stretched out like a sandy canvas, a meeting point of land and sea. It was adorned with vibrant hues, as parasails of every colour imaginable dotted the cerulean sky, their billowing canopies adding splashes of red, blue, and yellow to the natural palette. The sea was a vivid azure, its waves inviting and playful, enticing visitors to explore its depths or ride its swells.

The heart of the beach was a scene of organized chaos. Watersport enthusiasts and thrill-seekers thronged the shoreline, eager to partake in the diverse array of activities on offer. Jet skis whizzed across the water's surface, leaving frothy trails in their wake, their riders whooping with joy as they revelled in the sensation of speed and freedom.

Parasails filled the sky like graceful, floating kites, their occupants soaring high above the beach, suspended between the heavens and the earth. The colourful parachutes bobbed and danced in the warm breeze, offering breathtaking views of the coastline and the azure expanse of the Indian Ocean.

Motorboats, their engines growling with power, towed parasailers into the sky, their occupants shrieking with excitement as they ascended to dizzying heights. These boats ferried tourists to and from their aquatic adventures, their crews skilled navigators of the bustling waters.

The beach was alive with the laughter and chatter of tourists from around the world, their voices blending into a symphony of excitement and anticipation. Families built sandcastles along the shoreline, children giggling as they dug moats and sculpted turrets. Sunbathers basked in the warm embrace of the sun, their bodies adorned with bronzed skin and minimal swimsuits.

Beach vendors plied their trade, offering an array of snacks and refreshments to the sun-kissed crowds. The aroma of grilled seafood and exotic spices filled the air, tempting taste buds with the flavours of Bali. Souvenir stalls displayed an assortment of trinkets and mementos, each a tangible memory of this island paradise.

As the team observed this vibrant spectacle, they couldn't help but be captivated by the energy and vitality of Tanjung Benoa Beach. It was a place where the spirit of adventure danced on the shimmering waves, and the allure of the ocean beckoned all who sought excitement and escape. Yet beneath the surface of this idyllic paradise lay the mysteries and dangers that they were determined to uncover.

Tuck and Colton wasted no time and decided to indulge in a day of watersports as part of their cover. Tuck opted for parasailing, while Colton pushed a rented jet ski to its limits. The beach was a frenzy of activity, with jet skis zooming across the water, parasails dotting the sky, and motorboats ferrying excited tourists to and from their aquatic adventures. Basmati, on the other hand, had discovered a secluded spot on a rocky outcrop further down the beach. He unpacked his drone and prepared to capture aerial images of the bustling beach scene.

As the drone soared into the sky, Basmati watched the live feed on his iPad with a mix of amazement and shock. The sea was churned into frothy chaos by the numerous jet skis and motorboats towing parasails. The beach was a mass of humanity, and the white sand was almost entirely hidden beneath the throngs of people. It was a wonder that accidents and mishaps weren't more common in such a crowded and chaotic environment.

Tuck had managed to gather valuable information during his conversation with Adi. It was now evident that Mayan and his gang held sway over Tanjung Benoa Beach, controlling a variety of activities, from watersports to illicit dealings involving drugs, chemical enhancers, marijuana, and prostitution. This confirmed their suspicions that they were on the right track, especially given that Mayan and his associates were on Fabienne's list of suspects.

Inside a nearby bar that Fabienne had identified as Mayan's central control hub, Cutler observed the enigmatic figure closely. Mayan sat comfortably in an oversized reed chair beneath a rotating ceiling fan, exuding an aura of authority that intrigued Cutler. It was a phenomenon he had noticed before—the power of certain individuals, regardless of their physical stature, to command respect and loyalty.

Beside Mayan sat his younger brother, Tut, who handled the cash transactions involving drug vendors and pimps. It was clear to Cutler that these two were deeply involved in criminal activities.

Multiple Indonesians approached the bar, openly exchanging stacks of Bali rupiah notes with Tut. The lack of discretion suggested that they were possibly paying off local law enforcement. While Cutler had no doubt about their criminal affiliations, it remained unclear whether they had the infrastructure to steal and move high-value yachts worth millions of dollars.

As the team reconvened after their respective activities, Tuck shared his findings from his aerial perspective. He had observed drug dealers and pimps openly conducting their business on the beach. Furthermore, he had spotted a peculiar structure at the far end of the beach—a boat repair shed built on stilts in the water. It was guarded by two individuals, one stationed at the rear and another on the pier.

Colton had also attempted to get a closer look at the boathouse from a jet ski but had been warned off by an unfriendly guard. Tuck had noticed that buoys marked out a route leading into the boatyard, resembling a deep-water channel, which seemed odd given the beach's recreational nature. The area appeared equipped for large ships, even boasting a small mobile crane.

With their collective observations in mind, they couldn't ignore the significance of the guarded boathouse. It was evident that access to the boathouse was controlled from a road behind the beach, and the entire area was under constant surveillance. The presence of guards and the uncertain possibility of weapons heightened their caution.

"We need to investigate that boathouse," Colton stated. "But we have to be prepared for hostiles. We're unarmed."

Cutler pondered their options as they sat in a nondescript local café nearby. The mission was taking a dangerous turn, and the team needed to tread carefully if they were to uncover the truth behind the missing yachts and the criminal activities on Tanjung Benoa Beach.

The sun dipped low on the horizon, casting long shadows across the serene waters of Tanjung Benoa Beach. The team's mission had led them to the precipice of a hush-hush operation, one that would require utmost secrecy and precision. Cutler, his mind a whirlwind of tactics and strategy, outlined the plan to his comrades.

"This will have to be done quietly and from the sea. Let's get in touch with Old Joe and get his boat. Basmati, retrieve our scuba gear," Cutler instructed, his voice low and determined. "One more thing, they rule this area. We are not going to get close to them without having a heap of trouble descending down on us."

"Fucking bring it on," Tuck responded with a grin.

"Tuck, you nearly got through the whole morning without swearing," Colton remarked.

"When did you start hiring choirboys, Cutler?"

They all shared a laugh, the camaraderie of their team evident.

The exchange with Old Joe had been surprisingly smooth. A wedge of greenbacks had satisfied the old sailor, and he handed over the ignition keys to the cat ketch—a sturdy vessel with a faded white exterior and a navy-blue hull.

As the afternoon sun started to dip toward the horizon, Cutler assumed control of the cat ketch, acquainting himself with the controls and giving Basmati some impromptu training. The team anchored the boat approximately a mile from Tanjung Benoa

Beach, with their intention to carry out a secretive underwater mission once nightfall provided them with cover.

Cutler carefully inspected the scuba gear, ensuring that every piece of equipment was in perfect working order. The sun's diminishing warmth gave way to the cool embrace of twilight, and the beach, once teeming with tourists, began to empty, leaving only the die-hard drinkers behind.

Basmati, lacking experience in scuba diving, was assigned the crucial task of staying with the boat. He perched on the deck, gazing out at the tranquil sea, which seemed like an oasis of calm amidst the chaos of their mission.

Cutler's dive bag contained not only scuba gear but also an arsenal of listening and tracking devices sealed in waterproof plastic bags. These military-grade tools would allow Fabienne to monitor conversations and movements in real-time, providing a crucial advantage.

Colton, tasked with keeping an eye on Old Joe, would remain on land and maintain a watchful presence, his keen instincts on high alert. He had a mission to ensure Old Joe stayed loyal and, if necessary, inebriated.

With the stage set, Cutler and Tuck prepared to dive into the warm, inviting waters of Bali. The sea, an inky expanse under the dimming sky, beckoned them with its secrets and dangers. As they entered the water, they followed a path along the surface for the first mile, occasionally riding the gentle swells. But as they drew closer to their target, they submerged, finned flippers propelling them through the depths.

Meanwhile, Basmati basked in the solitude of his maritime vigil, seeking a moment of solace. He reached for his headphones and played Abba's "Dancing Queen" at near full volume, an incongruous choice of music.

Unbeknownst to Basmati, the calm of the sea was about to be shattered. The approach of a small cargo ship, the MV Fremantle, went unnoticed amid the music. This ship had conducted secret trips to the area several times before, approaching the pier without lights, guided by GPS signals from buoys.

Basmati's heart raced, its thunderous rhythm echoing in his ears like a war drum as he grasped the gravity of the impending catastrophe. The MV Fremantle, a looming behemoth of steel and menace, bore down upon them with relentless determination. Its massive steel hull cleaved through the water with a chilling, deadly precision, like a predator closing in on its unsuspecting prey.

In that heart-pounding moment, instinct and sheer survival instincts took over. With the swiftness of a cornered animal, Basmati sprang into action. There was no time for hesitation or second thoughts. He hurled himself over the side of the cat ketch, his body becoming a blur as he plummeted into the water below.

The sensation of cold seawater enveloping him was a shocking contrast to the warm tropical air above. But the urgency of the situation left no room for discomfort. Basmati's desperate strokes propelled him away from the impending collision, his limbs working in perfect synchronization with the primal instinct to survive.

As he fought the currents, adrenaline surging through his veins, Basmati's thoughts raced. His mind was a whirlwind of fear and determination, each heartbeat echoing a silent vow to defy the odds and emerge from this watery ambush unscathed.

The collision between the MV Fremantle and Joe's cat ketch was swift and brutal. Old Joe's beloved vessel, a sturdy companion for over three decades, was reduced to shattered debris beneath the hull of the cargo ship. The cataclysmic impact drew Basmati deeper into the water, where survival teetered on the edge of a propeller's deadly blades.

Amidst the chaos, Basmati fought for his life, battling against the relentless suction created by the MV Fremantle. His struggle for air and his harrowing brush with the propeller's menacing blades would test his mettle in ways he had never imagined.

Cutler and Tuck had reviewed the ship movements scheduled for that night and found no registered activity. They realized something was off when, swimming just below the surface, they heard the low hum of approaching propellers deadly advance pierced through the cacophony of their expelled breath echoing within their masks. In the darkness of the night, where the moon remained obscured by heavy clouds, they operated in silence and secrecy. Cutler's gloved hand discreetly signalled to Tuck to ascend, and they emerged from the water with only their heads breaking the surface. The vessel they sought had no lights to guide their way.

Cutler's gaze wasn't fixed on the approaching ship itself; instead, he sought out the buoys that marked the deep-water channel. One of these buoys was positioned just twenty feet to his left, a vital clue that any vessel of importance would have to traverse this precise path. As they converged by the buoy, the ominous silhouette of the vessel silently cruised past them, shrouded in darkness and mystery.

They had to contend with the strong swells generated by the ship's massive bulk before reuniting near the buoy. Cutler removed his mouthpiece and raised his voice slightly above the gentle lapping of the waves. "Go back and ensure Basmati is safe. That ship just came from his direction," he instructed Tuck.

With Tuck on his way back, Cutler swam stealthily towards the boatyard where the ship was in the process of mooring. The stars shimmered brightly overhead, a double-edged blessing that increased visibility but also raised the risk of being spotted. Cutler submerged once more, kicking his way towards the boatyard. The ship that lay before him appeared weathered and worn, a shadow of its former self. As he emerged in the shadow of the boathouse, he witnessed several Indonesians aboard a yacht, busily engaged in lifting cradles around the vessel. Two individuals were in the water, working together to sling the cradles beneath the yacht's hull.

From the waterproof bag secured around his waist, Cutler retrieved a handful of tracking devices. Silently, he swam towards a nearby ladder, allowing him access to the boatyard's interior.

However, as he observed the yacht more closely, Cutler recognized it was not the one he had been seeking. Conrad Ford's Coca V1 yacht bore distinct features that were unmistakable, whereas the vessel in front of him was an American-built LSX 92 Lazzara yacht. Its name had been concealed beneath masking tape, but Cutler had no doubt that this was not the yacht they were after. It bore a striking resemblance to the yacht leased by Sonny and Rosie Trench from Florida. Their sudden disappearance had sparked Cutler's interest, leading to background research that ultimately connected their case with Conrad Ford's.

Cutler submerged again, gliding beneath the water's surface. He swam towards a nearby pier and positioned himself discreetly behind the shelter of the first floating buoy. From this hidden vantage point, he observed Mayan's presence aboard the cargo ship, involved in a discreet transaction with the apparent ship's captain. A sizable package exchanged hands, containing a remarkable sum of 250,000 US dollars. Compared to the LSX 92's steep six-million-dollar price tag, the amount was a mere fraction. Yet, he would have to pay the full fee to Asfour as compensation for his carelessness in handling the situation with Robert Ford and his fiancée.

With a tracker in hand, Cutler submerged once more, shadowing the two Indonesians who had fitted the lifting slings onto the yacht. In the shroud of darkness, he clambered up the anchor chain of MV Fremantle, his movements executed with the precision of a seasoned operative. Cutler had to secure the tracker well above the waterline, taking into account potential swells or storms that might dislodge the magnetic device. Twenty feet above the water's surface, he fastened the tracker securely onto the vessel's side, wrapping his legs around the anchor chain to maintain stability.

Leaving nothing to chance, Cutler extracted a small tube of superglue concealed within the top of his wetsuit. With meticulous care, he applied the adhesive in a seamless circle around the tracker's edges, ensuring its steadfast attachment to the ship. Satisfied with his cryptic manoeuvre, he descended the anchor chain and once more vanished beneath the water's surface, a phantom in the night.

Mayan and his brothers remained engrossed in their activities aboard the cargo container, blissfully unaware of the vulnerability they had left behind at the boathouse. Cutler couldn't help but regard them as arrogant and inexperienced, placing undue confidence in the razor wire and security guarding the gate.

Mayan hadn't considered the possibility of a scuba diver infiltrating his territory, a peculiar oversight considering that he offered legitimate scuba training services on the very same beach. It was a lapse in judgment that now came back to haunt him.

Cutler, dripping with seawater and determination, resurfaced further inside the dimly lit boathouse. The air was thick with the acrid scent of diesel and the pungency of grease, creating an oppressive atmosphere. The storage facility's dimensions were ample enough to accommodate a full-size yacht comfortably. A platform along the left side of the boathouse stood elevated above the water, supported by concrete stations firmly rooted to the seabed. It served as the access point from the main door, granting a strategic viewpoint.

Five brand new Yamaha quad bikes occupied the platform, inconspicuous in the dim light except for one that stood out in vivid blue. Cutler was well-versed in quad bikes, having owned one himself back in the Everglades. These were Raptor special edition road-legal quads, each bearing distinctive features. The blue one boasted additional perks such as a mobile phone holder, a satellite navigation system, and even a digital radio with a Bluetooth music adapter. Cutler couldn't help but wonder how one could hear music over the deafening roar of the engine. His curiosity was satisfied when he discreetly made his way to the back of the bikes, discovering a set of helmets hanging on a rack. Each helmet bore a name, with four of them in standard black and one in striking blue with a white lightning stripe. It was immediately apparent that the blue helmet belonged to Mayan himself, as Cutler discerned the name inscribed on it.

A closer examination of the blue helmet revealed a built-in headphone system, presumably equipped with shortwave or Bluetooth technology for communication during rides. With utmost caution, Cutler discreetly attached his final tracker beneath the seat of the blue quad bike. Its placement was strategic, ensuring visibility without adhering to the non-metallic composite upper body. For the listening bug, Cutler delicately removed a section of the lining within the helmet and concealed it in a niche, ensuring it remained inconspicuous to the wearer. He couldn't be certain of the reception quality, but he had full faith in Fabienne, who would work her magic with filters and computers from her base in Geneva.

Having dedicated himself to the task at hand, Cutler's thoughts now drifted to Basmati, a gnawing concern that weighed heavily on him. As he descended back into the water, he swam to the outer edge of the buoys, watching as the container ship gradually moved away from its mooring. The journey underwater, covering a mile and a half, was uneventful. As he approached their designated rendezvous point, Cutler checked his wrist-mounted GPS and adjusted his course slightly, turning left by five degrees. Before long, he spotted the remnants of the cat ketch. Splintered wooden planks, a diesel slick on the water's surface, and sails suspended like a stratus cloud in the sky told the story of its unfortunate fate.

Cutler's gaze fixed on two sets of legs submerged in the dark waters above him. He swam toward the suspended limbs and, resurfacing slowly, surveyed the area for any potential threats. Finding none, he turned his attention to Tuck, who was assisting a semi-conscious Basmati. It was evident from the gaping wound on Basmati's left shoulder and the blood that oozed from it that he had sustained a severe injury.

Their predicament was exacerbated by the absence of medical supplies, which were several miles away at their hotel. The first aid equipment they had brought in haversacks had been lost with Old Joe's cat ketch. However, Cutler had instituted a crucial protocol. Each team member carried a waterproof satellite phone secured in a waterproof swim bag, tethered to their Speedos, along with a single morphine capsule. They administered the morphine from Tuck's pouch to alleviate Basmati's pain.

With his legs kicking gently to maintain buoyancy and riding the swells, Cutler managed to retrieve his phone and press '3' on the keypad, connecting him directly to Colton.

"Colton, we have a problem. There was a Zodiac moored alongside a yacht anchored off the beach earlier today. I doubt they would have left in the late afternoon, so it should still be there. Hotwire it. We're a mile offshore, adjacent to the boatyard. Get here as soon as possible," Cutler instructed urgently.

For a tense and agonizing 40 minutes, they grappled with Basmati's injury, battled against the swells, and fended off inquisitive fish drawn by the scent of blood. Colton, using his experience and dead reckoning, adeptly navigated the Zodiac Cadet 285 rigid inflatable boat to their location. Cutler tossed his scuba gear onto the back of the Zodiac and clambered aboard. Together, they hoisted the now unconscious Basmati onto the boat, followed by Tuck. Colton wasted no time in accelerating away from the scene.

As Tuck continued to apply pressure to Basmati's wound, there was little more they could do. The first aid kit on the Zodiac contained only Tuak, a local alcoholic concoction, which held no benefit in this dire situation. With the need to avoid being seen, they decided against heading directly to the marina. Instead, they grounded the craft 400 feet away, relying on the cover of darkness and shadows to conceal their landing.

Cutler swiftly donned a T-shirt and made his way to the marina. Meanwhile, Colton and Tuck maintained the pressure on Basmati's substantial wound. Tuck administered another phial of morphine to Basmati, the only solace they could offer in the absence of proper medical supplies. Cutler intended to seek Old Joe's assistance but was wary of being seen, opting for a discreet approach. He located Old Joe within the bar and quietly ushered him outside, away from prying eyes.

Old Joe's question about his missing boat hung in the air, but Cutler had no time for explanations or apologies. The urgency of their mission took precedence over small talk.

"No time for small talk. Are you looking after any of these yachts while their owners are not here?" Cutler pressed, his voice firm and direct.

Old Joe, somewhat taken aback by Cutler's urgency, hesitated for a moment before responding. "Two," he finally replied.

Cutler wasted no time in making his decision. "Which one is the furthest away from the bar and civilization?" he enquired.

Old Joe, still somewhat bewildered, pointed to a yacht. "The Aero 20 at the end of pier six."

"Good. Come with me," Cutler said, guiding Old Joe by the arm. There was no room for hesitation or negotiation.

Meanwhile, Tuck used a flashlight he had acquired from the Zodiac to light their way as they made their way back toward the marina. Colton, carrying the injured Basmati over his shoulder, followed closely behind. The darkness shrouded their movements, keeping them hidden from prying eyes.

When they arrived at the Aero 20, most of the boat owners were either at the bar or elsewhere, providing them with the cover they needed. Old Joe struggled with the keys but eventually managed to open the rear patio doors.

"First aid kit," Tuck instructed, his tone no-nonsense. "And a sewing kit if they have one. If not, a stapler."

Old Joe disappeared into the yacht for several minutes before returning with a first aid kit and a box housing a sewing machine. "This is their sail repair kit," he explained. "It's got thread, patch fabric, and a sewing machine. If you take the needle out and sterilize it, you can use that."

Tuck acknowledged the makeshift supplies. "It won't be pretty, but it will do," he remarked, getting ready to tend to Basmati's wounds.

Cutler knew they had to act quickly to save Basmati's life. He also understood that medical attention was urgently needed, and it couldn't be sought in Bali. With a sense of urgency, he stepped out onto the deck and reached for the satellite phone.

"Hi Fabienne, we have an unmounted cyclist," Cutler informed her, using their code to signal a man down and in need of immediate assistance.

Fabienne, on the other end of the line, grasped the urgency of the situation. "Received, what are your instructions?" she replied, ready to coordinate their rescue operation.

Cutler wasted no time. "Phone Julie Birch, Ford's head of security," he instructed. "They have a plane in the area ready for rapid deployment for when we get Roberts Ford's killer. Tell her we have an emergency and need it, preferably with a doctor on board. Tuck tells me he will last an eighteen-hour flight if he has medical assistance, so the destination will be Geneva. There will be too many questions if we aim for Singapore."

"On it straight away," Fabienne assured him, her voice cool and efficient. "And get him booked into the private hospital we use and have an ambulance waiting."

Cutler powered down the phone, knowing that they had taken the necessary steps to save Basmati's life. But there were still questions to be answered, and Old Joe, who had remained with Cutler, seemed to be hiding something beneath his gruff exterior.

Old Joe handed Cutler a beer, and the two men took a moment of respite amidst the chaos. The old mariner couldn't hide his curiosity any longer.

"You're no damn insurance agent, Cutler. Who and what are you? And where's my boat?" Old Joe finally voiced his questions, his tone a mixture of frustration and resignation.

Cutler took a sip of the beer and leaned in closer to Old Joe, a determined glint in his eyes. "The boat's gone. Don't worry, the guy I am working for will replace it," he reassured the old man.

As Old Joe drooped his head, Cutler couldn't help but feel that the mariner was keeping more secrets than he let on. There was a storm brewing beneath the surface, and Cutler was determined to uncover the truth.

With Basmati's life hanging in the balance, the night was far from over, and the mysteries surrounding the island's criminal activities were deepening by the minute.

With Fabienne's confirmation that Julie Birch had dispatched transport to pick up Basmati and coordinates for a private airfield to the north of the island, their plan to save Basmati was set in motion. The night was far from over, and Cutler had questions that needed answers.

Colton's face was framed by the window screen of the jeep, his steely gaze fixed on the road ahead. In the back of the vehicle, Basmati lay in a foetal position, his fate hanging in the balance. Tuck remained vigilant, monitoring Basmati's condition closely.

Cutler chose to stay behind with Old Joe, determined to uncover any secrets the old mariner might be harbouring. The black cloud that seemed to shroud Old Joe was a puzzle Cutler was eager to solve.

Their journey to the airfield took them across a mix of well-maintained roads and rough tracks, navigating the challenging terrain of the island. As they approached the aerodrome on the eastern side of the island, they parked and waited.

Fifteen minutes passed, and then a small Learjet touched down on the runway. Conrad Ford's retrieval team emerged from the aircraft, ready to assist. On the steps of the jet stood a modest Indonesian man, clutching a black doctor's bag.

The doctor and two security guards approached the jeep, with one of them helping Tuck carry Basmati up the aircraft steps. The second security guard remained in the shadows at the rear of the jeep, his presence concealed.

Tuck, never one to mince words, turned his attention to the doctor. "Is the doctor qualified?" he enquired, pointing at the man.

The security guard replied, "Best we could do at such short notice. He's a paediatrician. Big bodies, small bodies, it's all the same, I suppose."

Colton interjected, emphasizing the urgency of Basmati's condition. "He needs blood straight away. He's O negative."

The doctor acknowledged the gravity of the situation. "Looks like he needs a complete refill," he commented. "Take him to Geneva. I have one of my people organizing a pickup from the airport. She will have arranged the paperwork, and as far as immigration is concerned, it's a boating accident victim with the means and money to receive treatment in one of their top clinics," Tuck instructed.

The security man assured them, "We will be back within 48 hours, on standby should you nab the gang in that time."

Tuck responded, giving them a directive for their time in Geneva. "Take some R&R in Geneva. We are at least a week from lifting them."

The security man hesitated for a moment before replying, "Mr. Ford is getting impatient."

Tuck didn't waver in his response. "Mr. Ford will have to play with his cock for a week. Cutler's plan, Cutler's schedule."

The security man nodded reluctantly. "Very well, but I may slightly rephrase that when I brief him later."

As the Learjet prepared to take off with Basmati onboard, Cutler couldn't help but wonder what the next week would bring. The pieces of the puzzle were slowly coming together, but the dangerous game they were playing was far from over.

chapter seven
Hidden Agenda

Under the cold, watchful lights of Sandiford Airport in Orlando, Kurt Beaumont's steel-blue eyes held their gaze, unwavering. The intense border control officers saw a Canadian security expert who called the Dubai sands home. Yet beneath this meticulously carved mask was Kasim Asfour, an enigma the world wasn't ready for. As he slipped through the web of advanced biometric systems, an invisible hand had wiped his true face from every US database.

The airport was a tapestry of joy and anticipation, with families cocooned in their excitement, visions of Disney characters dancing in their children's eyes. Yet Asfour's destination was not among these fantasies. He sought refuge at the Hilton DoubleTree, strategically chosen for its proximity to the Orange County Convention Centre.

As dawn broke, casting long shadows over the Middle East Security Convention, he became just another face in the crowd.

Professor Charles Noble, an intellectual titan from Oxford University, dominated the morning's discourse, his silhouette accentuated by the haunting images on the screen behind him. The conference room, a modern-day coliseum, was abuzz with anticipation. Asfour, however, chose the shadows, settling at the farthest reaches of enlightenment.

Noble's narrative wove through the decades, capturing the transient peace that once cradled the Middle East. However, tranquillity was a mirage, shattered by the ruthless ambition of the entity known as the Islamic State (IS)—a chameleon constantly redefining itself, its name a subject of global contention.

The professor painted a grim picture, highlighting the fear seizing the hearts of adventurers and tourists alike. Once-coveted destinations now stood abandoned, echoes of laughter and wonder silenced by the horrific acts of terror and violence. The region's once-thriving economic arteries were choking, starved by the world's reticence to face potential perils.

In the electric hum of the convention, Asfour stood detached, a lone wolf among eager beavers. It was only the quiet buzz of his device that snapped him back, a concise, cryptic message slicing through his feigned apathy.

Stepping into the sharp sunlight, the world seemed almost too ordinary compared to the web he'd left behind inside. Yet parked amidst the ordinary was a black Mercedes SUV, its nondescript driver holding the door open.

The ride was a quiet one, their convoy slicing through the air with a wordless urgency. They left the known streets for more exclusive ground, a hidden haven for those whispered about in the corridors of power—a fortress of solitude and opulence. As Asfour stepped into the secluded lakeside abode, he was met by a single, armed man.

Asfour was ushered by a duty guard through the hushed opulence into the heart of the residence, the main lounge. There, around the dining table, sat the triumvirate of power: two men in suits sharp enough to draw blood and a woman whose elegance matched her evident authority. The fourth chair awaited him, and into it, he sank, his eyes locking onto a familiar player—Deputy Director Allen of the CIA. This was the man, the handler, who had sold Asfour's audacious plan to the highest echelon, straight to the president's desk. But with the seats of power now occupied by a new president, Asfour felt the frigid fingers of uncertainty grip him.

Allen's voice sliced through the tension. "This man before you is known to us as Kasim Asfour," he began, command wrapping around each syllable. "His birth name is inconsequential. What you must know is that he represents one of the most triumphant intelligence penetrations in over half a century. For eleven years, he's been our eyes and ears within the serpentine depths of Al-Qaeda, climbing its treacherous hierarchy."

A nod from the impeccably dressed woman, and she introduced herself, her voice calm, assertive. "I trust you recognize Vice President Treisman," she said, her gaze unwavering. "I steer his ship through the tumultuous waters of his office. Maria Sysco, chief of staff."

With a measured nod, Asfour acknowledged the vice president's chief of staff. "Treisman's reputation precedes him, but I hadn't anticipated seeing you here," he said, his voice touched with the gravel of suspicion.

Allen's voice held an edge of finality. "Maria Sysco isn't just another name on a sheet. She's been part of this programme since the beginning. She's been a pillar of strength and knowledge, and Vice President Treisman has total trust in her. Speak to her as you would to me."

"I had already woven myself into the Al-Qaeda's hierarchy. Eight years it took to get there," his voice carried a quiet force, an affirmation to the years of danger navigated in the perilous climb to the pinnacle of power." he remarked, the calm in his voice belying the seriousness of his words. "In those days, four people knew the about the operation. But then, the numbers began to climb—first five, and now we stand at six." He paused; the weight of his concern palpable in the growing frost of his tone. "Each addition, you must understand, punctures a fresh hole in the cloak of invisibility that is paramount to this mission's survival," Asfour declared, the words not just a statement but a challenge, a tension that stretched taut throughout the room, quivering with unsaid implications.

"Let's dispense with the theatrics, Asfour," interjected Vice President Richard Treisman, his voice a blend of steel and silk. "This group has bound themselves beyond the point of return. None within this room would hazard the peril of revealing you."

Asfour's response was measured, but the undercurrent of raw tension was unmistakable. "Gentlemen, you're cushioned by your stations, your reputations," he said, locking eyes with each person around the table. "A scandal, at worst, might dent your reputations, you have a cloak of powerful people not willing to see you fall. But for me," he paused, the room hanging on the precipice with him, "Can you even fathom what awaits me if Al-Qaeda uncovers who I really am?"

His words, though quietly delivered, resonated with the heavy truth of the perilous existence Asfour walked daily.

"You are seeing gremlins where there are none. We have a firm grip on this situation," Allen assured him, his voice a steady balm in the thickening air of tension. "The vice president, however, has several queries for you."

"What's the current status?" Vice President Treisman enquired, leaning forward, the steeple of his fingers indicating the gravity of his attention.

"Mr. Vice President," Asfour began, recognizing the weight of the moment, "the timetable of the operation has been moved up. In recent months, with cruise ships operating at half capacity following the Russian jet incident, there's an urgency we hadn't anticipated. We must act before the cruise lines abandon the region entirely."

Vice President Treisman's nod was slow and thoughtful. "Has there been any progress with the Warhead Command Unit?"

"Pleased to report, sir, that the WCU is now in our possession," Asfour confirmed.

"Excellent. And the strategy for its deployment?" Treisman probed further, the room's atmosphere thickening with anticipation.

Asfour leaned in slightly. "The cruise ship Reef Explorer is the perfect vessel for our needs. It is from an older generation of cruise ships, lacking the advanced security measures now commonplace. Recent events, particularly the disappearance of Gareth Cummings, one of their officers, have precipitated the exact reaction we expected," Asfour continued, each word measured and deliberate. "On receiving the news, the proprietors have moved out from the Red Sea and changed port destinations towards the Mediterranean waters, precisely as we had anticipated."

Throughout this exchange, Maria Sysco, the chief of staff, leaned to whisper a sequence of quiet, urgent words to Allen—a sotto voce commentary lost to the others but seemingly pivotal, given the solemn nod it extracted from the deputy director.

"We've got intel suggesting they've recovered Cummings' body. Word is that MIDAS, the outfit that found him, is spearheaded by a former Secret Service player, Max Cutler," Vice President Treisman disclosed, the information hanging like a sharp hook in the air.

Asfour's mind raced, recalibrating, assessing threats. "This is fresh info, landed in my lap just hours ago. Need to slice it, dice it, understand it before I can shoot any solid commentary your way," he responded, his tone all business, the gears in his head visibly turning.

"Cutler's not just some run-of-the-mill investigator. He's tooled up with former Special Forces, top-tier combatants, and investigators. Got to wonder, does this curveball pitch us off our game plan?" Treisman drilled; his stare as intense as a laser beam.

"Look," Asfour started, leaning back, every word deliberate, "if your angle is whether this can get traced back to you or the bigwigs at Langley, that's a hard no. And making the jump from stumbling across a corpse to unravelling what we've got cooking? That's a chasm too wide for anyone. MIDAS is small fry," he dismissed, his confidence unyielding.

Vice President Treisman gaze hardened, the stakes getting higher by the second. "This whole op was concocted three years back. You were knee-deep in the Al-Qaeda quagmire, and Syria was a chessboard soaked in blood. The landscape's shifted since.

New guy in the Oval, new chief at the Agency. They're both out of the loop. MIDAS is a threat, a clear threat," he asserted, the severity of his words underscoring the room's building tension.

Allen, catching the ball, pitched in firmly, "We're all on the same page, sir. As laid out, this circus is limited to the faces here, Julie Birch, and the ex-commander-in-chief. Odds of a springing a leak? Slim to none. As Asfour's flagged, MIDAS doesn't make the radar."

"No, that doesn't sit right," Maria Sysco cut in sharply, her voice slicing through the tense air. "If we were all playing the same game, Robert Ford and Samantha Gooding would not lying on a slab in Bali. The chatter from Bali? It's not just troubling; it's a damned red alert," she asserted.

"Collateral damage is part of the game," Asfour stated, his tone flat but carrying an undercurrent of resolve. "You don't get results without getting your hands dirty."

Treisman's face was a mask of barely restrained fury. "The one man left in the dark about our backdoor dealings and this whole shebang is Conrad Ford. He's not just a colleague; he's like family. So you've got to give me something, Asfour. Why in hell's name did you put his kid in the ground?" he bit out, the anger simmering in his words.

Asfour's expression didn't flicker. "I had a hunch there was more to this impromptu pow-wow in the middle of a live op," he began, his voice a steady monotone. "Allen here drew a couple of lines in the sand right at the start. First, Armitech was the go-to for our hardware needs. Second, no official funds were available, traceability. Keeps the money trail from leading back to your doorstep," he explained."

Allen nodded, a grave look crossing his features. "Right. Armitech was our one-stop shop. They had the research to put together the WCU we needed. After we pulled Ford's ass out of the Justice Department's sling, he's been our guy on a leash. But hearing about his boy," Allen shook his head, the shock genuine, "that hit all of us out of left field."

"Conrad Ford sees me as nothing more than a face in the crowd of extremists, a transaction on his ledger," Asfour began, his voice low and measured, the calm epicentre of the storm that was this conversation. "Sure, you greenlit the sale, but in his eyes, I'm just another mark, another risk worth taking for profit. He doubled the price of the WCU on what we agreed. And let's not kid ourselves, the higher-ups in Al-Qaeda? They're not taken in by smoke and mirrors. They track the arms, the cash flow. They're not just dots on a map; they're the mapmakers."

"I'm not wading through fields of gold or skimming off the top of some clandestine government operation," Asfour stated, his tone laced with a raw kind of irony. The room's ambiance shifted, adapting to the harsh realities his words conjured. "I'm down in the shit. High-end grand theft, extortion, cyber shakedowns, arms dealing—that's my day-to-day. It's dirty cash, and it's a grind."

He leaned in, the shadows cast by the room's dim lighting playing across his face. "When Ford tried to squeeze me for the extra million dollars, he wasn't just pressuring a businessman; he was threatening an entire facade I've risked my life to build. Al-Qaeda's not a boardroom of suits, worried about stock prices. They're warriors, zealots, criminals. Retribution isn't just expected; it's respected."

"There had to be another way," Vice President Treisman insisted, his voice a blend of frustration and disbelief.

Asfour's hands clenched unconsciously, echoes of the life-or-death tension he navigated daily. "I handled Ford the way my cover would, the way I had to. Sold his precious yacht right from under him. It's a message: nobody cheats us. Nobody undermines us. In this world, you retaliate, or you're just another body in the ground. I did what I did to survive, to keep this operation alive. Out there," he gestured vaguely, indicating the world beyond the room, "there's no playbook, no rules of engagement. There's just the hunt… and the very real chance of becoming prey. "His gaze locked onto Treisman, unyielding. "The decision wasn't about indulgence; it was about preservation—of credibility, of the role I've bled to maintain. You don't maintain deep cover by playing it safe. You do it by playing the part, even when that means making the hard calls."

As the reality of the operative's world settled over the room, Asfour's next words were almost a whisper, "And sometimes, those calls involve doing what your enemy expects, even when every fibre of your being resists. The deaths? A message—to Ford, to my 'comrades,' to anyone watching I'm committed. Because anything less is a bullet with my name on it."

In the terse silence, Treisman's words dropped like stones in a still pond. "Conrad Ford's employed Cutler and his MIDAS outfit for the investigation into his son's death. They're on the ground in Bali as we speak."

Asfour's calm didn't waver. "I was aware Ford deployed his assets, but Cutler's involvement is news. Irrelevant, though," he continued with icy precision. "Post-operation, my cover's compromised, my network expendable. That includes the gang in Bali. They know me only as Kasim Asfour, a terrorist or a criminal. They lack concrete intel to link back to us or thwart our agenda," he clarified, the danger in his tone almost palpable.

Sensing the escalating tension, Allen intervened, his voice a moderating force. "I believe we've addressed the pertinent issues," he stated, steering the conversation back to neutral territory. Asfour was not ready to let the argument drop.

Asfour's voice took on a steel edge, the calm before a storm. "Let's not mince words; what comes next will be drenched in blood."

Vice President Treisman's response, a fervent declaration more than anything, sliced through the room's tension. "Gentlemen, and lady," he glanced briefly at Maria, "in the service of our nation, certain sacrifices are indispensable. The Russians are rising again, Syria, Afrika, Serbia and Ukraine, its time the bear retreats to its cave."

The gravity of their undertaking hung heavy in the air before Allen, seeking tangibles amidst the rhetoric, intervened. "Where exactly do we stand with the operation?"

"We anticipated Reef Explorer diverting to safer waters—Tel Aviv, Haifa, then a stretch to Cyprus and the Aegean," Asfour began, the details flowing with the precision of a man who had visualized every step. "The recent chaos in Istanbul forced their hand, making Limassol the port of choice. It's a tender port."

Allen's brow furrowed. "And the significance?"

"Infiltration," Asfour said succinctly. "Standard ports are fortresses—IDs, scanners, endless checks. Tender ports? They're our back door in."

Maria Sysco, until now a silent observer, leaned forward. "Your teams, the timetable?"

"Groundwork's laid," Asfour responded without missing a beat. "Aziz heads the groundwork; our Somalian associates join shortly. After a week's prep, it's straight to Limassol to intersect with the Reef Explorer's itinerary."

Vice President Treisman's final words, underscored by resolve, sealed their grim covenant. "If any obstacles arise, they'll be swiftly neutralized. This operation is paramount."

* * * *

Asfour embarked on a whirlwind journey, spanning half the globe, to reach Hurghada in a mere twenty-six hours. At the airport, he was greeted by Aziz, who piloted a weathered Ford that had seen a decade of service. They departed from the airport, veering southward toward the remote premises Asfour had secured.

"Is the farm suitable for your men?" Asfour enquired.

Aziz responded, "There are ample rooms, two occupants per room. Our pantry is stocked with rice and vegetables, and chickens roam freely on the grounds. It's quite comfortable compared to the Bedouin camp."

"Excellent. Has Awaale and his men arrived at the farm, Aziz?" Asfour asked.

Aziz replied, "Yes, there was some grumbling about the sleeping arrangements on the transport ship, but once I handed them twenty cartons of Marlboro cigarettes, their spirits lifted."

"And you've placed them in the separate building, as we discussed?" Asfour enquired.

Aziz affirmed, "Yes. I've initiated their training, though it takes longer since none of them are literate. It's more of a 'show and do' approach. I gather the Somalis with my men for three hours each day, and then I train my men separately."

"Good. It's crucial that the Somalis continue to believe this is solely a financial hijacking. They are pivotal for positioning the ship and deterring any potential threats during the required period," Asfour emphasized as they arrived at the farm. The entrance gate was promptly secured behind them by one of the Arab guards assigned to security.

Asfour's boots crunched on the gravel as he stepped out of the vehicle, the heat of the day still lingering in the air like a shroud. The farm, a sprawling compound hidden away from prying eyes, was alive with activity and an undercurrent of urgency. Moving forward, he was immediately struck by the discordant range of aromas wafting toward him, a rich tapestry of scents that spoke of distant homelands and simpler times.

The Arab contingent, a band of men tempered by conflict and survival, had established their domain outside a nondescript building. Their presence was a fusion of resilience and nostalgia, evident from the smells of cinnamon, allspice, anise, and nutmeg that hung heavy in the air. They were men displaced, clinging to fragments of a culture they carried with them in the form of cherished recipes.

Navigating through the throng, Asfour made his way toward Aziz, located on the opposite side of the farm. Here, open fires roared, and portable gas stoves hissed, men huddled around them in camaraderie and necessity.

In this makeshift kitchen under the stars, when the relentless dust storms were at bay, they conjured up dishes that were memories manifest. With a refrigerator salvaged for their quarters, their culinary options expanded beyond the limitations often imposed on the Somalis.

Above the hum of conversations, the diesel generators coughed and spluttered, their rickety rhythm showing their age. They were indispensable, banishing darkness and driving the stifling heat away with whirring fans. But their clamour was a constant in the background, forcing Asfour to elevate his voice as he began coordinating with Aziz.

In the dimming light, Asfour motioned for the Arab contingent to follow him to a more secluded part of the compound, ensuring they were out of the Somalis' earshot. With a backdrop of the rugged landscape, the fading sunlight casting long shadows over their faces, Asfour began speaking, his voice low and commanding.

"Every single one of you is privy to the truth of my involvement here, by the grace of Allah," he initiated, his gaze intense, capturing each man's eyes to guarantee focus and connection. "Yet, for the Somalis, my identity assumes a different facade. I am to them but the financier. It's crucial you grasp this."

He paused, "As we move forward, ensure your actions and words reflect that. Treat me as the financier, the backer—not as your commander," Asfour concluded, his tone leaving no room for debate.

One by one, each member of the Arab group nodded in silent understanding, solidifying their allegiance to the mission and the secrets it held.

Surveying the fields surrounding them, once fertile with tobacco plants, now laid barren for generations with topsoil scattered by the winds, Asfour grew reflective. "This land," he began, "is a stark reminder of our homelands, despoiled of their natural riches by Western powers. Now, you are chosen to reclaim the soil, to nourish it with your blood. You have been carefully selected to strike a resounding blow for Islam." His words resonated with the attentive men, who regarded him with profound respect.

Once the inspirational talk had concluded, with each man personally addressed by Asfour, Aziz led him across the baked mud terrain to where Awaale and his group were stationed. The Somalis had been provided with substantial provisions, including ample supplies of rice, spaghetti, semolina, and teff flour. The combination of sour bread and eggs, post-digestion, created a distinctly pungent atmosphere in the enclosed space they shared.

Aziz formally introduced Asfour to Awaale as their financial supporter, just as a contingent of Arabs carried over several crates and placed them near the Somalis. The covers were removed, revealing Heckler and Koch G3 assault rifles.

Asfour picked up one of the rifles and extended it towards Awaale. "These weapons aren't brand new, but they're in excellent condition, and each one has been thoroughly tested. We selected them for their user-friendliness, whether you're left or right-handed. The rifles come equipped with flip-up rear sights and ventilated metallic handguards. Aziz will provide you with training on their use over the next few days."

Awaale examined the rifle and commented, "They're lighter than I expected."

"Weight is a critical factor, as you'll need to carry your rifle and magazines. We hope it never comes to using them, but preparation is essential. Don't hesitate to employ them if Aziz gives the order. Remember, this operation ensures that you and your family will never go hungry or be without shelter again," Asfour reminded them, evoking a unanimous murmur of agreement from the Somalis.

Aziz then uncovered a second crate. "This is C4 explosive. I will instruct you on where to place it throughout the ship and how to activate it."

"Why do we need explosives for hijacking? We've never used them when hijacking container ships. And why do my men have to handle them?" Awaale questioned, expressing his concerns.

Asfour fabricated an explanation, "You raise valid points. Firstly, there will be passengers from various countries involved, and some of their governments might contemplate launching a rescue operation. The presence of explosives will deter them. Secondly, these Arab comrades, much like your men, are here for a substantial payday. If they are spotted by satellites or a helicopter camera, some nations might misinterpret this operation as a terrorist plot, which it certainly is not. I've invested a significant amount of money in this endeavour, and I need to reap a profitable return. Somalis and Arabs must collaborate to maximize their earnings when we sell the ship and release the passengers."

Several discussions took place among the Somalis, and it became evident that they were pacified once Awaale voiced his understanding. "I get it. When do we begin?"

"In three days, you'll be concealed within the containers arriving tomorrow. You'll be transported to Hurghada port and loaded onto a container ship bound for Cyprus. Absolute silence must be maintained during the loading and unloading processes. The containers are equipped with soundproofing materials to minimize noise. So when you're at sea, keep your conversations in whispers, and there shouldn't be an issue," Asfour instructed.

A member of Awaale's group enquired, "How long will we be trapped in these metal coffins?"

"You'll transit through the Suez Canal, with a twelve-hour wait at Bitter Lake until the southern convoy clears. After you pass through the channel, you'll arrive in Limassol three days later. You'll have beds, clean clothes, drinking and washing water, as well as food—although not hot meals. A week in these conditions is a small price to pay, considering the wealth awaiting you at the end," Asfour explained.

Awaale sought further reassurance, "What about security at the canal? It sounds too simple."

"Awaale, all security matters have been handled. As long as you don't draw attention to yourselves, there shouldn't be any problems," Asfour assured him. Another member of Awaale's group raised a concern, "Can we breathe in there?"

Asfour addressed this concern, saying, "There are numerous air holes, and the containers are retrofitted with noise and odour filters. The air might become a bit stale, but there will be sufficient oxygen. Try to get as much sleep as possible; you'll need your strength once you disembark in Limassol."

After Asfour and Aziz departed to rejoin the Arab group, Awaale's second-in-command spoke quietly to him, "He's no mere financier, Awaale. Look at how the Arabs treat him."

"Maybe that's how they treat money men. We have a lot riding on this; let's not start with doubt and suspicion, my brother," Awaale replied.

Asfour led Aziz into a farm building where the crates of weapons were stored. Aziz expressed his curiosity, saying, "It's about time you told me more about what we have to do."

Asfour explained, "Secrecy is of the utmost importance for the success of this plan. The fewer people who know the details, the better. You'll need to select one of your men and train them on the primary objectives and how to use the new weapons."

As the dust swirled around the makeshift camp, Asfour's face was set in grim determination under the merciless heat of the Middle Eastern sun. The men around him, hardened by battles and a life steeped in a cause they deemed bigger than themselves, leaned in, sensing the gravity in Asfour's tone.

"The Russians," he began, his voice barely more than a rasp, yet commanding complete attention, "have manoeuvred a nuclear barge into Tartus, Syria. They claim its reactor is a benign giant, tasked with desalinating water and providing electricity," Asfour paused, letting out a derisive snort.

"Do we believe that? Hell, no," he spat out the words as if they left a foul taste.

"You reckon there's more to this?" Aziz interjected; his brow furrowed.

Asfour's eyes flashed with an intense fire. "It's about asserting naval prowess, pure and simple. They're erecting a fortress on water, a bastion for their fleet. And the day it stands completed, it'll be a sword hanging over our heads, ready to slice at will."

He paused, scanning the faces etched with lines of questioning and concern, ensuring his words sunk in deep.

"They might have their aircraft carriers," he continued, "but this? This is a whole new ball game. Imagine the sea teeming with their vessels, their power quadrupling virtually overnight. Plus, a massive base in Syria. We're not just talking about dodging the Americans anymore," Asfour's voice grew steelier with each word. "This is a second superpower, breathing down our necks, ready to unleash hell like they've been raining on ISIS in Syria and on their brothers in Ukraine. They have not time or love for Islam, in some respects they are worse than the Americans."

A murmur rippled through the group. The implication was clear, and the threat loomed larger than the desert sun. This was a new frontier of their struggle; one they had not anticipated—one they could not afford to ignore.

"But won't there be a nuclear catastrophe if we proceed?" Aziz questioned; concern etched on his face.

Asfour nodded solemnly. "Yes, a small one. The reactor will leak, and the Russians will have no choice but to scuttle the barge, blocking the port for years and costing them dearly. It's a sacrifice we must make to safeguard our interests."

Aziz contemplated the enormity of their task. "So are we to ram the barge with the Reef Explorer? That's a suicide mission. We wouldn't get within twenty miles of the port before they blow us out of the water, passengers on board or not."

Asfour's expression remained enigmatic as he approached a nearby crate. With a crowbar, he cracked it open and retrieved a small black box and a container housing a small black box with several terminal extensions.

"We have a plan, Aziz," he said, placing the WCU down between them. "This holds the key to our success. Our mission will require cunning and precision. We'll need to infiltrate, manipulate, and strike when the moment is right. It won't be easy, but it's our only chance."

Aziz ran his fingers over the WCU, realizing the gravity and intricacy of their mission. The stakes were high, and failure wasn't an option. He glanced up, a question evident in his eyes, "What's this thing capable of?"

Asfour smirked, a hint of menace in his eyes. "The better question is, what isn't it capable of?"

chapter eight
Calm before the Storm

Life has a way of throwing curveballs, even for a seasoned man like Stahmer. The journey from Sharm El Sheikh to Corfu had been an exhausting drag, stretching across two long days. In that time, he could have circled the globe from London to Hawaii and back. The route had taken him from the Middle East to the southern edge of Europe, with layovers and transfers that seemed endless.

The moment the trio stepped into the hotel grounds, exhaustion weighing heavily on Stahmer's shoulders, they were met with an unexpected sanctuary. The garden was a vivid oasis, colours bursting forth in defiance of the urban surroundings, set against the eternal expanse of the Ionian Sea. Mature palm trees stood sentry, their fronds dancing to the rhythm of the sea breeze, orchestrating a dynamic interplay of light and shadow over the rustic sitting areas below.

Stahmer, usually indifferent to such trivialities as nature's palette, found himself momentarily disarmed by the tranquillity. The garden was not just a place; it was a feeling. However, the weight of his fatigue, the mental fog from hours of relentless travel, dulled his ability to fully embrace the serenity offered to him on a platter.

Ghislaine and Shultz, on the other hand, absorbed what Stahmer couldn't. Ghislaine's eyes lit up, a stark contrast to the weariness in her gait, as she took in the surroundings. The scent of the flowers, almost hypnotic, seemed to weave through her senses, lightening her fatigue-filled limbs. She could hear the whispered lullaby of the waves caressing the nearby shore, a sound both alien and familiar, grounding her in the here and now.

Shultz, the silent observer, took a moment to close his eyes, the gentle sea breeze brushing against his skin like a promise of comfort.

Stahmer collapsed onto his hotel bed, his body weary from the journey. As he recounted the events and the attempt on their lives in Sharm El Sheikh, he typed up his debrief for Cheryl. He knew he needed to catch up with Fabienne to see if there were any further developments. Stahmer assumed that both Ghislaine and Shultz were already sound asleep in their beds.

However, when he entered the dining area at 5:30 am, he was surprised to find Shultz and Ghislaine already seated, enjoying a hearty breakfast. Both looked fresh and ready for the challenges that lay ahead.

"Morning, Robert," Ghislaine greeted him with a warm smile.

Stahmer simply nodded in acknowledgment.

"Make sure you have all your equipment ready," Ghislaine continued. "We'll be on the Reef Explorer for several days, perhaps even longer, depending on what we discover."

Shultz cut through the speculative haze that had settled in the room, his voice assuming a hard edge, the steel in it commanding attention. "We're not grasping the gravity of the situation," he began, his eyes scanning the expressions around him, ensuring he had every shred of their dwindling focus. "The intel from the

Egyptian authorities doesn't just suggest foul play; it's a goddamn neon sign for it. Cummings didn't just die; he was murdered. Drowned, for Christ's sake, in the middle of a desert."

He paused, letting the absurdity of that fact sink in. "This wasn't some low-level scuffle, or a deal gone wrong. He was tortured. And not for his bloody pocket change," Shultz continued, the urgency in his tone climbing. "Cummings was a straight arrow, a man who dedicated his life to the maritime. No vices to exploit, no dark secrets. His life, was tethered to that ship, the Reef Explorer."

The breakfast table remained silent; the tension palpable as Shultz delivered his final, chilling deduction. "Someone extracted information, something critical, it's related to the Reef Explorer. This is a warning. A prelude to something serious. We're potentially looking at a hijack scenario or, worse, a full-scale terrorist assault."

His gaze locked onto Stahmer and Ghislaine. "They're telegraphing their moves, and it's only a matter of time. It could be today, tomorrow, a week, or even a month. But make no mistake, something's coming. And that ship," he said, his voice lowering for emphasis, "is in the eye of the goddamn storm."

"I agree. We can't just sit on this information," she asserted, her voice a mixture of resolve and burgeoning urgency. "Part of what we need to do is alert the captain and the crew. Something's brewing, and they need to be on high alert, possibly even tighten security measures on board."

Stahmer's eyebrow arched upwards, a silent cue for more, and Shultz didn't disappoint. "And what about us, our own security?" he chimed in, the practicalities of the situation weighing heavily on his mind. "Shouldn't we consider being armed? If the threat is as real as we suspect, we're like sitting ducks without some sort of protection."

It was Stahmer, weathered by years of field experience, who shook his head, his gesture cutting through the building anxiety. "We're not just boarding a pleasure cruise; we're walking into what might be a volatile situation. We can't waltz on armed, not without the captain's express permission, which we've sought and been denied. Our play here is subtle: get on, blend in, observe, and extract whatever intel we can."

He paused, his eyes scanning the room, reading the quiet apprehension in each set of eyes. "We're there to assess and inform, to hopefully convince the captain to take the necessary precautions. We have to be quick, thorough, and inconspicuous. We disembark within a couple of days, max. Our strength isn't in our firepower; it's in our wits and our ability to piece together this puzzle."

Stahmer's gaze hardened with resolve, the seasoned grit in him surfacing. "Let's not kid ourselves; we're stepping into unknown territory. We're not Max Cutler or Tuck, we know something's on the horizon, and it's our job to anticipate and counter it without causing a full-blown panic."

The day promised to be a scorcher, and even at this early hour, the taxi's air conditioner was running at full blast. The trip to the port was smooth, as tourist coaches were sporadic, and the roads were empty due to the decline in tourism, fuelled by economic concerns and misconceptions about safety.

As they approached the port, Stahmer contemplated the fare charged by the taxi driver, deciding not to engage in a futile argument.

A little over an hour later, they had navigated several immigration checkpoints and were finally aboard the Reef Explorer. A petite Philippine waitress served them coffee and croissants, assuring them that the cruise director would join them shortly.

Within half an hour, a bald, myopic German named Eric Sheller, with an air of arrogance, arrived to provide them with a ship orientation. While he appeared to consider this duty beneath him, Stahmer knew better than to challenge the authority of the ship's master, who held the key to their investigation.

The Reef Explorer stood towering, a behemoth silhouette etching the horizon, her once-gleaming lines now hinting at a bygone era of luxury—a vestige from the days she was Elite Cruises crown jewel, now slightly diminished in her old-world grandeur. They started their reconnaissance at the summit of this floating relic, the ninth deck, under the vast expanse of the unblemished sky.

As they descended through the levels of the ship, they navigated a network of leisure—areas dedicated to human indulgence and relaxation. They passed by swimming pools that sparkled like oases amidst the sea of sun loungers, tempting all with a mirage of respite under the relentless sun. Nearby, Jacuzzis bubbled, their frothy waters a whisper of promised relaxation, an escape perhaps from the mundanity of seafaring monotony.

Further along, they encountered the spa, a sanctuary veiled in a semi-mystical allure. The area was populated with resin figures, static guardians of well-being, their forms harking back to the ancient Olympians. These effigies, frozen in moments of mythical might and ethereal grace, seemed to watch over the inhabitants with a promise of rejuvenation.

Each deck unravelled a new layer of the ship's identity, a narrative of past splendour slightly frayed by the passage of time. Stahmer, a man attuned to the silent language of vulnerability in even the most imposing structures, couldn't help but take a mental inventory of the ship's frailties.

It was no stronghold. The very design, intended for leisure and luxury, spoke little of defence or fortification. Amidst the laughter of patrons and the soft hum of the ship's heart, he noted the unguarded expanses, the insufficient surveillance points, access through the mooring deck—rope ladders with grapples could be thrown onto the lifeboat deck- potential entry points and he had only just begun to assess the ship.

As they descended to the sixth deck, a sense of opulence enveloped them, marking a distinct transition from the functional nature of the cabin decks. The air here seemed more refined, and the ambient lighting cast a soft glow on the surroundings, highlighting the understated luxury.

They stepped into the main reception area, a welcoming space that exuded elegance and comfort. The floor was laid with intricate marble designs, and the area was crowned with a stunning chandelier, which cascaded light, creating shimmering patterns on the surfaces below. Plush seating areas provided guests with spots to relax, converse, or simply marvel at the ship's interior beauty.

Adjacent to the reception, boutique shops lined the walkway, offering high-end goods and souvenirs. Each shop boasted its unique character, with polished glass fronts and tasteful displays of merchandise, from designer clothing and jewellery to fine perfumes and limited-edition collectibles. The attendants within were as elegant as the wares they were peddling, all smiles and discreet sales pitches, adding to the upscale ambiance.

But it was the grand staircase that truly captured their attention. A marvel of craftsmanship, it connected multiple decks, its sweeping curves adorned with polished wood and gilded handrails. The steps were carpeted with plush fabric, softening each footfall. It was easy to imagine guests pausing on these stairs for photographs, creating memories against the backdrop of affluence.

Off to the side, Eric Sheller, who had maintained a professional but clearly fatigued disposition, seemed to breathe a sigh of relief as he gestured towards John Cribb, the head of security. Cribb himself was a figure of authority and reassurance, his stance confident as he awaited to take over the tour. His presence seemed to signify a shift from the overt luxury to the behind-the-scenes strength and control necessary to maintain order and safety on such a grand vessel.

Cribb, a man in charge of a team of fifteen security personnel, oversaw the ship's access and ensured the safety of everyone on board.

"Our security team receives thorough briefings for each shift, and they are organized into teams to cover all entry and exit points when we are in port," Cribb explained. "Passengers are equipped with digitized swipe cards that contain the individual's details, including a photograph for easy identification."

Stahmer took the lead in the conversation, enquiring further. "What about the supplies?"

Cribb elaborated, "All food and supplies undergo rigorous inspections, including waste and bunker transfers. In addition to these duties, my team is responsible for ship security in case of rare fights or disagreements, and they ensure that areas potentially linked to a crime scene are properly secured."

Shultz, who had been diligently documenting the positions of security cameras in his notepad, turned to Cribb with a question. "Have there been many instances where these measures were needed?"

Cribb recounted the ship's recent history. "In the past year, we've had two cases of suspicious deaths, both involving spousal abuse, resulting in one serious injury and one fatality. There have been other deaths, most attributed to age, illness, or suicide."

Shultz didn't probe further, understanding the practical implications—murder on cruise ships could significantly harm business. If no concrete evidence suggested foul play, such cases were typically classified as suicides.

For nearly six hours, the MIDAS team meticulously reviewed the ship's floor plans. Stahmer and Shultz delved into the smallest details with Cribb, while Ghislaine diligently recorded their findings. When they were satisfied with their understanding of the ship's layout and security measures, they requested interviews with the officers, starting with those who had close connections with Gareth Cummings.

Initially, the captain hesitated to grant their request, citing the ongoing return of passengers from excursions and the officers' responsibilities in preparing the ship for departure from the port of Rhodes. However, he agreed that the officers would be made available to them over the next three days, depending on their schedules. Eric Sheller made another appearance to provide them with their swipe cards and assured them that their luggage had been delivered to their cabins.

Captain Carl Nordstrom, of Norwegian descent (who playfully referred to himself as 'Viking'), was informed about the MIDAS investigators' presence on board. Stahmer was designated as the team leader, and the captain assigned him a mini suite on deck seven, selected for its reduced vibration compared to lower decks. Shultz and Ghislaine received cabins on deck four, which were smaller and less luxurious than Stahmer's, and Shultz was disappointed to discover that they lacked the complimentary mini bar that Stahmer enjoyed. As the ship's engines roared to life, vibrations from the aging vessel reverberated throughout.

In each of their cabins, they found invitations to dine with the captain at 8 pm in the Windstorm dining room, a venue used by the master and guests alike. Some passengers anticipated the captain's presence at least once during the cruise, while others were indifferent.

The following morning, Stahmer conducted interviews with the senior officers, with Ghislaine providing translation when needed. Stahmer was particularly interested in their knowledge of Gareth Cummings and whether the kidnapping had been specific to him or if any officer of the Reef Explorer would have sufficed. Cummings had a broad range of expertise, responsible for various tasks, including navigation, operating the ship's computers, handling security matters, and being knowledgeable about the ship's vulnerabilities. As Stahmer gathered more information, his concerns grew.

Meanwhile, Shultz continued to probe the ship's weaknesses and successfully gained access to areas off-limits to guests. On one occasion, he ventured down to the engine room and encountered an engineer who questioned his presence.

Stahmer and Ghislaine visited the bridge and received an induction into the ship's computerised systems that governed most aspects of its operation. After the presentation, Stahmer couldn't help but feel like the elephant in the room. The captain took great pleasure in describing the ship's operation, even letting Ghislaine take control of the ship for several minutes, guiding her hand as she navigated. She didn't mind the attention, as she was accustomed to commanding the fascination and obedience of men like the captain with subtle gestures, touches, or hints of her allure.

Dan Williams had a close relationship with Gareth Cummings, their families socialising together. Dan had been closer to Cummings than anyone else on board. He recounted a visit to the market outside Sharm El Sheikh two weeks before Cummings' abduction, where he felt they were being followed and watched. He had warned Cummings, who had dismissed his concerns as paranoia. Dan provided Stahmer with a detailed description of the men who had been observing them closely.

That evening, the meal was served in Stahmer's mini suite, set up for three people with two sets of wine glasses. Stahmer, Shultz, and Ghislaine discussed their findings, their focus clear. The conversation continued until the butler entered to remove empty plates and replace them with the next course, fit for a Michelin-starred restaurant. The red wine was left to breathe on the table, and the white wine rested in an ice bucket. They opted for mineral water during the meeting to keep their minds sharp. All three MIDAS operatives were on the same page: Cummings had been tortured for information that would aid an attack on the Reef Explorer.

A meeting with the captain was scheduled for 3 pm the following day, but Stahmer decided to utilise the extra time. With Shultz and Ghislaine, he devised various attack scenarios, some seemingly outrageous at first glance but still within the realm of possibility. Shultz and Ghislaine played the role of devil's advocates, questioning and probing the weaknesses of the ship's security measures.

The knowledge they had accumulated about the Reef Explorer left them with more questions than answers. They contemplated scenarios involving aerial assaults, parachute landings on a moving ship, attacks from suicide boats loaded with explosives, and even the infamous Al-Qaeda-backed attack on the USS Cole in December 2000. They also considered the possibility of a lone wolf suicide bomber or attacker, as well as the presence of a sleeper agent already on board, possibly a transient worker or waiter, implanted by those with plans for the Reef Explorer.

One thing was certain: the individuals responsible for Gareth Cummings' death had a purpose, and their conclusions, along with Fabienne's data, all pointed in the same direction. It was inconceivable to undertake the risks associated with kidnapping and murder for any other reason, as no person or group had claimed responsibility for Cummings' death.

At 1 am, their brainstorming session concluded, just as the storm outside abated. Shultz and Ghislaine, exhausted, retired to their adjoining cabins. It was midnight in Geneva, and Stahmer had to speak with Fabienne. When she answered the secured video link, her image filled his laptop screen. She wore a loose, multi-coloured kaftan and held a Swiss version of a Dunkin' Donut in one hand, with what appeared to be a strawberry milkshake by her side.

"Good evening, Robert. Nice to see I'm not the only one awake at this hour," she greeted him.

Stahmer adjusted his eye patch, subconsciously affected by the rainbow and pastel colours of her kaftan. "Evening, Fabienne. Did you receive the report I sent a few minutes ago?"

"I certainly did, and you and your team have been quite busy," she replied.

"How is Basmati doing?"

"Basmati has developed a secondary infection from his wounds. He's under the care of the best doctors and receives daily visits from me. Fingers crossed, he'll recover," Fabienne updated.

"Please give him our best wishes. Have you had a chance to review my recommendations?" Stahmer enquired.

"Your conclusions align with the data I've gathered, and I find no fault with your recommendations. However, authorising some of them may be above my pay grade. I'm going to connect you with Cutler in Bali, as your main recommendation might have implications for his case," Fabienne explained as she blew Stahmer a kiss just before Cutler appeared on the screen.

"It sounds like you're having more excitement there than we are," Stahmer remarked wryly.

"If your report is accurate, things are about to get much livelier," Cutler responded as he glanced back at the secure report on his iPad.

Breakfast was brought to Stahmer's cabin by the butler at 6:30 am. It fell short of a full English breakfast, as cruise ships often served streaky bacon that resembled pure fat rather than the Danish smoked back bacon that Stahmer preferred. Ghislaine opted for items from the sideboard, helping herself to muesli, yogurt, and croissants. They all skipped the alcoholic Buck's Fizz that some cruise guests indulged in, settling for fresh orange juice. It may not have been too early for alcohol for the passengers, but it wasn't what the trio needed before starting their work.

As they enjoyed their coffee, the ship gradually slowed to a halt, and they could hear the rattling of chains as the anchor was lowered into the sea, followed by the sensation of it gripping the seabed. Ghislaine stood and went to the balcony, gazing at Limassol in the distance. The warm breeze and rising sun signalled a completely different day from the one before when Sahara sand had covered the ship's decks. When the announcement called for passengers to assemble at their designated meeting points for disembarkation, Stahmer, Shultz, and Ghislaine went in separate directions to observe how the guests were being transferred to shore.

Hull doors on deck four, starboard side, served as the disembarkation point. Gantry platforms were lowered to create standing areas, and tender boats circled off the bow, coming in one by one to ferry passengers to the port.

Guests who had paid for excursions disembarked first, followed by those who planned to explore the port on their own. Stahmer noticed that while most guests patiently queued, some believed in their self-entitlement and attempted to bypass the lines, leading to arguments. One elderly gentleman grew increasingly irate as a French woman brushed past his protests to board the boat, saving herself time in the queue and securing what she deemed a better seat on the tender.

Two security officers flanked a small Dutchman and physically escorted him off the ship, with his demure wife following him. When Shultz enquired about the situation, he was informed that the man had struck someone who had moved his laundry from a machine to dry his own clothes. The assailant claimed he had handled his wife's undergarments, and this had led to the altercation. Shultz couldn't help but shake his head at the foolishness of some people. The security officer explained that they often dealt with minor disputes among passengers, citing the challenges of bringing 3,000 strangers together.

Meanwhile, Ghislaine observed the opening of a hull door amidships, an exclusive access point for passengers participating in the snorkelling excursion. Twenty enthusiastic passengers, burdened with towels and bags, soon boarded a catamaran for an afternoon of snorkelling over the reefs. Security was present at all exits, scanning passengers' cruise cards to register their disembarkation.

After most of the guests had left for various excursions, Stahmer took the opportunity to explore the nearly deserted ship.

A few die-hard passengers, unwilling to stray far from the buffet offerings, sat sporadically around the pool or engaged in card games on the nearly empty upper open decks. Some of the less mobile guests took advantage of the deserted pool and jacuzzi.

Stahmer had quit smoking three years prior and had replaced cigarettes with vaping tobacco substitutes. The ship, like many others, had prohibited smoking in cabins and guest areas, with a few exceptions. One side of the casino allowed smoking due to the significant revenue it generated. Another designated smoking area was discreetly tucked away to the right of the bar on deck nine, a hidden nook. The billowing tobacco smoke was a giveaway to its purpose.

As Stahmer enjoyed his e-cigarette, he struck up a conversation with a charismatic man in his fifties. Based on the man's mannerisms and a certain velvety quality to his voice, he judged the man to be from money. Stahmer listened to the constant chatter, occasionally guiding the conversation toward topics of interest. The man turned out to be a prolific gossip, but Stahmer realised it often came with a touch of embellishment.

Once all the disembarking passengers had left the ship, the MIDAS operatives were summoned to the captain's cabin for a meeting.

"We have six hours before the excursion tenders return and eight hours before we set sail, so I would like to keep this meeting as brief as possible," Captain Carl Nordstrom began, his eyes openly admiring Ghislaine's bronzed, glistening legs, which contrasted sharply against her bright white shorts.

"Thank you for your time, Captain; we understand your busy schedule, and we'll be concise," Stahmer responded. Shultz and Ghislaine nodded in agreement.

"This ship is like a fortress, Mr. Stahmer. Nothing gets on or off without my officers knowing about it," the captain asserted.

"We don't doubt your professionalism or your crew's competence, Captain. However, we believe we're dealing with a serious situation," Stahmer said. Shultz and Ghislaine nodded in agreement.

"You're on a ship with radar to detect anything nearby, cameras monitoring every inch, and the ability to outrun most vessels. We also have strategically placed water cannons to deter potential threats," the captain replied confidently, unaccustomed to civilians questioning his ship's security.

Stahmer, though, pushed forward. "I spoke to a man on deck nine who claimed he walked onto the ship without being stopped by security. He said he was hailed before the ship left port because they thought he was still onshore due to his card not being scanned. Perhaps the ship's security isn't as foolproof as you believe?"

The captain bristled at the suggestion. "If that did occur, it's an exception, not the rule, Mr. Stahmer."

Shultz chimed in, "Your security cameras aren't manned 24/7. They're used mainly for reviewing incidents reactively, not proactively. If, for example, someone was to jump overboard or commit suicide, the cameras would record the event, but they wouldn't alert security to an ongoing situation. It's passive and insecure surveillance."

"The cost of monitoring all those cameras around the clock would be exorbitant and impractical," the captain countered defensively. "We employ active monitoring where it's most needed, based on a hazard analysis assessment."

Shultz pressed on, "You have security officers monitoring the casinos for signs of collusion or fraud during operating hours. Don't you think the vulnerable areas Mr. Stahmer has highlighted deserve the same attention, Captain?"

"We do what's necessary. Our surveillance techniques are thoroughly discussed and agreed upon," the captain retorted, his patience wearing thin.

Stahmer interjected calmly, "While Oceanic Enterprises conducts background checks on all staff, including photographs and personal histories, they don't employ biometrics like fingerprints or retinal scans. If we were so inclined, we could place an agent on board without your knowledge in less than a week, Captain."

The captain's face tightened. "My primary responsibility is to operate this ship safely and securely, ensuring it reaches its destination on time regardless of the weather. It's not my role to micromanage Human Resources. I assume that will be your task, Mr. Stahmer?"

"You have tenders staffed by your crew, shuttling between the ship and the port. Sometimes, they are dependent on filling up the tenders before moving off, leaving them isolated and out of sight of the ship or other tenders. It might be more prudent to organize the tenders so that they are always in sight of another boat. Additionally, you have private excursion boats approaching the port side, which are not manned by your crews, and this could also be considered a weak point in your security," Ghislaine pointed out.

Captain Nordstrom locked eyes with Ghislaine and said, "Young lady, I've been in this profession for many years, and this is the way we've always operated, without incident, I might add."

"Captain, my team and I are not here to undermine your efforts, and if we have offended you in any way, please accept my sincere apologies. We are here to assess security on behalf of your company, Oceanic Enterprises. The three of us concur that, with the disappearance of your officer, you are under an immediate threat," Stahmer emphasized.

"Communications Officer Cummings was an excellent man, both professionally and personally. He was simply unlucky, in the wrong place at the wrong time. Tragic, yes, but we shouldn't jump to conclusions based on one incident. "Replied the captain.

"I was attempting to spare you the gruesome details, Captain, but it seems I have no choice. Mr. Cummings was deliberately targeted and subjected to hours of torture. You may have heard of waterboarding, but his captors used a variant with a weak bleach solution. Not enough to kill him outright, but sufficient to inflict excruciating pain. After they obtained the information they wanted, they killed him and left his body to be consumed by animals. When we found him, he was covered in flies," Stahmer revealed, his tone grim, as the captain looked visibly shaken.

"They were intent on concealing his death. As we approached, they severely injured two Egyptian police officers and had previously killed another. They even attempted to kill us when we arrived at the scene. Captain, there is a very real and imminent threat now," Stahmer asserted. "In fact, I spoke with Max Cutler last night. Cutler heads MIDAS and serves as the senior partner and investigator. He concurs with our assessment and has relayed this information to Oceanic's board. He has a few loose ends to tie up in Bali, but he and his team should be joining us in the next couple of days. That's how convinced we are that you are a target."

"Captain, while this is an older ship, there are more valuable targets out there. Ships worth a hundred times more than this vessel," Shultz added.

"May I enquire if you have any weapons on board, Captain?" Shultz said.

"We don't carry weapons. We see that as a greater risk," the captain responded.

"Any tasers, pepper sprays, or any objects that could be used for self-defence?" Shultz pressed.

"Mr. Shultz, we are a cruise ship, not a naval vessel, and we do not carry weapons expecting riots or anarchy on our ships. We deal with inebriated passengers and spirited high jinks," the captain explained.

"We will need your permission for Mr. Cutler and his team to bring weapons on board when they arrive, Captain," Stahmer stated.

"Absolutely not. Mr. Cutler and his team are welcome on board once I receive clearance from our head office, but no weapons will be allowed on my ship, now or ever," the captain asserted firmly.

"Let's return to the topic of passenger safety ashore. What precautions are in place?" Ghislaine redirected, attempting to ease the growing tension.

"Those who pay for excursions are accompanied by security-cleared drivers and representatives to guide them. Those venturing ashore are under the protection of local law enforcement until they return to the port. In any case, there are always risks, and we rely on passengers to exercise common sense," the captain explained.

"Captain, I must reiterate the matter of weapons. Your board of directors has informed us that the captain has the final say on what is allowed on his ship, and that captain is you. I cannot emphasize enough the urgency of this issue, as we believe an attack is imminent within the next couple of weeks," Stahmer stressed.

"Mr. Stahmer, I believe you may have indulged in one too many Agatha Christie novels," Captain Nordstrom quipped.

chapter nine
Path to Redemption

The situation was a ticking time bomb, and Cutler felt the seconds slipping away like sand through his fingers. Basmati was down, they had a major operation underway and not enough agents to carry it out.

Cutler's voice, steady yet laced with an undercurrent of pressing haste, sliced through the tense air as he addressed Tuck and Colton. "We're flying blind," he declared. "Fabienne's just given me a heads-up. The tracker's pinged the Freemantle's location. They're docked down under, same name as the town they're in—Freemantle."

"Tracks right," Tuck chimed in. "Australia's a huge draw for the trade-in and resale of yachts, new and used."

"As we all know It's ferrying the LSX 92 Lazzara, Sonny and Rosie Trench's boat—both of whom have vanished from the radar since it went missing. Mang and his gang are e undoubtedly the same crew behind the hijacking of the Coca V1 yacht and the cold-blooded killing of Robert Ford. It's a fair shot they've killed the Trench siblings too," Cutler imparted.

"So which one of us is heading to the land of Oz?" Colton quipped, attempting to slice through the palpable tension.

"We're running on fumes, team-wise," Cutler admitted, his customary cool conduct fraying ever so slightly with evident irritation. "But Fabienne's played a card we had up our sleeve.

Pulled in a favour with an old contact of Tuck's. A Scot, former para, goes by the name of Jock, based now in Sydney. He's going to be our boots on the ground. His task—tail the cargo, monitor its berth, and stay alert for any ripple in the water."

"We're short on hands here with Basmati down," Tuck pointed out.

"I'm aware and have a plan. Timing is crucial," Cutler asserted. "Sunday presents an opportunity when they're preoccupied with their quad biking. Things are escalating with the Reef Explorer, and we need to act swiftly. "I might have just the solution," Cutler interjected.

"We've got a tight window, then. Four days. Without Basmati, we're flying blind on drone coverage," Tuck observed, glancing at Cutler.

"I might have just the solution—Old Joe," Cutler interjected.

"The old bastard practically knocking on death's door. What good can he do?" Tuck remarked, scepticism evident in his tone.

"He can handle a vehicle, maybe even the drone, and keep a lookout; we need someone for overwatch," Cutler interjected. "And after we've just turned his boat into splinters? Good luck getting him on board," Colton retorted with a mix of sarcasm and realism.

"Ford's signed off on replacing his cat ketch. Had a couple of talks with him, and I sense he's hiding something, but willing to help," Cutler responded, though an instinct told him Old Joe hadn't laid all his cards on the table.

Cutler made his way to the marina, finding Old Joe sipping a pink gin, in no time. They settled on the edge of a quiet pier, basking in the sun. To Old Joe, there was something about Cutler that echoed his former captain's resolve, a dash of that cinematic James Bond flair.

"What's off, Joe? Something doesn't add up. When we discussed the Trench kids' disappearance, not to mention Robert Ford and his fiancée, I saw a shift in you, a hint of guilt. Don't tell me you're tangled up with Mayan and his crew," Cutler pressed, his voice steady but probing, eyes searching Joe's for any flicker of truth.

Old Joe stirred uncomfortably, pausing for several long moments as he gathered his thoughts. Finally, he began, his voice a low, reflective timbre, "Three weeks before we were set to sail from England, life threw us a shit shot. Annie was diagnosed with leukaemia. But she… she was a force, you know. 'We're still making this trip,' she told me, her eyes fierce with determination. And so, we did."

He sighed, the weight of his memories pressing visibly on his shoulders. "She was incredible, surpassed what any of the doctors predicted—sixteen months. Sixteen months of bravely navigating through that illness and in those final months," he paused, swallowing hard, "I was her nurse, her protector, doing my best to keep her pain at bay with the morphine."

His eyes, lost in the past, shimmered with the recollection, the sorrow, and undeniable respect for her courage mingling in his narrative.

"I wasn't aware she accompanied you for part of that time," Cutler responded softly, offering a respectful nod.

"In the beginning, it was manageable. Our doctor anticipated she had about a year, providing us with a two lots of six-month supply packs of morphine. But Annie fought for sixteen months That's when the struggle for additional pain relief began. I ventured down paths I never imagined, some within the law, others… not so much," he admitted, his eyes dropping away.

"And you found a way to get the money… What did you do, Joe?" Cutler asked, his voice gentle yet insistent, urging the older man to confront what was clearly a painful chapter in his history.

"They used my weak point, my wife, used me then the stakes changed," Old Joe's voice grew rough like gravel, the weight of his past pressing evidently on his chest. The sun overhead seemed to dim as his story unfolded. "They started using to identify high value yachts. I was no longer just a runner; I was a smuggler, handling stolen goods, It wasn't just drugs anymore; it was these luxury yachts, stolen from the sea and marinas."

The air between them tensed, the earlier calm shattered by the gravity of Old Joe's involvement. Cutler's jaw set, a flicker of betrayal and calculation cold in his eyes.

"So, you are involved?" Cutler surmised, his voice steely, masking the turmoil within—the conflict between his respect for this old sailor and the stark, jagged edge of the criminal confession.

"Yes," Old Joe confirmed, his voice barely more than a whisper as if he were talking to his own soul. "Then Annie… she left me." His voice fractured, breaking on the jagged edges of his grief, which, despite the passage of time, remained as devastating as the day he lost her. "She passed only three days following one of those cursed runs. I… I wasn't even allowed the space to grieve her. They didn't care. To them, I was just a tool, valuable only for my knowledge of the sea routes and the vessels."

He shook his head, the shadows of his memories playing across his face. "They had me trapped. Said I was in debt, that I knew too much. They even threatened my life, claimed I still owed them a fortune. Corruption is rife here; they've got the cops in their pockets. There was no way I could escape this island with a breath left in me."

Drawing a ragged breath, he looked up, his eyes a mix of anger and deep regret. "I was the one who tipped them off about the Trench yacht. But harming those kids? No, that was never part of the plan. I assumed it was just another yacht theft, nothing more. They were supposed to only take the yacht." His last words were drowned in a sorrow so profound it seemed to echo around them, the guilt he carried laid bare for Cutler to see…"

Cutler's fists clenched, the anger for Old Joe's tormentors simmering beneath his skin. He needed to channel it, to use it to fuel their next moves. "You are waist deep in this Joe, no matter the cause you are indirectly responsible for people getting killed," Cutler acknowledged grimly. "But right now, you have a chance to put it right, Joe. Help us nail these bastards."

Old Joe looked up, the fight reigniting in his old, tired eyes. The confession, it seemed, had lit a long-extinguished flame.

"Tell me how you got involved and from the beginning," Cutler pressed, leaning in, the hunt now coursing through his veins. The predator in him, ever present beneath the surface, had awoken, hungry for retribution. "Tell me everything."

The air crackled with intensity as Old Joe, motivated by a newfound purpose, began to spill all he knew about the dark operations he'd been forced into. The information flowed like a torrid river between two.

We moored in a marina in Phuket, it wasn't cheap, and my money and Annies's medicine was running out quickly. The morphine was all I was worried about, I needed to make sure the pain was manageable," Joe's voice was a raspy whisper, the weight of his desperation hanging in the air. "Nine months, that's all the meds lasted, I had to increase her dosages because of the pain. We were bleeding cash, every last penny going to keep her pain at bay. I was frantic, told my son to sell the house back home, but the damn process takes time, and Annie… she was suffering right then and there."

"So you went looking for morphine, with no cash to purchase?" Cutler's voice was steel wrapped in velvet, pushing, probing.

Joe's eyes, hollow and haunted, met his. "One of the local dealers, he knew I was cornered, offered me a way out. 'Simple runs,' he said. Just me, the boat, and a stash of narcotics from one island to another. It was supposed to be easy money."

Cutler leaned in, the predator in him recognizing the desperation of a man with nothing left to lose. "But it wasn't simple, was it, Joe?"

A shudder ran through the older man, memories flooding back. "No, it wasn't. The first month, everything went smooth. Then they started asking for more—more runs, riskier jobs. I wasn't just the captain anymore; I was part of their damn underworld Things turned worse when the boss an Aussie turned up." His voice cracked, the terror of entrapment raw and palpable in the growing darkness.

Cutler could feel the shift, the moment the confession turned from a mere recounting of facts to a living, breathing nightmare.

The air around them charged with the electricity of truths too long buried, and secrets that were never meant to surface.

"Spill it, Joe. I need the full picture," Cutler pressed, his voice shifting from enquiry to outright demand, compelling the truth to emerge from the dark recesses where it hid, trembling.

"I was played, Cutler. Played like a fucking fiddle," Joe exhaled, his words laced with a mix of fear and anger. "That Aussie cornered me, forced me to mark the luxury yachts. It wasn't just a request; it was an ultimatum. No deal no drugs."

"So this Aussie pays you with fuel and morphine, all in exchange for the intel on those yachts?" Cutler's tone dropped, turning into a menacing rumble, his icy professionalism crystallizing into something far more dangerous with the unfolding revelations.

"Level with me, Joe. The yachts, their coordinates. You handed them over?" Cutler's interrogation sliced through the tension that hung like a heavy fog, his words keen-edged, carving clarity from a jumble of evasion and murky confessions. "He baited you with the morphine, even had a stash waiting in Bali, I take it," Cutler added, the pieces starting to ominously click together.

"Damn it, yes," Joe confessed, his fists balling in impotent rage as if he sought to physically restrain his own demons. "The Aussie, he downplayed it all. 'A few fancy boats,' he'd coaxed. 'Nobody gets hurt. It's all insured anyway.' But it was all crap. Nothing but damn lies."

As Joe's story unfolded, the cogs in Cutler's mind turned furiously, the sinister jigsaw beginning to form a ghastly picture. "An Aussie?" he drilled further, his gaze sharpening with suspicion. "You're telling me Mayan wasn't the one pulling your strings from Phuket?"

"The Aussie, was my point man in Phuket," Joe elucidated, his energy waning with every word as though each syllable leached his life force. "But here, it was Mayan calling the shots. I was running on fumes, Cutler. No fuel, no cash, no morphine."

The atmosphere turned leaden, the full weight of Joe's predicament, and his entanglement in this nefarious web pressing down on them, oppressive and relentless. Cutler's resolve solidified, his voice dropping to a steel-hard timbre, each word laden with promise and menace. "Listen up, I need everything you've got on this Aussie once we're through with this mess. Every last memory. My tech is going to strip this network down to the bone. Got it?"

Cutler's voice dropped, a softer note in the hardened melody of their gritty discourse. "When did Annie pass?" he asked, the question hovering delicately in the air like a fragile truce.

Old Joe's eyes glazed, his pain tangible. "Two months back," he rasped, his voice a cracked whisper. "We were at sea, and she… she just slipped away. God, it was just her and me, like it's always been." His eyes lost focus, staring into the abyss of his memories. "Couldn't part with her, not straight away. She was my whole damn world, you know. Together over four decades…"

The cabin seemed to shrink, suffused with a heartache so raw, so profound that even the walls seemed to mourn. "But then," Joe swallowed, a shudder running through him, "the cabin started reeking of death. I took one of the sails, wrapped her in it. Tied it with reef knots, strong and tight." His voice broke, tears breaching their banks and streaming freely. "I let her go, into the deep. My beautiful Annie, swallowed by the ocean."

The shift was almost palpable, a tangible change in the air as Cutler's professional facade snapped decisively into place, his empathy receding behind a wall of duty. The question came like a bullet, precise and unyielding. "The LSX 92 Lazzara, the Trench yacht, you've admitted to that. What about Ford's Coca V1? Were you the one who tipped them off? Who did you tell, Joe?"

Each syllable was a cold blade, stripping away the layers of evasion and self-pity that Old Joe might have hidden behind. There was no room for gentle prodding, not with the stakes this high.

The older man seemed to deflate further under Cutler's intense scrutiny, his soul laid bare by the relentless pressure of those probing, demanding words. There was nowhere to hide now, not from Cutler, and certainly not from his own conscience.

Joe's voice was a husk, the confession dragging out of him like the worst kind of agony. "I did," he murmured, almost drowned out by the relentless assault of his own grief. "It was the same procedure, I reported it to Mayan. The contact... I just pressed 'one.'"

The despair was a living entity between them, but Cutler didn't let it sway him. This was the ugly side of justice, the part where the lines blurred, where the horrors that men did in the darkness came to light, often carried on the whispers of those who, in another life, might have been simply old men mourning their wives.

Joe, still trapped in the grip of his grief, seemed to fracture further under the weight of confession. "Yes," he whispered, an echo of a man broken beyond repair. "The contact in Phuket, he handed me a burner phone. Told me to press 'one' and report.

The voice on the other end, I discovered was Mayan. I didn't know people would die; I swear. When I heard, it was already too late." His tears were a silent downpour now, words choked out between sobs. "Annie… she'd never forgive me."

The air thickened with unspoken peril as Cutler leaned in, his voice a low, fierce growl. "Listen up and listen good. The man who hired us… is Conrad Ford. He's not the understanding type. He finds out, you're dead. It's that simple. I won't include this in my report, but you keep your mouth shut tight, understand? No more chats, no confessions. Your life's on the line, Joe. You speak, and there's no hole deep enough for you to hide."

"Joe, let me be clear. We have two, possibly four, dead kids, and we are determined to get the killers. You owe them, and you are going to do whatever I ask of you. You seem a genuine guy, who has been caught in a bad situation. I think this is going to eat you up, you need to make amends for what you've done. I am a man down; you know this island and can drive. What about it?"

"I know, I hardly sleep thinking about them, I drink like a fish now and get by on gin and biscuits. Whatever you want I will do, I am sure the guilt will kill me off sooner rather than later."

"I guarantee you, help us bring Mayan and his lackies and you will feel a whole lot better. First, stop drinking today while you work for me, eat properly, and go and get me the contacts mobile phone," Cutler finished.

Cutler informed the rest of his team and Tuck's team later that day that they had a recruit. He decided not to share Old Joe's secret, for the moment.

Time wasn't just flying; it was racing, each second hurtling into the next as if trying to outrun the very clock. In the relentless march of hours and days, Old Joe found himself caught in a maelstrom of new age warfare—drones, not bullets, cameras, not eyes.

Colton, through the unpredictable hand of fate, had drawn the short straw, becoming the impromptu tutor in drone operations despite his own relatively green experience in the field. He found himself in the peculiar position of instructing a man ten years his senior, a twist that left him both bewildered and inadvertently impressed.

Old Joe, with a legacy steeped in naval mastery, surprisingly pivoted with an almost youthful dexterity to grasp the nuances of this new-age technological battleground. Here was a veteran, his hands weathered from years grappling with coarse ropes and steering through tempestuous seas, now deftly manoeuvring joysticks and parsing data on sleek touchscreens. The old dog was indeed learning new tricks.

However, the journey was far from smooth sailing. Two practice drones, caught in the crossfire of Old Joe's rigorous education, succumbed to the harsh lessons of trial and error. They plummeted from the sky, one after the other. Each crash, a cacophony of splintering plastic and technology, heralded a leap in Old Joe's understanding, a costly but necessary sacrifice on the altar of progress.

Despite the setbacks, Colton couldn't help but marvel at the old sailor's adaptability, the way old instincts were repurposed for warfare's modern frontiers. It was a stark reminder that, beneath the wrinkles and tales of bygone battles, lay a tactical mind still sharp as a tack.

The old sailor metamorphosed before their eyes. The wrinkles and liver spots didn't vanish, but now when they looked at Old Joe, they saw not just an old man, but a drone pilot, his hands steady as he executed intricate manoeuvres, his focus unyielding as he adjusted zoom lenses and camera angles with the deftness he once reserved for riggings in a storm.

The military-grade drone, a beast of a machine that they had brought along, was no longer a sophisticated piece of tech in Old Joe's hands but an extension of the man himself. It soared and dipped at his command, its electronic eyes his own as he scouted the terrain, they would soon tread themselves.

By the third day, Old Joe was more than they could have hoped for, filling a void they hadn't realized would be so gaping in Basmati's absence. They didn't speak of it, but they felt it—a tinge of awe, a sliver of gratitude, and, for Cutler, a rare sense of relief in the searing tension that coiled around them as D-Day approached. The old sailor wasn't just making do; he was becoming indispensable.

chapter ten
Blood Sea

The morning bore down with an oppressive heat, humidity clinging to the skin like a second layer, the sky an unrelenting bright orb. The sea shimmered mercilessly, as if flaunting its untouchable diamonds under the blazing sun. The ironic strains of Bob Dylan's *Knockin' on Heaven's Door* ripped through the stillness from the loudspeakers of the chalk-white catamaran, a mockery or perhaps a premonition. A specific line from the track, 'The long black cloud is coming down,' felt like a chilling prophecy on this deceptive day.

Paccar, the hardened skipper and catamaran owner, expertly steered the sleek vessel, guiding it with calculated thrusts of the engine and deft twists of the rudder. His target: the anchored leviathan known as the Reef Explorer. The distance closed until the fenders grazed its colossal side, a gentle kiss. Romano his son was drying the deck from the sea spray.

From the deck, a figure moved with coiled grace—Guano, his towering frame a silhouette against the blazing day, muscles honed from a life that knew of struggle more than comfort. The Ivorian wasn't just muscle, though; every movement was calculated, the result of a life forged in adversity. His past was a far cry from the passengers on the cruise ship. Despite his misfortune to born in poverty, he was a seeker of fortunes in a world that offered little to men from places like his.

Guano's throw was precise, the mooring lines snaking through the air to the waiting hands on the Reef Explorer's starboard platform. As crew members scrambled, securing the connection, Paccar dialled back the roaring engines to a predatory purr.

Guano, unlike the desperate souls fleeing horror, had been driven by economic hunger, a different kind of desperation. He'd found himself in the anarchic wasteland of Libya, a hell born from a rebellion that Europe had instigated but couldn't control. After being stripped of everything he owned, he'd been herded onto a floating deathtrap, more coffin than vessel, by remorseless Libyan smugglers.

The nightmare had only worsened when the smugglers, devoid of any semblance of humanity, abandoned them barely half a day into the voyage, leaving them to the merciless sea. By some miracle, more divine than luck, they'd been found days later by the Royal Navy, more walking corpses than men, ravaged by thirst and starvation, and had been ferried to the relative safety of Cyprus. They were the lucky ones who survived the trip.

Now, on this catamaran, Guano stood as a symbol of survival, a far cry from the broken man rescued from the sea's unforgiving expanse.

Guano had braced himself for the suffocating confines of an internment camp, a limbo of razor wire and watchful eyes. But fate, in a rare moment of mercy, dumped them instead in makeshift shelters—a sea of tents on the outskirts of Limassol. It was a holding pattern, a waiting game for the faceless bureaucracy to either shove them back into the hell they fled from or very unlikely, propel them into the churning mass of the European mainland.

But Guano was a man carved of hard edges and impatience. He thrived on certainties, tangible targets. The indefinite waiting gnawed at him, a slow torture. He knew all too well where he stood in the pecking order—right at the tail end. He was an economic migrant, a seeker of fortunes in the eyes of those holding the clipboard and pen, not a desperate refugee fleeing the scythe of war. His path, he knew, would be choked with red tape, a slow bleed of days, or worse, a ticket back to square one.

So he chose the unknown, preferring its sharp teeth to the slow devouring jaws of bureaucracy. Security had been a steel net as they were herded off the Royal Navy vessel, a web of uniforms and firearms. But during the chaotic shuffle to the camp, amidst faces marked with the same fear and uncertainty that mirrored his own, Guano seized his moment. He became a fleeting shadow, leaping from the lurching wagon into the embrace of the wild Cyprus terrain.

Paccar was a man steeped in history, his lineage a tangled root stretching back to the era when the Knights Templar laid claim to Cyprus in the distant year of 1192. The land knew his ancestors' footsteps, and the stone of his estate, having been in the family for over four centuries, bore the marks of rebuilds and renovations. Paccar himself was a sturdy Greek Cypriot, his frame robust, a reflection to the land that nourished him and a life reaped from the sea's bounty.

Commanding a modest fleet of three vessels, Paccar carved a living from the turquoise waters, ferrying sun-chased tourists and wide-eyed cruise passengers on excursions into the sea's embrace. His empire was small but his own, built on sweat, salt, and an understanding of how to ply the delicate trade of tourism.

It wasn't compassion that stayed Paccar's hand when he caught Guano, thin and desperate, pilfering one of his chickens. Nor was it kindness alone that saw him offer the man a job and a roof over his head. Paccar was a businessperson, through and through, and in Guano, he saw opportunity. Here was a man who'd cost considerably less than the local labour, a man whose circumstances had honed a work ethic sharp as a cutlass.

The accommodation Paccar provided was humble—a one-bedroom room fashioned from what once served as a storage barn. By the glossy standards of European comfort, it was a shadow of a dwelling. But through Guano's eyes, it was a fortress, a bastion of safety, and a far cry from the uncertainties that had dogged his journey from the Ivory Coast.

Guano's earnings, modest as they were, weren't frittered away on the fleeting comforts of the present. Each coin was a brick in the foundation of his future, safeguarded with the ferocity of a man who understood the true weight of currency. He had left behind a wife, young in years but old in hardships, her body heavy with the promise of new life. He had pledged himself to a singular goal: to toil, to save, and to ferry her from the suffocating poverty that strangled his homeland, bringing her into this new world he was painstakingly building, one saved coin at a time.

Gratitude tethered him to Paccar, manifesting in the relentless dedication he poured into his work. Guano was more than just an employee; he was a loyal, guarding the generosity that had granted him this second chance. Each day, he stood defiant, a bulwark against the tides of fate that sought to drag him back into the depths of destitution.

The blistering Cypriot summers ushered in a thrum of activity, with cruise liners lumbering into port thrice weekly, their arrivals dwindling with the cooler embrace of winter. Yet geopolitical unrest in distant Egypt had rerouted the tides of tourism, and with this shift, Paccar found his docks teeming and his excursions swelling with eager faces. The landscape of opportunity had broadened, and he was poised to seize it.

Guano, a steadfast fixture on the deck for three seasons now, played his part with the precision of a well-oiled cog in this vast machine of maritime commerce. He was the bridge between the behemoth cruise ships and the sleek catamaran, his seasoned hands securing the vessel with an ease born of repetition, his voice a buoyant welcome cutting through the salty sea air.

"Welcome to paradise. Watch your step," he'd call out, his tone a mixture of warmth and rehearsed courtesy as he ushered twenty-two souls from the cavernous belly of the Reef Explorer onto the catamaran's sun-drenched deck. They came in search of adventure, of escape, their anticipation palpable as they chattered about the morning's promises of crystalline waters and the underwater ballet of marine life they'd witness off the island's southern coast.

Paccar's fleet, a trio of Italian-crafted jewels, cut through the water with the grace of creatures born to the sea. Fashioned from cutting-edge composites, these multi-hulled marvels boasted a symmetry that promised velocity and assurance in each sleek line and curve. He'd chosen these beasts with a gambler's cunning and a sailor's insight, knowing well that their wide beams spelled stability on the capricious sea. After all, tourists with faces turned green, leaning over the side to pay homage to the ocean's sway, did little for reputation and less for the gratuity they were inclined to leave.

In this game, Paccar was a master of experience, understanding that the thrill he sold, the escapism tourists bought, hinged on the illusion of adventure—wild, yet tamed by the assured safety and comfort of his vessels. Every smooth sail, every delighted laugh was currency in the bank of survival in this trade. And amidst it all, Guano stood, the once-desperate stowaway now an essential pillar in the day-to-day dance between routine and adventure.

The catamaran's anatomy was a feat of nautical engineering, its twin hulls bridged by a Spartan frame, its sinews of high-tensile webbing a cradle for sun-seekers. Above, the superstructure loomed, housing a generous cabin, its skin dappled with the generous embrace of the sun. Aft, the deck was a sprawl of indulgence, loungers scattered like the aftermath of some luxurious battle, the command post nestled centrally, providing a vantage point that cleaved the ocean vistas in two.

These vessels, these gleaming predators of the sea, bore the colour of purity, their flanks adorned with the playful imagery of dolphins in mid-leap. They were sisters, christened 'Marion 1st', 'Marion 2nd', and 'Marion 3rd' in a tender homage to his lifelong anchor, his wife. Today, only the 'Marion 1st' would breach the waves, her sisters lying dormant.

Paccar's voice, seasoned by salt and command, cut through the background of wind and wave. "Today, our course is set for Agios Georgios Alamanou. Renowned for its bleached cliffs and welcoming embrace, it promises a spectacle of marine life below the tide. Today you will see parrot fish darting amongst the coral, while turtles swimming gracefully, we call them ancient mariners, crabs scuttling on the seabed. In short, ladies and gentlemen, a day that will live with you forever."

The catamaran cleaved through the water, before coming to rest a mile from the promised land. "Anchor away, Romano," Paccar commanded his thirty-year-old son. "I'll lead the dive today. Romano you take the second. Guano, the guests will be hungry when they resurface. See to the meal."

Each word was more than a directive; it was a thread in the fabric of a well-rehearsed operation. In this isolated slice of the world, away from the shores from which they'd embarked, hierarchy and purpose were as crucial as the tide itself.

In minutes, Paccar was overboard, snorkel and fins equipped, leading the first batch of adventure-seekers into the aquamarine depths. A couple, deep into their years but basking in the thrill, chose the comfort of the catamaran's deck and the sun's warm embrace over the allure of the deep.

Back on board, Guano, under the meticulous tutelage of Paccar's wife, had mastered the art of prepping the local fare. Sea bass, filleted to perfection, and sea bream awaited the searing kiss of the grill. He'd risen with the stars, at 5 AM, to craft pasta fresh enough to make Italian grandmothers nod in approval. A salad, rich with the tang of Feta, balanced with the sweet sharpness of balsamic, was ready to accompany the fish. The culinary secret weapon was the salt, heavy-handed yet cunningly masked with vinegar and oil, designed to fuel a thirst that would turn mere break-even into profit, with beer and coke being peddled at six euros a pop.

Paccar, with seasoned eyes, herded the first group through the underwater spectacle, his son Romano taking up the rear. Their vigilant guidance ensured every snorkeler's path was safe but drenched in wonder. Twenty minutes in, with the sea's treasures still unfolding below, Guano, amidst prepping the first sizzling batch of fish, caught sight of an uninvited guest. A fishing trawler, nondescript and innocuous, was inching its way from the west, closing the two-mile gap.

This wasn't an uncommon sight, especially this season. But Guano, ever diligent and schooled in the unsaid rules of the sea, paused his preparations. He reached for the ship's radio, hailing the approaching vessel. No response. He tried again, a tinge of concern creeping into his tone, his eyes never leaving the sight of the encroaching boat as it bore down upon the blissfully unaware snorkelers.

"Unknown vessel on the horizon, be advised, we have snorkellers in the water," Guano's voice crackled through the radio, slicing through the static that answered him. Switching frequencies, he repeated the message, but the radio spat nothing back but an unnerving silence.

The trawler loomed larger now, half-mile away, and it wasn't alone. Behind the first, a second vessel carved through the Mediterranean, its presence betrayed by the lift of its bow as it rode the wake of its predecessor. They moved in tandem, an unusual maritime ballet that Guano had never witnessed, and one that ratcheted up the tension knotting his muscles.

In the sun-dappled waters, Paccar was shepherding a cluster of eight from the Reef Explorer, their faces submerged in the silent world where only bubbles spoke. They were oblivious, entranced by the undersea realm, unaware of the shadow of danger inching ever closer.

Romano, vigilant in his charge, corralled his group of ten towards a reef, a kaleidoscope of marine life beneath them. He surfaced, saltwater trickling down his face, counting heads, making sure no one had drifted. That's when he saw them—the trawlers. Like steel-grey predators of the deep, they bore down on his unsuspecting flock.

The tension ratcheted up inside Romano, sharp as a razor's edge, the moment crystallizing around him with piercing clarity. His heart thudded in his chest like heavy fire, his breaths short, controlled bursts in the humid air, the taste of salt and imminent threat filling his mouth. The sea, moments ago a peaceful expanse, now felt like a minefield, with every ripple increased the danger.

Adrenaline coursed through him, hot and urgent, tightening every muscle. The trawlers' dark silhouettes loomed on the horizon, growing larger and more menacing by the second. They were steel behemoths, their shadows stretching across the water like sinister fingers, the thrum of their engines a growl that promised nothing good.

This wasn't just close quarters; this was a red zone, a potential kill radius. Romano's mind raced, instincts that lay dormant now snapping to the fore, triggered by the smell of danger, a primal, metallic scent that overshadowed the ocean's brine. His father's voice echoed in his skull, a litany of survival instructions from years gone by, merging with the rigorous discipline of his own past life's training.

Every part of him was wired, coiled tight, as his eyes sliced through the glare of the sun on the water, assessing trajectories, speed—the cold, hard math of disaster. Those vessels weren't aimlessly cutting through waves; they were weapons, their courses deliberate, slicing through the water towards his unsuspecting group.

Time warped, each second ballooning into a pulsing eternity, amplifying the sounds of his own blood coursing and the distant, muffled splashes of his charges' carefree movements. They were vulnerable, exposed, targets in a sudden, silent standoff.

Every muscle in Guano's body was a live wire, his senses sharpened to a razor's edge as Rod Stewart's voice was abruptly sliced away, replaced by the urgent wail of the catamaran's alarm. Five long, piercing blasts cleaved through the serenity, a desperate cry that seemed to ripple across the water's surface. It was a sonic flare, a call to arms, and a scream of warning all rolled into a harsh melody that set every nerve alight.

The calm sea, a traitor in its stillness, offered no camouflage for the advancing trawlers. Their steel hulls glinted menacingly, slicing the water with a determined ferocity that left no room for doubt. They were on a collision course with disaster, and every stroke of his arms sent a surge of desperation through Romano.

His voice, raw and edged with urgency, became the herald of doom, slicing through the idyllic air. "Back to the catamaran, now!" Each word was a hammer strike, driving the panic-stricken snorkellers into action. But the sea doesn't heed mortal terror, and their frenzied splashes were pitifully slow against the backdrop of oncoming monstrosities.

Panic was a contagion, and it spread through the water faster than any current. Muted screams bubbled through snorkels, a chorus of fear and confusion that grew louder even as it went unheard over the catamaran's relentless horn. They were a scattered flock of prey, and Romano was the shepherd, driving them back, his heart thundering a brutal cadence in his chest as he propelled the last of his group toward relative safety.

Then, he was surging through the water alone, his father's group still dangerously oblivious. The trawlers were beasts, their growling engines a death knell that drowned out reason and hope alike. The swell of chaos built around them, a tangible shift in the water as the churn of the approaching vessels disrupted the sea's natural rhythms.

The air was electric, charged with a primitive fear that clawed at the snorkellers. The rumble of the trawlers' old diesel engines was the soundtrack of nightmares, the vibration through the water a prelude to an executioner's stroke. And then, with a stomach-dropping inevitability, the peaceful ebb and flow of the sea rebelled. The water around them became a maelstrom, the trawlers' wake an unyielding force, indifferent to the fragile lives thrashing within its surge.

In those eternal seconds, with disaster a hair's breadth away, the world narrowed to heartbeats, breaths, and the white-knuckled struggle of man versus fate. They were all ensnared in a deadly washing machine, where the clothes were iron and flesh, and the stage was a once-tranquil sea now hungry for tragedy.

A nightmare unfolded in real-time, a merciless collision of innocence and metal. Guano, alongside the shell-shocked passengers on the catamaran, witnessed the unfathomable. Lives, moments ago vibrant and buoyant, were snuffed out within heartbeats, dragged beneath the steel behemoth. The trawler, unyielding and monstrous, swallowed them whole before the merciless churn of its propellers spat out only death and crimson chaos into the wake.

The air filled with terror—screams, cries for help, the haunting plea of a young girl, barely more than a child, her voice a shredded whisper across the waves, "Mama, help me!" The words lanced through Guano's heart, etching into his soul as hot tears carved tracks down his battle-hardened face. There was no playbook for this, no training that could have prepared him for the utter helplessness that clawed at his insides.

Then, as if the ocean hadn't suffered enough, the second trawler adjusted its deathly course towards Paccar's group. It sheared through the water with mechanical indifference, homing in on the thrashing snorkelers. These were no longer people to the cold machine, just obstacles, their terrified screams smothered by the gurgling sea. Blood and despair clouded the water, a churning grave of those who'd just been living, breathing human beings.

Disbelief and rage erupted from Guano's core, his voice raw as he howled to the uncaring sky, "How could they not see them?" But the only response was the roar of engines, the sea's cruel laughter, and the fading echoes of a tragedy that would haunt him to his dying days.

Like predators of the deep, the trawlers executed their next pass on the two groups, cold and methodical. The sea became a mortuary, peppered with the remnants of lives cut savagely short.

Bloodied survivors, barely recognizable as human, wailed in their watery purgatory, clutching wounds that spoke of unholy unions between man and machine. Yet even as death clasped greedily, it was their spirit that sputtered and died amidst the circling steel sharks.

Through this maritime massacre, Romano propelled himself forward with a fury that burned hotter than the sun. Each stroke through the macabre debris field brought a fresh surge of hellish realization. It wasn't carelessness; it was carnage by design. The silhouettes of armed men adorned the trawlers, their intentions written in the language of cold, lead-spitting death. This was no accident, no tragedy at sea. It was a slaughterhouse, an execution of innocence.

Romano's mind reeled, sanity fraying with the understanding that they were not victims of circumstance but targets in a most barbaric game. Every splash, every cry, was a grotesque note in a symphony of annihilation. Around him, the ocean didn't just claim bodies; it devoured souls, an abyss of madness where human depravity plumbed new, unfathomable depths.

The trawlers, engines roaring like beasts of prey, carved a merciless arc through the ocean, looping back with deliberate, homicidal intent towards the floundering remnants of humanity in the water. Their cold, mechanical precision contrasted starkly with the frantic struggles of the few survivors, now hunted in their watery domain.

Another pass, and death reigned supreme, plucking lives away with heartless ease. A family, united in their final moments by sheer terror and futile hope, were torn apart under a hail of indiscriminate gunfire. They became just three more casualties, their bodies buoyant and broken on the sea's uncaring swell.

As one death-bringer veered towards the catamaran, its twin prowled the blood-stained waters, Romano, every muscle screaming, reached Paccar and less than a handful of petrified snorkellers. Their strategy was primal, a desperate game of breath and evasion, as they submerged exploiting the meagre refuge offered by the water's surface tension. They propelled themselves towards an uncertain salvation onshore, lungs burning and limbs flailing in silent screams beneath the waves.

Onboard, Guano, driven by some mix of morbid duty and shock, dashed for the binoculars, only to be confronted by a spectacle that would haunt his nightmares forever. The trawlers had become platforms of execution, shooters lining their sides, firing with mechanical indifference into the water. The sea was no longer blue but a mottled canvas of red and terror.

Paralysis gripped him, the binoculars his only tether to the unfolding carnage, as each crack of gunfire orchestrated a symphony of real-time horror. It was no longer just a scene of survival; it was the ninth circle of hell, unfurling in merciless crescendo on the open sea. Every bullet, every lifeless body, intensified the chaos, the catamaran a lone spectre of safety in a suddenly meaningless world.

The trawler, an agent of death on the serene ocean, was relentless, cutting through the waves with sinister precision. It bore down on them with the inevitability of a nightmare, its shadow enveloping Romano, Paccar, and the terrified newlyweds as they desperately neared the shore. Only 200 yards away from the deceptive safety of the beach, the vessel throttled down, its engines throbbing ominously as it fell into a deadly parallel course with the swimmers.

Romano's heart was a hammer in his chest, adrenaline coursing through his veins as raw, primal fear took hold. "Please, please don't do this!" he screamed, positioning himself protectively in front of his father, his voice choked with desperation, every word a vice around his throat.

From the deck, an unfeeling face framed by the trappings of warfare peered down, eyes cold, a twisted smile corrupting his features. "Seek solace in your gods," the figure taunted in accented English, the sentence a death knell. The world slowed down, a surreal pause, before the deafening report of a gunshot punctured the moment. Romano's world went dark, a bullet robbing him of life before he even felt the impact.

Nearby, two newlyweds, paralyzed with the clarity of their impending doom, clasped each other's hands, their fingers intertwining in a bond that sought to transcend the horror enfolding them. They shared a final, despairing kiss, a silent, heartbreaking vow in the face of oblivion. Then, the air was torn by the sound of gunfire, short, loud, and final, shredding their embrace and extinguishing their future as precisely as it had begun exactly one week prior.

Paccar, momentarily blinded by grief and disbelief, swam towards his son's floating body, a keening wail escaping his lips. "My son, my son!" His voice was a raw scrape, barely audible over the trawler's engines and the high-pitched ringing in his ears.

The assassin, a man known to his comrades as Khalid, showed no mercy, no hesitation. "Your time has come, old man," he declared, void of any empathy, before unleashing a rapid, brutal fusillade into Paccar. The bullets, cruel and efficient, tore into flesh and bone, leaving destruction in their wake. Paccar's life slipped away on the back of a bloody tide, his fingers rigid in death around his son, their bodies together in a final, tragic embrace.

Blood pumping, heart slamming against his ribs like a war drum, Guano seized the filleting knife, its blade glinting with a sinister promise. As the trawler's shadow loomed over the catamaran, every survival instinct screamed within him, urging haste, demanding action. He bolted back to the helm, the deck vibrating with the growing roar of the trawler's engines, a grim reaper on their tail.

The catamaran, a sleek beast built for slicing through waves at breakneck speeds, was his only chance. The sea around him had turned into a watery grave, and the screams of the dying clawed at the edges of his frantic mind. They were beyond saving, beyond any hope but for swift vengeance.

Adrenaline surged as Guano wrestled with the keys, fingers slippery with sweat and sea spray. The engine coughed to life with a low growl, a sound that was almost drowned by the blood roaring in his ears. His hand, slick with fear, shoved the throttle forward, willing the vessel to respond, to fly across the water away from the carnage.

The sharp, jarring crack of the Perspex splintering tore through the tense air, followed by a sensation that was more shock than agony. Guano's eyes dropped to his left shoulder, registering the macabre bloom of red, the bullet having punched clean through. The pain was distant, a delayed echo, but his body understood the language of trauma. His movements faltered, legs buckling as he stumbled from the helm, the world tilting around him.

He collapsed against the railing, metal biting into his flesh, his breath coming in ragged gasps. The trawler was there, its presence an oppressive force ready to unleash hell. The figures on it, agents of chaos and cruelty, prepared to board, their intentions written in the coldness of their guns and the efficiency of their movements.

Desperation lent him strength, raw and frenzied. Guano hauled himself upright, the world swaying violently in his vision. Summoning every last reserve, he lunged to his right, his wounded body colliding with the railings. Momentum carried him over, and for a heart-stopping moment, he was suspended in a freefall, with the knife still firmly grasped in his right hand.

The collision with the sea was brutal, a bedlam of shock and disorientation. As he plunged beneath the waves, the salt water was a cruel invader, rushing into his mouth, clawing down his throat, and threatening to claim his lungs. In the chaos of the churned waters, with his senses reeling, Guano fought for life, each gasping breath a rebellion against the darkness that sought to pull him under.

Aziz, a figure carved from the ice of indifference itself, transitioned from the trawler to the catamaran. On the webbing between the dual hulls, two middle-aged passengers were frozen sculptures of terror. Clumsily, they fumbled with their snorkels, a pathetic attempt to flee into the dubious sanctuary of the water. Their every movement screamed silent pleas, the horror in their eyes an echo of witnessed atrocities.

They were late, oh so tragically late. Their mouths moved, soundless over the sea's relentless choir, bargaining in whispers for each other's existence. Guano, despite the pounding of his heart in his ears and now under the webbing, caught fragments of the husband's frantic urging. He was desperate to shepherd his wife to the relative safety at the catamaran's rear, a futile endeavour drowned by her paralysis of fear.

Aziz approached them, his presence an oppressive force. "Peace," he lied with the ease of a man to whom truth was malleable, "you shall be united in eternity." The words were barely past his lips when his gun roared, the husband crumpling like a puppet with cut strings. The wife, a portrait of despair, reached for the fading warmth of her life partner just as death claimed her with an echoing blast.

"Clean this place!" Aziz's command to his subordinates, who emerged behind him like shadows, was devoid of humanity. The couple, their lives snuffed out, were nothing more than detritus to be disposed of their bodies unceremoniously dumped into the sea's hungry embrace.

Amidst the horror, Guano clung to survival by the thinnest thread of resolve. The final cries of the couple rang in his ears, a chorus soon joined by the guttural cadence of Arabic commands. His only lifeline was opportunity, and it presented itself as chaos unfolded around him. Not a life jacket—an orange beacon of capture—but something… anything that could buoy him in the ocean's dark clutches without betraying his position.

As the bodies of the newly deceased splashed grotesquely near him, Guano propelled himself towards the vessel's edge.

Each breath drew him closer to a chance, a slender chance, that he might yet evade the clutches of the abyss.

Guano, each breath a razor in his chest, grappled fiercely with a tyre lashed to the catamaran's side, a makeshift fender for docking procedures now a potential lifeline. Muscles quivering in protest, he wrenched it free, his right arm anchoring into the centre void of the rubber ring, forcing it beneath the vessel's sanctuary.

Resurfacing in the ghostly corridor between the catamaran's twin hulls, he found a macabre shield in the overhanging netting—a frail barrier between him and the death dealers' mere feet away. The sea's grim harvest drifted eerily by—bodies of the fallen guests. One, a man to whom he'd served refreshments in what felt like another lifetime, bobbed grotesquely by, his snorkelling mask a final, futile protection.

Seizing a ragged scrap from the tyre, Guano, with hands trembling from pain and adrenal surge, stuffed the rubber into his searing wound. His flesh screamed in protest—a white-hot lance searing through his senses. But survival trumped agony. His blood, a beacon for the predators above, had to be contained.

Through the haze of torment, he moved the tyre against the catamaran's inner hull. Clinging to the desperate hope it would remain trapped; he gulped a lungful of air that tasted of salt and fear and plunged beneath the waves. Each powerful kick towards the grisly flotsam off the stern was a countdown to the inferno in his chest.

Shadowing a corpse, Guano used it as a morbid bulwark against the scrutiny from the boat. Air—precious, life-giving air—flooded his lungs as he broke the surface in a careful gasp.

A quick, perilous glance revealed a gunman's back, preoccupied with a second trawler's approach. In one fluid motion, born of urgency, he stripped the lifeless body of its snorkel gear, submerged once more, and darted back to the deceptive safety of the under-hull.

The tyre, a dark guardian angel, still swirled in the restless current. Ignoring the chorus of agony from his abused body, Guano wrestled the mask and snorkel into place. His hands, wedged within the tyre's rigid embrace, hidden in the tyre he kicked out from the boat. With painstaking care, he aligned the snorkel, ensuring it barely pierced the tyres shroud.

The first trawler disgorged its lethal shipment of armed zealots onto the catamaran before being cast adrift, making room for the second vessel to tether itself to the starboard flank. From his precarious hideaway, Guano discerned the ominous silhouettes of four armed men through the catamaran's webbing. The lilt of Arabic, harsh and unmistakable, pricked at his ears—a dark remnant from his days in Libya and confrontations back home. Engrossed in their macabre mission, the shooters paid no heed to the world beneath them, where Guano lay shrouded by the deceptive refuge of the tyre.

Aziz deployed his chess pieces with cold precision. Four of his pawns embarked from the first trawler, four more from the second, their souls as dark as the ocean depths. Eight Somalis, confined below deck on the second trawler, had been kept ignorant of this phase of Aziz's plan—a sagacious move, given their predictable dissent. They remained caged, the doors bolted, a precaution ensuring their forced neutrality.

Meanwhile, on a third trawler carving cold waves around the catamaran, Aziz kept his elite, four Arabic-speaking operatives, untainted by the bloodbath. They were pivotal for seizing the Reef Explorer, preserved from potential revolt. As the second trawler shored up portside, the air crackled with Aziz's commands, doors were unlatched, and a new phase of the nightmare began to unfold. He summoned Awaale from the bowels of the cabin to the catamaran's blood-stained deck.

Aziz's strike force was swelling: twelve Arabs, ferocious and unswerving, awaited the emergence of the Somalis. The moment was knife-edge tense—a volatile cocktail of mistrust and ambition. Above the deck, the night sky bore silent witness to the human treachery, while beneath it, amidst the ocean's lull, Guano steered the tyre towards the beach.

As the deathly stillness settled over the water, Aziz, with the clinical detachment of a surgeon, deemed the operation purged of any survivors. He commanded Khalid to unleash the remaining Somalis from their confinement. Awaale's eyes, hardened by countless skirmishes, couldn't mask his horror at the grotesque ballet of bodies drifting in the catamaran's wake. The distant echo of the massacre had reached them below deck; what began as percussive warnings had morphed into a chorus of death, the true purpose of the gunfire revealed in a symphony of screams.

Emerging into the ghastly aftermath, Awaale and his men were met with a scene of carnage: seagulls, like feathered vultures, descended, feasting on the ravaged remains of the passengers. With a voice gritty as crushed glass, Awaale confronted Aziz in English, the lingua franca of their dark trade.

"You're insane, Aziz. These lives carried worth, ransoms! Your bloodlust is wasting fortunes. What twisted logic drives you to this senseless slaughter?"

Aziz, unflinching, his eyes steely slits, replied, "Necessity, Awaale. These Kafirs are collateral damage. Imagine the horde awaiting us on the ship—ransoms far surpassing this. Even if we killed every last one, the vessel itself would fetch us millions. Your shortsightedness disappoints."

"You're playing a dangerous game, Aziz! Murder turns negotiators into hunters. We've marked ourselves for death, sabotaged the mission before it's begun!"

"Awaale, your vision is narrow," Aziz countered, his voice a venomous hiss. "Fear, my friend, is a potent currency. The world will recoil at our ruthlessness, yes. But then, they will come crawling, wallets in hand. Now, compose yourself; we can't afford panic in the ranks."

Uncertainty laced Awaale's defiance. "And what of our men, Aziz? The mouths they feed. If this gamble of yours marks them for the grave, who'll feed their families? You've changed the plan, it's a bloodbath. This… this isn't business, Aziz. It's a massacre."

In the charged silence that followed, even the sea seemed to hold its breath, awaiting the reply of a man whose orders had turned the Mediterranean crimson. The Mediterranean sun beat down on the chaotic scene as Aziz, cold and unyielding, turned to face Awaale. "There's no path but forward, Awaale. Rally your men. The third boat approaches, and with it, our future. Riches beyond measure await your people," Aziz declared, his voice was iron sheathed in silk.

Awaale's heart hammered a brutal, frenetic rhythm in his chest, the sea breeze chilling the sweat on his brow. He was entangled in a lethal web, spun by the ruthless cunning of Aziz. The trust that had been the foundation of their alliance crumbled away, irreparably fractured in the aftermath of betrayal and bloodshed. Aziz's men were armed to the teeth, a stark contrast to his own unarmed Somalis, whom Aziz had convinced needed no weapons until they were aboard the Reef Explorer.

Memories of whispered conversations, meetings without the presence of his Somali brothers-in-arms, haunted Awaale. Aziz had isolated them, a tactic he now realized was deliberate, leaving them vulnerable and ensnared within this deadly scheme. Kasim Asfour's manipulations echoed in Awaale's mind, a sinister refrain that had dictated their current predicament.

Some way off, Guano fought for survival, the tyre his only lifeline in the turbulent sea. Each breath through the snorkel was a gasp for hope, the rubber barrier his only concealment from the carnage above. The catamaran, now a vessel of death, drifted further away, and to the unsuspecting eye, the tyre was nothing more than debris lost amidst the commotion.

Suddenly, Khalid's voice cut through the tension like a knife. "Aziz, a tyre's come adrift. Must've happened in the scramble with the boats," he called out, unwittingly casting a spotlight on Guano's fragile sanctuary.

"Put a magazine into it !" Aziz's voice cut through the air; a command wrapped in deadly calm.

The tyre bobbed innocently over 100 yards from the catamaran. Khalid, his weapon raised, unleashed a salvo. The first bullet zipped through the air, missing the target. Under the water, Guano's eyes followed the lethal tracer, a harrowing dance of death. The next two rounds were on mark, piercing the rubber just above his submerged head, one round tearing the snorkel from his mouth with violent force. Pain exploded in his jaw; a crimson cloud unfurled in the water around him as he spat out blood mingled with fragments of teeth.

Clutching his ravaged mouth, blood streaming between his fingers, Guano dared a desperate move. No longer shielded by the tyre's embrace, he surfaced, scanning the horizon where the catamaran was now a diminishing point. The sea around him was a grim gallery, bodies of the fallen passengers floating grotesquely. Pain radiated from his bullet-torn shoulder, throbbing in cruel rhythm with his heartbeat, his left arm useless and trailing limply in the blood-tainted waves. Summoning the remnants of his strength, he clung to a floating body one good hand and began a laborious, one-legged kick towards a distant salvation: the shore.

Elsewhere in the water, Moira battled her own nightmare. Clinging to the lifeless body of her friend, she'd endured beneath the waves, the leaking snorkel a tormenting lifeline. Saltwater burned her insides, each breath a rasp of fire. A rogue wave crashed over her, flooding the snorkel. Coughing, spluttering, she let go of the cold hand she'd been holding in a death grip.

As the sea claimed the bodies around her, diluting the horror with indifferent tides, Moira realized she might be the sole survivor of the massacre. That's when she spotted the Guano.

Guano, his back to the shore, didn't see the rocks lying in ambush to his left or the insurmountable cliffs to his right. He had one goal: reach the beach. Each kick was a defiance, a refusal to surrender to the sea's cold embrace. It wasn't until he sensed a movement through his haze of pain that he saw her—a figure swimming towards him, red hair painting a fiery trail in the water.

As Moira reached Guano, her fingers, white-knuckled, gripped the corpse Guano was using as a float, and the dam within her broke. Tears, indistinguishable from the saltwater on her cheeks, cascaded down. Through his bloodied, toothless grimace, Guano offered what was meant to be a reassuring smile. Words were superfluous; their shared trauma spoke volumes. Together, in silent pact, they kicked through the swells towards an unseen sanctuary.

For 40 excruciating minutes, they battled. Every stroke through the water was a fight against the tide and a show of their raw determination. Guano's mind raced despite the searing agony in his shoulder and the metallic taste of blood that filled his mouth. He was an undocumented illegal in this country, a man without the luxury of legal existence. Seeking help from authorities was a gamble with his very freedom.

When the shore finally welcomed them, they were two battered souls crawling from the surf, their bodies etched with scars of survival. Collapsing on the sand, Guano, his voice a guttural rasp marred by the absence of teeth and the constant flow of blood, recounted the horror. He spoke of the carnage, the cold execution of commands, and the perpetrators' language he understood all too well. He repeated details, a mantra against forgetting, his words slurring into one another.

Moira, her gaze hollowed by shock, could only nod sporadically, her mind teetering on the edge of comprehension. It was only after she regained a shade of her former strength that Guano left her, making sure she could stagger towards the road, a lone figure with the mission to summon aid.

But Guano's path veered into the shadows. Wounded and vulnerable, he evaded the open road, driven by a single resolve: to find Marion, Paccar's wife, Romano's mother. She had been his anchor in turbulent times, and now, he navigated through agony and fear, indebted to the woman who had given him shelter.

As he approached what was once a haven, now blackened by loss, he knew Marion would be there, innocent to the day's slaughter, anticipating a family reunion over dinner. A knot tightened in Guano's stomach; a dread heavier than the lead that had torn through his flesh. He was to become the bringer of destruction, destroying the thread of hope that kept Marion's world intact.

Telling her would shatter more than her heart; it would be an act of breaking something within himself. Yet, in the settling dusk, amidst the constant chirping of crickets, Guano steeled himself for delivering the news that would forever cleave before from after.

chapter eleven
Rumble in the Jungle

Cutler initiated the recon on Friday, a strategic move three days ahead of the impending ambush aimed at ensnaring Mayan and his cohorts. The Bali jungle, an autonomous universe, pulsated with an ancient rhythm, its vital beats reverberating through an expanse of impenetrable greenery and penetrating the very core of those brave or foolhardy enough to penetrate its secrets. Gigantic trees stood as venerable sentinels, their twisted roots burrowing aggressively into the fertile soil, forming a complex web designed to ensnare those who tread carelessly. Above, the forest canopy emerged as a chaotic yet harmonious realm, where foliage and creeping lianas battled ruthlessly for the sun's rays, weaving a verdant mosaic that subdued the harsh light of day into ethereal half-shadows.

The air around them was a tangible force, dense and intoxicating with the musk of damp soil intertwined with the fragrant exhalations of vivid flowers, their hues a defiant spectacle amidst the overwhelming emerald dominion. This moisture-laden breath of the jungle enveloped Cutler and his team, an unyielding embrace that underscored the relentless pulse of life teeming within this verdant maze.

Tuck leased three high-octane quad bikes. Colton, Tuck, and Cutler would drive these mechanical beasts through treacherous terrains. Their training ground. The unforgiving jungle corridors notorious for being Mayan and his brutal entourage's stomping grounds. Yet the jungle's heart was a patchwork, its veins were unpredictable, and the exact path Mayan would take was anyone's guess. So they roared through every conceivable route, eyes peeled for the perfect ambush spots and potential kill zones, the engines growling like caged animals waiting to pounce.

Their strategy was to execute a jarring halt that would scatter the wits of Mayan and his thugs, making them easy pickings before fingers could even twitch towards triggers. Cutler had laid down the law—no black-market hardware. Too hot. The mere thought of getting nabbed with unlicensed firepower was enough to conjure visions of rotting away in a sweltering, rat-infested cell, the stench of despair heavy in the humid air.

Navigating local law was another minefield. Their rides? A battered Nissan truck showing twelve years of abuse and a slightly fresher Land Rover from Kuta Rent, both hauling quads and exuding not-so-subtle badass vibes. Checkpoints were a gamble, with local cops requiring their share of 'hush money.' Any slip-up could blow the mission wide open, sending them spiralling into diplomatic hell.

All day Saturday, they huddled over maps, intensely strategizing on the possible paths Mayan could take through the treacherous terrain. Two routes—the 'red' and 'amber'—were narrow veins through the jungle's heart, their oppressive foliage like walls that could easily turn into a death trap. These paths demanded a single-file approach, a tactical nightmare if there were any need for rapid, evasive action. An ambush here meant waiting for the prey to step out into the open, risking collateral damage among locals and tourists, an unacceptable mess that could blow the mission wide open.

Then there was the 'navy blue' route, a deceptive serpent of a path that transitioned into a watery gauntlet for about five miles. Here, the attack would have to be precise, amidst a jagged sea of rocks and boulders, with the water's deceptive tranquillity hiding lethal threats beneath. Any engagement here meant a high-octane chase, matching Mayan's men throttle for throttle, with the peril of being violently unseated by a hidden rock looming every split second.

The 'green' route, in contrast, was a relative walk in the park. It snaked out of the jungle, cleaving through a vast sugar plantation. Any deviation by Mayan into the sugar cane would leave a telltale path of destruction, offering no real cover or advantage.

Tuck brought in another layer of complex information; the season's first monsoons had begun their siege on the landscape. The 'red' route was a no-go—transformed into a vicious slide of mud, more a trap than a trail. 'Amber' could still be an option for those wanting to flirt with disaster, its treacherous mire potentially seen as a thrilling challenge for adrenaline junkies. The sugar plantation on the 'green' route was still immature, devoid of workers, and exposed. Most crucially, the 'navy blue' was a ticking clock—its waterway swelling, a sign that nature would soon reclaim it, making it impassable.

The tension was razor-sharp; everything hinged on Mayan's mood on the day of travel. Was he up for a reckless thrill, challenging nature, and man, or would it be a day for an easy ride? Lives hung in the balance, and time was a luxury they were fast running out of.

The air crackled with tension as Cutler scanned the faces of his team, each locked in their private calculations and gut-driven guesses. "Which route?" The question hung between them like a loaded gun.

"Red, for pure, unadulterated adrenaline," Tuck threw in with a dangerous gleam in his eyes.

"Green," Colton countered, the word slicing through the testosterone like a warning shot.

"Amber. A hell of a ride, but not a death wishes like Red," Cutler weighed in, the tactical part of his brain ticking over.

"Navy blue. It's now or never with the waters rising," Colton added, his voice steady, his gaze distant.

Cutler's mind was a war zone, strategy and instincts battling it out. "It's down to Amber or Navy Blue. Tuck, we need intel before Mayan even makes up his mind. He's the alpha—where he goes, they follow. Tuck, Cortez—you're on sabotage duty. Take the Land Rover, Joe's driving. Get a chainsaw and drop a tree at the start of the Amber trail. Make it an act of God, not man," he ordered, stabbing a point on the map with decisive force.

Cutler's jaw set. "There's rain coming tomorrow, heavy enough to wash out any thoughts of Red. With Amber conveniently blocked, thanks to Tuck's artistry, it narrows down the odds. Navy Blue becomes the default, unless Mayan loses his nerve and goes Green. But nothing about that man reads 'coward' to me."

"You're gambling. What if they roll the dice in another direction?" Old Joe remarked.

"Then we improvise," Cutler snapped, the steel in his voice a clear. "Your eye in the sky will be our early warning. I'll strategize for the other paths, but right now, every sinew, every neuron fires for Navy Blue.

Cutler swatted an insect feeding on his neck. "Joe, double-check the drone. I want eyes sharp enough to spot a flea on a dog. And comms needs to be crystal. No garbles. Understand?"

Without waiting for a nod, Cutler swivelled towards Colton. "This operation is raw, it's rough around the edges, but it's what we've got. A hard stop on this godforsaken terrain is a one-way ticket to a world of pain. I need a med kit that'd make a combat medic weep. Neck braces, stretchers, the works. Throw in needles and sutures. We're not losing anyone to shoddy field medicine."

Colton's eyes narrowed. "And our arsenal?"

"Like I said, no local guns. We need headlamps. catapults. knives, too. All in black titanium," Cutler's demand hung in the air.

"Black?" Old Joe's question was a flicker of confusion in the charged atmosphere.

"No reflections," Cutler shot back, the explanation as terse as a bullet. Tuck snorted, the sound jarring against the high-octane tension. "I see not all of us got the memo on covert kills, eh, rookie?"

Old Joe bristled. "Didn't realize I signed up for a masterclass in assassination etiquette."

"You're in the big leagues now," Tuck's retort was icy. "That kind of know-how isn't a luxury. It's a lifeline. It could mean the difference between a ticket home or a body bag."

The next hours were a blur. Sleep was a fleeting visitor. As the pre-dawn darkness clung to the world, they convened outside the hotel. Old Joe, bags under his eyes, handed out illicitly acquired toasties. The morning was a frenzy of preparation. Retrieving quad bikes, loading gear—they were a unit, a machine fuelled by sheer determination.

The convoy of a battered Fiat van and a Land Rover, trailers in tow, wound through the hinterlands, the modern world dwindling in their rear-view mirrors. They ascended tortuous roads etched into the island's heart, past timeless hamlets and ancient temples, guardians of history. Dawn, rather than bringing clarity, unveiled a brooding sky, the cumulus clouds like dark, coiled fists ready to pound the earth.

Cutler felt the oppressive weight of the clouds in his chest, an omen. Rain could unravel everything. What if the heavens broke before Mayan's gang embarked? The mere thought of another stagnant week, of their prey slipping through the fingers of time, was a poison in his veins.

As 7 am approached, they breached their destination, a secluded clearing ensconced in a thicket of banana trees, their lush leaves whispering secrets. The tang of impending rain was a sharp note against the heady scent of ripeness, the first sighs of wind like restless spirits among them. Concealed from prying eyes, this natural alcove was merely a stone's throw from the jungle's edge— their extraction point.

Old Joe stood on the rugged terrain outside the forward operating base, the pre-dawn light. In his hands, he held "Specter," a state-of-the-art military drone with a wingspan of less than five feet. Despite its compact size, Specter was a marvel of engineering, packed with high-resolution cameras, signal interceptors, and a cutting-edge stealth system that rendered it nearly invisible to radar.

The drone's lightweight composite materials, coupled with a matte grey finish, minimized its visual footprint against the sky. Every edge and contour were precision-crafted for aerodynamics and stealth, giving it an almost predatory appearance.

With a practiced motion, Old Joe held the drone high and performed a final systems check. The small LED indicators along its fuselage blinked back at him in a sequence of green lights, signalling all systems were go. The electric motors hummed softly as the carbon-fibre propellers spun, generating just enough lift.

He took a moment to scan the horizon. The base, hidden from casual observers, was a hive of silent activity as operatives monitored various screens, awaiting the vital real-time intelligence Specter was about to provide. With a smooth, practiced motion, he launched the drone into the air with a firm throw, releasing it into the wind like a bird of prey. Specter soared, its propellers seamlessly taking over to propel it forward as it climbed sharply into the pink-tinged sky.

As soon as the drone was airborne, it became a near-silent whisper in the sky, dipping and turning as it sought the optimal altitude and heading for its reconnaissance route. Within seconds, the drone switched to autonomous mode, using advanced algorithms and real-time data analysis to dodge any potential threats or detection methods employed in the area. It was a delicate balance between cutting-edge technology and human expertise.

Old Joe watched the sky where the Specter had disappeared, knowing that the fate of the mission was now in the hands of the technological marvel he had just launched.

Within the quarter-hour, the operatives—Cutler, Colton, and Tuck,— were skirting the jungle's embrace, mounted on their quad bikes. The world they entered teemed with life yet lay cloaked in shadow, the feeble light from the storm-laden sky devoured by voracious foliage. Flicking on their headlamps, they penetrated deeper, their path a serpent of diffused light in the undergrowth. As their eyes waged war with the gloom, the jungle's symphony, distant roars of thunder and nearby rustles, played around them.

A half-hour saw them adapted to the jungle's half-light; the lamps redundant. Cutler signalled a halt, the rest crowding in, engines a growing chorus in the heavy air.

"This is it," Cutler's voice sliced through the din. "Fabienne's intel confirms Mayan's on the move. We hold position until Old Joe gives the green light on their chosen path. Any deeper, and we risk blowing our cover if they take an alternate route."

"Storm's close," Tuck declared, nostrils flaring as if tasting the charged air. "Ponchos."

Inside the Fiat, Joe, eyes glued to the drone's feed after its smooth launch, the images sharp despite the dim light.

Mayan's SUV skidded to a halt at the precipice of a cliff. Below, steep terraces of rice paddies cascaded down like steps for giants. The Kopi Luwak café teetered on the edge, an audacious affront to gravity above tiered rice paddies. As if summoned by the growl of engines, two boys bolted out, their lithe bodies swerving around the Raptors being offloaded, dodging Mayan's curt, sharp commands.

With a proprietary air, Mayan and his brothers occupied a table with a king's view over the toiling paddy workers, miniature from this vantage. They indulged in the infamous coffee, its origin a journey through the entrails of civet monkeys, pairing the bitter swills with local bread, honey sweetened. Oblivious, they revelled there, under the gaze of eyes in the sky, their movements choreographed for an unseen audience.

Two clicks sounded, a silent void, then two more from Old Joe's s transmitter, painting the airwaves with urgent news yet withholding the path chosen by their marks.

Engines roared to life beneath the gang, machines purring with restrained power. Mayan led the procession on his Raptor, a mechanical monster at his command. They carved a route through the paddies, locals casting wary glances at the display of horsepower and bravado. The jungle swallowed them whole, only to regurgitate them minutes later, deterred by Tuck's cunning blockade.

Unfazed, Mayan charted a new path, vanishing into a gap in the treeline that promised obscurity. Old Joe, in tandem, plunged the drone into the verdant maw after them, now a shadow on their trail, its presence betrayed by eight urgent clicks on the transmitter.

"Navy blue," Cutler's Cutler's voice rumbled low, more felt than heard in the dense atmosphere, just as he intercepted Mayan giving the order through the hidden microphone, a fact that Old Joe confirmed using the drone.

Tuck's silent concession, a twenty-dollar bill passed to Cutler, was a whisper of normalcy amidst adrenalines hum.

The quad bikes beneath them were more beast than machine, responding with growls as they navigated through nature's barricade. Cutler forged ahead, eschewing the obvious paths, their tyres evading betraying imprints. They were ghosts in the greenery, chasing phantoms.

Hovering between the predators and their prey, the drone danced a delicate ballet. It dipped and swayed, threading through nature's obstacles, the drone's electronic heartbeat pulsing in sync with the humans below. Light was a capricious ally, dappled sunbeams breaking through the canopy in fickle flashes, casting an ethereal glow on their pursuit.

The ambush site was not chosen lightly. Cutler required the tactical superiority of elevation, a sweeping vista for the impending snare. He and Colton scaled a knoll, positioning themselves for the imminent strike. Below, the stream's path was a natural guide, leading their quarry into the trap.

Engines died, the jungle's chorus swelling to fill the void as they lay in wait. Cloaked by verdant ferns, Cutler's hands were steady as he carved into an ivory nut, the act almost meditative, grounding him in the moment before the storm.

Tuck and Colton had a problem getting through the Coffee and Ginger plants due to the root systems that spread out above the surface. Tuck managed to find a spot forty yards further on up the stream than Cutler on the left flank. The bank was nine feet above the level of the water and covered in several different types of low ferns, different shades and textures of green, intermixed with red- and yellow-coloured flowers of Birds of Paradise.

Tuck and Colton pulled down palm leaves that were twice the size of a man to shield themselves from view. Colton muffled a sneeze as the aroma of ginger infused their locality. Tuck removed several coffee beans from a plant nearby, pressed out the bean and discarded them and began munching away on the husks. He had picked up the habit from his time on a three-month sortie in Venezuela. Tuck and Colton had a limited view of the stream which meant they were reliant on seeing Cutler emerging from the other bank before acting.

Fork lightning lit up the horizon for an instant, flooding the gaps in the canopy in light. This was quickly followed by a massive explosion above, as the gods expressed their anger. Seconds after the thunder, Cutler felt the first large spot of rain as it bounced off his head gear and ran down his nose. The raindrop turned into several and then a shower followed by a deluge minutes later. Cutler and his crew were grateful for the camouflaged rain covers they wore, even though the humidity turned them into mini saunas.

Tuck had undertaken training with the SAS in the Arctic and had jumped into ice holes that he swore had shrunk his bollocks for life. He had tabbed through the jungles of Borneo with a fifty-kilo kit bag on his back, he had fought in the sewers of Iraq, so very little surprised him anymore. However, even Tuck was taken aback of how quickly a dry rut next to him turned into a small waterfall and how the stream bed which had eight inches of water minutes earlier, now rose to over a foot. What had been almost a stagnant stream now flowed at a rapid rate, containing water, mud and foliage debris.

Cutler observed the changes in the dynamics of the watercourse and fretted for a moment on whether Mayan would turn back. He assessed he would not, as they had been driving for forty minutes on a single track and trying to turn the machines around in what would be a mud heap would be tough. The stream increased its energy and sound level but was still driveable on these bikes and Mayan knew the area and knew the capabilities of his machines.

The jungle was a living, breathing entity, its pulse thrumming with hidden dangers as the dense canopy above formed a cocoon of emerald, green. The air was a tapestry of exotic scents, damp earth mingled with the rich, heady aroma of decaying vegetation. It was a world unto itself, where every rustle in the underbrush could be a predator lurking and every shadow held a whisper of menace.

Mayan, wearing the blue helmet had a keen sense of responsibility for his brothers trailing behind, navigated the treacherous terrain with heightened caution. Their journey through the stream was difficult, driving over slippery stones and deceptive currents. The water, which had seemed a tranquil companion, now betrayed them as the environment shifted ominously. The stream began to murmur secrets, a cryptic language that spoke of turmoil beneath its serene facade.

The Raptors they rode were robust machines, but even their engines seemed to protest against the elements, churning the once-placid water into furious bow waves that lashed at their legs, a stark reminder that nature was an adversary not to be taken lightly. Steam hissed and spat as it rose, a serpent from a watery lair, the heat from the engines warring with the coolness of the stream, creating a fog that threatened to cloak them in vulnerability.

The receiver on Cutler's bike blinked. All the LED lights lit up at once, the lights cutting through the torrential downpour. This was the code for "No Eyes on Subjects." He knew at once that the drone was no longer operational. The monsoon rain was difficult enough for Old Joe to fly the drone, the canopy above would collect the water until the foliage could no longer contain the weight and it would drop instantly. The first time the liquid avalanche from above descended on the drone, Old Joe through his newly developed skill, managed to keep the drone airborne some seven feet off the ground. The next deluge forced the drone into the bank of the stream and after contacting Cutler, he spent the next forty minutes teasing it back to life and back to the van, unsighted and unaware of the events being played out.

Cutler pressed once on his transmitter; Tuck's quad bike receiver blinked.

Tuck grunted, expelling the gritty remnants of the coffee husk from his mouth. The words he formed were silent but carried the weight of imminent peril. "They're here" Rain ponchos were shed in a fluid motion, a mirrored response to Cutler's earlier actions. The quad bikes underneath them thrummed, metallic beasts awaiting the spurring of their riders.

In the waterway, Mayan and his contingent throttled back, respect paid to the treacherous terrain. Bow waves surged, besieging them, while steam hissed a warning from the Raptors' engines. Seventy feet ahead, within striking distance of Cutler's ambush, they paused. Protective leggings were drawn over their limbs, a barrier against the searing mist.

A fleeting window opened, and Cutler nearly succumbed to the impulse to strike pre-emptively. Yet the moment waned as Mayan and his squadron regained their momentum, driving headlong into the snare. A mere twenty feet away, engines roared to life under Cutler and Colton, a thunderous decree of the hunt's climax.

Paranoia struck Mayan like a physical blow; his senses rebelled, detecting an anomaly amidst the engine's growls and the relentless assault of rain. His instincts screamed a warning, deciphered a heartbeat too late. From the embankment, phantoms materialized into predatory bikers, Cutler charging down with mud-spattered fury.

Controlling the bike was a battle, the mud beneath Cutler a living entity, striving to unseat him. He wrestled with the machine, a dance on the edge of chaos.

Mayan, in a desperate pivot, caught the image of their descent. His world narrowed to the menacing form of Cutler, just as his and his brothers' bikes slipped by. A rearward glance revealed the adversary now splashing into the streambed, the distance between them a shrinking lifeline. With a frantic twist, Mayan unleashed the Raptor's full fury, his attention riveted over his shoulder, the path ahead a secondary concern.

Cutler's emergence was the signal for Tuck and Colton, their engines screaming to life as they plummeted down the opposing bank, an unseen threat. Colton, the novice biker, was ill-prepared for the treachery of the terrain, a fact made brutally clear as his quad bike betrayed him, refusing to yield to his frantic steering. Mud dictated his trajectory, hurtling him toward disaster.

Tuck, a figure of vengeance, surged between Mayan and the second rider, his machine a roaring demon in pursuit. Adrenaline obliterated sensation, the steam's scalding touch reduced to a trivial nuisance as he became one with the deluge, a force of nature unto himself.

Into this maelstrom, Cutler followed, mere feet behind the third adversary, his proximity to Tut on the fourth bike a whisper of imminent doom. Engines screamed defiance, the gap between them a promised confrontation.

Then chaos crowned itself king.

Colton collided with catastrophic force against Mang's bike, the world erupting in a cacophony of metal and agony. Catapulted into a grotesque ballet, Colton's body described a harrowing arc over Mang, gravity reclaiming its due as he crashed onto the bank.

Disorientation battled shock; Colton's breath was a stolen treasure, his lungs clawing for air in the vacuum of his chest. A symphony of screams rent the air, a chilling serenade that he realized, with detached relief, were not his own. His collision had wrought carnage, Mang's leg a crushed ruin against his bike's unforgiving engine.

The stream was barely wide enough for two bikes abreast. Cutler's right footrest channelled out the mud along the bank as he pulled alongside. Tut looked petrified as the grinning Cutler pulled up alongside him, sweeping his left hand across his throat to explain what he was going to do to the fourth born member of the gang.

Tut used his left hand to try to pull something from a side bag on the bike and Cutler was not willing to wait to see if he had a weapon. In one fluid motion, he lifted his left foot of his footrest, at a downward angle slammed it on Tuts foot, which jammed the gear pedal down. The engine roared once as the bike decelerated instantly, it was too much for the machine to handle. The rear end of the bike lifted off the stream bed and tried to complete a three-hundred-and-sixty-degree loop. Tut fell from the bike into the fast-flowing water as it hit vertical, the machine twisted and hit the bank before tumbling over itself, narrowly missing the back of Tuck's quad bike.

Summoning every reserve of strength, Colton hauled himself upright, his surroundings a blur of chaos. Tut's unconscious form lay nearby, a grim marker on the battleground. Ignoring the scream of pain from his own bruised body, Colton lunged forward, vaulting over the carnage with a soldier's resolve.

His objective, the capsized quad bike, lay like a wounded animal amidst the mire. Each attempt to right the heavy machine drained precious seconds and shards of his waning strength, the mud beneath forming a treacherous foundation. Gritting his teeth, Colton braced, muscles quivering in protest as he heaved the bike upright.

Ragged breaths tore from his lungs, the sound of exertion in the rain. Though pain hammered through him with each heartbeat, the fire in his veins was not to be quelled. Mounting the resurrected machine, Colton throttled the engine to life—a growl in the storm, announcing his indomitable spirit.

With a warrior's grimace, he kicked the bike into motion, the world narrowing to the path ahead and the relentless pursuit of his fleeing quarry. Bruised, battered, but unbroken, Colton roared back into the fray.

Cutler glanced back to see the machine back in action and gave Colton the finger as a thank you. Kadex realized there was nowhere to go, behind him was his screaming brother Mang, he was trapped by another bike which cut off any route to bypass the tangled mess. Easily the best rider amongst the four brothers, although Mayan would never acknowledge that any of his brothers were more skilled than him, he realised he had only one option.

Considering the rain was pounding down, they were obviously under attack and the stream was now a raging torrent. Kadex pulled off a half turn that a world champion would be proud of. He was now facing the advancing Cutler and thought of his favourite movie 'Mad Max 2'. His favourite scene, was the one with two vehicles heading towards each other playing 'Chicken', seeing who would flinch first. Kadex opened up the throttle and sped towards Cutler.

Not one to ignore another's skill, Culter was impressed with Kadex's manoeuvre. In different circumstances he would have bought him a Budweiser, sat down and talked through how he had completed such a turn in the worse of conditions, but not today.

Cutler maintained his speed as the two machines raced towards each other. Kadex was ecstatic as adrenalin saturated his blood cells, Cutler had flinched first, or so he thought. Cutler stood upright on the bike, and Kadex believed Cutler was about to jump off. The next move surprised Kadex. Cutler while still holding the handlebars did a little jump so his feet were now on the seat, and he was squat over the handlebars.

Through the matrix of pain and sheer will, Mayan, battered but unyielding, had retrieved his firearm from under his poncho. With a primal roar, more beast than man, he unleashed a tempest of lead towards Cutler, the detonations echoing like thunderclaps through the foliage.

One rogue messenger of death found its mark, burrowing into the heart of Cutler's quad bike. The machine, loyal until its last breath, shuddered and convulsed beneath him. It spewed its lifeblood of oil into the waters, the liquid mingling with the stream's purity.

In the deathly waters of the jungle, betrayal came in the form of steam and metal—a mechanical death rattle as Cutler's vehicle breathed its last, leaving him vulnerably exposed in the maw of the wilderness. The air vibrated with the threat of impending violence, the hiss of steam a sinister whisper against the chorus of the jungle. And then, there was Kadex—hell-bent on vengeance, bearing down on him with the fury and pain inherited from his brother Mayan's downfall.

Every muscle in Cutler's body coiled tight as a compressed spring, a live wire of raw energy and survival instinct. He leaped onto his seat, a lone figure challenging the inevitable, his eyes locking with Kadex's. In that fractional moment, amidst the roar of engines and the jungle's haunting chorus, Cutler issued a silent challenge, questioning Kadex's resolve. But death swerved at the last second—Kadex, unwilling to become a martyr, veered away, missing by mere inches that might as well have been miles in the dense, charged atmosphere.

Adrenaline was both curse and ally as Cutler launched himself into the maelstrom, his body a missile targeting Kadex. They collided with the force of their collective rage, momentum sending them spiralling into the muddy embrace of the riverbank. Gasping for air, Kadex was a stunned serpent in a helmet, momentarily robbed of his venom, his fingers fumbling for the gun beneath his poncho in desperate retaliation.

The struggle for supremacy was brutal and intimate. Cutler seized Kadex's wrist, his other fist hammering into the man's ribs with punishing force. Yet Kadex, fuelled by vengeance and untold reserves, was an adversary not easily bested. Their grapple for the weapon was a savage ruck, each man a mirror of the other's determination and survival instinct.

Then, salvation came in a shout. "Gun, six o'clock!" Tuck's warning cut through the melee like a knife through the dense air. Instinct and training melded within Cutler as he executed a move as ruthless as it was effective, flipping onto his back and dragging Kadex into the line of fire. Time slowed, a trio of shots rang out, punctuating the jungle's soundtrack of chaos. Bullets, unforgiving and impersonal, buried themselves into Kadex, his body jerking atop Cutler in a grotesque embrace.

The weight of death was heavy, and as Kadex's life seeped into the waterlogged earth, Cutler shoved the carcass aside. It drifted, a corpse in the torpid stream before being ensnared by the greedy roots of the jungle. Rising, every movement etched with the urgency of battle, Cutler faced the final act of this brutal drama.

Mayan, trapped and mangled, was a portrait of agony, his leg a ruin amidst the steam and twisted metal. But even through the haze of pain, his focus was unerring, fingers grappling for a fresh magazine, for one last stand. He hadn't seen Cutler approach, until it was far too late. With a swift, jarring motion, Cutler seized Mayan's arm, snapping it back to break not just bone, but spirit. The sound was lost in the jungle.

The jungle transformed into a living entity, the pulsating heart of danger, as Tuck hammered his quad bike through the stream, hot on the leader Mang's trail. The world blurred into streaks of green and brown, with only the roaring river as his guide, a violent serpent winding through the landscape. Over a mile they clashed in this high-speed duel, man and machine versus nature's raw, untamed power.

Then, the serpent made a sudden twist—a sharp curve to the right that swallowed Mang whole. Tuck's survival instincts, homed in a crucible of combat and carnage, screamed a premonition. He throttled down, the engine's growl dropping to a wary purr. Caution overshadowed the urge to pursue. His senses stretched to their apex, reading the ominous hymn of the storm and the jungle.

Adrenaline was both a curse and a lifeline as Tuck eased around the deadly curve. Time seemed to manipulate itself, stretching out in an excruciating slow-motion sequence. Mang was there, a phantom emerging from the rain's curtain, his semi-automatic spitting venom. Bullets tore through the air, a lethal storm in their right, each whizz and crack a reminder to Tuck's proximity to death.

The dense thicket of the jungle, with its choral hum of insects and distant rumbles, was suddenly shattered by the staccato bursts of gunfire. The very earth seemed to tremble beneath Tuck's feet. As lead rained down, each bullet was an arbiter of fate, a merciless herald of death.

Every trained fibre of Tuck's being knew there was no sanctuary on land. With a heart still steady, he chose the river's dark abyss over the murderous sky above. Diving headlong, the world transformed instantly. The din of battle gave way to an eerie silence, the water wrapping around him like a cocoon, both shielding and smothering. The chill of the river seized him, a stark contrast to the sweltering heat of the jungle, but it was the inky blackness that truly disoriented—a void where vision was a luxury.

But Tuck wasn't a novice. Trained for scenarios even more grim than this, his every sense was hyper-attuned. The gunfire above, though muted, created ripples that caressed his skin, telling tales of danger and direction. The thrumming in his ears was not just from the pressurized depths, but from the adrenaline coursing through him, making seconds feel like hours.

A sharp pang gnawed at his chest, his lungs rebelling against their unnatural deprivation. But panic was an enemy Tuck couldn't afford. His fingers, numbed by the cold, moved deftly over the contours of the backpack. Every object felt, analysed, and discarded in split-second decisions until he touched upon salvation—the unmistakable texture of the catapult's rubber grip, the icy coldness of its metal frame. It was then he found himself along the river bank and he sought refuge in the dense reeds.

The weapon in his grasp, Tuck's mind raced. Emerging too soon would spell disaster; The outline of his foe, a transient apparition, played upon the water's shivering surface, illuminated by the erratic gunfire's ghostly strobe. But too long beneath the surface and his own body would betray him. It was a precarious balance, a deadly game of patience in the crucible of combat.

As the gravity of his decisions anchored itself in his chest, the realm above simmered with peril, a lethal cauldron ready to explode. In his hand, the primitive tension of a catapult; above, the cold, mechanized death promised by a semi-automatic. The imbalance did not escape him, a David-and-Goliath duel where modernity and firepower were not in his arsenal. Each breath a precious commodity, he acknowledged the stark contrast between his slingshot's humble elasticity and the gun's impersonal precision—a chasm measured not just in technical disparity but in the sheer, pulsating urge to survive.

Seconds were currency, and he was going bankrupt fast. The riverbed offered its arsenal—pebbles, cold and smooth. A childish weapon in his grasp, but in the language of warfare, all tools were tongues of potential destruction.

Above, Mang was a statue of deadly intent. His eyes, portals to a soul forged in the furnace of relentless battle, scoured the scene. The gun, an extension of his will, pointed where his gaze directed, ready to end lives at the whisper of a movement.

Tuck was pinned, a beast in a trap. No clear shot, the roots a prison now. He couldn't risk the telltale splash of emerging, couldn't gamble on his oxygen-starved body not betraying him with its desperation.

Tuck's world narrowed to a tightrope of survival. Through the skeletal lattice of the roots, his eyes, adjusting to the murk, caught the ominous silhouette of Mang. There was that fatal second, a shard of time where their eyes met through nature's barricade. Recognition, sharp as the crack of a gunshot, flared in Mang's gaze. Tuck's instincts screamed danger—he'd been spotted.

With the surge of adrenaline lending him ephemeral strength, Tuck inhaled deeply, believing it might be the final breath he would ever take, and dove deeper into the water's deceptive embrace. The pebbles in his grip and the catapult seemed like relics from a distant reality, almost absurd amidst this deadly dance.

Yet, with the calm that only the deeply trained can summon, Tuck forced the increased drumming of his heart into submission. Each beat echoed in the stillness of his submerged cocoon, a countdown to an inevitable end. He fumbled, his fingers numb and disobedient, to load the primitive weapon.

In the aqueous gloom, Tuck was a statue of coiled potential, the muscles in his legs tensed like steel springs, waiting for Mang to spend his round and forced to reload. The water around him, an insidious force, tugged and pulled as if to betray his position to the deadly predator mere feet away. He commanded his body to meld with the water's flow, becoming a fragment of the stream itself.

Then, with a predatory grace, Tuck surged from beneath the roots and flowing water. The action was an eruption of intent, his body breaking the surface with the abruptness of a suppressed memory bursting forth. Droplets of water caught in the frenzied air around him seemed to freeze, a tableau of a warrior reborn from the river's depths.

Mang's reaction was a viper's strike—swift, certain, deadly. The turn of his body wasn't just physical motion; it was the honing of a lethal trajectory, his weapon an extension of his intent to end Tuck's insurgence right there. In the spit of a second, the tableau shattered. Mang's finger flirted with destiny as it tightened on the trigger, the sound of murder barely a breath away.

But Tuck, the man carved from the same stone as war itself, was faster by a lethal margin.

The catapult, a primitive tool in a modern killing field, sang its tensioned note, and the pebble, inconsequential in any other context, became an envoy of destruction. It tore through the rain, a minor detail in the grander scheme, yet, at that moment, it was the entire story.

Targeting the only vulnerability, the unprotected face between helmet and goggles, Tuck wagered it all on this singular, frantic gamble. The odds were lunacy, the distance and the motion, the rain, and the peril—all weaving a narrative of almost certain demise.

Yet as the pebble made its meteoric impact, smashing into Mang's face with the wrath of retribution, the world telescoped to the echo of that strike. It wasn't the hit; it was the shockwave, the message it carried. In the milliseconds it took for pain and surprise to register, for Mang's neural pathways to scream error, the trigger's promise went unfulfilled.

The reality was stark and unforgiving: Tuck's next breath was borrowed from the devil himself. In the kill-or-be-killed creed of their brotherhood, there was no room for a second shot, no quarter for hesitation. As Mang stumbled, the river's cacophony was a death knell, and Tuck knew—there was only forward, only the mission, only survival.

Tuck towered over him, his silhouette cast large against the backdrop of chaos, the contours of his figure sharpened by rage. The air around them was heavy, a mix of gunpowder and vengeance, a volatile concoction that made the scene even more surreal.

"That's the price you pay for spilling innocent blood, motherfucker," Tuck's voice was steel wrapped in venom, the words not just an accusation but a judgment, delivered at the barrel-end of justice. Every syllable was a tribute to the lost young lives, a final epitaph for their unnamed graves. His breaths were ragged, torn from a place deep within after seeing the autopsy report on Smantha Gooding and the grief of the Trench's mother.

This was retribution, a small measure of balance restored in a world thrown into the throes of indiscriminate violence. The river's edge was a scene straight from purgatory, with Tuck, a bastion of warfare, perched on the bank, meticulously peeling back the Clingfilm around a cigar like he was disarming an intricate explosive device. His hands, those instruments of death, were oddly gentle, a poignant contrast to the carnage around him.

Colton emerged like a wraith through the tempest, his form a dark omen amidst the torrential downpour. The world around him was a maelstrom, rain slashing down in relentless, punishing sheets that turned the landscape into a blurred watercolour of turmoil. Each droplet was a prism, refracting the scant light and casting the world in a blurry sheen.

The storm itself was alive, a roaring entity of unbridled wrath. Thunder boomed like the drums of war, a deep, resonating sound that seemed to echo from the very bowels of the earth, shaking the ground and rattling even the sturdiest of nerves. Lightning forked, a serpentine dance across the bruised sky, illuminating Colton's features in stark intervals, casting his countenance in sharp relief one moment and shadow the next. The wind howled, a fierce combatant in the elemental turmoil, ripping through trees, sending branches, leaves, and unsecured debris spiralling into the tumult.

And there, stood Colton. His voice when it came, was a battle cry, a defiant roar against the storm's tempest. "Need a light?" he bellowed, the words torn from his lips and flung into the vortex.

"Nah, it's just habit," Tuck shouted back, his voice a gravel road of combat and survival. "Haven't lit one of these up in a decade. Your boy on the bike took one hell of a beating, you need driving lessons."

Cortez's gaze slid to the ruin of Mang, the grotesque artistry of his end a reflection to the savagery they had all embraced. "Seems he's faring better than yours," he retorted.

"Fucking made in Hong Kong," Tuck scoffed, disdain colouring his tone. "Helmut visors these days are supposed to withstand hell and high water. Instead, this one just capitulated, channelling the pebble and shards straight through. Blew up like a grenade in a trench."

Colton, despite the storm and the ordeal they had just endured, couldn't help but feel a hearty laugh well up within him. "Taken down by a stone launched from a forsaken catapult. You, Tuck, are like one of those geezers out of the Old Testament—," he exclaimed.

"Don't forget to bring me a body bag when you return from dropping off our limping friend," Tuck called out, nonchalant in the face of what they had wrought.

The aftermath stretched over an hour that seemed to cower under the weight of eternity. They salvaged what remained: four battered bikes, two dead, one unconscious and one broken. The van, a hearse of their own making, swallowed the wounded and dead, the black bags within an echo of the darkness they all shared.

Within the cramped confines of the van, Mayan's form took on the appearance of a grotesque masterpiece of human resilience. His body, a tableau of survival and agony, bore the brutal testimony of the ambush they had narrowly escaped. His leg, mangled beyond recognition, was a chaos of torn fabric, exposed flesh, and jutting bone—reminiscent of meat haphazardly torn asunder on a butcher's block. His arm, bent at an unnatural angle, confirmed a break, the swelling already beginning to discolour with the ominous hues of a severe bruise.

Beside him, Tut was silent, unconscious since the crash. He was slumped against the side of the van, his chest rising and falling with shallow, uneven breaths that were hardly reassuring. Every so often, a pained groan escaped his lips, or his eyelids would flutter, betraying a battle fought within the dark recesses of his unconscious mind.

The air in the van was a cloying miasma of blood and gunpowder, an oppressive cloud that they could neither escape nor ignore. It was a metallic tang that clung to the back of their throats and settled in their lungs, a constant reminder of the violence that had just transpired. Each inhale was a struggle, as if the van itself was reluctant to offer the oxygen they so desperately needed.

Despite the chaos, there was a strained orderliness among the remaining team members. With hands that shook from the cocktail of adrenaline and raw fear, Colton administered first aid with the efficiency born of desperate necessity. Makeshift tourniquets were applied, wounds were hastily covered.

Cutler's eyes flicked to Colton, his voice dropping to a conspiratorial whisper. "Status on the drone?"

"I can resurrect it, but it'll be deaf, the mikes are beyond anything I can do," Colton responded, frustration evident in the tight lines of his face.

"No matter. I need eyes on that police checkpoint. I want to know their numbers," Cutler insisted, the steel in his voice belying the danger of their proposition.

Minutes ticked by each second amplifying the palpable tension that hung around them like a shroud. Then, the intelligence came through: a solitary police cruiser, three officers—a detail that could either spell a stealthy bypass or a bloody confrontation.

Tuck operated with the precision of a surgeon, his hands deftly assessing the most robust of the bikes. It was more than a machine now; it was their lifeline, a metallic beast that needed to roar flawlessly. He ensured its veins were pulsing with enough fuel and its nervous system, the brake cables, unmarred by the day's brutality. His focus was absolute, the world narrowing to the task, each movement practiced and assured under the jungle's oppressive gaze.

chapter twelve
Revelations

In the simmering heat of the Balinese night, sweat and tension were indistinguishable allies as Cutler watched Old Joe prepare for the gamble of his life. The scent of gasoline mixed with the raw, alcoholic fumes rising from Joe's drenched clothing. The old man's hands, though steady, betrayed the gravity of his task as he unscrewed the whiskey bottle's cap and took several deep gulps. His eyes, a mirror of resolve shadowed by the knowledge of what lay ahead, never wavered from Cutler's.

Cutler approached, the scene around them a tableau of calculated urgency. Tuck and Colton were moving with grim efficiency, hoisting Mayan's and Kadek's lifeless bodies into the inconspicuous blackness of the body bag. The sound of the zipper seemed unnaturally loud, a harsh finality under the vast, indifferent expanse of stars.

"Joe, it's go-time," Cutler's voice was low, barely above the ambient noises of the night, but it carried an undeniable weight. "Remember, you need to reek like a distillery for this to work."

Old Joe nodded, sloshing more of the whiskey over his already damp clothes. The liquid darkened the fabric, and its pungent odour assaulted the senses. "If all goes to hell, Cutler," Joe began, his voice a gravelly whisper, "my boys all I got. Tell him I died doing good. Promise me you'll reach out. He's gotta know her old man stood for something in the end."

The intensity in Joe's gaze anchored Cutler to the spot. "You've got my word," he affirmed, clapping a hand on Joe's shoulder. "But plan on telling him yourself."

A semblance of an alcoholic smile tugged at Old Joe's weathered features before he revved the quad bike's engine to life, the growl of the machine slicing through the thick, humid air. And with that, he was off, a determined man hurtling toward a nebulous fate down the rain sodden road to Denpasar.

Cutler's eyes followed the quad's red taillights, his jaw set, mind racing as they receded into the distance. Every second counted. They had Indonesian bodies in their van where corruption ruled, and their enemies were legion. Mang's laboured breathing was a morbid metronome in the background, Tut's silent form a reminder of the tenuous thread by which their plan hung. One misstep, one unforeseen variable, and it would unravel in deadly fashion.

Old Joe barrelled toward the inevitable roadblock, a beacon of feigned inebriation. The police, likely bolstered by power, would be hungry for any excuse to exert their twisted sense of authority. Each vehicle was a potential victim, a chance encounter with fortune or ruin, dictated by the whims of greed.

As he neared the checkpoint, the scene played out in the harsh glare as the sun finally peeked through the clouds. Officers, predators in uniform, flagged down random targets, their hands itching for the feel of crumpled bills. They were merchants of fear, selling passage at the cost of whatever they fancied.

Old Joe thundered into this den of vipers, the whiskey and adrenaline a volatile cocktail in his veins. He swerved, a picture of reckless intoxication, straight into the police nest.

From a distance, Cutler and the others held their collective breath, the night air electric with silent prayers. This was the fulcrum upon which their fates would tilt, in the hands of a brave old sailor, possibly on his final, blazing ride.

Cutler's voice was steel-clad determination over the white noise of the drone's feed. The ghastly tableau of the explosion, coupled with Old Joe's beating, was a gruesome reality to the dark labyrinth they had waded into.

Beside him, Tuck's features tightened, the hardened soldier momentarily eclipsed by a glimpse of the humanity behind. "He's one tough bastard," he muttered, respect evident in his tone.

The drone's camera panned as Cutler guided it, capturing the chaos below. Police officers who had been basking in the thrill of the chase now scrambled to douse the roaring flames of his quadbike, their uniforms casting elongated, ghostly figures in the firelight. The charred remnants of the quad and the surrounding greenery created a stark contrast to the tropical beauty they had witnessed upon their arrival. Old Joe was obviously alive, the police usually done waste their time kicking a dead man.

"We have our window," Cutler announced, his voice a razor-sharp edge of concentration cutting through the tense air. "Old Joe's drunken antics has drawn them. We're going to hit the gas and turn off just after the checkpoint. There's a secondary route," he continued, tapping aggressively on a road that snaked like a shadow through his plastic-encased, weather-beaten map.

His finger traced the thin line that represented their slim chance, a backroad, perhaps barely more than a dirt track that meandered through what looked like dense foliage. "This pathway here is our ticket.

Cutler's eyes were aflame with the kind of manic determination that only appeared when every cell in his body was ignited with adrenaline. He knew the risks; they were the kind that could end with them in a ditch, or worse, in the firm grasp of authorities who were no doubt under the sway of powers far more dangerous than standard law enforcement.

"This isn't a Sunday drive," he cautioned, his gaze locking onto each of his team members, instilling in them the severity of their situation. "He folded the map with brisk, precise movements, the plan set, their window fleeting. "We have Old Joe to thank for this chance. Gear up.

Both drivers moved quickly, their training kicking in. They knew that speed was of the essence. The local police force, though corrupt, was vast and had a long reach. And with Mang in their custody, time was a luxury they couldn't afford.

As the vehicles sped through the winding roads, the tropical landscape flew past them in a blur. The verdant jungles, interspersed with the occasional village or settlement, played witness to their escape.

All the while, Cutler's mind raced. Old Joe had made the ultimate sacrifice, ensuring their escape route was clear. But it wasn't just a strategic move; it was a play for redemption. A quest to rewrite past sins with one final, defining act. The realisation weighed heavy on Cutler's conscience, but his men were paramount.

As the vehicle emerged from the dense forest, the vast expanse of the ocean stretched out in front of them, the horizon a shimmering line where the sky kissed the sea. Their extraction point was some way ahead, but Cutler had other plans.

Cutler and Tuck made their final checks, ensuring everything was in place. The drone, their silent observer, descended gracefully, landing in its designated spot in the back of the vehicle. Ten minutes later they cleared the road and off down their prescribed route and heading towards their safe house.

The atmosphere in the stone shed was as dense and heavy as lead, each breath seemingly more laborious to draw than the last. A thick silence hung low, an invisible fog, broken only by the sporadic grunt of discomfort or the restless shuffle of boots against the shed's earthen floor. This rustic hideaway, with its skeletal wooden beams and windows like shattered teeth, created an eerie tableau. The moon, a reluctant witness peering through the breaches in the timber, cast elongated shadows that danced across the rough-hewn walls, contributing to the macabre scenery.

Cutler stood in the centre of the room, his eyes scanning the interior he had reconnoitred with meticulous care barely three days prior. It had been a contingency, a strategic bolt hole, never meant to see the light of day unless circumstances twisted out of turn. Yet here they were, even though things had gone as hoped.

The shed, intended as a haven, now felt more akin to a tomb—a holding pen for the breathing yet battered bodies of his crew. His men and enforced guests' wounds varying from superficial scrapes to injuries that turned stomachs even amongst the hardened.

Every so often, a gust of wind would lament through the cracks in the structure, stirring the stale air and causing the shadows to shiver, as if even they were unsettled by the present company. The scant light from the tactical lanterns did little to lift the oppressive darkness, serving only to cast a ghastly pallor on the men's faces, highlighting the grim set of their jaws and the fatigue that haunted their eyes.

Cutler, feeling the weight of command heavy on his shoulders, allowed himself a moment to lean against the cool stone. This quiet solidarity amongst them was a balm, albeit temporary. They were, for now, out of sight, though he knew all too well that they were never beyond reach. The outside world—with its dangers—lay just beyond the fragile sanctuary of the shed's walls. For now, this was their reprieve, a chance to steel themselves for what was to come.

Tuck's gaze slid uneasily across the dim interior of the shed, finally settling on Colton, who returned his look with a noncommittal shrug. Tension hung between them like a taut wire, vibrating with the unspoken questions that ricocheted around the cramped space. The airstrip, their ticket out of this place, was barely ten miles away—a stone's throw away. Yet here they were, hunkered down in a decrepit stone shed that seemed to lean on its past memories for support, while precious minutes ticked by, unrecoverable.

Tuck felt the jagged edge of frustration gnaw at his insides. Cutler was not one to alter plans on a whim; his decisions were calculated, each risk meticulously weighed against potential reward. Every move was a carefully placed chess piece on a board that only Cutler fully visualized. So why the detour? What piece of the puzzle was Tuck missing, that Cutler seemed to hold between confident fingers?

He studied Cutler's profile, the set jaw and furrowed brow, the eyes that flicked with a restlessness that belied his outward calm. There was something amiss, an anomaly that had forced their leader's hand, steering them off the charted course and into unmarked territory.

With a quiet, almost imperceptible sigh, Tuck leaned back against the wall, feeling the rough texture of the stone through his clothing. He knew the drill—patience was as much a weapon in their arsenal as the firepower they carried. Trust in the hierarchy, faith in the man who had steered them through storms before, that was the creed they lived by.

"Hang Mayan's body up on the rafters," ordered Cutler.

Under the dim light filtering through the shed's dirty windows, Tuck and Colton set about their grim task with professional detachment. Mayan's lifeless body, still heavy with the last remnants of life, seemed an unwieldy burden as they hoisted it from the ground. The ropes, coarse and biting, were looped with efficient knots learned and earned from years in fields and operations that required such dark knowledge.

The air was thick with a silence that only the dead can bring, the kind that presses into your ears, a reminder of the finality of life. As they worked, the only sounds were the strained groans of ropes pulled tight and the soft, almost imperceptible swish of Mayan's clothes as his body was raised.

With a final tug, they secured the other end of the rope over one of the exposed beams that crisscrossed the shed's ceiling. The body hung there, an ominous pendulum, a silent confirmation to the fragility of life and the harshness of their current reality. Cutler observed the scene with a stony expression, his mind clearly turning over the implications of their situation.

The task done, Tuck and Colton stepped back, their hands and forearms aching from the exertion. They regarded Mayan with a mix of loathing and bile.

Cutler broke the silence, his voice grave. "We needed to do this. It's a message and a warning. For those two in there," he nodded towards the small room where Tut and Mang were kept, "they need to understand we mean business. They'll talk, or they need to think they will up end up like their brother."

Tuck wiped his hands on his trousers, a gesture more of fatigue than of trying to rid himself of the feel of death. "I don't understand why we have stopped, should be boarding the fucking plane by now," he said.

Cutler's gaze was hard, the glint in his eyes sharp as flint against steel. "The Fords are not just wealthy; they're connected. Arms dealing is a dirty business, muddied by secrets, lies, and betrayals. We've stumbled onto something bigger than a hijacking, bigger than ransom. Something worth killing for."

"Something's off; we're not seeing the whole picture here. The firearms, both from Tut's bag and retrieved from Mayan, are Armitech models. How likely is it that they're equipped with weapons from Conrad Ford's own firm?" Cutler mused aloud,

"They used to supply all over the world before the embargo," Tuck said.

Cutler passed one of the guns to Tuck, extracting it from the confines of his waistband. Tuck turned it over in his hands, examining the weapon with a professional eye.

"Seems pretty new, less than a year old, I'd say," Tuck noted, running his thumb over the space where a serial number should have been but wasn't. "And it's clean—no serial number."

He raised his eyes to meet Cutler's, a mutual understanding of the situation passing between them.

"Cutler's eyes narrowed, the gears in his mind visibly turning as he weighed the evidence before them. The stark room seemed to close in slightly, the tension thickening.

"It's more than just a coincidence, Tuck," Cutler began slowly, the weight of his years of experience lending a certain heaviness to his words. "Armitech under Conrad Ford's direction had a global reach, sure, but the specific absence of serial numbers? That's a tactic used to shield illicit transactions, to make weapons untraceable. It's the black market's signature."

He paused, letting the implication of his words settle in the stale air of the room, the body of Mayan suspended above them a grim reminder of the stakes at play.

"Robert Ford's death, these Armitech weapons in their hands, it's all part of a larger narrative we're not seeing yet," Cutler affirmed, his voice steel wrapped in velvet. "Before we even think about boarding Ford's plane, we have to know what's going on." Cutler declared, his determination etching into every syllable. "We're not just walking into a rescue mission; we're potentially walking into a spider's web. And I'll be damned if I'm going to let us get entangled without knowing who spun it."

"We're going to need more intel," Colton chimed in, the practicalities of their situation coming into focus. "Anything that can give us a clearer picture of what we're dealing with."

"Old Joe was told specifically to be on the lookout for Robert Ford's yacht. It wasn't just picked at random like the Trenches as we first thought; this was more than that, it was targeted," Cutler answered.

"So what's our move, Cutler? How do we trace these back without a serial number?" he asked, the urgency in his voice mirroring the severity of their situation.

Cutler's gaze was steely as he locked eyes with each of his team members, the decision made evident in his manner before he even spoke. "Let's find out what these boys know."

As they hauled Tut into the dim confines of the room, the tableau that greeted him was one ripped straight from a nightmare. Mayan, his brother, hung grotesquely upside down from the rough-hewn rafters, life having long departed from his body. The thick rope bit cruelly into the lifeless man's ankles, suspending him in an eerie, macabre display. His eyes, devoid of life, stared off into nothingness, bearing witness to the void that follows mortal existence.

The room, scantily lit, cast ghastly shadows over Mayan's features, accentuating the pallor of death that had washed over him. Colton and Tuck stood nearby, their hands grimy and crimson— pulling on the knots for effect, an unsettling but necessary part of the psychological war they were waging.

The sight of his brother, so inhumanely strung up, struck Tut like a physical blow, sending a jolt of horror that coursed through his veins. His eyes widened in abject terror, and a strangled cry tore from his throat, raw and piercing in the heavy silence that blanketed the room. It was a sound that encapsulated all the fear, the shock, and the profound sense of dread that bubbled up from his very soul.

His captors regarded him with a steely indifference, their expressions unreadable and their eyes hard. This was a method, a tactic, a necessary act in the pursuit of something far larger than the room they were in. They needed answers, and the scene they had orchestrated was designed to unsettle, to unhinge, to pry open the tight lid of secrets Tut had clamped down on.

As Tut's cry faded into a whimper, swallowed by the oppressive atmosphere, Cutler stepped forward. His figure, blocking the vision of Mayan's body, seemed both menacing and inquisitive.

"Now, Tut," Cutler began, his voice calm yet laced with an undercurrent of sternness, "we're going to have a conversation, and you're going to tell us everything you know."

In the stillness, with the chilling scene cast before him, Tut realized with sinking despair that his options were as limited as they were grim. The air, thick with tension and unspoken threats, waited with bated breath for the secrets he would divulge.

Outside, the hum of insects echoed in the night, punctuated by the distant croak of a frog. The otherwise serene sounds of nature juxtaposed the tension inside the shed.

Tut was a wreck of a human being at that moment, drenched in sweat, his eyes darting between the corpse of his dominant brother and the stony faces of the men who now controlled his fate. He seemed to shrink, the bravado and status conferred by his brother's presence now leeched away by the grim tableau before him.

Cutler, standing a head taller than Tut, leaned down into his personal space, his voice a gravelly whisper that contrasted sharply with Tut's ragged, panicked breaths. "I asked you a question, lad. Your answer determines a lot about what happens next."

Cutler's voice broke the silence, his tone low and almost conversational, yet within the confines of the shadow-draped room, it carried a chilling edge.

"Do you believe in the afterlife?" he asked, his gaze steady on Tut's face.

The shed was silent, save for the distant nocturnal sounds outside its confines. Even the air seemed to wait in anticipation for Tut's response. Colton and Tuck watched the exchange, their expressions hard and unreadable, adding to the weight that pressed in on Tut.

"I… I believe," Tut stammered, his voice barely audible, almost drowned out by his racing heartbeat. "We believe in the cycle… of death and rebirth."

"Good," Cutler responded, straightening. His silhouette seemed to loom larger as he spoke again, "Because your brother, Mayan, has started that journey. Where it leads, well…" he trailed off, gesturing to the suspended body. "That's up to the gods, isn't it?"

Cutler removed Mayan's eye.

His next words, deliberate and measured, cut through the tension like a knife. He took a step closer, the scant distance brimming with unspoken threat and promise.

"So your brother now begins his new journey without an eye, that's the belief, I'm told," he stated, his voice barely more than a whisper, yet every word struck with the precision of a well-aimed dagger.

The cultural reference, the notion of the deceased embarking on the afterlife marred by their earthly injuries, was a clear tactic, a calculated prod at Tut's spiritual and superstitious vulnerabilities.

It was a reminder, an emphasis on the finality of Mayan's death, and a nudge at the responsibilities that the living hold for the dead in many belief systems.

Tut's gaze remained transfixed on his brother's lifeless form, the harsh reality of their situation washing over him relentlessly. His brother's closed eye, now sealed forever, served as a stark symbol of their dire circumstances, a tangible reminder of the brutality and irrevocable conclusion that had engulfed them. This was more than just a man's passing; it was the rupture of a deep familial bond, a lifelong connection that had met a brutal and abrupt end.

Cutler's manner shifted imperceptibly, the menace in his tone casting a chilling message across the room. He leaned in, his face mere inches from Tut's, the gravity of his presence a palpable force in the confined space.

"I'm going to take his other eye, then his balls, and then I'll bring in Mang and do the same... and then you," Cutler threatened, each word laced with a cold, lethal calm that brooked no argument. His voice, low and even, was a stark contrast to the violent imagery he invoked, painting a picture of methodical, escalating torture with surgical precision.

Panic crashed over Tut like a tidal wave, his earlier resignation swept away in a flood of primal fear. His eyes, wide and terror-stricken, darted frantically, seeking any sign of mercy or reprieve.

"Wait, wait," he gasped desperately, his breath hitching in his throat as the severity of Cutler's words fully dawned on him. "What do you want?" The words tumbled out; a lifeline thrown amidst a sea of dread.

Cutler straightened up, the intensity in his eyes unrelenting. "Information," he said simply, his demand succinct. The unyielding edge to his voice hinted at no room for negotiation—Tut's options were painfully clear. Cooperation, or unimaginable suffering.

"You're going to tell me everything. Who you're working for, the plans for the weapons, the connection with Conrad Ford's company, and why Robert Ford was targeted. Everything, Tut. And you're going to start now," Cutler continued, his ultimatum hanging heavy in the air between them.

The remnants of Tut's defiance crumbled under Cutler's steely gaze, the weight of his predicament pressing down on him with suffocating force. Cornered, with the horrifying image of his brother's mutilated body seared into his mind, Tut's resolve shattered.

"Okay, okay… I'll talk," he stammered, the words barely audible, a stark capitulation in the face of overwhelming fear. As he began to speak, the details of the nefarious web in which they were all entangled started to slowly, horrifically, come to light.

He turned slightly, nodding to Colton. The larger man stepped forward, the sound of his boots on the wooden floor seemingly loud in the tense quiet. He pulled out a small device—a digital recorder—and placed it deliberately on a rickety table in the centre of the room.

"Start from the beginning, Tut. The dealings, the yachts, the killings—particularly information on Armitech and Robert Ford. We want names, places, transactions. Don't leave anything out," Cutler's command was calm, but it carried an underlying threat that was as menacing as the corpse swinging gently behind Tut.

Tut's gaze flickered between the men, the recorder, and his dead brother. The truth weighed heavily on him, a tangled web he never wanted to un-weave. But now, with his options depleted and his life hanging by the same precarious thread as Mayan's, Tut realized he had one last card to play—cooperation.

The atmosphere in the shed was thick with menace, every shadow seeming to pulse with the dark promise of violence. The air was heavy, each breath laden with the metallic tang of fear and the acrid stench of urine.

Cutler's voice cut through the tension like a knife, cold and precise. "Your life is hanging by the slimmest thread, Tut. A thread I'm more than ready to cut. But you have one chance to save yourself. Talk."

Tut, pressed against the wall as if trying to will himself through it, was a mess of terror. His body shook uncontrollably, sobs catching in his throat, eyes darting frenetically from Mayan's mutilated body to Colton's blood-stained knife, to the unyielding faces of his captors.

Tuck, towering and imposing, loomed over the broken figure, his expression one of disgust as he looked down at the dampness staining his boots. His hand shot out, fast as a striking snake, grabbing a fistful of Tut's hair and yanking his head back, forcing him to look at the macabre scene before him.

"Do you fucking understand your situation?!" Tuck growled, his face inches from Tut's, his breath hot against his cheek. "You're going to spill your guts, every dirty little secret, every fucking deal, every person involved in your twisted little operations. And if you even think about lying, it's going to be a long night for you, boy."

Tut's eyes were bloodshot, tears and snot mixing on his face, making him a pitiful sight. But this was beyond pity. This was about survival. His voice, when it finally came, was a broken whisper, each word a struggle, as though he was dragging them from the deepest, darkest part of himself.

The narrative that unfolded was a dark and unsettling account of avarice, treachery, and relentless ambition. He recounted secret meetings, whispered conversations in dimly lit corners, and financial transactions occurring under the cover of darkness. He unveiled names that prompted even Cutler's experienced team to raise their eyebrows—names that held considerable influence and authority, names that had the potential to be lethal for those involved.

Outside, the world was oblivious to the revelations happening within the decrepit shed. But inside, the very air seemed charged with the weight of Tut's words. They were words that could change everything—words that could indeed save him or, if they fell into the wrong hands, could sign his death warrant.

"Now tell me about the Barracuda and Robert Ford" ordered Cutler.

"It wasn't just any yacht; it was an order," he started, his voice trembling, "The LSX 92 Lazzara, Free Spirit. We had inside information. It was all planned!"

As if acting on a silent command, Tuck grabbed Tut, hauling him to his feet with terrifying strength. The urine puddle spread further, forgotten as Tut faced the monstrous reality of his interrogators' intentions. The chilling dance of death and domination played out, with Cutler orchestrating the grim symphony.

"Inside information? From whom? Speak up!" Cutler demanded, the dark promise in his voice sending shivers down even Tuck's spine.

"Mr. Sheldrake! He's the one behind it all. He told Mang to make them disappear, never to be found," Tut blurted, a sense of frenzied desperation taking over him as his survival instincts kicked in.

"And the couple on the Free Spirit?" Cutler's voice was dangerously soft, belying the storm that was building inside him.

Tut hesitated, a fatal mistake. Colton, ever watchful, seized the opportunity, his movements fluid like a predator's. The sound of the knife slicing through the stale air was a sinister prelude to the horror that unfolded. Mayan's remaining eye was deftly extracted, the gruesome trophy displayed before Tut's face, pushing him over the edge." We start working on Mayan next, alive or not"

"They're dead! We killed them," Tut screamed in hysteria, "Dropped their bodies into the sea. It was Mang!"

The shed was silent for a moment that seemed to stretch for an eternity, the only sound Tut's heavy, ragged breathing and the quiet drip of blood from Colton's knife. The stakes had changed. This wasn't just about information or confession anymore.

"Every detail, Tut. Don't you dare leave anything out. The Barracuda, the other operations, the routes, the contacts," Cutler's voice was a whip, each word lashing at Tut's sanity, "We will unravel everything, and if you lie, what we did to Mayan will seem merciful compared to what awaits you."

Tut's breathing became erratic, fear pulsing through his veins as he faced the relentless gaze of his captors. The words began to spill from him in a frantic, disjointed confession, as if releasing them would somehow lessen the burden he carried.

"Mang… Mang never wanted any Americans dead," he started, his voice trembling. "The thing with the Trenches, it wasn't supposed to happen like that. It was all a mistake, a terrible mistake. They… they just went too far," he stammered, his eyes darting anxiously from face to face, seeking a hint of understanding, of empathy.

He swallowed hard, continuing, "It was Sheldrake. He… he was, pulling his strings. I overheard them once," Tut admitted, his voice dropping as though sharing a secret he had long feared to reveal. "Robert Ford's father, he was involved in something shady. Tried to shake down Sheldrake for more money. I don't know all the details, but it was something big, something dangerous."

Tut's hands fidgeted nervously with the hem of his shirt as he delved deeper into his fragmented account. "I was in the next room. Mang sent me to spy, to find out what I could. Sheldrake didn't know I was there, couldn't see me. But I heard it all," he emphasized, his eyes wide with the intensity of the memory.

"Mang," Tut whispered through clenched teeth, his voice trembling with fear, "I need you to retrieve that damn package from the Ford's yacht, and I want you to set an example they'll never forget. Those were Sheldrake's exact words," he revealed, the room now suffused with an electrifying tension that seemed to vibrate in the air." After we killed them…"

Tuck's rage erupted like a volcano as he lunged at Tut, his fingers wrapping around Tut's throat with an iron grip. "You sick, twisted bastard! Don't you dare downplay it!"

"I had nothing to do with that!" Tut gasped, his eyes darting desperately to the lifeless body of his own brother, suspended in front of him, a grim reminder of the brutal consequences they were all entangled in.

"Let him finish, Tuck," Cutler intervened, his voice dripping with cold calculation, and Tuck reluctantly released his stranglehold, but the tension in the room continued to escalate, an ominous cloud hanging over them.

"What was in the package?" Cutler's eyes bore into Tut, a dangerous curiosity gleaming in them.

Tut swallowed hard, beads of sweat forming on his forehead. He hesitated for a moment; the weight of his betrayal heavy on his shoulders. "Sheldrake had warned Mayan not to open the package," he confessed, his voice barely above a whisper. "Mayan knew better than to go behind his back. But he put me in charge of minding the package, and I couldn't help it. I carefully opened it and looked inside, then closed it and resealed it. You couldn't tell it had ever been opened," he admitted, the revelation hanging in the air like a dark cloud, thickening the tension in the room to an almost unbearable level.

"What was inside?" Cutler's eyes bored into Tut; his curiosity matched only by his growing suspicion.

Tut hesitated once more, each second stretching out like an eternity. "It was a small computer and a USB stick," he confessed, his voice quivering as he revealed the contents of the ominous package.

Cutler's sharp mind wasted no time in probing further. "Did you turn it on?" he enquired, a sense of urgency underlining his words.

"No," Tut replied swiftly, his eyes darting nervously around the room. "I didn't dare. Sheldrake would have known, I think," he admitted, the fear of Sheldrake's wrath palpable in his voice.

Cutler leaned in, his voice low and insistent. "What was on the computer, any logos or writing?" he demanded to know.

Tut gulped, his voice trembling as he divulged the disturbing details. "Yes, Weapons Control Unit and a badge, 'Armitech'," he said.

Cutler's eyes were icy, the gravity of their situation mirrored in his stoic expression. "You're already in the kill zone. I want a description of Sheldrake and I want you to tell me where the Trench kid's bodies are."

"I have a picture on my phone," Tut whispered urgently, his voice barely audible above the tension in the room. "I took it when he met us last time. It's from a distance because I didn't want him to know. As for the bodies, Mang got rid of them. I don't know."

Cutler's gaze bore into Tuck, who wasted no time. He raised the smartphone to read Tut's face, he opened the camera and started scanning the photos. Tuck thrust the phone right in front of Tut. "Is this him?" he demanded, his eyes narrowing.

Tut's throat constricted as he nodded slowly, beads of sweat forming on his forehead. The room seemed to tighten around them like a noose.

"You know where the bodies are," Cutler growled, his voice dripping with menace, "tell me. It's the difference between you hanging from these rafters or walking out of here."

Tut hesitated; his fear palpable. "We had them buried out back of the boatyard," he confessed, each word heavy with the weight of his guilt. "But when the trawler dragged up the Ford kid, and the security team from Armitech turned up, Mayan was worried. We dug them up and put them in barrels of acid and dropped them ten miles off the coast," he revealed, the room filled with a chilling silence broken only by the distant sound of waves crashing against the shore.

Tuck's fury boiled over, and he unleashed a brutal punch to Tut's gut. "Not even a body for their Mum to bury them, you fucking animals" he seethed, the tension in the room reaching its zenith, threatening to explode at any moment.

Tuck's steely gaze bore into the trembling young pirate, a wordless message of dire consequence, leaving no room for doubt that cooperation was his sole salvation. "Know this," Tuck whispered, his voice dripping with menace, "Ford's father is going to crucify you."

Tut's desperation surged as he cried out, "You said you would let me go if I told you!" His voice trembled with fear, echoing through the dimly lit room, where shadows danced in macabre silence.

With a ruthless efficiency, Tuck seized Tut, his fingers gripping with a brutal intensity, and swiftly secured him with unforgiving plastic ties. He dragged Tut to the room where Mayan lay writhing in agony. "We were never letting you go, you little fucker," Tuck hissed, his eyes ablaze with vindictive fury. "You see your brother there? That's what awaits you when Conrad Ford gets his hands on you," he declared, the room's tension escalating to a boiling point, the air thick with impending doom."

The humid air in the shed seemed to congeal, thick with anticipation. Cutler's expression hardened; each piece of information they extracted pointed to an intricate network operating under Sheldrake's command, a network that was alarmingly well-organized and extensive. The revelations about the 'Lotus Leaf,' the detailed planning, and the use of real-time intelligence highlighted a level of sophistication that sent a shiver down even the most seasoned operative's spine.

Cutler's secure phone buzzed, and he swiftly answered the call, his voice lowering to a hushed tone without losing its razor-sharp edge. "Fabienne, report."

Fabienne's voice, typically calm and composed, carried a palpable strain as she spoke. "Cutler, we've got a problem, and it's on a couple of fronts."

Her words crackled through the line with urgency, her European accent more pronounced than usual, "Cutler, my intelligence software just intercepted news of an attack on passengers from the Reef Explorer. It looks like an entire group of snorkelers was slaughtered. If this is a precursor to an attack on the Reef Explorer itself, Stahmer, Cortez, and Ghislaine are on board. I've tried to contact them, but all communications to the ship have been severed, including the secure satellite phone."

Cutler's grip on the phone tightened, his knuckles turning white with tension. "Get the comms up and running, Fabienne. I need to know what's happening," he ordered firmly, his mind racing with the gravity of the situation. "Am about to send a photo. Clean it up and see what the face recognition software picks up. Also, find out everything you can about a Weapons Control Unit manufactured by Armitech."

"I've intercepted some critical information from the bugs you planted in Ford's home, and a WCU was mentioned gather this is the Weapons Control Unit you are referring to," Fabienne's voice crackled with tension. "This guy is in deep, Cutler, talking to some top-tier people, and there's something massive in the works. But he's not stupid enough to discuss it over the phone. So I've been tracking him, and trust me, you won't believe what I'm about to report."

Cutler's jaw tightened as he absorbed Fabienne's words. The situation was rapidly spiralling. "Send the report and I will read it on the plane. For now the Reef Explorer is our priority, Fabienne," he replied, his voice laced with urgency.

"Ford is acting as if we're adversaries, not just his subcontractor. He's up to something," Fabienne continued, her tone fraught with concern. "I've arranged for a leased plane out of Singapore to Cyprus. Do not board any aircraft he sends your way, Cutler."

"Understood," Cutler acknowledged, his mind racing. "What's the ETA for the jet?" he enquired, knowing that time was of the essence.

"Three hours, Cutler," Fabienne responded, her voice carrying a palpable sense of urgency that mirrored the ticking clock.

"Last thing, Fabienne," Cutler added. "Access the border controls here and erase any data that could trace us back to Bali."

"We're moving," Cutler declared with a commanding tone. "Get Tut and Mayan into the van. And make sure we secure that body discreetly." The tension in the air escalated as they hurried to execute their high-stakes plan while navigating a web of intrigue and danger.

Tuck acted swiftly, seizing Tut first, while Colton helped him carry Mayan, who had been administered another vial of morphine to ease his suffering. As they prepared to leave, Tuck stopped Cutler, his expression grave. "Ford's mixed up in this, neck deep."

Cutler nodded; "You're right, he's in the dark about our knowledge of the WCU. It seems he was using his son as a delivery method for something crucial. Don't know the full details yet, but it seems it was due to be delivered to Sheldrake, as he had prior knowledge of the delivery. For whatever reason, that deal must have soured, and through Mang, Sheldrake not only retrieved the package but exacted his revenge. However, Ford won't remain in the dark for long, especially after his henchmen debrief Tut on that plane," Cutler remarked, the weight of the impending showdown evident in his words and the tension in the room.

"What's the plan Once he knows we have a target painted on our back?" Tuck asked, a sense of urgency in his voice.

"Fabienne reckons that target has already been painted Tuck."

As they approached the isolated landing strip, the two Learjets, having idled for hours, came into view like silent sentinels in the darkness. Julie Birch, her face etched with a mix of frustration and impatience, stood waiting for them. She closely monitored the grim process of loading Mayan and Tut onto the first Learjet, their limp bodies a stark reminder of the perilous situation they found themselves in. Behind them lay the lifeless forms of Mang and Kadex, their presence serving as a wakeup call to the brutality of their circumstances.

Julie Birch, clearly vexed by Cutler and his team's refusal to board the second Learjet, attempted to employ her own security detail to coerce compliance. However, Tuck and Colton moved with a swiftness and precision that left no room for negotiation. They disarmed the security personnel effortlessly and left them nursing physical reminders of their encounter, effectively quashing any further attempts to sway their decision.

The engines of the Learjet roared, breaking the eerie silence of the night as it cut through the inky blackness above. On the ground, Cutler, Tuck, and Colton remained, watching as the aircraft became nothing more than a speck in the dark sky, carrying away its cargo of death and treachery.

The silence after the jet's departure was almost deafening—a stillness that didn't sit well with men accustomed to the cacophony of the battlefield. Two hours later the jet Cheryl had organised landed and headed towards Cyprus.

During the flight Cutler received Fabienne's report, Cutler's intrusion into Conrad Ford's private residence after Robert Ford's funeral had been a goldmine, but one particular discovery stood to pivot their entire operation: an encrypted phone, subtly hidden within the confines of Ford's ultra-secure home office. It wasn't just the phone's high-level encryption that intrigued Cutler; it was its isolation. It was charged separately, had its own secure storage, and seemed prepared specifically for conversations meant to be deeply buried from prying ears and standard surveillance.

Understanding the gravity of this find, Cutler had cloned the device and retreated undetected from the fortress-like residence. Once safely away, he initiated a secure, encrypted communication link with Fabienne, who was patiently awaiting details from the field operation. Her skills as a digital warfare specialist were unparalleled, and Cutler knew if anyone could breach the phone's defence's, it would be her.

As Fabienne received the phone's data remotely, she initiated a cryptographic assault on the device's defences. The phone, designed to self-destruct its data if an unauthorized access was detected, proved to be a formidable opponent. It was an intricate dance, a battle of wits against a digital adversary, fought in the language of code and cyber-manipulation.

Among the deluge of intercepted data, it became glaringly evident that the phone in question served as a direct, channel of communication between Conrad Ford and an exclusive circle of individuals. One of these shadowy figures was none other than Vice President Treisman. Their conversations were shrouded in secrecy, laced with cryptic jargon, and hinted at a sinister web of intrigue that extended far beyond the surface.

Yet it was a particular conversation that sent a shiver down their spines. In hushed tones, the vice president and Conrad discussed a name that resonated with ominous significance: 'Sheldrake'. The connection was undeniable. Was Sheldrake an intelligence operative, operating in the shadows of Black Ops? Or was he the very criminal he appeared to be, working under the employ of Robert Ford, and, on the surface, Vice President Treisman himself?

As they approached their landing destination, a chilling sequence of images sent by Fabienne appeared on Cutler's screen, each one more unsettling than the last.

The first image, taken from Tut's phone and expertly cleaned up, displayed the same mysterious man they had been tracking. He was captured entering the Orlando Convention Centre, his presence there raising questions they couldn't ignore.

The subsequent slide showed the man being discreetly guided to a waiting chauffeur-driven car. Nothing seemed unusual at first, but then the next image sent a shockwave through Cutler. The car, they discovered, was unmistakably government-issued, allocated to none other than Deputy Chief Allen of the CIA.

The next image was displayed—a snapshot from traffic CCTV, positioned outside a conspicuous residence in the area. It revealed the government-issued car departing the residence approximately an hour later, closely followed shortly after by the vice president's vehicle and a convoy of secret service cars, forming a protective shield around the vice president.

chapter thirteen
The Hidden Alliance

Conrad Ford meandered by the time-weathered fishing pond; the air thick with latent tension that seemed almost incongruous with the serene setting. His gaze lifted toward the familiar sight of his retreat, nestling boldly on the hillock's crest, silhouetted against the verdant grandeur of mountains so spectacular they'd been immortalized in cinematic epics like *Jurassic Park*, *Windtalkers*, and *Pearl Harbor*.

This secluded haven in Hawaii had been his chosen sanctuary, a place sought for sunshine and solace, intended as a healing balm for his wife's shattered soul after the earth-shattering loss of their son, Robert. It was more than a holiday home in Honolulu; it was a fortress of memories, a tentative step towards a semblance of peace Ford's wife was desperately clawing for.

The villa itself was a pledge to opulence and a fortress-like stance against the outside world, a white jewel ensconced in meticulously curated grounds that seemed to span for eternity. Its security was airtight, a necessity that Ford never skimped on. Surveillance cameras stood like silent sentinels, their electronic eyes unblinking, while motion detectors formed an invisible web around the palatial haven. Every square yard of the expansive five-thousand-yard estate was under vigilant watch, a silent promise of safety.

Within the villa's walls, the trappings of luxury were equally matched by functional fortitude. Ford's personal office was a technological stronghold, bristling with advanced computing and communications systems, a nerve centre where global connections were just a keystroke away. This was not merely a home; it was a command post.

While the tranquillity was the villa's facade, vigilance pulsed in its veins. A duo of security professionals was the permanent shadow of the estate, their number swelling to a formidable six whenever Ford took residence. His staff, a well-oiled machine, included housekeepers, a culinary wizard of a chef, a discreet butler, and critically, a nurse whose presence was a solemn nod to the lingering heartache that Mrs. Ford bore silently. Every need was anticipated, every potential risk assessed and mitigated.

The day took on a charged edge with the arrival of Vice President Treisman in the first blush of morning. Post the patio breakfast, where the first meal of the day was served amidst fluttering breezes, Treisman subtly motioned to his six-strong phalanx of Secret Service agents. They understood, receding to the estate's edges, close enough to respond at a shout yet far enough to grant confidentiality.

Maria Sysco, ever the VP's shadow, was a silent overseer. Together, Ford, Sysco, and the vice president traversed the manicured landscape to the pond's far reaches, where a stone bulwark stood as the only divide between them and the vast, churning Pacific beyond. Here, in this secluded corner where whispers were drowned by the ocean's susurrus, crucial words would be exchanged, weighty with consequences that extended beyond the villa's fortified seclusion.

The tension was palpable, a living entity that seemed to breathe along with the men, as the ocean's relentless waves crashed against the stone bulwark. Vice President Treisman voice cut through the charged air, a sharp-edged blade of accusation pointed squarely at Conrad Ford. "You've ignited a tinderbox, Conrad. One that threatens to upend our plans."

"Nonsense," Ford retorted, his voice laced with defiance.

"What on God's green earth compelled you to jack up the price of the WCU, demanding a king's ransom for it?" Vice President Treisman pressed, his patience wearing thin.

"We overran development costs. I had to recover them," Ford responded, his tone filled with irritation. "You tasked me with delivering a weapon, but you provided no budget and expected me to sell it to whoever? I'm a businessman, not a charity. I don't care about the specifics of what or who you want it for. What I do know is that it's not official US business, or they would have slapped an embargo on anything we do for them," he spat out, his disdain for the situation palpable.

The vice president's gaze was unwavering, the disappointment in his eyes overshadowed by a hard, political pragmatism. "Your insatiable greed severed your ties with Defence, Conrad. Don't think I'm unaware. It's only through my intervention, leveraging my CIA networks, that you've managed to keep your head above water, peddling your death tools to buyers who shy away from the light of legitimacy."

Ford's stance softened, a note of genuine contrition in his voice. "I'm well aware, and my gratitude knows no bounds. The windfall was meant to settle my accounts with Justice, to scrub the slate clean. I've had my fill of fraternizing with the dregs of humanity. I intend to re-enter the fold, legitimate and unencumbered."

"Don't delude yourself with revisionist history, Conrad. It was your dalliance with these 'dregs,' as you so eloquently put it, that carved your path to where you stand. You sowed the wind, and now, the whirlwind is at your doorstep," Treisman countered, his words carrying the weight of years of secretive dealings.

"No longer. I'm stepping into the light," Ford asserted with quiet resolve.

Maria Sysco, who had remained silent until now, interjected, her voice a cold harbinger of unvarnished truth. "Wishful thinking won't erase the past, Conrad. Justice isn't known for its forgetfulness. You're ensnared in a web of your own making, and now, your lifeline is us. Your contracts, your future—they're in our hands."

Ford straightened, defiance sparking in his eyes. "The WCU changes everything. It's revolutionary. I may have strayed from the sanctioned path, but Defence will be clambering for my alliance once they witness its capabilities."

VP Teasman's expression hardened, the politician surfacing above the friend. "A weapon of that calibre, Conrad, has a single use shelf life. It's a weapon that will haunt only briefly. Once it's unveiled, once the Chinese and Russians discern its potential, they'll engineer antidotes to dull its edge, to render it impotent. Your leverage is fleeting."

"So you intend to use it?" Ford replied.

In the charged silence that followed, the ocean's roar seemed to underscore the gravity of their stand-off, a reminder that they teetered on a precipice, with allegiances as unpredictable as the churning waters below.

The atmosphere crackled with a tension so thick it was nearly suffocating as the words hung heavy between the men. Maria Sysco's voice had the edge of a cold blade, her words not just a warning but a promise laced with danger. "Your curiosity is a luxury you can ill afford if you harbour any fondness for the sanctity of your life and the splendour of your estates, both here and on the mainland," she said, the latent threat weaving through his words like poison.

"Your dog is barking; we have been friends to long to start falling out now. I recovered my costs. What you do with the WCU is your business. I didn't mean to overstep," Ford said, as the vice president watched several large humpback sperm whales surface in the sea, clearly visible from his garden. He let Maria Sysco answer Ford's apology.

Maria Sysco's Treisman's words were pointed, a sharpened spear aimed straight at Ford's conscience. "Those whales are an echo of you, Conrad: rising briefly into the light before diving back into the deep to continue your predatory games. Considering the murky waters you tread, what insanity compelled you to welcome outside examination, MIDAS, to pry open the door to your operations?"

"You're talking about Cutler?" Ford's voice was a low rumble, the name stirring a storm within him.

"Exactly. Cutler isn't just some run-of-the-mill sleuth. He's a craftsman of investigation, a tactician. He's amassed a cadre of virtuosos in tech, linguistics, and field operations, poaching from elite military units. Does that sound familiar? He's running a compact mirror of an intelligence agency albeit a maritime one, and you've foolishly drawn him into our world." Sysco's tone was laden with a mix of frustration and foreboding.

Desperation crept into Ford's stance, his usual composure fracturing. "My options were limited when my son was murdered. I needed eyes and ears in places I no longer had reach. I wanted—no, needed—to know who took him from me," his words were laced with a father's raw grief, the façade finally crumbling.

Treisman's next words were a verbal coup de grâce, delivered with unflinching resolve. "You set your son's fate in stone, Conrad. You used your only son to transport the WCU, then tried to strong-arm the client into paying a whole lot more than agreed, you signed his death warrant."

Confusion warred with shock in Ford's eyes. "What are you implying? The WCU and the death of my son is linked. I had been told there was a gang who was operating out in those waters that targeted yachts. I thought the WCU was at the bottom of the ocean. Robert knew the package was of a delicate nature and at the first sign of trouble he would have thrown it overboard?"

"And yet the client has not come back to you, asking for the hefty deposit back," Sysco replied.

"Spot on, Conrad. And now, the very men you've been hunting, the ones entangled in your weapons fiasco, the murderers of your son and his future bride—they're all part of the network to take custody of the WCU."

"If what you say is true, I will soon know; Julie Birch has them on a Learjet on the way back from Bali," Ford said.

"And you sent a second jet for Ford and his team Conrad," VP Treisman said.

Maria Sysco stepped in. "Do you think we would let you transport the Bali gang or whatever was left of them back to Malysia where you could interrogate them? Do you think Cutler has not already done that, who knows what he unearthed?"

A tremor of disbelief shook Ford. "What have you done?" His world was fracturing, slipping through his fingers like grains of sand.

"Cleaning up your mess, Conrad. Both those jets are now resting at the bottom of the Java Sea, or whatever's left of them after the explosions," Sysco declared, her voice tinged with a cold, calculated edge.

Ford's veneer of vengeance momentarily cracked, replaced by raw anger. "You killed my security team, and Julie Birch—those bastards who took Robert from me were mine, mine to do whatever I wanted!"

But Vice President Treisman, with an air of ominous authority, cut through the brewing storm. "There's far more at stake here than your personal vendettas, Robert. You and your wife need time to heal. Forget about the WCU, forget about the gang, and forget about Cutler. They've all been taken care of." He hesitated briefly before adding, "I might note some reluctance regarding Birch. She was Deputy Chief Allen's agent, tasked with keeping an eye on you, such a shame."

"You're my friend, or supposed to be, and you put someone in, somebody I trusted as a snitch," Ford said.

The room crackled with palpable tension, each word a spark that fuelled the electric charge hanging heavy in the air. Vice President

Treisman's words were deliberate, each one a calculated step on a treacherous path. "It's truly remarkable, Conrad, how a man of your intellect can often remain blissfully unaware. Your own operatives, they know the truth. They've merely chosen to keep you in the shadows. Did you honestly believe we'd support you without keeping our own eyes on the field?"

"You had no right," Ford seethed, his voice dripping with indignation.

"Once you brought Cutler into the fold, we had every right," Maria Sysco interjected, her tone unyielding.

"I already had plans to deal with Cutler as well," Ford retorted, attempting to assert control.

"All sorted," Maria Sysco replied, her response a stark reminder of their ruthlessness.

Struggling to leash his fury and wounded pride, Ford distanced himself, pacing down the embankment as he fought to regain control. The waves crashing in the distance mirrored the chaos brewing within him. With each step, he battled to realign himself in a world where the rules had just been rewritten. When he returned to face the vice president, his voice was a low, controlled calm. "For someone who claims to have all the answers, you can't even get their facts right. Cutler and his team… they refused to get on the jet," he spat out, a hint of desperation in his voice.

Vice President Teasman's eyes were like flint, his mind strategizing several moves ahead. "He's likely pieced together that you're compromised, embroiled in something far dirtier than simple arms dealing. The WCU might be on his radar, but its capabilities remain our ace in the hole. The issue is, Cutler has a penchant for digging deep—relentlessly so. He'll tear this open if we give him the chance."

Ford's retort was edged with bitterness. "A situation you can't afford, right? Even your reputation or the CIA's wouldn't survive a scandal of this magnitude."

Vice President Treisman's face hardened, the severity in his eyes chilling. "Listen closely, Conrad, because I won't repeat myself. This operation doesn't fall under the CIA's official purview. It's a black op. If Cutler connects the dots between us, we're both compromised. So, the way I see it, I have two options: I eliminate the liability—that's you, my friend—which I'm reluctant to do, considering you might still be useful, or we join forces and eliminate them."

The words were a proposition laced with as much threat as opportunity. It was a stark reminder for Conrad Ford: in this world, friendships were transient, and survival wasn't granted—it was leveraged. As the gravity of his situation sank in, Ford understood that this chess game of espionage and shadow wars had no room for loyalty, and he was precariously close to checkmate.

The atmosphere was thick with menace, the undercurrent of danger weaving through each word, each calculated pause. Conrad Ford's voice was frigid, a stark contrast to the tropical warmth surrounding them. "As you've pointed out, you still require my services," he stated, each syllable dropping like ice.

Maria Sysco, her attitude as unforgiving as the situation they were mired in, didn't miss a beat. "If their Everglades office were attacked, the WCU may be put on the back burner, and time is our friend."

Ford's eyes narrowed, the implication hanging heavy between them. "You're suggesting killing his employees."

Sysco's expression remained impassive. "Your words, not mine. But understand this, Conrad: your involvement needs to mirror our own commitment. If not, you'll find yourself just another loose end in the eyes of our task force," Treisman interjected, his tone a warning wrapped in the guise of counsel.

Ford's mind raced, tactical gears turning. "Cutler's reach isn't limited to one place. He has resources, people working other angles," he countered, seeking a semblance of leverage.

Vice President Treisman's retort was as sharp as a whip. "A snake dies once you cut off its head. Any lingering threats, those curious souls who might continue their prying, can be systematically eliminated. Our immediate concern is Cutler and his core team, especially those tied directly to the Bali situation. Their hub in the Everglades can't just be neutralized; it needs to be obliterated, leaving no trace behind."

A new thread of information unfurled as Ford continued, "We've encountered a woman, Fabienne. Is she stationed in the Everglades?" Ford asked.

"Fabienne Asper is a more elusive target," Sysco interjected with a professional chill. "She's not there. MIDAS operates out of Europe too, but pinning her down is challenging. She's operating somewhere within France or Switzerland, but her exact location remains a mystery."

Vice President Treisman's face was an impenetrable mask as he responded, "Cutler is a seasoned player in this arena. He knows how to cover his tracks, knows how to keep his operations hidden.

But everyone has a breaking point, Conrad. Once the Everglades operation is dismantled, and Cutler is out of the picture, the rest of his network will start to unravel. And when it does, we'll find her," he asserted, the steel in his voice leaving no room for doubt.

Ford's mind raced back to a recent development. "We recently had to transport one of his injured men to Geneva."

"Yes, and we've been combing through every possible lead, trying to pinpoint the medical facility they used. But so far, it's like chasing shadows. Cutler knows the value of operational security," Sysco admitted, his tone begrudgingly respectful of their adversary's competencies.

"Conrad, I can't stress enough the importance of acting quickly. I need you to resolve this within days. Go back to your fortress up there," he gestured towards the imposing villa on the hill, "and start pulling the strings you need to pull. This all ends now."

Once back at his villa, Ford summoned David Sumner to his private study. Sumner was a dark piece in Ford's human chess game, a man he had recruited for his ruthlessness and lack of scruples. A bodyguard by title but an enforcer by nature, Sumner had a weakness for alcohol and harboured dark, violent cravings that he satiated far from prying eyes. His predilections led him to the seedy underworld of the Philippines, where he indulged his sinister appetites without restraint.

Ford was privy to the lurid details of Sumner's exploits, thanks to comprehensive dossiers kept by Birch. The files were a source of control, a means of ensuring absolute loyalty. Sumner had crossed a deadly line the previous year, his brutality resulting in a young boy's death. The incident had sparked an manhunt in the Philippines, but Ford intervened, erasing the legal threat hanging over Sumner's head. From that moment, Sumner was ensnared, fully aware that disobedience wasn't an option.

Ford's voice was glacial as he briefed Sumner. "I have an assignment for you," he said, sliding a piece of paper across the desk with an address written on it. "I don't want any details. I don't want any survivors. I want that place erased from existence, and its inhabitants… they're just going to be collateral damage in an unfortunate tragedy."

Sumner's face was impassive, but there was a flicker in his eyes—the dark thrill of the hunt. "I'm going to need assistance," he stated flatly, the implication clear: this was not a one-man operation. The gravity of the task was understood, and the machinations of their deadly intent were set into motion, ready to cut a swathe through the heart of Cutler's operations.

"Do you have contacts outside our circle? This operation needs to be contained, leaving no trails back to us," Ford's words were more than a simple question; they were a stipulation, his tone leaving no room for error.

Sumner's mind sifted through the repertoire of shadowy figures he knew he could rely on for a job as dark as this one. "I know a guy out of Miami," he said after a moment.

"I don't want his name," Ford cut him off sharply, "and it's imperative he remains in the dark about who's pulling the strings. Your acquaintance does the job, he gets paid, and his part in this story ends. Permanently. Is that understood?" The icy command layered within Ford's query was unmistakable.

Sumner gave a curt nod, recognizing the lethal seriousness in Ford's directive. "What about gear?" he enquired, knowing well that an operation of this size required firepower that couldn't be traced back to Armitech or any of Ford's known associates.

Ford's response was to tap his finger on the desk thoughtfully. "Use whatever your contact can scrounge up. I don't want a single piece of our inventory involved. No links, no loose ends," he instructed, his voice a low growl. As he spoke, he slid a hefty envelope across the desk toward Sumner. It was nondescript, but the contents were anything but—packed with crisp bills, the currency of the underworld.

"That should cover your expenses," Ford continued, a sinister undertone in his voice suggesting a finality beyond mere financial transactions. "Your associate's compensation, the hardware, and whatever's left… consider it a bonus."

Sumner's eyes flicked down to the envelope, and a slow, understanding grin crept over his features. "Appreciate it, boss," he said, the words laced with dark implication.

As Sumner left the study, Ford remained seated, the gravity of the operation sinking in. They were now committed to a path of no return.

chapter fourteen
Twilight Ambush

The dim light from the laptop screen cast an eerie glow on Sumner's face as he scrutinized the blueprints. This wasn't going to be a walk in the park; the Everglades office was a fortress, designed to withstand all kinds of conventional threats. But every fortress had its weak point, and Sumner thought he had found this one's. The structural flaw gleamed on the screen like a beacon, guiding the way to chaos.

Exiting the artificially bright interior of a McDonald's fast food café, Sumner stepped into the sultry Honolulu night. The air was thick, and the sounds of distant traffic were a low hum in the background. He dialled Marc Portishead, a man whose reputation for ruthlessness was only eclipsed by his eccentricities.

Portishead answered on the second ring, his voice gravelly, betraying a life lived precariously. The man was an enigma, a walking contradiction—his ostentatious appearance and the understated danger he exuded were worlds apart. With his vibrant tattoos and unmissable Mohican, he was a man meant for the spotlight, yet his profession demanded shadows.

As Sumner briefed him, Portishead's mind wasn't on the details of the job; it was on the pay. Sumner caught the next flight to Miami, his mind racing through logistics and potential pitfalls. His encounter with Portishead would be brief, clinical.

They were two sides of the same coin, both moulded by a world that demanded toughness, devoid of the luxury of trust.

Portishead, meanwhile, prepared for the task. His ritual was simple: a joint, enough to calm the nerves but not dull the senses, and a thorough check of his tools. He was an artist in his own right, and destruction was his canvas. The cannabis was his muse, the slow burn of the roll his companion through countless nights.

The world knew Oxford as a scholarly haven, a picturesque postcard of academic excellence. But it was oblivious to the underbelly that churned in the shadows of its spires. It was here that Marc Portishead was forged, amidst the despair of a crowded council estate and the brutality of neglect. The British Army was supposed to be his salvation, a way out. Instead, it was just a gateway, a place where he honed his craft, the craft that now defined him.

Marc Portishead, the boy from the forgotten streets of Oxford, was a name man who had slipped away from the norms of society. A man who could make problems disappear, leaving nothing behind but smoke and echoes.

The parade ground in Portsmouth back in 1980 was a sea of uniformity, every soldier an identical representation of discipline and conformity. Every soldier but one. Underneath the starched uniform that Marc Portishead wore, the rubberised suit clung to him like a second skin, a silent rebellion against the order he had been forced into. It was his armour, not against bullets or shrapnel, but against a world that had continually tried to grind down his edges and remould him into something more palatable.

The Falklands War was a turning point, a crucible that would either make or break the men who fought in it. Portishead, with thoughts of desertion swirling in his cannabis smoke-filled mind, chose to stay, not out of duty or patriotism, but out of a primal aversion to a caged existence if caught deserting. As his unit yomped across the unforgiving terrain of the islands, Trekking because the helicopters that should have carried them lay twisted and broken at the bottom of the sea, something within him crystallized.

At Mount Longdon, death became an acquaintance. The enemy soldier's life slipped away under Portishead's hands, inconsequential as a passing thought. Yet, in the aftermath, he sat in a shell crater, sharing a joint and whispered confidences with a corpse, a vision that unsettled even the hardened men around him. It wasn't the act of killing that marked this as a pivotal moment in his life; it was the profound disconnection from it.

Returning to a nation of flag-waving patriots, he found himself an anachronism. The Army, eager to maintain the polished image of their victorious campaign, quietly severed ties with the man who had become an uncomfortable reminder of the war's savagery. On the day of his discharge, the metal ring he placed in his lip was not just an accessory but a sign the shackles that anchored him to discipline was not a thing of the past.

Thailand was an escape, a place where the rules blurred, and Portishead could blend into the chaotic tapestry of expat life. From the lush, tranquil landscapes of Chiang Mai to the neon-drenched decadence of Pattaya, he thrived in the underbelly of the Land of Smiles, profiting from the hedonistic appetites of tourists. Yet this life, too, had its dark corners.

Revenge, when it came for him, was not a fiery, passionate affair. It was cold, calculated precision. The drug dealer had made a fatal error, adulterating Portishead's products, and disrespecting his business. The retaliation was swift and brutal, the makeshift wooden weapon speaking a language understood across all cultures. As blood seeped into the dust, Portishead felt not the thrill of victory, but the satisfaction of equilibrium restored.

Before he fled Thailand, he committed to a ritual that would become his gruesome legacy. The tattoo that adorned his arm was not mere ink but a silent mark to his life's path, each one a milestone etched into his skin, a permanent reminder of each life he had taken.

Now, as he ran his fingers over the increasingly crowded canvas of his skin, Marc Portishead acknowledged a stark truth: he was running out of skin, but his work was far from done. Each mark was a story, a memory of flesh and blood, and there were still more tattoos to add.

Portishead ran a finger over the edge of his crystal glass, the muted sounds of Miami nightlife seeping through the window. His former life in Las Vegas seemed worlds away, the glittering Strip now replaced by the glitzy boulevards of South Beach. But the transition wasn't just about lights and glamour. The receding waters of Lake Mead had once hidden his handiwork; now, as Miami's humid air embraced him, he felt exposed.

His phone vibrated, disrupting his thoughts. It was Sumner.

"Got a job for you," the voice on the other end said, the hint of a smile detectable. Portishead's heart skipped. The money was running dry, and Sumner's call couldn't have come at a better time.

"Details?"

"You'll be partnered up," Sumner began. A pause, intentional. "With Fidel."

Portishead nearly choked on his drink. Fidel? That upstart had been taking contracts out from under him for years. In their profession, being a competitor wasn't just about snatching business opportunities—it was personal, and it often got bloody.

"Why him?" Portishead spat out.

"Because this job's bigger than your petty feuds," Sumner responded sharply. "You both have unique skill sets that are needed. Meet tomorrow, 5 AM. Warehouse 12, Dockside. And play nice."

The line went dead.

Portishead leaned back, thinking of the times he and Delgado had crossed paths. While they had never exchanged blows, their underground reputations had been the stuff of legend. Two experts in their trade, now forced to work together.

The next morning, as the sun's rays began to pierce Miami's skyline, two figures approached Warehouse 12. Their eyes met, two pros sizing each other up.

"Portishead," Fidel nodded.

"Fidel."

"Now you've introduced yourselves, in the car and let's be on our way Fidel you drive" Sumner ordered.

The black Buick ate up the miles, the swampy wilderness of the Everglades flying by in a blur of green and brown. Portishead, now grizzled and marked by the passage of time and vice, felt the weight of his years heavy upon him. The cannabis that had been a constant companion had also stolen chunks of his life, leaving smoky voids in his memory. This job, he promised himself, would be the last. He'd become a ghost, a story whispered in the criminal underbelly, nothing more.

Fidel, a wiry man whose life stories were etched into his weathered skin as clearly as ink, was an enigma. He smiled with the assurance of one who had death at his fingertips. There was a coldness in Fidel's eyes that even Sumner, no stranger to the world of assassinations, found unsettling.

Sumner shifted in his seat, the money in his briefcase a tangible reminder of the job's stakes. Forty thousand dollars. It was no small sum, and it came with the kind of strings that could tighten around a man's neck with alarming speed. Sumner knew they were playing a high-stakes game, one that required keeping his client details close to his chest.

"Here's what you need to know," Sumner broke the silence, his voice low and even. "The target's location is a fortress, state-of-the-art security. Our window of opportunity is narrow. We get one shot at this, and it has to be clean We have a grenade launcher in the boot."

Portishead nodded, his mind already assessing strategies, angles, risks. "Grenade launcher, too loud, will attract attention?" he said, his voice raspy from years of smoke inhalation.

"Non-negotiable," Sumner replied firmly. "It's the only way to guarantee the job gets done. No loose ends."

A silence settled over them as the Buick continued its relentless journey. Portishead and Fidel exchanged a glance, an entire conversation held in a look. They were professionals in a world where mistakes cost more than just money.

The gleam of dawn began to caress the horizon as the outskirts of Everglade City loomed in the distance. As the first rays of sunlight punctured the still darkness, swarms of mosquitoes reluctantly retreated, leaving behind the emerald canopy that had shielded them throughout the night.

The close call with the county sheriff's patrol who followed them for several miles before turning off into the glades, was a stark reminder of the fine line they were treading. Sumner felt a surge of adrenaline, the kind that came not from danger but from the threat of it.

In the car, the atmosphere tensed perceptibly after they passed the patrol car. Even the air seemed to constrict, heavy with the swamp's musk and the sharp tang of human alertness. Fidel's hands, though steady on the wheel, betrayed the coiled readiness of a predator, every sense sharpened, not by fear, but respect for the potential havoc a single misstep could wreak.

"You think they'll be more patrols?" Portishead asked, the rearview mirror reflecting his piercing gaze as he watched the sheriff's car shrink into the distance.

Sumner's gaze was steely, and his voice held a chilling edge as he spoke. "Maybe," he conceded, his thoughts racing through the myriad of scenarios that lay ahead. "If they pull us over, they won't live to regret it. With that launcher in the boot, it's not as if we're toting around a duck-shooting shotgun. It's a one-way ticket to a cell."

Portishead, feeling the itch he always did before a job, flipped open a tobacco wallet, a worn case. From it, he produced a hand-rolled joint, the scent pungent and familiar. It was his ritual; one he didn't break even as the stakes were as high as they'd ever been.

With a flick of his lighter, he inhaled deeply, the smoke clouding the interior of the car.

"No smoking," Fidel grunted, his first words in hours. His disapproval was palpable, his belief in clarity of mind before a job unyielding.

"Relax," Portishead exhaled the word in a smoky whisper, his poise not changing despite the rebuke. "It's medicinal."

Sumner didn't intervene. He knew men like Portishead had their quirks, especially before a dangerous operation. If the hitman needed this to steady his nerves or sharpen his focus, Sumner wasn't about to object. They were, after all, mere fifteen minutes from a confrontation that would end in death.

The bite-sized white chapel stood proudly, edged by large palms. Its bells rang out eight times, announcing the hour to residents and visitors alike. As the sound floated away on the wind, Marc Portishead parked the Buick behind a small garage, out of view from the main road in Everglade City. They were less than 100 yards from their intended targets and had a little time before taking action. Portishead was always cheery, in stark contrast to Sumner, who had failed to raise a smile in years.

"Every time I do wet work, I get a new tattoo; the problem is, I'm running out of skin," Portishead began the small talk to pass the time.

"Fascinating. These bloody bugs are in a feeding frenzy," Sumner replied, slapping the back of his neck in annoyance at a long-gone bloodsucker.

"I'm going to get outlines of an arc etched on the back of my neck. Each time I finish a job -"

Sumner opened his eyes and cut Portishead off mid-sentence, outlining his plan of attack. "Retrieve your weapons from the backpacks. Fidel, you take the rear of the building, Portishead the front, and I'll take the south side. Keep your faces covered, as there are two CCTV cameras outside the MIDAS building."

Sumner's meticulous planning ensured that every detail was taken into account. The weapons were discreetly hidden within three innocuous-looking backpacks. To any onlooker, they appeared as any other bag carried by tourists, which was particularly advantageous in Everglade City. This place teemed with thrill-seekers, each eager for an exhilarating airboat ride across the marshy waters, making them blend in seamlessly.

They leaned casually against a garage's faded brickwork, a little way down from the office, but in clear sight. To anyone passing by, they were just three tourists perhaps waiting for their next adventure or taking a rest from the increasing humidity.

However, Portishead, the most experienced of the trio, took extra precautions. His seasoned instincts made him choose a smaller, handheld bag for the grenade launcher; the Glock semi-automatic he securely tucked into his waistband. His casual attire and the deceptive bag did well to hide the potent weapon, ready to be deployed at a moment's notice.

With an almost imperceptible narrowing of his eyes, Sumner watched Cheryl's every move. There was something about her—a confidence, a purpose—that was hard to miss. As she neared the entrance, the bulky figure who unlocked the door caught Sumner's attention. The way he moved, the economy of motion, the alertness in his eyes—this was a man who had seen his fair share of action.

As someone who left no stone unturned when it came to safety, Cutler was meticulous. It was no surprise that he had brought on board a former Marine, a local named Colin Falser, to manage the security for the office and to be Cheryl's personal shadow on assignments. Falser had served tours in Iraq and Afghanistan, built like a tank, and loyal to a fault.

Every time Cutler and Tuck would leave for a mission, Falser would be a step behind, his watchful eyes scanning the environment. They were an odd pair to any outsider—the sophisticated and sharp businessperson and the gruff, stoic Marine. But those in the know understood that it was Falser' experience and unwavering commitment to duty that made him the perfect guardian for Cheryl.

Sumner discreetly pulled out his phone, scrolling through a series of photographs with practiced ease. There she was, unmistakable even in the candid shots—Cheryl, photographed at a recent gala with key figures from MIDAS.

The trio of assassins waited for five minutes before making their approach, pulling their scarves up around their faces. Just as Sumner had instructed, Fidel went to the rear of the building, Portishead waited at the front, and Sumner positioned himself on the south corner, watching as the interior window blinds cracked open.

Falser immediately noticed the three men stationed around the building as she entered the first-floor office. The four television screens on her inner wall provided a 360-degree view of the structure. Observing the men, he saw that they appeared to be watching their office. The tattoo-covered man to the south held what seemed to be a grenade launcher. He called out a warning to Cheryl, who was in the process of opening the blinds when the warning rang out.

Sumner aimed the Howa type 89 assault rifle with the Japanese 06 rifle grenade attachment. The final sound was the noise of an explosion and the window shattering as Portishead opened fire with the automatic. Falser and Cheryl, in different rooms, both hit the floor. Fidel fired warning shots toward two onlookers who had been alerted by the noise, causing them to run in the opposite direction as fast as they could.

Falser's instincts kicked into overdrive, his adrenaline pumping as he dashed into Cheryl's office. With a firm grip, he pulled her out, forcefully pressing her against a corridor firewall, shielding her with his body. Each heartbeat resonated with the fear of the unknown danger that lurked around.

Ascending to the second floor, Falser hoped to gain a vantage point over the attackers. The everglades heat betrayed him, the swipe lock remained an unyielding barrier. Cursing under his breath, he realized his pass was in the jacket he'd discarded downstairs, a victim to the overwhelming humidity. As he tried to make his next move, the devastating force of a grenade explosion knocked him off his feet. Vision blurring, ears ringing, he registered two more heart-stopping blasts before an eerie silence ensued, broken only by a haunting crackle.

Outside, the drama continued. Portishead, cold and calculated, hurled another grenade into the SUV parked perilously close to the building's foundational stilts. The vehicle erupted into flames, threatening the entire structure's integrity. Without missing a beat,

Sumner, Portishead, and Fidel sprinted to their getaway car. The engine roared to life, tyres screeching against the tarmac. In the dance of the fiery reflections, Sumner's eyes caught the menacing inferno they left behind—a grim affirmation to their ruthlessness.

In the heart of Everglade City, a place renowned for its tranquil wetlands and majestic egrets, an unspeakable horror unfolded. The MIDAS offices, once a shining example of modern architecture, stood tall with three stories of pristine glass and sleek steel. Now, it bore the scars of devastation.

The initial smouldering of the edifice served as a deceptive calm before the storm. As the fire protection systems roared to life, torrents of water rained down, hissing into steam upon meeting the relentless flames. But just when it seemed the worst was over, a series of violent explosions ripped through the structure, magnifying the catastrophe tenfold. Offices that once housed desks and computers were obliterated. The reception area was now a haunting wasteland of debris. The once-clear panoramic windows were shattered into a million pieces, allowing the thick, ominous smoke to escape and cast a dark shadow over the serene landscape.

Yet amidst the chaos, a beacon of hope remained. By some miracle, the explosions had spared the server farm housed within the building.

As the city's skyline faded behind them, the trio thundered down the highway, each heartbeat mirroring the rhythm of the roaring engine. Portishead white-knuckled, clutched the steering wheel, every ounce of his focus intent on pushing the car beyond its limits. The powerful hum of the engine reverberated, and the gas pedal felt the weight of desperation.

Alligator Alley stretched out before them, seemingly endless, but just as they began to believe they might make a clean escape, Portishead's sharp eyes caught a lurking danger in their rear-view mirror. The ominous silhouette of a patrol car was unmistakable. News of the turmoil at MIDAS they thought had clearly reached law enforcement faster than they had anticipated. A whisper of panic set in.

Sheriff John Roach, a seasoned officer with instincts honed by years on the force, immediately sensed something amiss. Without a second's hesitation, he switched on his siren and flashing lights, declaring his intent. With a masterful swiftness that spoke of countless high-speed chases under his belt, he spun his patrol car around in a dizzying 180-degree arc, now hot on their tail. The chase was on. Blue and red lights flashed ominously in Sumner's rear-view mirror.

Falser regained enough composure to get back to Cheryl. He kept low to the ground, the building engulfed in flames and smoke. He coughed involuntarily, as the fumes invaded his lungs, knowing that the gases were more likely to kill him than the fire that was spreading up the walls of the building. His instincts told him to go left, toward the draft coming in through the broken window, hoping he could navigate the fire. He turned right on his hands and knees and crawled toward where he had left Cheryl. She was there, prone and unconscious. Falser dragged her through the corridor with flames on either side of them. Once inside the room with the smashed window, Falser grabbed hold of Cheryl's blouse to get leverage to lift her out of the window and onto the balcony, which had remained untouched by the fire until now. Without warning, a hot piece of material from the window blinds landed on Falser's right leg, and his trousers immediately burst into flames.

On fire, Falser pushed Cheryl out and followed her through the window and onto the balcony. He tore off his shirt and did his best to smother the flames that engulfed his right leg and hip. Falser was in agony, and he wasn't sure if the burns were life-threatening, but he knew they were life changing.

Sheriff John Roach, born and raised in the Everglades, was an ex- green beret, married to a local Indian girl from the Seminole tribe. Together, they had been blessed with three children. Roach lived and breathed his family and his extended family and was a cherished adoptee among the Seminole. Roach was fair, tough, and always polite. Sheriff Roach had never fired a shot in the ten years he had been in office; most of his work involved sorting out domestic abuse cases and issuing tickets to alligator hunters, and drivers who treated Alligator Alley like a Grand Prix racetrack.

Reports of the fire in Everglades City crackled through his radio as he followed closely behind the black Buick.

With one hand gripping the steering wheel, Sheriff Roach unclipped his holster and retrieved his .38 revolver, flicking the safety to the 'off' position. Using his elbow, he activated the button on the door to lower the window, which swiftly retracted into the door housing. His foot pressed firmly on the accelerator, closing the gap on the Buick. Sheriff Roach understood that his options were limited; he needed to halt the speeding vehicle.

Balancing the patrol car with his right hand on the wheel and his gun in his left, he rested his forearm on the open window, aiming through the windshield. Roach slightly adjusted his shooting hand, targeting the Buick's tyres. He hesitated for a brief moment, waiting for the Humvee he had just spotted to pass them on the opposite side of the highway. Then, in rapid succession, he fired off two rounds. The first lodged in the wheel arch, and the second struck the rubber, causing the tyre to disintegrate rapidly due to rapid depressurization and the car's speed.

The patrol car's brakes responded immediately to the pressure, coming to a stop just short of the skidding Buick, which had turned at a right angle about ten yards ahead. The patrol car's front windshield shattered abruptly as a bullet whizzed past the sheriff's left ear. Sheriff Roach instinctively swung open the driver's door. Bullets pounded into the driver's side door, showering him with glass shards as the window screen exploded inward. His front nearside tyre was the next casualty as bullets pierced it during the onslaught. The sheriff cautiously lifted his head and fired two more rounds in the general direction of the car.

Sumner and Fidel quickly exited the Buick and took cover behind the tailgate and bonnet, intending to flank the sheriff once he ran out of ammunition and had to reload. Marc Portishead remained in the front seat of the Buick, providing covering fire. He knew that with just two more bullets, the sheriff would need to replace his magazine.

Fidel was s city-dweller, with little experience. Portishead and Sumner had travelled the world and wouldn't make the mistake Fidel was about to. He shouted warnings, but the relentless gunfire drowned them out. Fidel positioned himself near the bonnet and moved to flank the patrol car on the left-hand side, intending to present the sheriff with a target. He spotted what appeared to be a drainage ditch and stepped down onto the bank as he advanced. Fidel was about to learn the harsh reality of why the highway was called Alligator Alley. In the blink of an eye, a fourteen-foot behemoth lunged from the foot of water in the ditch, clamping its massive jaws around Fidel's chest and dragging him into the channel with agonized screams. The reptile twisted and writhed, crushing and drowning Fidel simultaneously. With the body held between its fangs, the alligator slithered away, saving the remains for a later, more fetid meal.

Sumner quickly moved to the right, flanking the patrol car. If Sheriff Roach hadn't been momentarily distracted by the screams, he might have spotted Sumner in time. As Roach spun on his heels, sensing someone behind him, a bullet pierced his side, tearing through his left lung. He dropped his weapon immediately, slumping against the car as he coughed up frothy, crimson blood. Meanwhile, Sumner watched over him, his presence cold and calculating.

Sumner kicked the sheriff's gun into the ditch while taking out a Marlborough from a pack. He passed a cigarette to Portishead, who had joined him. Portishead declined, preferring his reefer. Sumner enjoyed the nicotine hit, while Portishead indulged in the marijuana, both men silently witnessing the life slipping away from Sheriff Roach.

The twisted metal and shattered glass painted a grim picture on the highway—the aftermath of a chase gone wrong. Both the Buick and the patrol car were rendered useless hunks of metal. The distant wail of sirens served as a stark reminder to Sumner: time was not on their side.

Desperation heightened his senses. Every second mattered. He swept his gaze over the vicinity, hoping to spot a potential getaway vehicle, but luck wasn't with them—the area was barren of any means of escape.

Portishead, his face shadowed with grim determination, leaned over to the incapacitated Sheriff Roach. In a gesture dripping with dark irony, he placed a cannabis joint between the lawman's lips, lighting the end, letting the acrid smoke coil upwards. The surreal moment hung in the air; a heavy silence punctuated only by the approaching sirens. Then, with cold detachment, Portishead delivered a point-blank shot, sealing the sheriff's fate.

"We have to get going. Follow me, Sumner," Portishead urged, beginning to trot into the reeds on the other side of the highway. In seconds, they had vanished into the swamp, wading through the shallow, tan-stained waters, weapons at the ready, alert for both human threats and reptiles.

The Humvee that had passed the patrol car minutes before navigated a slight bend on Alligator Alley, unaware of the encounter to follow. The commotion behind him remained out of sight for the driver. If the bend in the road hadn't been precisely where it was, Sheriff Roach might still have been alive. The man behind the wheel was Philip Cortez, who had flown in from Spain on Cutler's orders. Cortez was a MIDAS operative but had taken a six-month sabbatical after marrying the Italian beauty he had met through an internet website the previous year.

Cortez had returned from Madrid after a conversation with Cutler, the previous day, charged with providing extra safety of Cheryl and Esme. Fabienne had filled in the gaps, and Cortez understood that there was a security risk to MIDAS. Arriving at the scene of the raging fire, Cortez reached the scene at the same time as the ambulance. He had seen combat and witnessed his fair share of injuries, but Colin Falser's condition was among the worst he had ever encountered. Falser's legs were all but gone, replaced by blackened, gnarled, scorched sinew and bone. Cortez doubted the man's chances of survival.

Cortez swiftly jogged around the burning building, his initial thought that it was a lifeless body proved incorrect as he discovered Cheryl, who was gradually regaining consciousness. Worried about the structure's potential collapse, he moved her another twenty feet away from the engulfed building. As Cheryl slowly came to her senses, the wailing sirens of the fire brigade filled the air. Cheryl's voice was croaky but audible.

"Cortez, what are you doing here?" Cheryl rasped.

Cortez leaned in close, speaking into Cheryl's ear, "Cutler phoned me, thought you needed a bit of protection. Seems he was right."

Cheryl mouthed, "Esme, get Esme, make sure she's safe," just as the police arrived. Cortez communicated with an officer who promptly dispatched a colleague to retrieve Cheryl's daughter from the local school and ensure her safety. Cheryl refused to get into the ambulance until she knew Esme was secure, a confirmation that came fifteen minutes later.

"Did you see them?" Cortez asked Cheryl, and she mouthed, "Even though they wore masks I could see the color tones of their arms. Heavily tattooed, white, another white male, and I think a Hispanic."

Once Cortez was convinced that Cheryl would have continuous police protection in the hospital, he drove the Humvee back along Alligator Alley to where Sheriff Roach's body remained. He parked a short distance from the shooting scene out of respect for the fallen sheriff, whose lifeless form still sat upright against the patrol car. Three local patrol cars and two Miami-Dade patrol cars were present at the scene.

Had an officer been shot in the city, every patrol car and law enforcement officer within a 50-block radius would have rushed to the scene. As it was in the Everglades, three cars amounted to a full contingent.

Cortez approached a young officer who appeared detached from the group and visibly upset.

"Heard they killed the sheriff," Cortez said, displaying his MIDAS credentials.

The officer bowed his head briefly. "Yes, shot him through the lung and finished him off with one to the head. He was a good man, like a father to us all in the department."

"The men responsible for killing the sheriff also bombed our offices. One of ours has extensive burns. Where are the bastards now?" Cortez enquired in Spanglish.

"We recovered one of the perps, or at least what's left of him, from the drainage ditch. Seems like a gator got him. They're searching the ditches now for it, planning to euthanize it and recover the rest of the bastard. I hope the gator's moved on, done us a service as far as I know."

"What's your name?" Cortez asked.

"Jim Mason."

"You gonna be okay, amigo?" Cortez added.

"We believe there are two more perpetrators out there. They had to withdraw the tracking dogs, lost one already to the gators. The Miami-Dade police have a helicopter with an infrared camera searching for heat signals, but it's a massive area," Officer Mason explained. "If these guys know what they're doing, they can hide and mask the heat signatures in a dozen different ways. These city cops don't know the Everglades like we do, and they have us patrolling the highway instead of letting us track them. Shitty office politics, we lost a friend and colleague."

"Do me a favour, if they get sight of them or catch them, let me know," Cortez requested as he handed Jim a contact card.

"If you want to find him, you should go see Bull—not his birth name, but the only one he goes by. He's Seminole; his sister is, I mean, was married to the sheriff," Jim replied.

"How can I find him, Jim?"

"He's the one standing over there, squatting alongside the body of the sheriff. Locals have warned the Miami cops opposite that it would be a mistake to try and remove him until he finishes his incantations."

"Gracias, Jim."

"One thing, if you use Bull to find the killers of his brother-in-law, they won't be coming out of the Glades alive."

"Shit happens," Cortez replied.

Cortez waited for 35 minutes until Bull concluded his farewells and moved to the ditch where the alligator had pounced on Fidel. Cortez scrutinized the Seminole Indian, his experienced eye searching for prison tattoos, but he found none on the well-developed exposed forearms or around the neck. Considering he ran an airboat company; he was no executive type; the muscle definition spoke of a man who had known hard manual labour. Bull's hair was black and tied in a ponytail that exposed his entire face, dominated by a large hawk nose. As he stood to his full height, Cortez assessed him at six feet three, every inch an alpha male.

"I'm sorry about the sheriff, I know you were family," Cortez began.

"You a cop?" Bull asked.

"No, I work for MIDAS. They firebombed our headquarters before the sheriff caught up to them."

"I heard about the fire. Nothing much happens here; a fire and a killing in one day had to be connected. Heard it was the MIDAS building, are Cheryl and her kid okay?"

"Cheryl suffered smoke inhalation; she's gone to the hospital. Esme was in school, thankfully. A security man didn't get off so lightly, better off dead by the looks of him."

"Shame Tuck is away; he'd be in there pointing into the Everglades, tracking those killers down."

"Heard you were a good tracker. Want to put some of those skills your ancestors handed down to you, Bull?"

"Damn right. My sister and the kids will be distraught; I'll need to see them before I head off."

"So you are going after them?"

"Those city boys aren't going to find them anytime soon," Bull replied.

"I want to go with you, amigo."

"When I find them, it won't be to arrest them."

"You have to do what you have to do, Bull. I am not going to lose sleep over a couple of hitmen meeting their maker. I just need to know who put them up to it. Find them, let me ask a few questions, then I am gone and never there, that's a promise Bull."

"I know Tuck and Cutler. If what you tell me pans out and they trust you, why not?"

"The three men are probably hired help—hitmen. If that's the case, I need to know who hired them. If I don't, the real killer of your brother-in-law will be drinking margaritas and enjoying the local attractions while you are burying the sheriff, Bull."

"I find them, you ask your questions, and then you leave. I have your word on that?" Bull's voice was firm.

"You have my word," Cortez promised.

"You break your word, and you will have the whole Seminole tribe out for your blood, you understand that?"

"I don't break my word."

"Give me one of your cards to check you out. If everything is okay, meet me in two hours at the bend in the river two miles west. Don't be late, or I will be gone."

"I'll be there."

Cortez, already feeling the weight of the journey, glanced at the dense vegetation ahead. The swamp looked impenetrable, a sea of green broken only by dark, still waters and occasional pockets of mud.

Two hours later they met at the river's bend. "Cover yourself in deet or the mosquitoes will eat you alive in there," Bull warned, breaking the seal of a repellent canister and tossing one to Cortez.

The sun hung low, casting long shadows He vigorously applied the repellent, making sure no patch of exposed skin went untreated. Bull did the same, the methodical nature of his application showing a man well acquainted with the swamp's perils.

As they prepared to delve deeper into the swamp, Cortez couldn't help but think that the mosquitoes might be the least of their worries. The buzzing already growing louder around them. over the marshy terrain. The sounds of the swamp echoed around them, a cacophony of croaking frogs, chirping crickets, and the occasional splash of unseen creatures in the murky waters.

Cortez's eyes, red-rimmed and heavy, scanned the surroundings with a focused intensity that belied his exhaustion. Seventeen hours awake, coupled with the mental weight of jet lag, had pushed him to the brink of his physical limits. But he was determined, drawing on reserves of strength he didn't know he had.

The swamp buggy had been a godsend for the initial leg of their pursuit. Its large tyres and powerful engine made short work of the wet, uneven terrain. But now, three miles in, the terrain became trickier, a maze of waterways and dense underbrush.

Bull, ever the expert tracker, jumped off the buggy and began examining the ground. Mud squelched under his boots as he bent low, eyes squinting as he deciphered the subtle signs left behind by their quarry.

"These guys are smart," Bull muttered, running a hand through his grizzled beard. "They've tried to mask their trail, but they've made a mistake here." He pointed to a faint footprint, half submerged in the swampy water, and a snapped twig not far from it.

Cortez moved closer, leaning down to get a better look. "They have four hours on us?"

Bull straightened up, scanning the horizon. "Doesn't matter if they did," he replied, determination evident in his voice. "They won't get far. Not from us."

With renewed vigour, Cortez nodded in agreement. Fatigue be damned, they had killers to track.

The urgency in Bull's voice was palpable. As the dust from the recently vacated scene swirled around them, the two men began piecing together the clues left behind. "They went this way," Bull declared confidently, pointing towards ain indistinct set of tracks leading away from the area.

Cortez studied the tracks and his map, his eyebrows knitting together in concentration. "Looks like they are heading towards the Rangers station," he surmised, gauging the direction.

Bull, ever the sharp observer, added, "Seven miles away from the ranger's station. Whoever's leading their escape knows the terrain well." He glanced at the nearby swamp buggy; its wheels mired in a patch unsuitable for travel. "Can't take the buggy that way, so it looks like we're on foot."

Cortez, always one step ahead, suddenly pointed to another set of faint tracks veering in a different direction. "Tracks going the other direction," he noted, his voice laden with suspicion. "Did they loop back?"

Bull chuckled, a hint of admiration in his eyes. "Old soldiers' trick. They're trying to double back and throw us off their scent." His gaze hardened, determination evident. "But not good enough to fool me."

Cortez nodded; respect evident in his eyes. "Lead the way," he urged.

"Let's go" Bull commanded, setting off at a brisk pace, Cortez right on his heels. The hunt was on, and neither of them intended to let their prey escape.

"Don't worry, I can keep up, amigo," Cortez assured him.

"Mangroves, swamps, hope you can," Bull replied, pulling a Remington 870 shotgun and a pack of cartridges from the vehicle.

"Remington 870, typically police issue," Cortez observed.

"The sheriff sure as hell doesn't need it anymore, just ask my sister."

It was a hard three hour forced trek to get there. On land, Bull could sniff out a carcass from over a mile away; in the Everglades, it was a little over 1,500 yards. Bull suddenly stopped, pulling Cortez close and gesturing for silence. He whispered into Cortez's ear, "The ranger's lodge is just a few minutes that way; they are or have been here. I can smell coffee and a human corpse. We go slow and we go quietly."

Bull took the lead, Cortez following closely behind. Bull's night vision was at its limit. The faint sound of an airboat engine starting up reached their ears, and then it roared to life. Bull stood up and moved toward the ranger's hut.

Cortez's face contorted with frustration. Even with the strong application of deet, it seemed as though the mosquitoes of the Everglades had evolved an insatiable hunger, unhindered by the repellent.

"Ah, shit," Cortez whispered, scratching the irritated patches on his skin. "Fucking mosquitoes seem to have gotten a taste for the deet."

Seeing Cortez's discomfort, Bull unzipped his backpack with a knowing smirk, revealing his knowledge of the land. He pulled out a cluster of American Beautyberry leaves, their vibrant magenta berries glowing in the dimming light. He crushed the leaves, releasing their natural oils, and handed them to Cortez.

"Rub these on your skin," Bull instructed. "Nature has its remedies. This plant has been keeping bugs at bay long before modern repellents."

As Cortez gratefully applied the crushed leaves, Bull's sharp gaze darted to the water's edge, catching a glimpse of disturbed water and fresh tracks. "They're gone," he declared, his voice filled with a mix of annoyance and admiration. "Took the airboat."

The low hum of an engine faded in the distance, merging with the symphony of swamp sounds. The chase had just taken a new twist, and they were already a step behind.

"Don't worry, these rangers always have a backup," Bull assured him.

"Will we be able to catch them?" Cortez asked, feeling a bit out of his comfort zone as jungle warfare wasn't on his resume.

Inside the ranger's hut, they found the dead ranger on the porch, his head crushed. A bloodied log lay nearby.

"They didn't want to use their weapons in case the noise travelled," Cortez noted.

Cortez's eyes widened, following Bull's gesture towards the overturned cup on the table. A dark stain marred the rough wooden surface where the liquid had spilled, steam still rising faintly. Beside it lay the limp form of the ranger, his uniform stained and face pale.

"It's fresh," Cortez murmured, touching the side of another cup, feeling the residual warmth. The haunting image of their adversaries calmly sipping hot coffee while a life ebbed away next to them sent a chill down his spine.

"Cold sons of bitches even had hot coffee over his body," Bull said, his voice dripping with a mix of disgust and grudging respect for their enemy's audacity.

As Bull moved to inspect the key cabinet, it was evident that the place had been hastily rummaged through. The small hooks, once orderly with labelled keys, now lay bare. Only a few scattered keys remained.

"They've taken what they needed," Bull mused, fingers brushing over the empty hooks, attempting to decipher which keys were missing. "The boat, of course, but there's more. Something else they're after."

"Wait, show me the keys you're looking for, and I'll get them. Remember, we were never here," Cortez said, donning a pair of latex gloves from his backpack.

Bull pointed to a specific set of keys on the bottom row, and Cortez retrieved them. He handed the keys to Bull and wiped down the door handles and their footprints on their way out, making sure not to step in the blood pool. Bull followed suit.

Bull walked to the edge of a small tributary and found the two-seater airboat tied to a post in the ground.

"They picked the wrong airboat," Bull declared. "The noise we heard from the airboat was from an old one, probably their backup. This boat has carbon composite fans, newer, faster, and more agile than theirs. I also know several shortcuts to where they're going that aren't on Google Earth. We can catch them with time to spare."

Cortez felt a sense of unease as Bull, instead of getting on the airboat, returned to the ranger's cabin. Several minutes later, Bull emerged with a machete in hand.

"To cut through the mangroves," Bull explained.

Bull revved the engine, trimming the blades, and the airboat roared to life. Cortez, in search of a seat belt, was met with a wide grin from Bull, indicating that such safety measures didn't exist on this vessel.

The airboat followed the waterway for several miles to the east before Cortez broke the silence. "Which direction do you think they're heading, Bull?"

"Our boys will know the police have checkpoints along Alligator Alley and Tamiami Trail, so they won't be going north toward Big Cypress Reserve or west to Naples. Rangers always keep a spare jerry can of fuel on their boats, so my guess would be east, toward Homestead, on the edge of the Glades. From there, they can pick up Highway 1 or 95, hijack a car, and be in Miami in no time. If they have a well-thought-out escape plan, there's a small airport at Homestead. Either way, if they make it there, you won't be finding them anytime soon."

"Homestead it is," Cortez agreed as Bull adjusted the airboat's course, veering away from the waterway and skimming over the swampland. They continued in silence for an hour before Bull cut the engine and stood up.

"I hear their boat," Bull said, slowly turning 180 degrees and settling on a direction slightly off-centre. "How can you be sure it's theirs, Bull?" Cortez asked.

"Nothing around here for the tourists and no moonshine stills," Bull replied. "It's got to be them." He restarted the airboat, adjusting their course. "They're using a compass and staying to the left of the waterway. They don't know the terrain, and they'll struggle in the mangrove swamps. We should have enough time to catch them."

Over the next 30 minutes, the sound of the fleeing airboat blades grew louder until it overtook the fans on Bull's airboat. Bull kept parallel to them, using the mangrove trees for cover. Suddenly, Bull swerved the boat through a gap in the mangroves and emerged just twenty feet behind the fugitives. For a few seconds, Portishead and Sumner were oblivious to the airboat trailing them. Portishead was controlling the airboat, and Sumner, the passenger, spotted the craft behind them. He nudged Portishead with his elbow and gestured backward.

Bull veered the craft left just as the first bullet whizzed by. He continued to the left, and the next shot pinged off the composite blade harmlessly, behind Cortez's head. Bull then moved the boat further left, taking out the branches of a mangrove tree. Another round missed its target. Cortez had managed to retrieve his weapon from its holster, but the collision with the tree had jolted him, causing the gun to slip from his hand and plunge into the swamp.

With one hand on the controls and the other reaching for the machete by his chair, Bull elicited an incredulous look from

Cortez. "You'll never hit him with that from here; there's a massive fan in the way!"

"Exactly," Bull replied. He let go of the control, swiftly stood up, and launched the machete. The blade soared straight and true, not deviating an inch over the fifteen-foot span between the two airboats. The impact was immediate, as the blade jammed the metal blades, filling the air with the sound of metal on metal. The fleeing airboat lost all thrust and control, wobbling from side to side while still moving forward, using the last of its momentum. Suddenly, the craft flipped right and spun several times.

Sumner and Portishead were violently ejected from the tumbling airboat during its chaotic flips. Portishead managed to resurface from the murky, tannic, acid-stained water first, his hand still clutching the gun, followed by his head and shoulders. Bull leaped out of the boat with lightning speed, mid-air delivering a powerful kick that sent Sumner's pistol flying into the distance.

Cortez leapt ashore from the boat with a primal intensity, his eyes darting like a predator, searching the eerie surroundings for any lurking danger. At the same moment, Sumner, drenched in muck and swamp water, clawed his way out of the treacherous quagmire, his nerves on edge, desperately trying to regain his composure. His trembling hands fumbled as he extracted a slick, concealed Glock 43 from his soaked jacket. He spun around, panic mounting, scanning the ominous shadows for any sign of impending threat.

But Cortez, with his preternatural reflexes, moved like a warrior of doom. He snatched Sumner's gun hand with a vice-like grip, his fingers crushing Sumner's hope. A brutal, bone-crushing elbow strike followed, sending searing pain through Sumner's skull as his left orbital bone shattered like glass. Sumner staggered backward, his world spinning, his fingers feeling as brittle as twigs. Cortez wrestled the Glock 43 from his grip with ruthless efficiency, and the weapon disappeared into the unforgiving depths of the murky swamp waters, leaving Sumner utterly defenceless in the face of impending doom.

Sumner retaliated with an overhand left hook, which Cortez anticipated, tilting his head downward to absorb the blow. Despite this, the punch still packed a punch, stunning Cortez and fracturing Sumner's knuckles. Dazed but not defeated, Cortez pivoted his right elbow outward and upward, catching Sumner under the chin and sending him tumbling backward. Swiftly, Cortez produced a plastic tie restraint from his pocket and secured Sumner before he could fully emerge from the water, gasping for breath.

Portishead's fate took a darker turn. Cortez turned his attention to Bull, who stood motionless with his right leg slightly raised. Bull's boot pressed heavily upon Portishead's heavily tattooed right arm, which flailed weakly in the water. It was evident that Portishead would draw his last breath under Bull's relentless pressure. Cortez realized he wouldn't be able to question him any further.

Cortez turned toward Bull, "You never mentioned you needed to interrogate both of them. You've got your prisoner for now."

The narrow gap between Bull's and Cortez's seats on the airboat was no more than two feet wide. Bull carefully positioned Portishead's lifeless body at the front of the airboat and secured Sumner's restrained form beneath his feet. Bull expertly steered the airboat over to the overturned vessel, leaped out, and with all his might, flipped it upright. Retrieving a rope from the airboat locker, he secured the two crafts together. Satisfied with his work, Bull refuelled and steered them back west.

After 45 minutes of navigating through a tight waterway flanked by tall mangrove trees, Bull halted the boat, advanced, and tipped Portishead's lifeless form into the brown, tannic-stained waters.

A surprised Cortez shifted on his seat to observe the floating body. "Aren't you going to weigh it down?"

"Watch," Bull replied as two alligators emerged from the mangroves. "Alligator Hilton around here, want to stop and watch?"

Cortez stared at Bull and said, "I don't need any more haunting memories, thanks."

Twenty minutes later, Bull docked at the ranger station and secured both boats. He meticulously washed and wiped down the composite and metal surfaces with a cloth soaked in petrol. "Deal's a deal; he isn't getting out of here," Bull declared as Sumner began to struggle against his restraints.

Cortez turned his attention to Sumner and sternly enquired, "Who sent you?"

Sumner, defiant despite his dire circumstances, retorted, "Why should I tell you?"

"You're going to die today," Cortez said with a cold determination, "and the big Indian over there will make sure of that."

Cortez's voice was cold and unwavering as he confronted Sumner. "It can be quick and painless, or Geronimo can feed you bit by bit to the gators. Your choice?"

Sumner struggled to clear his throat before responding. "I am entitled to justice. You have to take me back; I am entitled to a fair trial."

"Tell me who put you up to the MIDAS bombing, and I will see what I can do," Cortez offered.

Bull, growing impatient, interjected, "That's not the deal."

"Shut up, Bull, and let me do my job," Cortez snapped.

Sumner sat up, his silence hanging heavy in the air as he contemplated his dire predicament. The imminent danger of the present weighed more on his mind than the consequences Conrad Ford might inflict. "My boss is Conrad Ford. He gives the orders; I just follow them. Now get me back to civilisation and away from Geronimo over there!"

Cortez nodded, acknowledging the information. "Thank you for your help," he said to Sumner. "He's all yours now, Bull, and I do want to witness what happens to this puta," Cortez added in Spanish, relying on the language for emphasis.

"Hey, hey, hey!" Sumner screamed through the gag as Cortez walked away.

Bull swiftly tied a rag around Sumner's mouth and hoisted him over his shoulder like a rag doll. "Back to the buggy, I have a nice surprise waiting for him there," he said, and Cortez followed closely as they navigated through the dense mangroves.

Bull placed Sumner on the ground about ten yards from the truck. "Climb back into the cab; you'll get a bird's eye view, and believe me, you don't want to be on the ground." Bull moved to the back of the vehicle, lifted the lid on a black container, and began to extract a massive snake, an African rock python. Sumner, now witnessing this horror, began to struggle, his muffled screams filling the air. He glanced up at Cortez, pleading with his eyes, but Cortez's resolve remained cold and unyielding.

"The Burmese pythons we've been finding around here can swallow a kid but can't swallow a man; it's the shoulders they can't cope with. This baby is my pet African rock python," Bull explained as he dragged the reptile from its enclosure. He then climbed back into the truck.

The rock python slithered up beside Sumner, its twenty-foot body poised and ready. It was covered in blotches with irregular stripes, and its triangular head bore a dark brown spearhead outlined in buffy yellow. The snake examined Sumner's wriggling form, coiling around him several times as he screamed into his gag. With a final, powerful squeeze, the serpent constricted, the gruesome sound of bones and sinews breaking audible to all present. Cortez watched as Sumner's eyes bulged and ultimately popped under the immense pressure.

"It's rare for one of these to kill a man, but a hungry snake and trussed bait is too much of a treat for Rocky," Bull remarked. The snake released Sumner's lifeless form, then extended its jaw, exposing numerous backward-curved teeth as it prepared to devour Portishead.

Cortez had seen enough. "I've seen enough, Bull; one can only take so much revenge at a time."

Bull nodded, his expression stoic. "Not a problem. You kept your word. Rocky won't be going anywhere for twenty-four hours after that feast, so I'll pick him up tomorrow." Bull paused before adding, "One more thing, that guy Conrad Ford, he was responsible for my brother-in-law's death. Can you keep that to yourself?"

Cortez nodded, understanding the gravity of the situation. "Bull, Conrad Ford runs a multi-million-dollar business, and he has security. If you think of going after him, it's not like picking up a couple of hitmen in your backyard; they'll kill you stone dead."

Bull's eyes gleamed with determination. "I'm not thinking of doing it alone. When Tuck, Cheryl's man, finds out he attacked her; he's going to track them down and kill them. I'm good, and from what I hear, he's better."

The two men shared a silent understanding of the impending storm that would descend upon those who had caused so much pain and chaos. Revenge was a relentless force, and it seemed that justice would find its own way, no matter how treacherous the path.

chapter fifteen
Showdown on the Open Sea

Kasim Asfour had dedicated a decade of his life to the murky tapestry of Al-Qaeda, ascending from an inconspicuous arms peddler to a linchpin in the group's formidable hierarchy. His last four years were consumed by the orchestration of a bold heist, a masterpiece of subterfuge and guile. As an undercover agent, his allegiance lay with a black operation faction tacitly endorsed by power players within the halls of Washington—a cabal that included a former commander-in-chief and the sitting vice president, not to mention a deputy director of the CIA who pulled strings from behind a veil of secrecy.

Asfour, with the cold precision of a seasoned chess player, had choreographed through the ranks of the terrorist cadre, adopting their creed and methods with chilling indifference. His rise was marked by calculated brutality, where not even the lives of his compatriots were spared. There was an unnerving absence of empathy within him, a sociopathic strain that rendered his conscience barren—a trait that made him the perfect impersonator of an Al-Qaeda operative, undeterred by the moral weight of his actions.

The Reef Explorer, a colossal vessel with over 2,000 passengers and 500 crew members, presented a daunting challenge. Attempting to control such a fully laden behemoth with a mere 20 men seemed impossible, even with their substantial firepower.

Asfour recognized that since the tragic events of the Twin Towers, people had come to associate terrorist attacks with a singular outcome: their own death. Faced with the sheer number of potential adversaries on board, both men and women would likely fight back, believing they had nothing left to lose. Asfour had meticulously studied the heroic resistance on "Flight 93" and understood how it had inspired countless individuals to take action.

Based on the information extracted from Cummings, Aziz had learned that approximately 700 passengers and 200 crew members would disembark in Limassol for excursions or planned days ashore. Most would return late in the afternoon via tender, leaving behind around 250 passengers and 200 crew members who remained on the ship. The catamaran, with its morning and afternoon bookings, would return at 12:30 pm, bringing back a manageable number of people who could easily be accommodated in the 400-seat theatre nestled in the ship's bow on decks four and five.

Including Aziz himself, there were sixteen combatants aboard the catamaran, with four additional specialists set to join them at the appropriate moment. Asfour's men were well-versed in the plan; the eight Africans had been unwittingly used as pawns, believing themselves to be critical players but never knowing when or where the true leaders would enter the game.

Aziz issued orders for all the men to discard their green coveralls, replacing them with colourful speedo swimming trunks. The visual illusion was crucial; they needed to appear as though they were simply returning happy passengers to the Reef Explorer. Awaale translated Aziz's instructions for his seven comrades who did not understand Arabic. Command and control were Aziz's specialties, and he efficiently organized his men into distinct combat units. There were five units in total, and Aziz himself led cell one, with Ali from Egypt as his second-in-command. Awaale, who required close oversight, was placed in Aziz's group, along with Abel, who hailed from the same district as Awaale. Their primary objective was to secure the bridge of the Reef Explorer, located forward on deck eight, in anticipation of the specialists from cell three.

Cell two, led by Imran, consisted of two Arabs and two Somalis, and their role was to safeguard the members of cell three, who were currently approaching the Reef Explorer's side in a second boat. Omar, a zealous fanatic, led cell four, driven by the belief that all non-believers should be eradicated from the face of the Earth. Their initial objectives were to secure the starboard access platform and release the trawler that had transported them to the Reef Explorer, allowing the second terrorist vessel to draw near. When cells four and five eventually boarded the ship, the plan was for them to move to the port side and secure the tender platforms on deck four, which serviced returning passengers. The meticulously orchestrated operation was about to unfold.

Once the outer vessel doors had been sealed, locking the security detail in, Kasim Asfour's detailed plan was set into motion. He had spent years painstakingly preparing for this audacious raid, and now it was time to execute it.

Cell three, the specialist unit, was too valuable to risk in the initial assault. Led by Mouhamed, a French-born Algerian with extensive maritime experience, this team included Abdul, a skilled

French engineer, Hussain, a Syrian communications expert, and Saddar, a Libyan navigator. Each of them had long ago abandoned their surnames to protect their families from the consequences of their actions. Their critical mission was to take control of the ship from the bridge and the engine room once those areas were secured.

Mouhamed, once a third mate on a container ship and quietly linked to revolutionary circles, faced a career-ending dispute over an ISIS flag found in his cabin by his French crewmates. For a year, he tried to find employment elsewhere but was blacklisted. When recruited, radicalization came swiftly, and he understood that this mission was likely a suicide mission.

Born with a French birth certificate that belied his true origins, Abdul's ancestry could be traced back to Algeria, a fact he wore like a badge of honour. His devotion to the cause ran deep, and he had honed the art of radicalization to a sinister precision. It was Abdul who had recruited Mouhamed, the French-born Algerian now on a collision course with destiny. For months, Abdul had meticulously chipped away at Mouhamed's doubts and reservations, moulding him into a devoted follower of their cause.

Hussain, an ex-Iraqi military officer who barely survived the Gulf Wars, had found himself in the ranks of Al-Qaeda after escaping the second Gulf War. He had served as the head of the Elite Guard communication network and was forced into a revolutionary role when a targeted bomb eliminated his comrades. His skills were essential for this operation.

Saddar's life had once been a tranquil one, marked by the quiet expertise of a ship pilot guiding vessels safely into the bustling port of Tripoli. He had found contentment in his routine, a sense of purpose in the precision of his navigation. But all that had been irrevocably shattered one fateful day when the roaring engines of French and British jets had filled the skies.

Their target was a building housing Gadhafi's elite forces, merely a few blocks away from Saddar's modest home. In the chaos of war, a stray missile had struck with merciless accuracy, obliterating his family—his wife and two young sons—leaving nothing but fragments too scant to bury. Saddar, at the tender age of twenty-eight, had been thrust into a vortex of grief and rage, his world torn asunder.

In the pressure cooker of his despair, Saddar had turned to the siren call of Al-Qaeda's twisted ideology. He had come to believe that Christians and Jews were bent on the destruction of Islam, a conviction that amplified his readiness to sacrifice his life for their malevolent cause. For Saddar, vengeance had become a consuming fire, and he fostered a fervent desire to exact retribution on Westerners, willing to spill his own blood to achieve it.

As the catamaran sliced through the moonlit waters, Aziz's voice carried over the waves, instructing Khalid, who manned the helm, "Cut the engines and let her drift for twenty minutes. If we don't return within the allocated time, it will set off alarm bells and raise suspicions." The tension aboard the vessel was noticeable, a sinister prelude to the impending chaos that would soon engulf the Reef Explorer.

Aziz moved with purpose among his team, each step calculated and deliberate. His eyes swept over the array of weapons and gear, ensuring that everything was in its rightful place. The tension was a coiled anticipation of the impending mission.

Addressing Khalid, who manned the helm with unwavering resolve, Aziz provided clear instructions, his voice tinged with a sense of urgency, "Khalid, start the engines and chart a course that avoids the tenders approaching from the port side. We'll make a wide arc, skirting around to the starboard side."

As the catamaran glided through the tranquil waters, Aziz couldn't help but acknowledge the accuracy of Cummings' information. He had been right—the tenders clustered on the port side of the Reef Explorer, awaiting their turn to dock. The port tender platform, teeming with sailors, security personnel, and an officer, stood poised for action. The bridge of the Reef Explorer loomed above, extending on both starboard and port sides, affording a vantage point for the ship's officers to oversee the intricate ballet of tenders and catamarans. The pieces of the puzzle were falling into place, and Aziz's mind was a whirlwind of calculated moves and potential obstacles.

"Put on the music, Khalid," Aziz ordered, a calculated move to maintain the illusion of a routine tender operation. He gave a wave to the crew stationed on the starboard side loading platform as they neared the staging area. The welcoming party on the starboard side was notably smaller compared to the bustling scene on the port platform, as the catamaran was the sole vessel offloading on that side that day. The two security officers hailed from India, exuding an air of competence and readiness. An additional pair of Philippine guards stood guard at the hull door, accessible via a series of steps leading down from the staging area.

Among the guards, Naveed, stationed closest to the waterline on the platform, was a seasoned veteran aboard the ship. Having spent nine months on the Reef Explorer, he was on the cusp of a well-deserved three-month break at home in Mumbai. Naveed was intimately familiar with this port, having witnessed Paccar and Romano depart and return with passengers on numerous occasions.

Something about the posture of the man at the catamaran's helm was amiss—it didn't align with the usual conduct of either Paccar or Guano. There was an unsettling discrepancy, something different, and Naveed couldn't shake the feeling that someone or something on that catamaran didn't quite fit the expected pattern. None of the three original crew members had beards, yet the man steering the catamaran did. Moreover, the guests weren't engaged in their usual dance, an anomaly that raised suspicion in Naveed's vigilant eyes.

The catamaran glided closer, a mere twenty yards from docking with the platform, when Naveed's urgent shout cut through the air, "That's not the crew!" His words reverberated through the ears of the security guards stationed above him. Aziz, too, heard the warning and responded swiftly; his right arm shot up in a signal, prompting his men to shed their inconspicuous towels, revealing the deadly arsenal beneath.

Naveed watched in horrified disbelief as the gunmen aboard the catamaran took aim at the two security guards positioned above him. The deafening racket of bullets striking steel and flesh echoed in the confined space, followed by an eerie silence that settled over the platform. The two security guards, caught in a devastating hail of bullets, were violently propelled backward by the sheer force of the volley.

"Don't move!" Aziz's commanding shout pierced the tension-laden atmosphere. He needed at least one of his men to safely disembark onto the staging area to secure the catamaran—a calculated risk. However, Naveed had other plans. With a quick and determined motion, he seized his transmitter, intending to relay the alarming breach back to the bridge.

Just as Naveed's finger hovered over the transmission switch, his world plunged into darkness.

As the lifeless forms of the fallen guards drifted alongside the catamaran, they bore witness to a bewildered sailor, who had been hidden from view. Desperately, he attempted to close the hull door in a frantic bid to thwart the raiders. However, the hastily executed manoeuvre, compounded by the failure to raise and store the access steps from the staging, proved futile. The door was obstructed by the protruding steps, rendering it impossible to secure. Khalid acted swiftly, discharging his weapon with deadly precision. The seaman's head erupted in a gruesome explosion, drenching the staging with a macabre mixture of brain matter and blood.

Aziz clumsily navigated the catamaran as close to the looming bulk of the Reef Explorer as the surging swell allowed. The small vessel bobbed uneasily on the restless waves. Khalid, a steely resolve in his eyes, awaited the opportune moment. He timed his jump to perfection, leaping from the catamaran just as a wave lifted it to nearly the same level as the platform.

However, the sudden elevation caught Khalid off guard, and he lost his footing as the staging platform rapidly ascended by two feet in a split-second. Panic gripped him as he desperately grasped at the platform's edge, teetering precariously on the brink of a deadly predicament. Khalid's drenched form was now perilously vulnerable, with the looming threat of being crushed between the unforgiving catamaran and the unyielding staging platform. In a race against time, he hauled himself onto the staging just as the catamaran collided with it once more, its relentless momentum unchecked by the rising tide.

With the immediate danger averted, Khalid's dripping and sodden form quickly sprang into action. Awaiting him were his fellow hijackers, the Arabs and the Somalis, all bearing backpacks laden with their sinister cargo. Time was of the essence. In the cramped quarters behind the hull door, they swiftly shed their swimming costumes, exchanging them for matching green tracksuits. The uniformity of their attire was not only a mark of camaraderie but also a calculated move to minimize the risk of friendly fire—a perilous phenomenon known in the theatre of war as 'blue on blue'. Aziz had no desire to explain such a concept to his Somali comrades in the heat of battle, especially when dressed in green.

With the transformation complete, Aziz severed the mooring rope that had tethered the catamaran to the staging. The vessel, now untethered and straining against the line, surged forward with newfound vigour, bumping and scraping along the unforgiving metal hull of the Reef Explorer before finally breaking free from its grasp. The die had been cast, and their audacious mission was now irrevocably set in motion.

The abrupt eruption of gunfire sent shockwaves through the officers stationed on the bridge of the Reef Explorer. Third Officer

Dan Williams, his vantage point providing a sweeping view of the ship, cast a quick glance to the port side. To his trained eye, everything appeared deceptively routine. Reporting back, he assured the others that no immediate threat was evident on that front.

Meanwhile, the second officer turned his gaze toward the starboard side, his heart pounding as he beheld the unfolding chaos. The catamaran, liberated from its moorings, careened perilously along the ship's bow. His eyes widened in alarm as he spotted two figures clad in green tracksuits—an incongruity amid the expected security officers—standing on the loading platform. Panic clenched his chest as he realized the gravity of the situation.

At this crucial juncture, the ship's captain was absent from the bridge, dealing with matters among the crew. It fell upon the first mate to take charge. He issued a terse command, and the second officer, gripping a deepening sense of dread, raced to the ship's transmitter.

"Pan pan, pan pan, pan pan," the first mate intoned gravely into the radio, his voice a steady thread of calm in the maelstrom. With each repeat, the urgency of the situation thrummed through the airwaves—a coded incantation of imminent peril. The words, a discreet herald of piracy or armed robbery, rippled out into the ether, an invisible beacon of their distress.

He swivelled, eyes locking with the second mate, his directive crisp and laden with silent gravity. "Initiate the SSAS, now." His words were a baton passed in a relay race against time.

With deft movements, the second mate complied, fingers accessing the console to unleash the silent alarm. The Ship Security Alert System, a silent sentinel, coursed into life, sending its silent scream to the ship's flag state. This digital whisper, undetected by the marauders aboard, was a lifeline cast into the vastness of the sea, carrying with it the vessel's identity, its precise coordinates, and the unspoken truth of their dire straits.

"Attention, Team Bravo, please report to the meeting room for the daily briefing," the first mate announced coolly over the ship's tannoy. His voice, practiced and composed, gave no hint of the underlying urgency.

Below deck, the words 'Team Bravo' set a carefully trained group of security personnel into immediate, silent action. The 'meeting room,' a predetermined code for their strategically placed security hub, awaited their presence on the starboard side—the heart of the current unease.

'Daily briefing'—these words, so innocuous to the untrained ear, were the agreed-upon signal for a security crisis, an assault on their sovereignty on the open waters. It was a discreet call to arms, a summons to confront the shadow of danger that had stealthily crept aboard.

With the urgent call relayed, the first mate turned his gaze to the ship's radio officer, urging swift action. "Transmit a Mayday to Cyprus coastguard, let them know we are under attack, then notify head office."

"Aye aye, sir," the radio officer responded, his fingers flying over the controls as he initiated the distress signal.

The Reef Explorer's security teams had rehearsed similar scenarios in the past, but never during passenger embarkation or disembarkation. This was uncharted territory, and the crew were faced with a perilous decision.

Stationed at the forward port staging area, Duty Officer Abilene Shaw wasted no time when confronted with the confusion that rippled through her colleagues. She immediately took charge, her voice ringing out above the clamour.

"Go, go!" Shaw barked at the security team, marshalling them into action. With several crew members at her side, she swiftly issued orders to halt the approaching tenders.

Meanwhile, her counterpart stationed at the port amidships staging area, though less experienced, responded as best he could. He directed two of the security staff to react to the alarm while the remainder stood by at their post. Acting on orders from the first mate, four security personnel, accompanied by a junior officer, sprinted down multiple flights of stairs, converging on the breach point along the starboard side.

Aziz, with a cunning that belied his weathered features, picked up on the tannoy message that was meant to be a call to arms—a warning without the shrill pitch of alarm that would have sung of danger. It was an invisible thread, one he followed with a predator's intuition.

As his men worked, blissfully unaware, Aziz's hands, steady and sure, passed out the tools of their treacherous trade: guns gleamed darkly against the stark light, magazines clicked into place, smoke bombs and hand grenades were distributed with a solemnity reserved for sacred rituals. The anxious and slightly bewildered breaths of the Somali men mingled with the salt air, a silent warning to the tension that clung to them like the ocean mist.

"Awaale, ensure the men know this is no drill. Immediate action, shoot on sight, no second thoughts. Take control by any means necessary. Is my command clear?" Aziz's voice, a low growl, was a soundwave of tension that left no room for doubt.

"I understand," Awaale responded, his voice slicing through the humid air, sharp and unyielding. "But remember, the security onboard, they're unarmed. There's no need for a bloodbath."

Aziz's lips tightened, a shadow passing over his hardened features. "Listen and listen well. You strike hard and fast. Hesitation can kill us," he shot back, a steel edge of command to his words.

Their exchange, terse and fraught with the gravity of their intent, hung between them Awaale had been briefed on the ship's assault and the careful allocation of his men into units alongside Aziz's forces. Aziz had conducted meticulous drills, displaying diagrams detailing the ship's layout, gleaned from the intelligence gathered through the intense interrogation of Gareth Cummings. Securing the Reef Explorer was Aziz's ultimate priority, and he had identified the closure of the hull doors, along with the neutralization of the security personnel guarding them, as the first critical step in achieving their objective.

Aziz, Awaale, and the rest of cell one surged toward the nearest corridor opening, ascending the internal stairs that would lead them to the bridge. Two junior officers, their faces etched with valiant resolve, attempted to impede their progress. However, their courage proved futile as Aziz, wielding his weapon in semi-automatic mode, swiftly extinguished their lives. The remnants of their obliterated heads painted a grisly tableau across the door to the bridge. Aziz carefully navigated the macabre scene, affixing a small parcel of explosive to the door. Taking cover, he initiated the explosive's detonation. The bridge security door, guarding the entrance to the ship's control centre, was blown open instantly.

Meanwhile, several decks below, Imran, at the helm of cell two, detected the approaching footsteps of the ship's security team, echoing ominously down the narrow corridor from both directions. Seven security personnel, three converging from the aft and a formidable four-man security detail advancing from the forward section, charged forward with a potent blend of adrenaline and steadfast bravery.

In perfect synchronization, the two teams of security personnel accelerated toward the intruders, arming themselves with knives and meat cleavers sourced from the ship's galley. Two of them wielded powder extinguishers, gripping them tightly as they entered the line of sight of the armed assailants. With resolute yet desperate intent, the two Philippine security officers activated the extinguishers, attempting to conceal themselves behind a billowing curtain of powder and CO_2. It was futile, an act of collective self-sacrifice as the brave officers battled guns with knives.

Imran and his second-in-command from cell two took up positions back-to-back with the two Somalis, forming a deadly barrier against the charging security teams. This configuration provided them with a clear view of the frenzied advance from both the forward and aft directions. The billowing cloud of extinguisher powder served as both a concealing shroud and a temporary curtain of confusion for the approaching security personnel. In this chaotic moment, the opposing sides unleashed a relentless hail of gunfire, bullets ricocheting wildly off the unforgiving metal bulkheads, and piercing through human bodies.

The two Arabs leading cell two had extensive experience in armed conflicts, their nerves steely and their reactions honed by countless confrontations. In contrast, the Somalis had never encountered such brutality, but they followed Imran's lead with unwavering determination. Their weapons barked in rapid succession, discharging more than 40 rounds per second. Projectiles tore through the opaque veil of extinguisher powder, seeking out their targets with deadly precision. They advanced relentlessly through the crimson tide that flowed toward them, every downed body punctuated by a finishing shot to the head, ensuring that the seven security personnel posed no further threat.

With cell two having efficiently completed their grim task, they retreated to the staging area. Their green overalls bore the gruesome remnants of bodily fluids and tissue from the brutal firefight. Imran's boots occasionally lost traction in the slick blood that now inundated the corridor. The team proceeded to secure the second trawler to the Reef Explorer while the other team stood vigilant, ready to repel any potential threats.

Meanwhile, the four members of cell three scrambled onto the staging within the bowels of the Reef Explorer, each carrying crates laden with equipment. They made repeated trips to unload the cargo from the fishing vessel, diligently working to release the boat from its moorings. As the trawler gracefully glided toward the stern of the ship, Imran issued commands for the two Somalis to retract the exterior stairwell and firmly seal the hull door, completing this crucial phase of their operation.

Khalid led cell five onto deck nine, directing them to split into two groups—one forward and one aft. The pool area sprawled in the open, exposed to the elements, with deck ten hovering above like a silent observer. A massive TV screen hung suspended between the two levels, featuring the ever-present image of Elton John, his music serenading both the terrorists and their unsuspecting hostages. Tragically, as resistance flared among a handful of passengers and crew, they found themselves caught in a brutal crossfire, their bodies torn apart by a deadly hail of bullets.

Deck ten offered a promenade that overlooked the swimming pool below, extending along both the port and starboard sides. It encompassed a more extensive seating area with a bar located slightly forward of the pool, as well as a compact stage where the ship's band had once entertained passengers. Khalid carefully positioned the two Somalis on the port side and his Arab comrade on the starboard side, effectively blanketing the entire area. Their mission was simple: maintain their position and execute anyone who dared defy their commands.

Meanwhile, two members of cell four hastened to the forward tender station, sprinting through the chaotic scene. With ruthless efficiency, they employed the butts of their semi-automatic weapons to forcefully push passengers backward. Tragically, the impact proved fatal for some of the elderly passengers, their frail skulls no match for the brutal force. Crew members, along with a twenty-seven-year-old Swiss female engineering officer, courageously confronted the assailants, imploring them to spare the innocent passengers. However, Omar, the unrelenting leader of the team, showed no mercy, eliminating both targets with point-blank shots. The narrow corridor echoed with the agonized cries of the living and the mournful wails of the dying, while the walls bore witness to the grotesque aftermath, drenched in blood and gore.

Aziz had warned them about the bustling gangway, teeming with passengers arriving and departing. However, Omar had descended into a murderous frenzy, urging his men to open fire indiscriminately on passengers and crew alike, forcibly propelling them backward toward the hull door and the staging area. The Somali warrior had faced gunfights in his homeland, but nothing could have prepared him for this one-sided massacre. Awaale, during their mission training, had emphasized pushing the passengers and crew toward the hull door, but there had been no mention of the slaughter they were now enacting.

"Shoot them, or I'll kill you!" Omar's menacing scream compelled the terrified Somali to comply, his fear for his own survival overpowering any sense of moral objection.

The orchestrated carnage within the access area leading to the hull door yielded the desired outcome, precisely as Aziz had anticipated. The surviving passengers stampeded in blind panic, some getting wedged in the narrow corridor. Men ruthlessly shoved aside women, and the elderly, children, and the infirm were trampled underfoot as chaos reigned.

The surge of passengers and security personnel drove them back through the hull door and onto a gangway that led to the staging platform. This gangway, constructed of metal railings, netting, and a corrugated metal floor for added grip, proved inadequate for the sudden force and weight. It creaked and groaned under the strain before finally twisting and breaking loose. Sixty crew members and passengers plummeted between the hull of the Reef Explorer and the staging platform, with many meeting their deaths upon impact as the heavy gangway crashed down upon them. Others were left stunned by the fall, drifting beneath the superstructure, while some managed to swim clear, only to return frantically searching for missing loved ones amidst the ensuing chaos.

A few fortunate passengers and a single crew member landed safely in the tender boat, having been at the far end of the gangway. Unfortunately, others weren't as lucky and fell into the sea, trapped between the tender boat and the staging platform. They were crushed as the waves slapped the tender boat back and forth, with no security guards in sight—these guards had already left to respond to the breach. At the rear of the surge, Abilene Shaw and three crew members found themselves on the staging platform.

Those passengers and crew who managed to survive the initial onslaught resorted to a desperate escape—jumping into the sea. Nine passengers stood on the loading platform, while one elderly man, reliant on a walking frame, faced a daunting predicament.

His frail gait resembled that of a snail, incapable of quickening its pace even when his life hung in the balance—a life that now depended on swift action.

"Throw him over the side," Omar's command sliced through the air like a guillotine.

The Somali hesitated briefly, his internal conflict tangible. With a reluctant resolve, he hurled the elderly man with all his might in a desperate attempt to bridge the gap between the Reef Explorer and the staging area. The unfortunate man's skull met the unyielding side of the staging, leaving no doubt that he had perished in the fall. Omar promptly disposed of the old man's walking frame by tossing it out of the hull, then secured the ship's hatch door, sealing off the grim tableau in the corridor. The lifeless bodies remained where they had fallen, silent witnesses to the horrors that had transpired.

Omar's grip on the Somali's arm was unrelenting as he led him toward another tender access point, where Bharat and Aman awaited backup. The scene they encountered was no less gruesome as they approached. Aman, the youngest of the Somali team, sat with his head in his hands, overwhelmed by the brutality that had unfolded. Omar wasted no time in hauling him to his feet.

"Get to your station, or you'll be the next one over the side," Omar's chilling warning jolted Aman into action.

Meanwhile, crew members operating the other tender boats had witnessed the bloodshed and swiftly relayed warnings to inbound tenders. Their urgent messages informed them that the Reef Explorer was under attack and that passengers had lost their lives. The distressing news quickly reached the passengers waiting ashore, many of whom still had family members on board.

The bridge's security hatch proved no match for the small explosive device Aziz had used. Upon hearing the alarm, Captain Carl Nordstrom rushed to the ship's control centre. He issued rapid orders to his radio officer to alert the authorities and instructed his other officers to muster the men under their command to defend against the unlawful intruders. However, their efforts were in vain, as it was already too late. Aziz, at the helm of cell one, followed by Awaale and the remaining members of the team, stormed through the breached opening and onto the bridge, their semi-automatics menacingly displayed.

A brave third officer valiantly attempted to halt Aziz and his henchmen from seizing control of the bridge. Aziz derided him for his foolhardy courage, confronting armed men with nothing more than his bare fists. Captain Nordstrom, who had arrived on the bridge mere seconds before Aziz's entry, was a firsthand witness to the officer's tragic end.

"Enough, enough! Stand down, no more resistance!" Captain Nordstrom's commanding voice reverberated through the chaos. He then turned his attention to Aziz, his tone pleading, "Stop killing my officers!"

Aziz, briefly silencing his deadly rampage, addressed the captain, "Get your officers to sit in the centre of the bridge, hands on heads. If one moves, I will kill them all. Do you understand, Captain?" Aziz's words left no room for negotiation. The captain nodded, acknowledging the grim terms.

Cell two arrived, delivering three members of cell three. Mouhamed, Hussain, and Saddar joined the scene, noting the officers on the deck, each with their hands resting on the tops of their heads. Caleb, a member of cell two, was tasked with the gruesome duty of removing the remains of the fallen third officer, and he was later assigned the responsibility of cleansing the dark red bloodstain that marred the otherwise gleaming deck.

Cell four had successfully secured the tender areas and sealed off the Reef Explorer. With their primary duties accomplished, they turned their attention to secondary tasks—gaining access to the doors leading to the engine room, both forward and aft on deck one. Two members of the team guarded the forward entrance, while the cell leader and a Somali companion secured the rear.

Two maintenance electricians, one Serbian and the other Latvian, both employed on the Reef Explorer, had been diligently working on refitting lights in the stairwell leading to the engine room. The sudden eruption of gunfire from above had caused them to freeze in their tracks. Bharat, second in command of cell four, came hurtling down the stairs, and without a moment's hesitation, he dispatched them with a swift pull of the trigger. Their lifeless bodies served as mere obstacles as Bharat and his team proceeded to open one of the two access doors to the engine room.

The second pair of terrorists encountered no opposition as they made their way into the engine room ahead of the others. The relentless roar of the ship's engines masked the sounds of gunfire, leaving the twenty-two bewildered engineers with looks of confusion and anger as the armed intruders infiltrated their domain. Two more militants entered through the second access steel door, sealing the room in an aura of tension.

Khalid, leader of cell five, had positioned himself on deck nine, where his team swiftly began herding crew members and passengers into the pool and lido area. Their threats were underscored by the brutal execution of any passengers who dared to resist. Khalid's second in command, Salam, had been monitoring the port side of the ship, his gaze fixated on the tenders hastily returning to port. All of them were heading in the same direction, except for one vessel that stood out with its grey hull, a stark contrast to the customary red and white of the tender fleet. Salam quickly alerted Aziz to the situation.

"Coastguard approaching from the port side, 2,000 yards and closing!" Salam's voice rang out.

Beneath the cloudless sky, Khalid had an unobstructed view of the oncoming vessel. As part of his pre-mission responsibilities, he had meticulously researched the capabilities of the Cyprus police and coastguard fleet. With a discerning eye, he recognized the approaching ship as an SAB-12 patrol boat. He raised his binoculars to confirm the details, revealing the presence of an officer on the forward deck and two more in the bridge. The patrol boat surged relentlessly toward the Reef Explorer.

Salam, a skilled operator of the rocket-propelled grenade launcher, had seen action in Mosul and Kirkuk, gaining expertise in missile firing. He had taken out tanks, demolished buildings, and even brought down a Russian helicopter. However, this marked his first time aiming at a ship.

"Light them up, Salam," Khalid's command left no room for hesitation.

Salam steadied the launcher against the ship's port railings, donned his small, rounded glasses, and took aim. With precision, the first grenade found its target, striking the forward gun on the coastguard vessel.

The detonation reverberated through the air, leaving a twisted and charred weapon in its wake. On the coastguard vessel, one of the officers frantically tried to extinguish the flames that had engulfed a comrade who had been sitting behind the gun. Despite the chaos, the coastguard boat stubbornly maintained its course, steadily advancing towards the looming presence of the Reef Explorer. Salam knew that he had to make the next round count, as the ship's metal hull had been reinforced to withstand such attacks. Passengers and crew around the pool area, having either witnessed the grenade launch or heard the distant explosion, grew increasingly agitated. Khalid fired a couple of warning shots over their heads, coercing them into temporary submission.

Salam steadied the launcher once more, taking a deep breath and only exhaling once he depressed the trigger. The second grenade found its mark, piercing the bridge's window before erupting into a fiery explosion. Khalid's comrades erupted into cheers, fully aware that no one on the coastguard vessel's bridge could have survived such a blast. Thick, black smoke billowed from the shattered bridge, and the coastguard boat careened wildly to starboard, its speed undiminished as it spiralled out of control, completing a full circle before embarking on a second lap.

In the engine room, cell two had reached their intended destination, escorted by Abdul, the French-Algerian engineer from cell three. However, what met their eyes was a gruesome tableau of blood and violence.

The Italian chief engineer and three of his Philippine colleagues had valiantly fought back, wielding large spanners as weapons against the assailants, Omar and Bruk, the wounded Somalian. Bruk bore a deep, crushing wound from one of the tools. In that brief moment of hesitation before trying to defend himself, Bruk's fate was sealed. Omar and his men had shown no such hesitation, unleashing a hail of gunfire that left all four defenders and three other engineers dead, their bodies scattered across the engine room floor. The remaining engineers cowered, attempting to blend into the bulkhead, trembling in fear.

"Dispose of these bodies from my engine room deck. They'll soon fill the place with a foul stench in this heat," ordered Abdul.

Omar turned to one of his comrades, instructing him, "Go join your unit on deck nine and take the injured Somali with you." The injured Somali desperately sought help, having found a pulse in Bruk's wrist, clinging to the hope that they might be able to save him. However, his pleas fell on deaf ears as he was forcibly pushed out of the engine room by Omar.

"The injured Somali is of no use to anyone; his head is wide open. Get rid of him," ordered Abdul, sealing Bruk's grim fate.

Omar comprehended his place in the hierarchy of the operation; Abdul held a pivotal role and was one of the few individuals who could give him orders, aside from Aziz. With little hesitation, Omar raised his right foot, delivering a forceful snap kick that thrust Bruk's throat, ending his life in an instant.

The Somali, who had returned with Bharat, stood solemnly over his lifeless cousin. He vehemently refused to cast Bruk's body into the sea, declaring his intention to bring him back to his wife and children. Not eager to provoke a confrontation with the African or his comrades, Abdul reluctantly agreed to this condition, on the condition that the body be removed from the engine room before the pungent scent of diesel mixed with decomposing flesh.

Under instructions, Omar herded the surviving engineers, who had escaped the initial gunfire, into a secured cage located at the rear of the engine room. This enclosure also housed acetylene gas bottles necessary for welding tasks. It was a cramped space for the men, their confinement further ensured by a hefty lock secured by Omar. Abdul recognized the value of their expertise in keeping the engines and generators running smoothly, so he assured them that they would be released from the pen if any issues with the turbines arose.

Abdul secured both entrances to the engine room, and Bharat strategically positioned several packets of plastic explosives around the compartment. He informed the captive engineers that he would detonate the ordnance should any attempt be made to breach the cage or if an external threat materialized. Meanwhile, Omar perched on a large, warm water pipe, his weapon trained on the two engineers not confined within the cage, ensuring a continuous supply of electricity from the generators.

On the bridge, Hussain, the Syrian communication expert from cell three, occupied the communications console. His initial task was to swiftly isolate the ship from the internet and mobile phone networks, abruptly terminating numerous conversations between anxious passengers and their loved ones. Once he had successfully implemented the blackout, he shifted his attention to the radar screen, monitoring both marine and air traffic.

Aziz engaged in a hushed conversation with Awaale in a corner of the bridge, having just witnessed the explosions on the coastguard vessel.

"It's time to address the passengers, Awaale. Begin with English, then proceed to French. We lack German speakers, which could pose a problem with some passengers," Aziz advised. Awaale nodded and picked up the prepared speech Aziz had provided. After studying it for a moment, he made some notes to ensure he could deliver the message without hesitation. Satisfied with his grasp of the language, Awaale picked up the ship's phone, and Hussain connected him to the ship's internal transmitter.

"To all guests aboard the Reef Explorer, please understand that if you heed our instructions, we can guarantee your safety. We are a group of Somali and Arab pirates who have seized control of this vessel and its passengers. Our intention is to negotiate a ransom with the ship's owners for both the ship's release and your return to your respective governments and families. This is a financial hijacking, not a terrorist attack. We deeply regret the unfortunate loss of life, but sometimes such incidents are unavoidable, and we hope to avoid further casualties. All passengers are requested to proceed to the theatre located on decks four and five within the next fifteen minutes. Crew members should make their way to deck nine. Anyone found outside these designated safety zones after this period will be considered a threat and treated accordingly. We cannot guarantee your safety in such cases. Let me emphasize once more, this is a financial hijacking. If you are dead, we cannot secure your ransom, so we urge your cooperation. Please proceed to your designated rally points silently. Crew members will be transferred to lifeboats, and we strongly discourage any acts of heroism, as they may result in harm to those involved. Any communication with external parties will be viewed as noncompliance, and again, we cannot guarantee your safety in such instances. Please, for your own well-being, comply with these instructions."

Awaale repeated the message in French.

Reluctantly, under pressure from Kasim Asfour, Aziz had been forced to release most of the crew members. Asfour was well aware that they would likely pose a problem, being unwilling to patiently await their fate. He deemed it safer to remove them from the ship rather than risk compromising the operation.

On deck nine, eight armed hijackers were present, with four assigned to escort passengers down five decks to the theatre, while the remaining four guarded crew members en route to the lifeboat embarkation point on the starboard side of deck six. Non-essential crew members were grouped together and forcibly directed onto two lifeboats. Gunfire resonated throughout the ship several times as isolated crew members failed to comply with shouted orders.

Khalid's instincts screamed for a clean sweep, the ruthless part of him desiring to leave no witnesses, no wild cards. But orders from Aziz, underpinned by the steely directive of Asfour, dictated otherwise—no unnecessary casualties, for resistance from the crew could be fierce and costly, perhaps even tipping the precarious scales against them.

Aziz, with the foresight of a seasoned tactician, had painted the grim picture: the potential loss of their own in a heated battle. So, with a discontented frown etching lines into his brow, Khalid barked commands, corralling the crew into the lifeboats. His movements were brusque, driven by a mix of reluctance and urgency.

As the lifeboats, heavily laden with the forlorn figures of the crew, touched the churning sea, Khalid's hand lingered on the cold metal of his gun. With a dark sneer, he unleashed a spray of bullets over the bobbing vessels. "Let them resist down there," he declared, a bitter edge to his tone.

Aziz, standing by, observed the action with detached pragmatism. The shrug of his shoulders was nonchalant, betraying none of the conflict that played out before him.

Panic rippled through the passengers when they observed the bullet torn lifeboats, filled with crew members, sailing away from the

Reef Explorer. Many had witnessed the deaths of fellow passengers and crew and now saw the crew disembarking. Initially, there was resistance, and Khalid was compelled to use lethal force against the most agitated individuals. A handful of younger passengers attempted to rush toward Khalid and met a swift end from a hail of bullets. After a few minutes, the majority of passengers and remaining crew members complied and made their way to the theatre. However, some of the more daring hostages concluded that jumping into the sea from decks seven and higher offered a better chance of survival than remaining aboard the ship. Some made it to safety, while others met a tragic fate as Mouhamed started the engines, hoisted the anchor, and steered the vessel away from the coast of Cyprus.

A minority among the passengers did not comply. They had noticed Arabs among the Somalis and wisely doubted the message conveyed over the transmitter by Awaale. Some went into hiding, a few attempted resistances, but after twenty tense minutes, over three hundred individuals sat in the theatre under armed guard at each entrance. Tragically, over forty had perished in acts of futile bravery, and fifteen, including Stahmer, Shultz, and Ghislaine, remained in hiding.

Imran assumed command of the theatre's security, perched at the front of the stage, overlooking the captive hostages. He strategically placed two Somalis from Khalid's unit near each of the theatre's rear exits, maintaining a discreet distance to allow the hostages access to the restrooms on the right for men and the left for women. Two other Arabs guided passengers down from the upper decks, positioning themselves along parallel walkways that flanked the theatre. Aziz had devised this plan to keep most of the Somalis within the theatre area but separated, preventing easy communication.

Khalid and his team initiated a second sweep of the decks, systematically dealing with any crew or passengers who had failed to comply with the instructions. Aziz understood that some individuals might be holed up in their cabins, either out of sickness or fear, and as long as they remained there, they posed no immediate threat. However, should they venture out, they would become visible on the ship's CCTV cameras, which monitored the cabin corridors, public areas, and sides of the vessel. Mouhamed assumed the role of ship's mate, using the CCTV system to identify the location and deck of anyone entering a monitored area. He would then dispatch Khalid and his team to administer swift justice. Salam remained on deck nine, armed with the rocket grenade launcher, ready to repel any potential threats. Mouhamed would also monitor the radar for incoming ships or aircraft.

Aziz, accompanied by three of his fellow Arabs, escorted the ship's officers to deck six. He retained two crew members on the bridge to assist Mouhamed and assigned Abel to watch over them with his semi-automatic. Originally, Aziz had intended to bring any surviving security personnel along with them, but all had met their demise while resisting the attack.

On deck six, Aziz dismantled a section of the movable guardrail, which typically provided passengers access to the lifeboats during emergencies. These lifeboats had already been lowered and released after being loaded with crew members. The gap in the rail spanned four feet, leading to a precipitous drop into the ocean below. Aziz positioned two of his men on either side of the rail, their semi-automatics aimed at the officers, effectively corralling them around the opening in the guardrail.

Aziz closely monitored the helicopter, which hovered approximately two miles away. He had issued strict orders that any closer approach would result in it being taken down with the grenade launcher. Aziz hoped it was a news helicopter from Cyprus, and his assumption proved correct. Rod Jackman, a camera operator for Nicosia News, had been covering a forest fire some 30 miles inland when they received instructions to approach the Reef Explorer. Jackman adjusted his camera's zoom and observed the gathering of officers on the starboard side of the ship.

"Jump," Aziz ordered.

"You've let the rest of the crew go on lifeboats," Captain Nordstrom protested.

"Jump," Aziz repeated.

"This is suicide! Most of us will die! Where is your humanity, man?" Nordstrom shouted.

Aziz fired a shot into the deck, narrowly missing the captain and those officers with him.

"Jump, or the next shot won't be aimed at the floor, Captain."

Two junior officers leaped first, followed by the cruise director and hospitality officer. Captain Nordstrom was the last to drop. Three officers tragically perished upon impact, while two lacked the strength to swim away from the suction force of the propellers. Three suffered broken bones, and two of them succumbed to their injuries before a rescue boat could reach them. Out of the seventeen officers, ten managed to survive, but Captain Nordstrom was not among them. The entire ordeal unfolded live on Nicosia News, and within the hour, Al-Jazeera, CNN, and the BBC broadcasted these dramatic images to millions of viewers around the world.

Taking a break from their security sweeps, Khalid and his team surrounded deck six with plastic explosives, spaced twenty feet apart. They had practiced this task diligently back in Egypt, making them experts. The packages were bright yellow and clearly visible from the TV helicopter, which had been getting closer to the Reef Explorer. When the helicopter approached too closely, Khalid fired several warning shots to maintain a safe distance.

In a darkened room at a safehouse in Pakistan, Kasim Asfour watched the unfolding events on several television screens alongside other high-ranking Al-Qaeda leaders. Throwing officers from the ship and detonating a lifeboat full of the crew were not part of his plan. Aziz was going off the reservation, setting off alarm bells. Asfour sent a Snapchat message to Aziz, demanding an explanation, but received no reply.

A British Royal Air Force Griffin helicopter, usually based at RAF Akrotiri in Cyprus, began to veer erratically and descended to sea level. Mouhamed had previously identified the TV helicopter on the screen through Salam's report. Now, a second aircraft with a more prominent media presence was heading toward the Reef Explorer. Salam fired a rocket-propelled grenade towards it. The RAF pilot, experienced in evading missiles from past deployments in Iraq and Syria, found this to be the closest call yet. The rocket-propelled grenade missed its target and detonated ten feet above the water, causing the helicopter pilot to struggle for control against the blast's pressure. The helicopter sharply altered its course after receiving orders to stand down.

Aziz understood the urgency of getting a message out to the relevant authorities, even though it was unclear which country would take the lead, a process that would likely take several hours to formulate. Asfour and Aziz's plans were not focused on stealth; instead, they prioritized speed. Aziz had designed the operation to be completed within two days, as he knew that any longer would risk a counter-attack. Among the passengers on board were Germans, British, French, Italians, Swedes, Swiss, and some Americans. Given the proximity of British and French military bases in the Mediterranean and Cyprus, they were the most likely to respond swiftly. Aziz was keen to avoid elite units like the SAS or French special forces descending upon the ship.

Aziz called for Awaale to join him in the theatre, positioning himself on the stage before the seated hostages. Aziz enlisted one of the sound engineers to set up a camera to record the message. Awaale stood hesitantly, shuffling awkwardly before he began to read the statement Aziz had prepared for him.

"This message is directed to the owners of the Reef Explorer, Oceanic Enterprises, and the families of our guests on the Reef Explorer. We, Africans, have endured years of suffering as the West has grown rich by exploiting our lands' natural resources. We've struggled to feed our families, receiving nothing more than a couple of bags of grain when the media showcased our children's starvation, shaming you. It is now time for you to pay for your deeds. We—"

Awaale's chastisement was abruptly cut short as an American man in his sixties rose from his seat. Aziz, positioned just off the stage, gestured across his throat to signal the sound engineer to halt the recording. The American began shouting vehemently.

"I am an American, goddammit! I fought in Vietnam and Grenada to protect my country. I would strongly advise you to release the Americans because when our president learns of this kidnapping, he will rain down hellfire upon you, reducing you to the Stone Age!"

Another one of the American hostages shouted, "Hoo ha!" Aziz, showing a hint of surprise, walked onto the stage.

"Stop recording!" Aziz shouted.

"Sir, you are an American?" Aziz's enquiry sliced through the tension, his accent tinged with an African lilt, oddly polite in the midst of chaos. "Forgive our oversight. We seemed to have misjudged the… diversity of our assembly." The gaze that peered out from above the camouflaged fabric of his mask was sharp, intent on the American.

He beckoned with a deceptive calmness. "Please, join me on stage. It's imperative that your commander-in-chief hears from one of his own, lest we find ourselves in an unfortunate conflict of interests."

The American's posture, hardened by years of service, betrayed no apprehension as he complied, stepping into the harsh spotlight of the pirate's impromptu forum. With the world watching, Aziz handed him the grim role of a negotiator.

The American, a grizzled veteran with a spine forged in adversity, gave a terse nod, his 'damn right' less of an affirmation and more of a challenge. He mounted the stage deliberately, his tread heavy, each step, energy sapping. Aziz gestured him to the spotlight's unforgiving glare, an unspoken command to start his address to the world's most powerful leader.

Clearing his throat, the veteran barely formed a word before pandemonium ensued. A shot rang out—a deafening crack that froze the blood of all who heard it. The veteran crumpled, his message unspoken, his fall from grace a violent plunge into chaos.

The body, now an emblem of the terror they wielded, was dispatched from the stage with a callous swing of Aziz's boot. The act was barbaric, almost theatrical, and it tore through the already taut fabric of the hostages' fragile calm, eliciting a series of gasps and shrieks. Fear, raw and unyielding, clutched the hearts of everyone present as the grim reality of their situation set in.

"Anyone else with a message or who wishes to speak, please stand," Aziz calmly declared, though everyone remained seated, many weeping.

Awaale appeared uneasy and lowered his head. Aziz signalled to resume recording, and Awaale once again launched into the diatribe, this time amidst the blood and brain matter around his feet.

"This message is for the ship owners, Oceanic Enterprises, and the families of our guests. We've endured years of suffering as the West has grown rich and drained our lands of natural resources. We've struggled to feed our families, receiving nothing more than a couple of bags of grain when the BBC or CNN shows our children dying by the thousands. Now is the time for you to pay. We demand 50 million euros for the safe return of the vessel and its crew, plus 100,000 euros for each of our guests left aboard. We will provide a list of all passengers so that their governments or families can arrange a transfer of the money to an account we will notify you of later. Plastic explosives are placed around the ship, clearly visible. I'm sure several satellites are scrutinizing us. We intend to depart this ship within 48 hours. That's the time frame for you to gather the money.

"Some of my colleagues have detonator switches, and if we detect any signs of resistance or incursions, they have orders to sink this ship along with its passengers to the depths of the Mediterranean. There will be no negotiations or communication. Passenger names will be released in one hour, money must be deposited within 40 hours with account detail to follow. Failure to comply by certain governments or families will result in the death of citizens from that country. Those citizens will be returned if their countries do comply. Our destination is the port of Hurghada, where we will hand over the ship upon meeting our demands. You will ensure the Suez Canal remains open to us with no boarding attempts as we sail through. Your leaders will sign a treaty guaranteeing our safe passage back to Somalia. No deviations from these demands, no attempted boardings, or this ship sinks with everyone on board. 40 hours and counting."

Aziz downloaded the recording and swiftly sent it to the bridge, where Hussain immediately transmitted the message.

Meanwhile, Khalid and his team had reached the ship's top deck, deck ten. During their sweep, they stumbled upon several crew members who had sought refuge in a towel locker near the gym. Without hesitation, they were shot where they hid. Six other passengers had concealed themselves in their cabins, hoping to evade detection. Khalid's relentless search revealed their whereabouts, and they too met their tragic end on the spot. Tragedy seemed to haunt every corner of the ship, even causing the death of one elderly woman who suffered a heart attack when an armed intruder pulled back her shower curtain.

Recognizing the need for a larger security presence on the decks, Aziz reassigned Awaale and Abel to assist with the sweeps, keeping his own men available for other undisclosed tasks critical to their mission's success.

The moment the shots rang out, the ambiance aboard the ship transformed from one of subdued anticipation to one of acceptance. Shultz and Ghislaine, who had been in the supposed safety of Stahmer's quarters, felt a cold shiver of dread at the unmistakable sound of gunfire. The metallic resonance of bullet casings hitting the deck was an indicator of the violence that had been unleashed.

Stahmer, whose instincts had been sharpened over years, recognized the direness of the situation instantly—it was the attack he had feared, the calamity he had cautioned against. Wasting not a second, he propelled himself towards the captain's quarters. The door, which would normally stand as an impenetrable barrier to the uninitiated, gave way to his urgent need.

In the captain's sanctum, the master key lay almost expectant on the polished surface of the desk, a silent ally amidst the chaos. He retraced his steps with haste, the weight of each second growing heavier as he moved. Upon his return, the eyes of Shultz and Ghislaine met his, their gazes alight with the unspoken understanding that time was their most scarce resource. They had the keys to a temporary kingdom in this floating citadel, but now they needed a strategy, a plan that would shield them from the storm of violence that raged outside. And they needed it with an urgency that the ticking hands of a clock could never truly capture.

Stahmer quickly contacted Fabienne, informing her of the attack on the ship and their current hiding spot. Fabienne instructed him to check in again in two hours. Back on the bridge, Hussain picked up the signal, indicating that someone on board was transmitting via a satellite phone. However, it was challenging to pinpoint the exact location as the transmission was brief and elusive.

For an agonizing hour, Stahmer, Shultz, and Ghislaine remained hidden, their nerves on edge as they listened to the unsettling noises echoing in the corridor outside. Stahmer's cabin had balcony access, providing a potential escape route. Shultz took the initiative, carefully climbing over the balcony rails. He dangled perilously over open water, fully aware that a fall from such a height would be fatal. With calculated precision, Shultz swung his legs outward and, on the returning arc, released his grip on the rail. He landed heavily on the cabin patio below.

With Shultz safely below, Stahmer held onto Ghislaine's arms and slowly lowered her over the side, into Shultz's waiting embrace. In that critical moment, their connection went beyond survival, as Stahmer held onto Ghislaine slightly longer than he might have otherwise. Finally, Stahmer followed suit, gripping the balcony rails as Shultz and Ghislaine pulled him to safety, their daring escape from the encroaching danger marking the beginning of a new chapter in their ordeal.

Hussain closely monitored the escape operation via the closed-circuit television and swiftly turned to Aziz with his report. "We have three individuals who just descended from a balcony to the deck below."

Aziz wasted no time issuing orders. "Radio Awaale immediately and instruct them to proceed to deck seven and eliminate those intruders," he commanded. He was aware of Khalid's ongoing situation on deck four, dealing with defiant crew members who had refused to comply with the evacuation orders.

Shultz attempted to open the patio door, but it remained firmly locked. "It's locked," he reported to Stahmer, who retrieved the keys he had taken from the captain's desk.

Stahmer diligently tried eight keys, all to no avail. However, on the ninth attempt, the key slid into the lock and turned successfully. "The master key," he whispered to Shultz and Ghislaine.

As they entered the spacious double cabin, their focus immediately shifted to the door leading to the corridor. Ghislaine retrieved a small compact case from one of her shorts' pockets.

Shultz cautiously opened the compact, allowing him to partially slide the mirror side through the crack in the door to discreetly observe the corridor. He spotted the two Black men approximately in green overalls ten cabins down, forcefully using the butts of their semi-automatic weapons to break the locks on cabin doors before conducting brief searches. Shultz calculated that it took them roughly twenty-five seconds to complete each cabin search.

With a quick twist of the compact, Shultz examined the corridor from a different angle, seeking any potential escape routes. About six doors down on the opposite side of the corridor, he spotted a door marked "Crew Only." This door had a lock that differed from the cabin doors and appeared sturdier.

Shultz retracted the mirror and softly closed the door, then turned to Stahmer. He whispered, "There's a crew door, about six doors away on the opposite side. The lock looks different. Do you think the master key we found might work for all the locks?"

Stahmer considered the situation carefully. "It's possible, but I can't say for sure. It's the only one of this type among the keys we have."

Shultz weighed their options. "If it's not the right key, we'll be in trouble. It seems like our only escape route. The two men are just nine doors away. I think I can make it."

Ghislaine gripped the door handle firmly while Stahmer gently eased the mirror back out of the door's crack. He observed the two-armed intruders as they forcefully kicked in the door of a cabin eight doors down. Stahmer nodded to signal their opportunity.

Ghislaine quietly pulled the door open, allowing Shultz to slip out. Shultz hurriedly reached the crew door, his heart pounding with adrenaline, and took just under five seconds to insert the key. Unfortunately, the lock did not budge. Shultz swiftly retrieved his iPhone from his pocket, activated the camera app, and snapped a picture of the lock. The entire process took twenty-one seconds, and a further few precious seconds as he returned to safety.

Shultz showed Stahmer the picture on the iPhone without saying a word. Stahmer studied the lock and inspected the other keys in the bunch. He picked out key fourteen after a minute. He nodded to Ghislaine to slightly open the door, and they repeated the process with the mirror. The Somalis were six cabins away.

Shultz ran to the crew door again, when Stahmer had indicated it was safe to do so.

Shultz breathed a sigh of relief, as the key turned in the lock and he entered the stairwell with ten seconds to spare.

The Somalis were three cabins away when Ghislaine sprinted from the stateroom to the stairwell. Shultz ensured there was only a slight gap in the door as not to alert the Somalis, just wide enough so he could see when Stahmer was ready to come across.

It was difficult for Stahmer, as he had to wedge the door open with his foot and put the mirror out, before crossing the corridor.

The task took precious seconds, and Stahmer was not as agile, or as quick as Ghislaine and Shultz. He was mid-passage when the Somalis appeared and noticed him immediately.

The Somalis had only been in the cabin ten seconds when Hussein told them off their escape plan he witnessed on CCTV. Both Somalis raised their weapons; it was evident to Shultz and Ghislaine that they would shoot Stahmer before he could reach the crew door.

Ghislaine stepped out, hoping they would think twice before killing an unarmed woman. She put herself in between the armed men and Stahmer. Shultz grabbed Stahmer to safety inside the stairwell. Ghislaine walked back slowly as the two men eyed her up and down, they were mesmerised by her beauty.

"Halt, or we shoot," Awaale shouted.

"No, you won't," Ghislaine said with confidence.

Awaale and his comrade looked at each other; their hesitation allowed Shultz to grab her and instantly pull her into the stairwell and bang the door shut.

The noise reverberated around them, as Awaale attempted to smash open the door as they had done with the cabin doors. Rather than the composite material the cabin doors were constructed of, this one was steel; they would have needed a jackhammer to open it, not the end of a semi-automatic.

"Thank you, Ghislaine, that was incredibly brave," Stahmer said. "Bloody stupid if you ask me," Shultz said.

"Give it a rest Shultz, I just saved our asses," Ghislaine responded angrily.

"I am security on this team, Stahmer is the investigator, and you are a translator. If decisions are made regarding placing yourself in danger, that is my call, Ghislaine."

"I'm afraid he's right, Ghislaine, but I'm still incredibly grateful," Stahmer said.

"You're welcome, Robert," she replied with a smile, though her eyes remained fixed on Shultz, expressing her disagreement.

"Time to get in touch with Fabienne," Stahmer whispered as he retrieved the satellite phone from beneath his jacket.

Awaale felt the chill of the corridor seep into his bones, a stark contrast to the heat of Hussein's anger that now flooded his earpiece. "The damn gun locked up on me," he responded, masking the lie with a veneer of frustration.

Awaale, having allowed three passengers to escape, chose not to inform Aziz of his decision. Since they were only passengers, he believed no harm would come from his actions. Awaale had brought several packs of coca leaves with him to help his men stay alert. After completing his sweep, he delivered the coca leaves to his comrades in the theatre and then made his way down to the engine room. As he entered, Abel discreetly pushed Awaale out of sight, away from Omar's watchful gaze. He leaned closer to Awaale's ear and whispered, "They killed Bruk."

Awaale took a step back, his voice less hushed now. "Bruk is dead? What happened?"

"He had a head injury from one of the engineers but was alive when I left to throw the bodies overboard. When I returned, he was dead. There was a mark around his throat, a boot mark."

"Are you sure?"

"Awaale, they killed him. We're supposed to be working with them, and they're killing us like we're the enemy."

"Keep this to yourself, for now. I need to think."

Fabienne had been tirelessly working at her desk, managing multiple keyboards as she gathered as much information as possible. Stahmer's call brought relief to her tense shoulders.

"Thank God you're safe! Are Ghislaine and Shultz, okay?"

"We're all alive and well, Fabienne. I need to brief you on what we know."

Hussain signalled for Aziz to approach his console. "The rogue satellite phone is transmitting again."

Aziz swiftly reorganized the Somalis and his own men. He selected one Somali theatre guard to watch a small team of chefs in the kitchen, where they prepared sandwiches for the hostages. Another guard supervised the waitstaff as they transported bottles of water from deck four to distribute to the thirsty captives. Aziz's motives were not driven by altruism or concern for the passengers missing a couple of meals and water. Instead, it was a matter of practicality—well-fed and hydrated hostages were less likely to incite an uprising.

Aziz assessed the situation. The four toilet cubicles adjacent to the theatre exit were in constant use, each one guarded. Cell three's team was positioned to ensure the ship's smooth operation. He left two of his men on deck nine with rocket launchers. Additionally, he deployed two tactical teams, each consisting of two of his own men, with explicit orders to eliminate anyone using the satellite phone on sight.

Aziz's rebuke was sharp, a razor slicing through the tension. "You've been spotted by the press chopper during the skirmish with the coastguard. Our story of an African hijack is compromised," he chastised Khalid.

Khalid's retort came with the assurance of someone who had made a difficult, but necessary, call. "It's a lesser evil than letting an armed coastguard team onboard," he argued, standing his ground.

There was a pause as Aziz weighed the situation, the truth of Khalid's words sinking in. Reluctantly, he conceded, recognizing the inevitability of their exposure. "The world would have discovered the truth before long," Aziz admitted, the edge of frustration still lingering in his voice, yet now tinged with resignation.

Stahmer, Ghislaine, and Shultz descended the internal staircase, their senses heightened as they listened for any signs of the terrorists behind the steel doors. Decks ten through eight remained eerily quiet. The hub of activity appeared to be on decks five and six, judging by the sounds they could discern. They had two hours until their next contact with Cutler and needed to find an isolated place where they could plan without interruption.

Stahmer emerged into a corridor, followed closely by his companions. Deck two stood in stark contrast to the upper levels, devoid of any luxurious fixtures or fittings. The steel hull gave the area an eerie silence, and the lifeless bodies of crew members lay scattered around.

Using his master key, Stahmer tried several doors. One revealed a storeroom filled with dirty laundry and lacking space. Another door led to a room filled with pallets of bottled water, soda, and alcohol. Stahmer deemed this area high risk and moved on, leading them down the corridor until they reached the amidships section. There, he tried his master key on a large steel door, which swung open to reveal a room filled with bags of garbage, inundating them with the putrid stench of rotting and decaying food. Dim background lighting provided a faint glow to the surroundings.

"This will do," Stahmer declared.

"It's the garbage room," Ghislaine remarked, her face contorted in disgust.

"Any port in a storm, excuse the pun. You don't want to be in there. Neither will the bastards who want to kill you. We can make a hide over there, stack the bags up six high around us, and we'll have a perfect hideout."

chapter sixteen
Finding Guano

The unexpected ring of the telephone in Cutler's pocket was like the sudden squall that whips across the Mississippi, catching the unwary seafarer by surprise, and within moments, he felt as if he were navigating through his own private storm. Fabienne's voice, usually so calm and collected, had taken on a pitch that bespoke volumes of the chaos unfurling at their bastion in the Everglades.

Cutler's pulse raced, a staccato against the soft leather of the armrest, as he absorbed the synopsis of the incursion at their sanctuary. Though miles away, he could almost smell the acrid scent of gunpowder and feel the damp, earthy air of Florida's wild hinterland as Fabienne painted the picture of their compromised stronghold.

A sigh of deep relief, akin to a prisoner reprieved, escaped him when he was told Cheryl and Esme had skirted the edges of disaster. Fabienne transferred the call to Cheryl who was recovering at home from smoke inhalation.

With a nod that was as much about steadying his own nerves as it was about acknowledging Fabienne's silent command, he excused himself with a discreet elegance, rising from his seat. With each step towards the tail of the plane, he moved away from Tuck's prying ears and the inquisitive glances of others.

As Cutler absorbed the blow of each revelation, a subsequent call with Cheryl brought him a morsel of solace. Her voice, though steady, could not entirely mask the undercurrent of strain as she detailed the bolstered defences—ex-special services operatives now stood guard, a necessary bulwark against further onslaught.

The silence that followed Cheryl's pronouncement was heavy with implication. She would not let Tuck be blindsided by this attack on her and MIDAS, while he stood shoulder to shoulder with Cutler. The truth of the attack would bide its time, waiting until Tuck's return.

"Cutler," Cheryl's voice cut through the tense air once more, a blade revealing more treachery. "There's another layer to this. Conrad Ford masterminded the assault. And there's a trail leading to some highly placed individuals." Her words hung like a guillotine's blade, poised and lethal.

A growl simmered from Cutler's throat, a sound of visceral contempt. "Ford," he spat the name out as if it left a residue of poison on his tongue. "That duplicitous bastard just made the biggest mistake of his life." His fists clenched, the betrayal a visceral punch that tightened his chest.

"Tell Cortez to stand down, leave Ford to us" Cutler instructed, his mind already plotting Ford's downfall. "Tuck and I will sort this."

"Bull's got skin in the game, they killed his brother in-law" she said, her voice carrying a blend of sorrow and a hard edge of resolve.

There was a solemn pause as the reality of Bull's loss sank in, the loss of a brother-in-law who upheld the law in Everglade city and well known to all MIDAS agents.

"He was by Cortez's side when they confessed—it was Ford who marked us as targets," Cheryl stated.

Cutler's jaw set firmly, the new information cementing his resolve. "Ford made this personal for too many of us," he uttered, the words like flint striking steel. "He'll wish he hadn't."

Cutler's request was immediate, commanding. "Let Bull know we won't act without him. Also have Fabienne forward me the intel on Ford's accomplices. I want to know who's pulling the strings behind this puppet."

Cutler's voice was like steel, each word sharpened by the raw edge of betrayal and the instinct for survival. "Whoever's at the top of this ladder, they won't be out of reach," he said, with a hint of cold resolve.

Cheryl's tone matched his, "The Everglades… they hit us in our own backyard," she said, the disbelief still resonant in her voice. "It's a statement. They're trying to intimidate us, to show they can reach us anywhere."

Cutler's mind worked rapidly, piecing together the grim puzzle. "It's not just intimidation. After Bali, we know too much. Robert Ford's little delivery run… it was just the tip of the iceberg. They're scared we'll uncover the rest." There was anger in his voice, a smouldering fury.

"The Bali Learjet… it went down, all hands lost" Cheryl concluded, her voice hard as flint.

Cutler's response was icy, his usual charm now a distant memory. "They wanted to send us to the bottom of the ocean and kill anyone at our HQ. They failed," he stated flatly. "But this… this is a declaration of war. I think Old Joe might be at risk when

Fabienne sorts his release, phone him on his new phone and let him know to check the boat Conrad has supplied as a replacement."

There was a moment of charged silence before Cutler continued, "I want the base locked down. In Geneva too. Bulletproof the entire operation. I won't lose anyone else to these bastards," he commanded, the protective instincts for his team, his family, burning bright.

Cutler replaced the receiver, the click echoing slightly in the silence that had stretched out around him. Cheryl's commands dovetailed seamlessly with his own deeply held belief: the paramount importance of evacuating their comrades from the besieged Reef Explorer.

Tuck's keen observation didn't overlook the subtle clenching of Cutler's jaw or the stormy intensity building in his eyes. Inside the cabin, an unspoken tension hung in the air, serving as a silent confirmation of the drama unfolding, a situation that Tuck recognized all too clearly from Cutler's nonverbal cues. Ultimately, Tuck confronted Cutler, and for the sake of their friendship, Cutler chose to be honest and reveal the truth.

Cutler faced his old friend, the weight of leadership etching lines of determination on his brow. "There's been an attack," he admitted, the words falling between them with the heaviness of betrayal—not towards Tuck, but towards the sanctuary they had all believed impregnable. He held Tuck's gaze as he offered an out, a return to safety, to family. "You can go back, to Cheryl, to Esme," he said, the offer hanging in the air like a lifeline.

But as Tuck's eyes searched his, Cutler laid bare the final card. "She thought it best you do not know," he confessed, "believing that the key to all this may well lie in the job we are about to undertake." Cutler's revelation held the gravity of their shared past, the unspoken trust. Tuck decided to remain by Cutler's side and thanked him for his honesty.

Christensen's history with Cutler was as layered and complex as the geopolitical tapestry of the Middle East where they'd first collaborated. Back then, his knack for logistics had turned potential disasters into smoothly run operations, earning him the reputation of being a solid logistics supplier.

Now, under the warm, unforgiving Cypriot sun, Christensen found himself revisiting that role. Fabienne had been meticulous in her preparations, her list of necessities a precursor to what Cutler would no doubt need.

He was at the airport as the trio emerged, the drive to their hotel was uneventful, yet charged with an unspoken anticipation. Christensen kept his eyes on the road. His mind, however, was racing ahead, turning over the possibilities of what Cutler's extended shopping list might include this time around.

The hotel, an inconspicuous establishment that promised discretion, was well-chosen for its purpose. As they settled into the temporary base of operations, Christensen knew the game well: logistics in such operations didn't just mean equipment and supplies—it meant being ready for the unexpected, for the rapid shifts in plan and protocol that were the hallmarks of Cutler's missions.

Cutler let Tuck and Colton settle in for fifteen minutes before summoning them to his room.

Cutler's voice broke the silence, his tone low and even, but the undercurrent of urgency was unmistakable. "This operation has just shifted gears. We're no longer observers or intelligence gatherers. We're now on a rescue mission, and it's personal."

The journey from the bustling coastal city of Limassol to the Troodos Mountains was uneventful but scenic. Thirty miles—that's all it took to swap the lapping waves of the Mediterranean for the stately silence of the Troodos range.

Christensen navigated the winding mountain roads with the same precision and calm he applied to all his undertakings. He had chosen the western slopes of the Troodos for their operation, an area where the peaks stood like custodians over the vast blue expanse of sea, a strategic spot removed from prying eyes.

The drone was stowed away discreetly amongst their gear. It was a marvel that such a small piece of technology could carry such weight—both in its construction and the implications of its mission. Christensen had supplied it, and like everything he supplied it met the specifications Fabienne had requested.

As Colton engaged in a clipped exchange with Fabienne, he sent the drone skyward, slicing through the crisp mountain air with mechanical precision. Moments later, Fabienne's voice, crisp and professional, crackled through the receiver, confirming the vital signs of their aerial envoy—the tracking device and camera were relaying clear images back to her station.

Meanwhile, Tuck, settled into the drone's controls. His fingers moved over the console with assured agility, his gaze was unyielding—a sharpshooter's stare fixed on the monitor, through which he would soon divine the placement of the Reef Explorer.

The drone, now a speck against the canvas of the sky, made its silent voyage towards its quarry. It was a thirty-minute ballet of technology and air currents.

"Tuck, talk to me. What do you see?" Cutler's voice broke the tension, his eyes peering over Tuck's shoulder in search of the truths held on the screen.

"The Reef Explorer… it's moving at pace, heading south."

Without missing a beat, Cutler extended his hand and the satellite phone transitioned from Colton's grip to his own. "Fabienne, I need you to assume command of the drone," he commanded with a calm authority. "Christensen has just briefed me—our bird has a seven-day lifeline before it requires recharging. I want you to ensure it keeps the Reef Explorer under its surveillance."

"Roger that, we've got two that made it off the trawler alive. The local law enforcement is on the hunt for one—a bloke named Guano. Disappeared into thin air. They've pegged him as crew on that overturned catamaran."

"Vanished, just like that?" Cutler's question was sharp, a blade cutting through ambiguity.

The crackle of the speaker preceded Fabienne's seasoned tone. "Cyprus has become a magnet for those dodging the border controls. Illegals tend to blend in, working for next to nothing. I'd bet Guano's gone to ground, scared witless of being sent back."

"Any leads on him, Fabienne?" Cutler's voice was all business.

"Just one. He pulled a girl from the water—gave her a message. Told her to tell the police it was Arabs who hit them. But there's a twist—one of them, maybe the leader, spoke English to a couple on board before killing them, some odd accent, then switched to fluent Arabic with his mates," Fabienne briefed with a hint of intrigue.

"You reckon the head honcho could be British?" Cutler's question sliced through the static, his voice carrying the weight of a new and pressing suspicion.

Fabienne's response was quick and sure, not a flicker of doubt in her tone. "I'd stake my last dollar on it," she asserted. The certainty in her voice suggested she had more than just a hunch.

"Where could Guano be now?" Cutler prodded.

"Best guess—he's bolted for familiar ground. The skipper of the catamaran, a guy named Paccar, he died in the raid, but his wife might be shielding him. I'm sending you Paccar's address," Fabienne offered.

"And the police, they've checked this out?" Cutler pushed for operational clarity.

"They went there but Paccar's wife is a mess, said she's not seen him You'll have Paccar's details in a moment," she assured.

"Appreciate it. Out for now," Cutler signed off, the line going dead as he pivoted to the group of men beside him.

Cutler nodded, processing the information. "We move out in five. Christensen, you speak Greek, we'll need you as interpreter."

Paccar's place was straight out of a Greek travel magazine. The main house stood proud, its white walls gleaming under the Cypriot sun, fresh blue tiles crowning its roof. A patio complete with a water drinking fountain suggested a life of simple luxuries. But it was the second, shabbier structure that drew Cutler's eye—a storehouse bulging with marine paraphernalia, its peeling paint and sagging roof. The grounds were a camouflage of domestic normality; olive trees and aloe vera plants dotted around, but the centrepiece was different—an ancient fig tree, its limbs contorted with time.

As Cutler's boots crunched on the gravel, he noted the figure huddled on the terrace. Paccar's wife, a picture of grief-stricken abandonment, didn't even twitch at his approach. She was lost in her own world of sorrow, clutching a teddy bear—likely an emblem of her son's youth, now lost—and an old jumper belonging to her husband that must've carried his scent.

She murmured through her tears, a litany of heartbreak, her voice barely rising above the whisper of the leaves. "Romano…" she sobbed, pressing her lips to the plush toy as though it could answer her. "His first toy," she wept, drowning in the fabric of the jumper as if trying to inhale her husband's presence from its threads. Her laments were in English; Cutler would not need Christensen to translate after all.

Cutler's past was a relentless instructor; experience had etched into him that in the face of such raw grief, words were futile. He left the widow to her sorrow and made his way to the outhouses, knowing that time and action were the currencies he now traded in.

The outhouse greeted him with the acrid tang of diesel that clawed at the back of his throat, a sharp contrast to the open air outside. A constellation of light pierced the dilapidated roof, revealing workbenches cluttered with mechanical entrails. At the far end, hidden behind a metal rack hid Guano. His bare torso was a canvas of toil and pain, marked by a crimson stain that seeped from his shoulder. Blood on the floor gave away his position.

The man's gaze lifted weakly as Cutler approached. "Are you here to deport me?" he asked, his voice a hoarse whisper of defeat.

"I'm here for answers, not your extradition. But first, we stop you from bleeding out," Cutler replied, his voice low and even. "Your name's Guano, right?"

Affirmation came with a nod.

In swift, practised motions, Cutler was back from the car with a first aid kit. The course from Miami hadn't just been another box to tick—it was preparation for moments like this. Cutler didn't wait for consent; his hands were already assessing Guano, fingers probing for hidden damage, the pulse under his fingertips spelling out the urgency of the situation.

Cutler worked with the deft precision of a seasoned veteran. The wounds on Guano's body were telling—the bullet had carved a clean path through flesh and bone, but fortune had favoured the man; the damage was not beyond the reach of makeshift field treatment. Cutler's hands, steady and resolute, moved with an urgency that betrayed no hesitation.

However, the battered state of Guano's face spoke of violence that had left deeper scars than the bullet had. Cutler's gaze momentarily took in the ragged damage to Guano's mouth—the shattered teeth, the torn lip, the bruised gums, all mute testimony to brutality. There was an intimate horror to such injuries that could unsettle even the most steeled operative, but Cutler had long learned to lock away such reactions. These were injuries beyond his ability to remedy in the field.

For a moment, his hands paused, recognizing the boundary of his capabilities. Cutler focused on what he could fix, bandaging the shoulder with practiced efficiency, staunching the flow of life from Guano's body.

There would be time later for surgeons and dentists. For now, Cutler's task was to keep the man alive, to hold onto the thread of Guano's story that could help them find out who was responsible for the attack.

Guano's words tumbled out, each one slurred by the trauma to his mouth, each sentence an effort as he recounted the nightmare. His English, usually articulate, was now distorted, the sounds struggling to find their shape around the injuries.

"I pushed the throttle as hard as I could," he began, the recollection darkening his eyes with the memory. "The catamaran jolted forward." He paused, wincing as he relived the moment. "That's when the bullet hit me."

The shed fell into a tense silence, punctuated only by the sound of Guano's laborious swallow, a sound that carried the weight of his agony. "The men," he resumed, voice barely above a whisper, "they didn't hesitate. They… they ran over the clients, shot them without a second thought, and then… then they turned to us."

Cutler listened, his expression hardening with each word. The horror of what Guano described was stark, brutal, the kind of violence that left a permanent mark not just on the bodies of those who suffered it, but on the souls of those who survived to tell the tale. He absorbed every detail, every piece of the jigsaw that Guano's testimony provided, knowing it was vital intelligence.

Cutler's grip tightened around the needle. He could picture it, the chaos, the screams of terror mixed with the staccato rhythm of gunfire.

The raw admission came from Guano, a murmur of lingering shock and pain that threaded through the dim space of the outhouse. "They thought I was dead," he uttered, each syllable heavy with the weight of his ordeal. His gaze seemed to drift, lost in the horrific replay of that day.

Guano shifted, a wince crossing his features as he recounted the harrowing moment. "I was beneath a tyre, hidden from their view," he continued, his voice a haunted whisper. "One of them… he shot at it." His hand hesitantly rose to touch his mouth, fingers trembling as they hovered over the destruction left in that moment of callous amusement.

"It tore out my snorkel, and the bullet—" Guano stopped, the memories visibly fighting their way past the barrier of his pain. He didn't need to finish; the wounds spoke the grim remainder of the story. It was a grim testimony to the savagery he had endured, a cruel twist of fate that had saved his life while mutilating his body.

Cutler's face remained an unreadable mask, trained to keep his emotions in check, but his eyes were sharp with empathy and rage.

Guano shuddered, his body quaking with the intensity of the memory. Cutler resumed his stitching, the motion automatic."

Guano's voice held a desperate edge, the words tumbling out in a frantic cadence as Cutler worked with methodical precision on the exit wound. His hands were steady, but his mind was attuned to the urgency in Guano's plea.

"The police, they can't find me. I can't go back," Guano's eyes flickered with a wild fear, the kind that came from harrowing memories and the threat of being thrust back into them.

Cutler didn't look up from his task, but his response was immediate and calm, designed to install a measure of confidence in the man before him. "The local authorities are stretched thin, Guano," he assured him, his tone carrying the cool surety of someone who had assessed every angle.

"You'll be on your feet before they even start to close in on this place. Once I've patched you up, you're free to disappear. They won't get the chance to drag you anywhere you don't want to go," Cutler continued, his focus unyielding as he secured the final piece of gauze.

"Tell me about the leader, the one with the weird English accent" Cutler probed.

"The leader, he didn't fit in, not like the others," Guano's voice was low, but it carried the weight of his conviction. "He moved with a certainty, a swagger—you could tell he wasn't born to that desert heat, that his roots were set in cooler climates."

"Hear and names"

"Yes, 'Aziz'—it was said with respect, maybe even fear. And 'Awaale,' he spat it out like a curse."

A heavy silence settled as Colton snipped the last of the thread. Names were leads, and in their line of work, a lead was as good as a lifeline. "Aziz and Awaale," Cutler repeated to himself, etching the names into his own memory.

"Can you give me a description of the men?" Cutler asked.

Guano's revelation of his artistic skill added an unexpected asset to Cutler's operation. Even as the last stitch was tied off and Guano's wound was bandaged, Cutler could see the beginnings of a plan taking shape. The sketch would be invaluable—evidence it was the same man who Fabienne had identified as Birmingham born and bred an now calls himself 'Aziz.'

"Colton," Cutler called out, his voice firm with the urgency of their task. "Get that paper and pencil, fast as you can."

"Listen carefully, Guano," Cutler's voice was low, deliberate. "Every piece of information you give us helps to build the bigger picture. Helps us stop them from doing this again."

Guano nodded, his eyes reflecting the turmoil of his memories. He continued, "The African, Awaale, he was clearly terrified of the man he called Aziz. There was power in the way Aziz stood, a certain…

. "Did you notice anything else? Any specific features or behaviours that stood out?"

Guano's gaze shifted to the ground as he thought. "The Arab men, they followed Aziz's orders without question. The guns… they were like extensions of their arms, always ready, always pointed."

"And Awaale? After he was silenced, what did he do?" Cutler pressed, understanding the dynamics of fear and command.

"He… he backed down. He just nodded and went along with the rest of them. But I saw it in his eyes—hesitation, maybe even regret."

Cutler absorbed the information like a sponge. The complex hierarchy, the interplay of fear and power—it was all vital intelligence.

"Guano, you've done well," Cutler affirmed, locking eyes with the injured man. "You're a brave man."

Colton was back in moments, handing over a notepad and a set of pencils from the car. Meanwhile, Cutler turned his attention to Christensen, who had come in with Colton.

"Christensen, we need a dentist, someone discrete," Cutler said, the gravity of the situation clears in his voice. "Someone who can patch up Guano without raising flags or asking too many questions."

Christensen nodded, his fingers already investigating his address book. "I might know a guy," he murmured, his connections in the local area proving their worth once again.

As Guano braced himself against the pain, his good hand took the pencil with a determined grip. He began to sketch, lines and shadows taking form under his skilled fingers, creating a likeness that would soon be scanned and land on Fabienne's tablet.

The men watched, a quiet tension among them. This was more than just a drawing; it was the first step in finding out who was behind the attacks.

Cutler watched the portrait emerge, knowing each stroke brought them closer to their quarry. This was what MIDAS did— turn the tables, find the threat, and neutralize it. And it all started with the face on the page, the artist's rendering of the enemy.

"Can I go now?" Guano asked, after competing drawings of Awaale and Aziz.

"You can, but I want you to hand yourself into the police, you have information they need, and I think it will help you. We have some clout and will do everything to help you," Cutler said.

Cutler could see the cogs turning in Guano's head, the weight of each option being measured against a scale of risks and chances. The lines of stress on Guano's face were like a map of the hard decisions he'd had to navigate in his life, and here was yet another. But this time, Cutler knew the stakes were higher, not just for Guano, but for the case at hand.

"Listen," Cutler added, his tone softening just enough to show his sincerity without losing the edge of command. "The information you've given us, the descriptions, the sketches, they could save lives. They could prevent the next attack or bring down these killers. That's not just a bargaining chip—it's leverage."

Guano's eyes lifted to meet Cutler's, a clear struggle behind them. "And you'll stand by me? Really fight for my stay?"

Cutler extended his hand, a pact without paper but with the weight of his word behind it. "You won't face this alone. MIDAS has resources and I personally will see to it that we follow through. If you help the authorities, it reflects well on you. They're more likely to be lenient if they see you as an ally rather than a fugitive."

A moment passed, heavy with the weight of what was unspoken—the countless stories of broken promises and shattered hopes that both men were well aware of. But then Guano's hand met Cutler's, a firm shake sealing the deal just as a police car arrived.

"Not us," Cutler said.

"I'll go," Guano said, his voice firmer now, a decision made. "I'll trust you What about Mrs Paccar?"

Cutler nodded, satisfied. "Good man. As for Mrs Paccar," he said, glancing at the forlorn figure still clutching the remnants of her shattered life, "I'll make sure the neighbour comes to look after her. No one should be alone in a time like this."

As the police officers approached, Cutler stepped forward to greet them, his temperament one of calm authority. He would handle the exchange, ensure that Guano's cooperation was fully understood, and that his role as a witness was valued over his status as an illegal immigrant.

"Officers," Cutler called out as he met them halfway, "we've got a survivor here who's ready to help you, please treat him with respect."

Cutler turned to Christensen. "Get the dentist and the best lawyer on the island to meet them at the police station."

Cutler scanned the sketches on his phone and a minute later Fabienne had fed the images into her facial recognition software.

chapter seventeen
Into the Abyss

The dank chill of the holding cell seemed to seep into Old Joe's bones, as he paced the narrow confines, the stench of urine and vomit almost palpable in the stagnant air. Sixty agonizing hours of uncertainty had crawled by, each one hammering at his resolve, before the solicitor—a sharp-eyed woman with a no-nonsense approach, dispatched by Fabienne, appeared. Her arrival was like a sudden beam of light, slicing through the murk of his dire situation.

Outside the suffocating cell, a more insidious game played out. In an illicit digital exchange, veiled by the highest grade of cyber stealth, Fabienne transferred a hefty sum from an untraceable account into the personal coffers of the senior interrogating officer. A man whose greed outweighed his duty. With the transaction, Old Joe's paper trail would evaporate, the bureaucratic maze conveniently forgetting he ever existed. The only condition tethered to his freedom: he had to vanish from the island by sunset.

Staggering into the blinding sunlight, freedom felt like a surreal dream to Old Joe. At the harbour, a sense of displacement washed over him as he was greeted by Kai, a shipping agent with a demeanour as calm as the sea on a windless day. Cutler had prepared for everything—a package and a credit card were evidence of that.

The cat ketch moored at the dock was not his beloved vessel, the faithful companion on his nautical escapes around the world, but it was sturdier, older, its hull, one of promises of safety and endurance. Cutler had forced Conrad Ford to replace Old Joe's previous ship.

Kai handed over a prepaid Mastercard. "There's $50,000 here," he explained quietly, "for fuel, food, and whatever else you might need." The sum was staggering, ensuring not just weeks, but years of survival if he so wished. "Fabienne from MIDAS wants you to contact her before you sail."

As the reality anchored in his mind, Old Joe's throat tightened, emotions swelling like a tide. "Thank you, Cutler," he whispered, casting his words into the salty breeze, hoping they'd find their way to whatever sanctuary his benefactor occupied.

The transition wasn't seamless. Old Joe wrestled with new controls, familiarizing himself with the updated navigation system's digital glow, and the boat's unique quirks. Two exhaustive hours slipped by in checks and rechecks before he dared to navigate into the open sea. His course was etched in mind and map: a southerly path skirting treacherous waters, through East Timor, and ultimately, the northern shores of Australia.

Night unfurled its darkened banner overhead as he coasted along Lombok, the world reduced to the creak of the ship and the lapping of waves. Above, a dome of stars gazed down, their light dying before it touched the glassy obsidian sea. In the serene isolation, Old Joe dared to breach Cutler's package. Inside, a satellite phone and a charger nestled among padding—his lifeline to the world he was forsaking. Beneath them lay a note, the handwriting undoubtedly Cutler's, each word a lifeline pulling him back from the edge of his lonely odyssey.

Old Joe's hands trembled as he unfolded the paper, bracing himself for whatever directives or revelations were penned in the stark, military-precise script of a man who had already altered the course of his life in unimaginable ways.

'Joe,

If you are reading this, you didn't die on the quad bike, which was highly possible, given the circumstances. You did some bad things, albeit with the best intentions for Annie. You have made good inroads for redemption, and I am sure you will continue to do so.

The lads and I can't thank you enough for your help and assistance. There's a man called Conrad Ford who wouldn't see it the same way. Suggest you never speak of what went on to anyone and don't draw attention to yourself.

If you ever need help, hit three on the phone in the package, and you will be put through to a lady called Fabienne, who will try to help you and will let us know. Hope we never get the call.

Remember it's not the goodbye that hurts, but the flashbacks that follow.

Regards,
Cutler
Your friends at MIDAS.'

Old Joe swallowed hard, a bitter cocktail of shame and disbelief coursing through him as he considered the immense help he had received from Cutler and his associates at MIDAS. Did he truly deserve this lifeline? The weight of his past actions pressed on him like a leaden shroud Fabienne—he needed to call her before making a move, he reminded himself.

Pushing those thoughts aside, he focused on the satellite phone. A flicker of curiosity sparked as he saw that it held half of its battery charge. Five missed calls from the same unknown number piqued his interest. He made a mental note that it was probably Fabienne from MIDAS, and he would call her back in the morning. For now, he stretched out on the deck of the boat, taking in the vast, star-studded sky that had unveiled itself after the earlier sea mist dissipated. The Big Dipper loomed brightly on the northern horizon, a stark reminder of the path he now found himself on.

Using the torch which he pressed by mistake on the satellite phone's screen, Old Joe meticulously planned his next steps. Australia was his destination, with stops in Darwin and Cairns to keep the promise he had made to Annie regarding the Great Barrier Reef. He would embark on a new journey, ultimately reaching New Guinea. There, he would sell the boat and offer his services to UNICEF or another humanitarian organization, fulfilling his newfound purpose for redemption. Annie would need to wait a little longer for their reunion, for Old Joe had forged new plans, infused with a newfound zeal thanks to his friend and benefactor, Max Cutler.

The satellite phone, unbeknownst to Old Joe, remained partially powered on, awaiting a call. Moments later, the display lit up, signalling an incoming call from the same unknown number that was probably Fabienne's.

"Hello?" Old Joe answered, his voice tinged with curiosity.

"Hello Joe, I'm Fabienne," a calm, measured voice on the other end introduced itself, "Did Mr. Cutler explain who I am?"

"Yes, in a note. Is there a problem? I have five missed calls from you."

The reply from Fabienne came swiftly, tinged with urgency, "Are you still in Bali, or have you left on your boat?"

"I left several hours ago, heading south-east, the man at the port told me to phone you, but I forgot" Old Joe responded, a growing sense of unease settling in.

"I don't want to worry you, but Mr. Cutler wants you to take the boat to the nearest port, but not in Bali, and have it checked over," Fabienne explained urgently, "His instructions were to do this immediately and have it thoroughly tested. Let me know the boatyard undertaking the inspection, and we will cover the cost."

Before Old Joe could fully comprehend the gravity of the situation, a deafening explosion shattered the calm. Fabienne's voice became a distant memory as the line abruptly went dead. Panic set in as he frantically attempted to reconnect, but the phone remained silent, offering no lifeline.

Fabienne, at her end, instinctively tried to trace the call, hoping to ping off the satellite and pinpoint Old Joe's location. But all efforts yielded nothing but static. She played back the recording, the tension in her chest tightening as she discerned the unmistakable sound of an explosion just before the line went dead.

The deafening blast had been as swift and brutal as a thunderclap. The explosion tore through the boat with the sudden fury of a tempest, shattering the night calm in an instant. Wooden splinters flew like lethal daggers, and the air was filled with the deadly bonfire of burning debris and shrapnel. The front of the vessel, once a proud symbol of nautical durability, was now nothing more than a grotesque sculpture of fire and destruction.

In the heart of this chaos, a colossal fireball was born, its ferocity untamed and voracious. This was no mere blaze; it was a ravenous beast, consuming everything with an unholy appetite. The inferno's core glowed with an intensity that turned darkness into a harsh, unforgiving daylight, casting a hellish glow over the churning sea.

As the flames surged skyward, they seemed almost alive, a demonic dance of destruction. They reached upwards, as if trying to tear the very heavens apart, their crackling and hissing a sinister requiem. In this moment of absolute devastation, the night was transformed into a scene of apocalyptic terror, unbridled power of destruction unleashed.

In an instant, Old Joe found himself ensnared within this fiery vortex, a hapless victim of its merciless grasp. The searing heat bore down upon him, scorching the air and searing his exposed flesh. His vision blurred and distorted as waves of scintillating heat rippled through the atmosphere. The world became a nightmarish canvas of flames and chaos, and time seemed to stretch into eternity.

Within the tempest of fire, Old Joe's agonized screams were swallowed by the roaring inferno, his cries a futile protest against the relentless wrath of the elements. His senses were overwhelmed by the acrid stench of burning fuel, the crackling fury of the flames, and the blistering, oppressive heat that threatened to consume him whole.

In an abrupt shift, the raging inferno dwindled as swiftly as it had erupted, its intense fury dissipated, leaving behind a scene of desolate ruin. What had been a tranquil, reflective sea now resembled a chilling, eerie tableau, with its once-clear waters tainted by a foreboding, blood-red hue—a sombre reminder of the catastrophic violence that had recently transpired.

Old Joe, battered by the explosion's wrath, his body scorched and broken, was miraculously cast clear from the fiery maw. He found himself plunging into the cold, dark embrace of the sea, his fall broken by the remnants of the boat's rigging. Clutching onto a fragment of the shattered mast and a piece of the burning sail, he floated amidst the wreckage, a lone survivor in a sea of destruction, his spirit clinging to life as tenaciously as his hands gripped the remnants of the vessel.

The ensuing agony was beyond human endurance, a merciless siege on Old Joe's every sense. His skin bore the brutal marks of third-degree burns, a vicious map of unrelenting pain etched across his face, each nerve ablaze in an unceasing chorus of agony. The impact had shattered his very being, collapsing a lung, fracturing bones, leaving him broken amidst the chaos.

His clothes, once casual and comfortable, had morphed into a prison of agony, melding grotesquely with his blistered skin, the fabric inseparable from the seared flesh beneath. And as the relentless waves of saltwater lapped against his ravaged body, they brought with them a fresh hell of pain. The salt, like countless needles, found every wound, every raw nerve, magnifying the torment exponentially. With each crash of the waves, the pain surged, pushing him to the very edge of consciousness, a thin line between life and an abyss of darkness.

Beneath the shroud of agony that enveloped him, Old Joe was painfully aware of the jagged wooden splinter that had become an extension of his body, a grotesque emblem of his survival. It pierced his abdomen with cruel precision, its cruel emergence from his back a stark reminder of the cataclysmic explosion that had thrust him into this nightmarish realm. Saltwater mingled with his blood, the cold tendrils of the sea weaving a chilling tableau of crimson and salt that clung to him like a gruesome baptism.

Alone in the inky blackness, his every breath an anguished gasp, Old Joe clung tenaciously to the thin thread of life that remained. His body, once sturdy and weathered by life's trials, now felt frail and battered, a mere vessel for his indomitable will to endure. The relentless sea, with its capricious waves and unforgiving depths, bore witness to his torment, offering no respite from the suffering that coursed through his veins.

Amid the relentless pain and the suffocating darkness of his dire predicament, Old Joe's mind began to drift back to a time when life had been simpler, brighter, and filled with the warmth of love. In his fading consciousness, he summoned the memory of his beloved wife, Annie.

Annie, with her radiant smile and eyes that sparkled with life, had been his anchor in a world that often felt tumultuous and uncertain. She had been the light that guided him through the darkest storms, and her laughter had been the melody that chased away his worries.

As the cold waters of the sea enveloped him, Old Joe found solace in the recollection of their cherished moments together— their lazy Sunday mornings spent in bed, their adventures on the open ocean, and the countless nights they had shared under a canopy of stars, just like the one above him now.

With each laboured breath, Joe felt himself slipping further into the abyss. He longed to be reunited with Annie, to feel her embrace and hear her laughter once more. As the memories of their love washed over him, he clung to the hope that, in death, he would find the peace and serenity that had eluded him in life.

As the frigid sea cradled him in its icy embrace, Old Joe's final moments approached with a solemn serenity. With the last remnants of his strength, he closed his weary eyes and whispered a silent farewell to the world that had been both his sanctuary and his prison. In that poignant moment, he found solace in the knowledge that, at last, he would be reunited with the woman he had loved so deeply, for all eternity.

The mast that impaled him kept him afloat. He wished it would drag him under, to end the agony. Summoning a guttural scream, he drew upon a wellspring of strength he never knew he possessed. With excruciating agony, he began to pull at the embedded mast, wrenching it free from. Each pull sent shockwaves of pain radiating through his battered body, but he refused to yield. Once free he emptied the buoyancy in his lungs and slipped beneath the waves.

As Old Joe sank deeper, the world he knew seemed to vanish into a distant past, its memories fading into a surreal haze. The boundary between the tangible and the otherworldly became indistinct, almost dreamlike. His vision clouded, blurring the line between consciousness and the looming void of oblivion.

In this dire moment, as he hovered at the brink of the abyss, the stark reality dawned on him—there was no reversing this descent into darkness. The depths called to him, an inescapable siren song, and with each meter he fell, the pressure against his chest mounted, a cruel reminder of his mortal limits. His lungs ached, starved of air, yet no breath would come in this watery grave.

Amidst this struggle, as his body cried out for oxygen, Old Joe's mind, driven by desperation, crafted an illusion. There, amidst the crushing depths, he saw her—his beloved Annie, suspended in the liquid abyss, her hand outstretched toward him. In that fleeting instant, as his body convulsed with the last vestiges of life, he reached out, his fingers straining to bridge the gap between reality and illusion.

The vision remained a distant, unreachable realm as his vision blurred, and the cold embrace of the ocean claimed him. With wide-open eyes, Old Joe stretched his arms toward the spectral form of his beloved Annie, ready to embrace her for all eternity. In that final, desperate act, he surrendered to the chasm, where the pain and torment of the world could torment him no more.

chapter eighteen
The Inner Circle

The rain lashed against the Oval Office's windows, an unrelenting storm that mirrored the turmoil encapsulating President's Shelby's administration. Sixteen months in the hot seat, and the world seemed to enjoy throwing flames his way. Inside, the tension was a tangible entity, weaving through the room, feeding off the whispered conversations and the restless energy of the president. Shelby, a man forged by crises, felt the familiar weight of expectation and dread settle on his shoulders.

His own party's sharks circled, baring their teeth with every dip in the polls, ready to tear him apart at the first sign of blood in the water. They'd been waiting, biding their time, and today, they smelled fear. The morning's news had hit like a sucker punch: his approval ratings had plummeted, carving record lows that whispered Nixon's ghost.

But what came next made his personal political crisis seem like a schoolyard squabble.

The hijacking news thundered into the world's consciousness, a storm of terror and demands blasting from every screen, every speaker, and every panicked phone call. Al Jazeera had broadcast Awaale's chilling message from the Reef Explorer, and hell broke loose. The veterans, those brave men he was scheduled to meet, would have to wait. History was in the making, and it was bloody.

Ryan Welt, the president's chief of staff, was an enigma wrapped in a riddle. A former high-flying exec known for steering Aragon Derivatives through shark-infested waters, he was as out of place in the West Wing as honesty in politics. Yet here he was, his cool logic and ruthless strategy the eye in the centre of this gathering storm.

The office was a nerve centre, screens split between CNN, Al Jazeera, and the BBC, their murmurs a dissonant soundtrack to the crisis at hand. Welt, ever the pragmatist, sat stoically, eyes flicking between the reports and the president, analysing, calculating.

"The British are moving," Shelby's voice cut through the tension, his words heavy with the burden of command. "SAS units are en route to Cyprus."

Welt nodded, the news no comfort in the face of the chaos unfolding thousands of miles away. "The situation's a quagmire, Mr. President. We're staring down the barrel, and it's not just money these bastards are after."

Silence hung thick as Shelby processed. "What's the play, Ryan?"

"It's dark, sir. They've slaughtered over fifty passengers and crew, deviating from the pirate playbook. We're blind on American casualties, there could be over twenty "Welt's voice was steady, a rock in the rapids. "But there's a card in play. Oceanic Enterprises has skin in the game—MIDAS, a private outfit with boots on the ground. Three agents, American."

Interest sparked in Shelby's eyes. "Go on."

"Max Cutler, that's the name, sir. Former Secret Service. He's the main guy at MIDAS, been snooping around the Reef Explorer since one of their officers disappeared. He's got his informants," Welt said, leaning in, sensing a kindred spirit in Cutler's predatory tactics. "I've just hung up with him. He's convinced it's not about pirates—says it's a terror strike, led by Arab operatives, not Somalis."

Shelby's jaw set, knowing he was dealing with a situation more complex than he first thought.

"MIDAS, Cutler... right, he's the one who cracked the case of the serial killer targeting cruise liners. I recall now, there was a piece about him in the *Times* a while back. Nobody else had a finger on the pulse like he did."

Ryan Welt slid a dossier across the table to President Shelby. "This is everything on MIDAS. It's like a roll call of top-tier intelligence and special forces veterans. Cutler's assembled an impressive crew—former British intelligence operatives, ex-GCHQ maestro, ex-SAS members, past DEA agents, and as I mentioned, he himself is ex-Secret Service. They specialize in investigating disappearances at sea—MIDAS stands for Marine Investigations Deaths at Sea."

"Background?" enquired President Shelby, seeking more details.

"I'll tell you this, sir, these MIDAS operatives are as formidable on land as they are at sea. What we're looking at is a dual-threat— an elite intelligence network and a strike force, all in one package. And there's Fabienne Asper, ex-GCHQ, in their ranks. We've been tracking her for years, long before MIDAS was even a concept in Cutler's mind. Her encryption skills are like a fortress, virtually impenetrable. And her software development capabilities?

We don't have anyone who can hold a candle to her. But she's loyal to MIDAS, won't leave them for anything."

"You make them sound more CIA than the CIA," President Shelby remarked, a hint of intrigue lacing his tone.

He paused, the screens' flickering light casting gaunt shadows across his face. "They're formidable. Their comms networks. Might as well be military-grade."

Shelby's brow creased; the implication clear. "We've been surveilling an American outfit?"

Welt's gaze didn't waver. "Mr. President, CIA, Homeland, NSA, even the space boys at NASA—they're all scavengers hungry for intel. MIDAS isn't just resolving sob stories; they're knee-deep in matters of national security. They've got a clearance rate that makes our best look like schoolyard bullies fumbling in the dark. They're a wellspring of information we can't afford to ignore."

The president absorbed this, his eyes hardening. "Continue."

"Cutler's not some desk jockey, Mr. President. He's Secret Service, down to the marrow. Made a name in anti-counterfeiting ops, then pivoted to MIDAS after tragedy struck. He's rallied a cohort of the toughest, most seasoned dogs of war—ex-commandos, detectives who've stared down the barrel more times than they can count, intelligence virtuosos, linguistic prodigies. They pinned down a phantom, sir, a serial predator at sea, right under our noses."

Treisman's interest was a live wire now. "Go on."

Welt edged closer, his voice low. "Cutler blurred the lines between myth and reality. He hunted down the bastard who killed his sister. Word on the grapevine is, he served his own brand of justice—chucked the scumbag right into the blazing guts of a volcano."

The president let out a low whistle. "He doesn't play by the rules."

"He writes his own, sir. MIDAS operates from the Everglades, but their intel hub. A ghost operation in Geneva. They're not just successful; they're unparalleled. And Cutler? He's still one of us at heart. Comes across something that smells like national interest, he's on the line with his old Secret Service ties."

"And now?" Shelby was coiled for action.

Welt's eyes were steel. "Cutler's in the eye of the storm, sir. His mentor, Wyatt Rockman, reached out, played the national security card. We needed a full debrief on the hijacking situation."

"And?"

"He didn't hold back. Langley's ears were all over the call—analysts confirm he's straight-shooting. His intel chief, Asper, she's compiled a hit list of potential targets, puts our analysts to shame."

Shelby's next words were granite. "Targets, Ryan?"

"The Suez, sir. It's the crown jewel. Sink the Reef Explorer there, and we're staring down an economic black hole stretching into trillions. It's a chokepoint, Mr. President. Eight percent of global maritime traffic, over 6,000 miles saved per passage. And these hijackers, they're charting a course straight for Hurghada, right through the canal's jugular."

"The Egyptians won't allow that vessel anywhere near the Suez," Treisman stated, his voice a mix of iron resolve and smooth assurance. "It's crucial for their economy, pumping over five billion dollars into their treasury every year," President Shelby remarked.

"True, Mr. President," Welt replied, the gravity of the situation darkening his features. "But they won't engage. They can't risk the international fallout. They'll look to us, expect America to take the helm."

"The other players?" the president pressed, his gaze never faltering.

"Russians are fortifying their position in Tartus, Syria. It's a chess piece on their board," Welt added.

Shelby scoffed, a flash of disdain crossing his visage. "That's a Russian bear trap, not ours."

"But if that ship becomes a death trap for Americans, sir, it'll be our downfall," Welt retorted sharply. "Public sentiment is like a raging inferno. If Russia makes a move on the Reef Explorer while we're just watching, we'll be toast. Our approval ratings will plummet."

"Other variables?"

"Israel, sir. They've constructed radar towers in Ashkelon, missile bases near Akko. They're worried about that ship making a beeline for Gaza, highlighting the endless conflict, and perhaps picking up Palestinian refugees, or even targeting the radar installations," Welt delivered the information swiftly, his tone reflecting the gravity of the situation. "Israel will take action, sir, international backlash be damned."

Welt drew a breath, every word heavy with implication. "There's chatter from years back—terrorists plotted to bottleneck the Straits of Gibraltar. It's a long shot, but if the Reef Explorer veers north, it'll tip our hand to the Brits. Alternatively, they could aim for the Bosporus, cage the Russian fleet in the Black Sea."

He paused, letting the stakes sink in. "But the Russians are steps ahead, deployed the aircraft carrier Siberia to safeguard their interests."

The president was a fortress under siege, absorbing the blows. "Tourist hotspots in Turkey, the Greek isles, Tel Aviv, Haifa—sitting ducks. Every leader in that tinderbox has a stake in this."

"Exactly, Mr. President. The clock's ticking, loud and clear. This isn't a game of days. We're down to hours, maybe less."

"Assets?"

"USS Lincoln's in play. MIDAS's eye in the sky spotted the Reef Explorer bristling with explosives. A direct assault would be a bloodbath," Welt's tone was solemn, forecasting doom.

"So, we're shackled," Shelby's fist clenched. "We can't greenlight an Israeli offensive on the ship. Can't stomach or risk Russians slaughtering Americans in a botched rescue. Can't sanction a suicide mission ourselves, igniting a powder keg and killing civilians. And you're telling me we're racing against a doomsday clock?"

Welt nodded, the motion a death knell. "That's the swamp we're wading through, sir."

A moment of oppressive silence hung between them, the eye of the storm.

"What's our move, Ryan?"

Welt's eyes, hard with resolve and a flicker of something raw and desperate, met the president's.

"Wyatt Rockman has Cutler on the line," he said, the weight of their last hope pressing into the words. "MIDAS isn't just our best shot; right now, they're our only shot. Cutler's playing this close to the chest, but he's got a plan. If anyone can navigate this hell storm, it's him. We need to hear him out."

Shelby's jaw set, the decision, and its monumental consequences looming before him. In the brewing storm, with darkness encroaching, they were down to a single, perilous gambit. The fate of countless lives, the delicate balance of global powers, and the legacy of his administration hung on the razor's edge of this moment, on the brink of irrevocable history.

Shelby's jaw clenched. He'd given explicit orders—no interruptions, a decree only breached for the most critical of crises.

"Mr. President," the secretary's voice cut through the tense atmosphere, "Russian Prime Minister Petrov is on the line, demanding to speak with you immediately." Shelby reached for the phone. Contrary to popular belief, it wasn't the mythical red phone, often depicted in movies as the direct line for crisis communication.

"Mr. President, President Petrov here. How's the family?"

"We're all doing well, Oleg. And yours?"

"Good, I'm calling about the situation in the Mediterranean, Mr. President."

"Ah, a real tragedy with those snorkellers."

"Indeed, tragic. But there's a bigger issue. Terrorists have hijacked a ship in a crucial shipping lane."

"I've heard. Seems like a money grab more than a serious regional threat," President Shelby said, bending the truth.

"Mr. President, we have interests in that area."

"You guys have your hands in a lot of pies, Oleg. What's the concern?"

"I can't go into details, but if that ship, the Reef Explorer, threatens our assets, we'll have to intervene."

"Slow down, Oleg. The British are leading the response. They've probably got an SAS team heading there now."

"The British presence is just for show. They don't understand the potential harm this ship could cause, and they don't operate with Russian interests in mind."

"Oleg, don't underestimate British intelligence. They're likely well aware of the situation and will act accordingly."

"That might be too late, Mr. President."

"Remember, there are Americans on that ship. Any attack on it is an attack on us. Let the Brits handle the recovery. You have enough troubles with Ukraine, Mr. President?"

"Ukraine is an internal problem, Mr. President. But if the ship poses a direct threat to our international assets, action might be necessary."

"I hope it doesn't come to that, Oleg. Goodbye."

"Alright, Ryan. Speak to Admiral Collins."

"On it, boss," Welt replied, shutting the door behind him.

Welt's first call was to Admiral Collins. The man was holed up in a Japanese-run dive in Waikiki, soaking up Pearl Harbour's sun. Collins picked up, half-dressed, with a local girl dozing in the background. Next up, Welt dialled Secretary of State Morris, who was already in the loop about the Mediterranean chaos. Morris promised to shake some trees in the area and report back.

Welt's subsequent call to Callum Rees of the CIA was more intense, delving into the nitty-gritty. They discussed 'Red Storm,' an operation that was currently being executed by the Russians.

Less than an hour later, Welt was back in the Oval Office, standing ramrod straight in front of the president's desk, as was his way since he got the job a year back. He waved off the offer to sit, again.

"Mr. President, we've got a new twist. Admiral Collins reports our birds in the sky have spotted an Israeli Dolphin-class 2 sub, the Abraham bolting from Haifa. It's ahead of schedule by a fortnight. Something's up."

"Get Prime Minister Baum on the line," announced President Shelby.

Tension snaked through the room, a live wire thrumming with each passing second. "The last thing we need is Israel stepping into this sticky situation," Shelby muttered, the weight of impending tension bearing down on him.

The connection clicked after an agonizing wait. "Shalom, Abraham."

"Shalom, Mr. President. To what do I owe this unexpected call?" Baum's voice carried an edge, a man braced for a storm.

"Your Dolphin submarine, Abraham. Its sudden departure from Haifa—should I interpret it as a move concerning the Reef Explorer debacle? "Shelby's voice was steel sheathed in velvet, a warning of the tightrope they were all walking.

A moment of heavy silence, filled with unspoken strategies. "Mr. President, we both know that in the middle east political chess game, Israel often plays the role of a cornered king. Even though we don't know the specific target, it's prudent to assume it could very well involve our interests."

"Abraham, this situation reads like a standard hijacking, unrelated to Israel."

"Let's not indulge in pretences, Mr. President. The Reef Explorer, commandeered by extremists, poses a direct, unequivocal threat to Israeli security. We've always maintained a stance of proactive defence. This scenario? It screams danger, immediate and lethal."

Shelby felt the conversation spiralling. "Hypothetically, if these terrorists aim for Israel, any offensive against the diverse international passengers aboard will ignite a firestorm, both domestically and abroad."

Baum's resolve was unyielding. "We'll confront that crisis if it arises. My paramount obligation is the security of Israel."

Tightness gripped Shelby's chest. "How soon before your submarine reaches a critical position?"

"Fifteen hours."

"I'm asking for twenty-four, Abraham. Commit to a hold until then."

A heavy silence ensued, the unspoken words within it thunderous. "They're on a trajectory past our borders, Mr. President. That ship has set its course."

"Twenty-four hours, Abraham."

"Mr. President," Baum countered, his voice steely. "Post that, they breach proximity to our northern outposts. Any compromise of our radar systems leaves us vulnerable— a sitting duck for an Iranian missile onslaught. This could all be a grand orchestration for an all-out assault on Israel. My military advisors are pushing for a pre-emptive strike in sixteen. You propose twenty-four. I'll meet you in the middle: eighteen hours."

Treisman's mind raced; eighteen hours to avert an international catastrophe. "Agreed, eighteen it is."

"Your success is in our prayers, Mr. President," Baum's voice softened, a stark contrast to the rigidity of moments before.

In Israel, Baum presided over a fortress, not an office—a strategic hub alive with the hum of national defences. Surrounded by military brass and Avi Cohen, Mossad's chief, the call's echoes filled the room.

"He's feeding you fairy tales, Prime Minister," Cohen's cynicism cut through the tense air.

Baum's nod was grim. "Undoubtedly."

"Why risk global condemnation by destroying the Reef Explorer? It's likely the Russians will handle our dirty work," Cohen posited, the realpolitik stark in his tone.

Baum considered, eyes hardening. "The Americans might intervene with Russia, triggering a stalemate at sea. Meanwhile, the terrorists, caught in the crossfire, retain strike capabilities."

The room pulsed with unsaid fears, every mind envisioning a nightmare: their homeland, exposed and defenceless.

The atmosphere in the room was a tinderbox, every breath like a spark against the dry kindling of nerves. "Exact time of engagement, Prime Minister?" Admiral Hirsch's voice cut through the dense tension, a blade sharp with urgency.

Baum's gaze was steely, shaped by the myriad conflicts that had left their mark on the region. "Tell Captain Moesha to set the clock for T-minus sixteen hours. But" he paused, the weight of the decision palpable, "we're in the dark about the firepower those terrorists are packing. Satellites caught them loading crates onto the Reef Explorer. If there's even a hint they're gearing up for a strike, Moesha has the green light to move up our timetable. We don't know what they've got, and if they veer even slightly our way, Tel Aviv is in their crosshairs."

The unspoken dread was palpable, every official in the room acutely aware of the hair-trigger reality they were grappling with—a reality where mere minutes could determine the fate of millions.

Meanwhile, in Washington, Ryan Welt was poring over a dossier, the contents of which sent shivers down his spine, when a courier burst in, urgency written all over his face. The CIA report he handed over was like a live grenade. "Project Red Storm," it read, an operation that reeked of subterfuge and ominous intent.

"Mr. President," Welt began, voice barely concealing his alarm, "Red Storm isn't just another military exercise. It's a smokescreen for Russia's naval tentacles reaching into the Mediterranean, a counterpoint to our own strategic posts. British intelligence caught wind of a significant asset movement to Tartus, Syria, following Aleppo's downfall."

Shelby, already on a razor's edge, snapped, "What kind of asset, Welt?"

"A floating nightmare—a nuclear barge. Essentially, a mobile Chernobyl," Welt responded.

Cold realization washed over Shelby. "A nuclear reactor on Middle Eastern waters? Why in God's name wasn't this flagged at the top of our intel briefs?"

"Sir, GCHQ identified this monstrosity two years back. Our predecessors confronted the Russian envoy, demanding clarity on why they'd sneak a reactor into such volatile territory."

"And?" Shelby was practically bristling now.

"They pitched it as a beacon of humanitarian aid, claiming the barge would serve as a dual-purpose power generator and desalination plant, bringing life to war-torn wastelands."

Selby's s scowl conveyed his scepticism. "And we bought that tale?"

"Not for a second, Mr. President. But diplomatic dance aside, our satellites have since spotted over 10,000 Russian personnel flooding the zone. They're erecting a naval stronghold, fit for a fleet, right under our noses."

Treisman connected the dots, his gut sinking. "So they're anchoring their influence, permanently, in the Middle East. And now, they're petrified of an assault on this reactor."

"The consequences are unthinkable, sir," Welt said, his tone heavy with seriousness. "If the Reef Explorer collides with it, we're facing a catastrophic radioactive disaster spreading uncontrollably across the Middle East, all the way to Israel's borders. "We'd witness human and ecological devastation on an unimaginable scale. It wouldn't just be a local catastrophe. Radiation would poison diplomatic relations, sparking international outrage and potentially even war. Imagine the horror of Chernobyl, resurfacing like a ghoul from the past."

In the silence that followed, the gravity of their predicament settled like a shroud over the room. They were no longer merely players in a regional crisis but key actors in a scenario threatening global stability. The next steps required a dance on the geopolitical tightrope, where even the slightest misstep promised chaos.

The room's atmosphere was electric with unspoken peril, each word dropping like a stone into the abyss of potential catastrophe.

"That entire seaboard region of Syria would be rendered a ghost land for generations, Mr. President," Welt's tone was grim, the weight of his words resonating in the thick, charged air of the Oval Office.

"Are we talking apocalyptic consequences?" President Shelby asked, the creases on his forehead deepening as if trying to contain the explosive gravity of the situation within the folds of his skin.

In the gritty, tension-filled room, Welt's face was etched with concern as he relayed the grim possibilities. "Sinking that breached nuclear barge? It's a double-edged sword," he said, his voice low and steady. "Think about it—water could keep the nuclear beast alive, feeding the reaction. And if they sink it, we're not just burying a problem; we're spreading radioactive poison across the sea. It turns into an underwater Chernobyl, untouchable and leaking death for years. The cleanup? A nightmare. We'd be fighting an invisible enemy, one that sneaks into the food chain, into the air, everywhere. This isn't a simple smash and grab; it's a complex beast, and we're walking a razor's edge trying to tame it." His words hung in the air, a stark reminder of the perilous tightrope they were walking."

"And the fallout?" Treisman's voice was barely above a whisper, indicative of the tension that gripped him.

"An environmental time bombs. Billions poured into a perpetual effort to contain the nuclear seepage. Tartus would turn into a modern Pompeii, and the Russian Mediterranean dream would crumble into radioactive dust. Their geopolitical gameboard would be kicked over."

Shelby's mind raced, "Is it possible to move the reactor away from the area? Away from Syria and the Reef Explorer?"

Welt shook his head, "It's a behemoth, anchored deep and tied to the land. Mobilizing it isn't like hotwiring a car and speeding off. It lacks its propulsion system, requiring a fleet of tugs for movement. Besides, its strategic mooring leaves it exposed with zero natural barriers—only their military hardware stands between the reactor and oblivion."

"So they're cornered. Hence their desperation to annihilate the Reef Explorer and its innocent lives—a necessary sacrifice in their twisted calculus?"

"Any of the scenarios we've theorized could be their nightmare, sir."

Shelby's jaw set, "I need to review Cutler's strategy, Welt."

Welt exhaled, delving into the precarious details. "Cutler foresaw an all-out SAS assault as a gamble. The likelihood of Aziz triggering a catastrophic blast in response is sky-high. He recommended a precision strike by the Special Boat Squadron on the rudder—a daring manoeuvre, given the Reef Explorer's breakneck speed over turbulent waves. Still, within the realm of possibility for those men."

"And if they board?"

"The terrorists could unleash hell before the SAS even set foot on deck. It's a high-stakes game of chess with human pieces, Mr. President. Every move could spell disaster."

"Why would the British entertain such a gamble?"

"The final call would rest with the on-site SAS commander—a judgment call in the heat of the moment," Welt replied, the burden of the decision echoing in his words.

Shelby was silent before finally speaking, "Cutler seems to wield quite the strategic mind. Patch him through, Ryan."

Across the globe, in a makeshift strategic hub at a Limassol hotel, Max Cutler, alongside operatives Tuck and Colton, was knee-deep in drone feeds and intelligence chatter. Fabienne's voice sliced through the concentration, "Max, you have a call."

"Can't it wait, Fabienne? If it's not Stahmer, I'm swamped," Cutler responded, the strain evident in his voice.

"It's the president of the United States. Verified and urgent."

Cutler's eyes widened in surprise. Gesturing apologetically to Colton, he switched the call to speaker mode. "Mr. President, this is unexpected. How can I assist?"

Shelby's voice, edged with the sharpness of strained patience, filled the room. "Cutler, I'm given to understand we're on a secure channel?"

"Absolutely, sir. If Fabienne says it's secure, then you're speaking from a digital fortress."

Their words, laden with urgency and world-altering decisions, traversed the secure lines. The tension was a live wire, crackling through the secure line, stretching taut between continents.

"Your expertise is invaluable, Cutler," the president began, his voice carrying the strain of a man upon whose shoulders the safety of the world precariously rested. "Wyatt Rockman briefed me. The Reef Explorer situation is a ticking time bomb, and it seems we're hurtling toward a geopolitical disaster. The Russians, the Israelis—they're on a razor's edge. And now, we've got a countdown. Sixteen hours. That's our window."

Cutler's pulse thrummed in his ears, the deadline casting a stark, foreboding shadow over the operation. "We anticipated complications, Mr. President, but this… This narrows our play considerably."

"There's no rerouting fate, Cutler. I wish there were. The strings of this debacle are being pulled far from our reach," the president admitted, a rare note of helplessness seeping into his tone.

Cutler clenched his jaw, thinking of the lives at stake. "We have over two hundred civilians aboard that ship, sir. Plus, my team. Three of my best are mingling with the unsuspecting guests and crew, all of them sitting atop a floating powder keg."

"Can we make a move on the ship? Is boarding an option?" Shelby's question was a thin veil over the desperation that threatened to overwhelm command.

"The extremists have it rigged to blow, sir. Any overt action from our end, and they'll not hesitate to turn that vessel into debris. They don't fear death—they embrace it."

Silence hummed over the line before the president spoke again, "Your men on the inside… you've got a strategy, Cutler?"

"Affirmative, sir. There's a contingency in place."

"I was told you'd have something up your sleeve," the president said, a hint of bleak humour amidst the crisis. "Rockman claimed it'd be audacious. That's you, isn't it, Cutler?"

Cutler's mind raced, scenarios, risks, and outcomes flashing through his tactical mindset. "We've figured out a way to board the Reef Explorer unseen. Once there, our first task is to neutralize the explosive threat."

"And after that hurdle?" the president pressed, urgency underscoring his words.

"We engage close-quarter combat. Either the SEALs or SAS will spearhead the assault. Yes, we'll face resistance, possibly casualties, but nothing compared to the carnage if those charges go off. We can secure the aft, establish a beachhead on the ship, and use grapple lines for the assault teams' ingress."

Shelby exhaled a heavy breath, the decision weighing on him like a leaden mantle. "It's as if we're damned to intervene, Cutler."

"Mr. President, we're already neck-deep in a larger scheme. This was never a sideline view. The Reef Explorer is just the opening act," Cutler's voice was steel wrapped in velvet, calm yet relentless. "If we don't act, the Russians or Israelis will, without a second thought for collateral damage. They'd cite national security and wash their hands of the bloodshed."

Cutler's words lingered in the air, serving as a stark reminder of the harsh reality they were confronting. "I hear you, Cutler. I can't authorize your operation without obtaining consensus from my chiefs of staff. Nevertheless, I can make preparations, ensuring everything is in place if we receive the necessary approval. Now, tell me, what are your requirements?"

"Equipment, Mr. President. Tools we can't source here, stuck in bureaucratic limbo at Nicosia airport. We need it out of customs yesterday. Time's slipping through our fingers. By my estimate, we have till midnight, European time, before all hell breaks loose. I also need an air asset, a USAF or RAF chopper on standby within four hours, equipped with a Zodiac and an outboard motor."

"They've demonstrated they can hit a helicopter, Cutler."

"We'll maintain a safe distance, sir. The goal is to stay off their radar."

Shelby's voice hardened, the steel of command reinforcing his resolve. "The Russian jitters are forcing my hand toward military deployment. If they strike first, we're caught in a maelstrom of retaliation. It's a chain reaction, Cutler. One we can't afford, especially with Israel in the mix. Right now, you're the ace up our sleeve."

The line seemed to thrum with the enormity of what lay ahead, the silence pregnant with unspoken fears, strategies, and the ghost of the catastrophe that loomed on the horizon.

The tension was palpable, even though the secure line. "Cutler, you have conditional permission to proceed, subject to the approval we spoke of" President Shelby's voice carried that unmistakable gravitas, the burden of a decision that could alter the course of history.

"Sir, we're going to need a base of operations, somewhere we can coordinate and mobilize," Cutler responded, his tone reflecting the urgency of their harrowing race against time.

"Understood, Cutler. The USS Lincoln is stationed nearby. She's a floating fortress and equipped with state-of-the-art tech. Have Fabienne relay your specs, and I'll have Welt expedite the clearance and transport of your gear to the Lincoln. But, Cutler, you said you needed something else?"

"Yes, Mr. President. I need eyes on Armitech Industries, particularly Conrad Ford."

The silence on the other end was heavy, laden with the unsaid and the political undercurrents that ran deep and treacherous. "That's wading into dangerous waters, Cutler. Ford has his tendrils wrapped around pillars in the Senate, even Congress. What's the play?"

"He's not just bending the rules, sir. He's flirting with disaster, peddling weapons in the shadows to anyone flashing cash, friends, and foes alike. We've picked up information about a 'WCU'—

Weapons Control Unit. Fabienne's digging deep to crack what it stands for. But I'd wager everything I've got that it's aboard the Reef Explorer, Mr. President."

"That's a hefty allegation, Cutler. We'll circle back to this post-mission."

"Sir, with all due respect, we might not have a 'post-mission.' Our exit bird, courtesy of Armitech, crashed and burned off Java. Not long after we unearthed their dirty deals. And just now, I received word of an assault on our Everglades outpost. My people are down, Mr. President."

"Are you pinning this on Ford?"

"Without a shred of doubt, sir and Fabienne Asper has information that he is not alone."

Shelby exhaled, a sound of steel sharpening steel. "I'll dig into this, Cutler. If Ford's hands are as dirty as you say, we'll bury him under the jail."

"Thank you, sir," Cutler acknowledged, just before the line cut out, leaving only the echo of promises that hung heavily in the charged silence.

Exiting the sanctity of the Oval Office, President Shelby and his national security advisor, Ryan Welt, were flanked by their Secret Service detail. The atmosphere was electric with unspoken urgency as they descended to the subterranean confines of the war room. Gathered were figures that composed the nation's backbone during crises: advisors, intelligence chiefs, military heads, all with the weight of the free world on their shoulders.

Treasures of trust had been exchanged with British Prime Minister Tess Wills since Shelby's rise to the office. Now, that relationship was put to the test as they navigated waters mired in threat and geopolitical intrigue.

"Tess, I'm briefed on the Reef Explorer nightmare. Your offer to deploy the SAS is a lifeline—we can't get the SEALs there in time. But there's a caveat. We have a private contractor, a key player on the ground. Your forces will need to blend operations with them."

A pause, then the hint of confusion from across the Atlantic. "Our SAS operates in solitude, it's their strength. I'm unsure about this synergy, especially with a non-military entity."

"I share your reservations, Tess, but the details are too sensitive to transmit. Our man will neutralize the onboard threat and prep for your team's entry. They're our best shot."

"I need to convene with my emergency response, the Cobra committee. This is… unprecedented."

"Time is a luxury we don't have, Tess. How quickly can you get Cobra on board?"

While Shelby anxiously awaited her response, the war room existed as a self-contained universe, with the stars of intelligence piercing the darkness of the challenges before them. It resembled a black hole, a potential disaster lurking ominously. Every passing second resonated with the reverberations of consequences, and the next actions were of paramount importance as they navigated the precarious terrain of international diplomacy and covert warfare, teetering on the brink of uncertainty.

The room was a cauldron of silent tension, everyone lost in the gravity of the situation. The strategists, military chiefs, and intelligence advisors each bore the weight of the impending crisis on their shoulders. The atmosphere was electric, charged with the potential energy of a thundercloud about to burst.

"We're currently hosting the Cobra committee," Tess's voice crackled over the secure line, her tone betraying the high stakes. "Who exactly are we coordinating with, Mr. President?"

"MIDAS. It's a private outfit led by Max Cutler. His point person on this is Fabienne Asper, ex-GCHQ," Treisman replied, his voice the calm in the eye of the storm.

"Very well. Give me twenty minutes to thrash this out with my team," Tess responded, the line going dead as she turned to confront the task at hand.

Selby set the phone down gently, pouring himself a glass of soda water, the fizz a stark contrast to the stifling pressure of the room. He turned to Welt; his gaze hardened by resolve. "Get the CIA on Ford and this 'WCU.' I want a full brief in an hour. Also, set up a meeting with the director today."

No sooner had the president set his glass down than the phone shattered the silence. It was Tess, back from her deliberations. "We're on board, with conditions. Our SAS takes command once they're on the Reef Explorer. Your contractors will comply."

"Understood and agreed. Have your team in Cyprus, and we'll arrange their reception on the USS Lincoln. They can set terms with Cutler directly," Selby negotiated.

"ETA 35 minutes they are out of Limassol, Mr. President," Tess confirmed before disconnecting.

Moments later, the phone erupted again, this time the Russian prime minister on the line after multiple failed attempts. The conversation was brief, laced with veiled threats and diplomatic sparring. The tension between the two leaders was almost palpable, a deadly game played with human lives.

As the call ended, President Treisman stood, his silhouette framed against the backdrop of the Oval Office window. His reflection superimposed on the view outside, a man standing against the world.

"Ryan, I want the USS Lincoln on full alert. They are to safeguard the Reef Explorer at all costs," he ordered without turning.

Welt executed the command immediately, his fingers flying over the phone keypad. As he finished, he looked up to find the president, still a statue at the window.

"What's the next move, sir?"

"Gather the chiefs of staff. War room, fifteen minutes."

As the advisors and military heads filed into the war room, there was a sense of grim determination. They had heard the recordings, understood the stakes. President Shelby took his seat, his eyes surveying the room, making contact with each person there. This was a council of war, and their decision could very well shape the future.

"We've all been briefed on the situation with the Reef Explorer, heard the stakes from the British and the Russians, and just getting to grips with the risk posed by Armitech and Ford. I need to know we're unified in this," he paused, his gaze locking onto each individual around the table. "Are we prepared to sanction this operation and stand against any threat to those civilians?"

The room was still for a heartbeat, and then, one by one, the members of the most powerful crisis committee in the world gave their assent. They were committed, come what may. The storm was coming, and they would meet it head-on.

As they exited, the corridor outside the war room felt oppressively quiet compared to the strategic hub they'd just left. The gravity of the decisions made within those walls carried a weight that seemed to silence the usual hum of White House activity.

"Sir," Ryan Welt ventured cautiously, respecting the heavy contemplation the president was undoubtedly in, "If I may, what's running through your mind?"

President Shelby walked with measured steps; his hands clasped behind his back. "History, Ryan," he replied, his voice low but firm. "I'm thinking about how history is a beast with an insatiable appetite. Today, whatever happens, it will demand that we feed it decisions that will shape the world for years to come."

They moved towards the Oval Office, the setting sun casting long shadows through the windows, mirroring the darkness creeping into their circumstances.

"Sir, the situation is precarious," Welt continued, glancing sideways at the president, "but you made decisions based on the best possible advice and real-time intelligence. The American people, when they know the facts, will understand the need to protect our citizens and uphold international stability."

The president halted, turning to face Welt fully, the evening light painting his profile in hues of burning seriousness. "Ryan, in that room, we juggled human lives, international relations, and the risk of a military confrontation. These aren't statistics, strategies, or chess pieces. They're lives, and the ripple effects of today's actions will be felt far and wide."

He resumed walking, more slowly now. "We've potentially put men and women in harm's way, not just those aboard the Reef Explorer, but also our service members and MIDAS operatives. We've poked a bear by engaging with Russia. Now, we brace for the consequences."

Welt, feeling the enormity of their conversation, remained silent as they entered the Oval Office.

The president moved to his desk, picking up a pen with a slightly shaking hand. Below it lay countless documents needing his signature, decisions requiring his approval, and letters from people whose lives were affected by his administration. But they all faded into the background, insignificant in the face of the current crisis.

He looked up, meeting Welt's eyes with a resolute stare. "Keep me updated on every move. I want to know the moment the SAS boards the Reef Explorer, the status of the USS Lincoln, any murmur from the Russians, and especially any more information on Conrad Ford and Armitech."

Welt nodded, the gesture solid and sure, understanding the mantle of his duty. "Absolutely, Mr. President. First-hand information, as it comes."

As Welt exited, President Shelby turned to the window, gazing out as the twilight danced on the horizon, pondering the lives in his hands. In the silence of the Oval Office, with the night drawing in, he felt the loneliness of command. He picked up the phone, ready to make more calls, to shore up international support, and to prepare for any fallout.

Outside, the world continued to turn, unaware of how different tomorrow might look.

chapter nineteen
Race Against Time

Aziz was deep in a high-stakes game of hide and seek. Fate had thrown him against a cunning and sharp adversary in Stahmer. They kept moving, always one step ahead, scanning escape routes and marking hijacker sightings. They ducked into the waste disposal, then to the crew canteen hidden in the ship's belly and slipped into the laundry at the hint of danger. They even snuck into the wheelhouse bar, now holing up in the life jacket storage on deck five.

They'd had a few close shaves with the Arab and Somali pursuers, but the run-in with the Africans earlier was hair-raising. Shultz was on watch, holing up in the lifeboat across from the storeroom, concealed within. He peered through a salt-battered Perspex window, keeping a vigilant eye on the life jacket store's entry. Armed with a hefty metal bar, he was poised to pounce from his lookout in the lifeboat if trouble came knocking. Meanwhile, Ghislaine was prepping for any showdown, pinning her long black hair into a tight, no-nonsense Swiss bun, not about to let it become a liability.

Stahmer was on the sat phone to Geneva. After a quick check-in with Fabienne, the line was switched to Cutler on the USS Lincoln.

"Stahmer, what's the situation?" Cutler's voice crackled through.

"Just keeping our heads above water," Stahmer replied.

Cutler, finding a secluded corner in the wardroom to escape the relentless noise of the Lincoln's flight deck, relayed the fresh intel. "Here's what Fabienne unearthed. This Umair Aziz, actually Richard Hussein from Birmingham. London radicalised him, then he did rounds in Al-Qaeda camps in Yemen, Afghanistan. Nabbed in Iraq, 2012. But then, there's this blank spot in his file, up until Abu Ghraib, just before the big jailbreak in 2013."

"And his expertise?" Stahmer enquired.

"Tech savvy, but he's seen combat in Afghanistan and Iraq. Was on a Most Wanted list, then declared dead. Interesting, eh?"

"What about the African, Awaale?"

"Only got the first name. Common in Somalia. Of the three we know, one's dead in Libya, another's too old. Our Awaale's the third, from Marka. Loose ties with Al-Shabaab, not a zealot, but plays ball with radicals for survival. And easy to spot—childhood leprosy scars."

Stahmer mulled over the details. "So we've bumped into Awaale already. Any family ties for either him or Azziz that we know of?"

"Aziz is a lone wolf, no ties left. Awaale, though, he's got a wife, four kids. Here's a twist—Kenyans tore through his village, Awaale was the main mark. Stripped him clean, Fabienne says. Happened two weeks before he met with Aziz in Jordan. My bet? Awaale was cornered, forced into this gig."

"Hmm, he's the fall guy, then," Stahmer pondered.

"Either that, or Aziz needed a black African face to paint this as a hijack, not terrorism, didn't last too long that fairy tale," Cutler suggested.

"Not exactly a smooth plan, was it?"

"They didn't count on Guano making it out to tell us Arabs were in charge. And they sure as hell didn't know you'd be on that ship, Stahmer. Without those, the world might still be buying the hijack story."

"Or maybe they needed time to rig the explosives. Any idea on the real target, Cutler?"

"It's a crapshoot. Could be the Suez, Israeli radars, Syrian nuclear site, prelude to an Iranian strike on Israel, or targeting tourist-packed beaches."

"A lot of variables," Stahmer acknowledged.

"There's another player—Sheldrake. Seems he's the brains. Fabienne's digging through Bali's immigration records for a match."

"She's hacking into it?"

"Fabienne's doing her thing. Back to you—seen any big guns on board?"

"We've spotted boxes on the upper deck, under constant watch. They've shown off grenade launchers and there's the explosives on deck six."

"Got it. What's the enemy layout? Arabs and Somalis mixed?"

"Last I checked Arabs on the bridge, mixed teams in the engine room, rear deck, and doing sweeps. An Arab on deck ten, sometimes with a launcher."

"So the back's heavily guarded, eyes on all approaches. And they're watching the explosives."

"That's the setup. We've got two plans. If you think Plan A is dead in the water, I'll back your call, you're the man on the ground."

"Plan A's talking to the Somali leader. Tell him the US president's offering a clean slate and a million per head for his crew. No backlash, now or ever."

"Hang on," Stahmer said, turning to brief Ghislaine.

"What's plan B?"

"No contact or help from the Somalis. Your team needs to take control of the poop deck, neutralizing the guards. We need this done sharp at 2000 hours. We'll need your team on the stern deck to assist our boarding."

"Boarding?" Stahmer clarified.

"Not fully greenlit by the president yet, but I expect it soon."

"Any special forces?"

"After the explosives are handled, SAS will move in," Cutler confirmed.

"Roger that," Stahmer responded, turning to Ghislaine. "We need to position ourselves on the poop deck. Grab some knives from the galley and meet me here in ten. I've got to get Shultz up to speed on the plan."

"Alright. I need a moment to plan this out," Ghislaine said, already mapping her route in her mind.

The ship's stairwell, a 'V' lying on its side, offered a tactical advantage for Ghislaine. With her shoes off for stealth, she hugged the wall as she descended. On deck four, Somali chatter made her pause. Peeking around, she spotted two guards, neither showing signs of leprosy.

She moved down to deck three, quieter, lined with cabins and laundry facilities but devoid of bars or eateries. Dead passengers and crew members lay scattered, a grim reminder of the situation's severity. She made her way to the galley, the tension palpable with each step.

In the galley, she swiftly collected two large knives and a meat cleaver, carefully placing them into a day bag, cushioned by an apron to silence any clinking. Exiting the kitchen, her heart skipped a beat as she nearly collided with a Somali guard. He froze, eyeing her curiously as he lit a cigarette, the semi-automatic rifle across his chest remaining untouched. It was his patrol area; encountering him was inevitable in the chaos of the hijacked vessel.

Ghislaine, prepared for such encounters, had developed a contingency plan back in the life jacket store, ready to adapt to the unfolding situation.

The Somali, mistaking her for just another crew member. She scooped up her breasts. "You like these?" Ghislaine taunted, feigning vulnerability.

The Somali's gaze didn't waver, his words crude. "Nice," he remarked, moving closer with a predatory glare.

"How about some privacy in the galley?" Ghislaine suggested, steering him away from the corridor.

Once inside the kitchen, the Somali maintained a cautious distance, his hand never straying far from his weapon. "Take off your blouse and skirt. Gotta check for weapons," he demanded, his tone leaving no room for argument.

Ghislaine complied, she put on a show for the Somali ensuring his eyes never left her body as she laid down her day bag and slowly shed her clothing. Ghislaine was left in her blue lace bra and matching high cut panties. "See? I carry no weapons; I am not here to hurt you."

The big Somali laughed, "Hurt me? Little girl could not hurt me."

"You are right; I could not hurt you."

The Somali still held the cigarette and moved towards her; with his free hand he began to unzip his pants. He dropped the Marlboro to the floor and crushed it with his boot. "Make me happy," he said and advanced towards her with his enlarged penis in hand.

Ghislaine dropped to her knees in compliant mode, which excited the Somali more. Ghislaine clutched the sizeable black member with her left hand; the Somali rolled his eyes in pleasure. She maintained the foreplay while using her right hand deftly searching her day bag. The Somali placed both his hands on the back of her head pushing her lightly at first towards him and then increased the force. Pushing her downwards for a second, he could not understand why it was not the pleasurable experience expected, and when he moved her back why her face was bloody. In her left hand, she held his penis and, in her right, was a kitchen knife. He looked down bewildered, and the pain hit him from where she had severed his manhood. His reaction was to drop both hands to the area to stem the blood, and his legs gave way.

Cutler had ensured all MIDAS agents who had not been in the forces had one-to-one combat training, using a variety of weapons and objects. Ghislaine had undergone the training with enthusiasm, impressing her instructors. However, that was under controlled conditions, and she had never had to use force before, let alone kill. Ghislaine comprehended she had to act quickly before the Somali's screams brought along uninvited guests or he attacked her. Before he could howl again, she thrust the boning knife into his throat. He collapsed, moving his hands from his groin to try to stem the aerated blood.

Ghislaine, with a steely resolve, dragged the Somali's body into the freezer. She quickly cleaned the blood from the deck and galley walls, then hosed herself down, redressing with haste. She armed herself with the Somali's semi-automatic and spare magazines. Retracing her steps with cautious precision, she moved past the lifeboat, slipping into the life jacket store unnoticed.

No sooner had she closed the door behind her than Shultz emerged from the lifeboat, following her in. Ghislaine placed the semi-automatic and the three knives on the table.

Stahmer, eyeing the weapons and her dishevelled state, remarked, "Looks like you had a bit of a situation."

"Just a minor hiccup," Ghislaine responded, fighting to keep her emotions in check.

Shultz, blunt as ever, asked, "Is the problem… permanently solved?"

"Yeah, hid the body," Ghislaine said, her voice steady despite the ordeal.

"Right, let's not get hung up on that. Good news is, we've got ourselves some weapons now, thanks to you," Stahmer acknowledged, nodding at Ghislaine.

Stahmer reached for the sat phone, punching in Fabienne's number, but instead, it was Cutler's voice that boomed through, nearly drowned out by the chaos around him—the unmistakable roar of a Pave Hawk helicopter prepping for the mission.

"Hold on, Stahmer, just need to find a quieter spot," Cutler's voice boomed over the din, giving Tuck a nod to keep prepping the bird.

A moment later, the line cleared. "Alright, I'm somewhere I can hear you now," Cutler said, having commandeered a space in the wardroom, much to the chagrin of a couple of sailors.

"We're set here. Got a semi-auto and a stash of knives, all courtesy of Ghislaine," Stahmer reported.

"Ghislaine?" Cutler echoed. "Got the green light from the top brass, we're a go," Cutler's voice crackled through the satellite phone.

"What's the play?" Stahmer asked, ready for the details.

"We'll be hitting the poop deck from the sky, 2030 hours. Need Shultz to guide us in; you're on point," Cutler instructed.

Stahmer frowned. "That's a tight spot for a landing. How you planning to nail that?"

Cutler's voice was calm. "We've got a strategy. But we'll need Shultz to secure the chutes, quick-like, or the wind will whip us overboard. We drop in 20-second waves."

Stahmer's scepticism was palpable. "That's a tall order, mate. Airdropping onto a moving target? Plus, any aircraft buzzing too close will get smoked by their SAMs."

"Two teams," Cutler confirmed, "One team will approach from the sea, we will be the second team and will jump from several miles out using the flying suits, then parachute down onto the deck."

Stahmer, Ghislaine, and Shultz moved like shadows through the Reef Explorer, their steps muffled against the ship's steel floors. The air was thick with tension, each turn a potential encounter with the Arab terrorists patrolling the corridors. Stahmer led the way, his eyes scanning every corner, every possible hiding spot. Ghislaine followed closely, her senses on high alert, her hand gripping the semi-automatic she had acquired earlier. Shultz brought up the rear, his experience making him the perfect rear guard.

They had to reach the poop deck unseen; a task akin to threading a needle in a hurricane. The ship, a labyrinth of narrow corridors and sudden open spaces, presented a challenge that Stahmer navigated with the precision of a veteran soldier. They ducked into empty cabins and utility closets, pausing to let patrols pass, their breaths held in unison. The terrorists, armed and on edge, were an ever-present threat, their voices echoing off the walls in a deluge of foreign tongues.

In one heart-stopping moment, they were nearly spotted. A pair of terrorists rounded the corner just as the trio slipped into a service alcove. Stahmer's hand signal froze Ghislaine and Shultz in place, their backs pressed against the cold metal, the terrorists' voices a mere whisper away. The tension was palpable, a tangible entity that gripped them until the danger passed.

Moving deeper into the ship, they encountered signs of the terrorists' passage—discarded ammunition clips, a hastily abandoned lookout post, a map of the ship with areas circled in red. Stahmer studied it briefly, memorizing the layout, before leading them on.

As they neared the poop deck, the sound of the sea grew louder, the smell of salt air stronger. The deck was their goal, but also their biggest risk—open, exposed. Stahmer peered around a corner, his hand signalling 'hold'. Two guards stood at the entrance to the deck, their attention focused outward, towards the sea. This was their chance.

With a series of hand gestures, Stahmer laid out a silent plan. Shultz would create a distraction on the opposite side, drawing the guards away. Ghislaine would then take point, her weapon ready, while Stahmer provided cover. It was risky, but it was their only shot.

Shultz slipped away, circling around to approach the guards from the other side. The sound of something crashing echoed moments later, the guards snapping to attention and moving off to investigate. Like wraiths, Ghislaine and Stahmer darted out, crossing the threshold onto the poop deck, the sea breeze a sudden slap against their faces.

Now concealed behind a sturdy steel door near the poop deck, Stahmer, Ghislaine, and Shultz crouched in the shadows, each moment stretching like hours. The door provided scant cover but was their best bet in staying hidden until Cutler's team made their daring entry. The sound of the sea lapping against the ship's hull was a constant reminder of both their isolation and the imminent danger.

Ghislaine quietly passed the semi-automatic to Shultz, who, with the deftness of a seasoned warrior, double-checked its readiness. Stahmer, meanwhile, kept his gaze laser-focused on the narrow view of the deck, his every sense sharpened to the ship's rhythm. Shultz maintained his vigil on the corridor behind, a human shield against any unexpected threat.

The wait was a mental warfare, each team member entrenched in their own headspace, strategizing for the impending chaos that Cutler's arrival would unleash. They were acutely aware that the fate of the hostages and the mission's success teetered on a knife-edge.

Each distant sound, each murmur of the ship's groan heightened their alertness. They were like coiled springs, hidden in the belly of the ship, primed to leap into action. This game of stealth and survival they played was critical, and they were the unseen force ready to strike against the terror that had hijacked the Reef Explorer.

Time seemed to slow as they braced for the climax of their operation. Stahmer exchanged a look with his team, a silent signal of their readiness.

chapter twenty
Farewell to a Friend

John Bruce, better known as 'Jock', was a force to be reckoned with—a blend of relentless determination and Scottish grit. His bond with Tuck was forged in the fires of Special Forces operations, a brotherhood built on shared experiences in combat and camaraderie in the downtime.

When Basmati was sidelined with an injury, and with Cortez on security duties in the Everglades, their team was at least man down. Cutler, a leader who valued trust above all in his field operatives, would only consider a new addition if Tuck or Stahmer vouched for them. Without missing a beat, Tuck threw Jock's.

Jock, a rugged Scotsman with a penchant for whisky and a thick brogue, was wrapping up a security gig in Kuala Lumpur, playing bodyguard to a tycoon's son—a job more about appearances than actual danger. When Tuck reached out with an offer from Cutler—a payout for his current contract plus a bonus to dig up dirt on the hijacked yachts in Bali—Jock didn't hesitate. Bags packed; he was on an internal flight to Freemantle within hours.

His mission was clear: trace the hijacked yachts and uncover the owner of the boatyard where they were being cleaned up. Fabienne, their intel ace, fed Jock satellite data and leads, pointing him towards Fremantle in Western Australia.

Fremantle, with its Victorian architecture, felt oddly familiar to Jock, reminiscent of Glasgow or Edinburgh, albeit under a relentless Australian sun—a stark contrast to Scotland's habitual grey skies. He familiarized himself with the locale, the watering holes, cafes, and potential exit routes—always the tactician.

Fabienne's package—a military-spec laptop and smartphone—awaited him at his hotel. The leads brought him to Fremantle, but the trail could lead to any number of boatyards. Jock spent his mornings poring over maps, aligning them with satellite images, his nights in the local bars, piecing together the puzzle.

His breakthrough came over a glass of Johnny Walker's Black Label. He pinpointed the last sighting to a spot by the Swan River. After a breakfast spat over the absence of porridge, Jock scouted the identified area, meticulously mapping out the long industrial road by the river.

Content with his day's reconnaissance, he settled for the evening with a local brew and his customary whiskey chaser. Back in his room, he shot off an email to Fabienne with his findings.

Soon after, his secure phone rang—it was Fabienne, confirming his suspicions. "Owens Marine Repair Boatyard, recently acquired by someone named Sheldrake," she informed. The same Sheldrake Cutler had flagged in Bali. Jock, listening intently, felt the pieces of the puzzle falling into place.

"Will check it out and get back to you," Jock said, his voice echoing the assurance and resolve that came with years in the field.

The return call from Jock came the next morning. In their line of work, patience was as critical as action. Jock knew the value of gathering the right intel, the importance of timing. He wouldn't make a move or share information until he had everything lined up perfectly.

When he finally got back to Fabienne, his report was loaded with fresh intelligence. His voice, steady and confident, relayed the details with precision.

"Seems we're on to something," Jock replied, a trace of satisfaction in his voice. "Guy's done a proper clear-out, hasn't he? Rounded up a proper band of misfits. Nice digging with those tax records and Crim-Trac, Fabienne." His Scottish accent added a rugged edge to his words.

"Thanks, Jock. Seems Sheldrake got a taste for the shady types," Fabienne added, detailing the criminal pasts of the boatyard workers. "Quite the band of misfits he's assembled."

Jock's chuckle was dry. "Bet they're a lively bunch. You sure know where to dig to get your information. Any chance you could dig up what my ex-wife's splurging my alimony on?"

Fabienne's laughter tinkled through" Counselling probably."

Jock couldn't help but chuckle at Fabienne's quip about his ex-wife. The light-hearted banter was a brief respite in their high-tension line of work.

For the next several days, Jock turned into a shadow, surveilling the boatyard employees. Each night was a new mission as he tailed one worker after another, blending into the background like a ghost. His notes detailed their living situations—who was alone, who had a family. Fabienne's intel painted a picture of a diverse crew, a melting pot of nationalities, all united under Sheldrake's shady operations.

Armed with scuba gear, Jock executed a series of unseen recon missions around the boatyard. He moved with the stealth of a seasoned operative, undetectable in the murky waters of the Swan River. The boatyard's security was a mix of passive and active measures, but to Jock's trained eye, there were gaps. He cleverly employed a pencil camera, mounted on a twig, to survey above the waterline, identifying a strategic entry point between two steel supports.

The shipyard was a sprawling complex. Two dry docks held vessels in place, while concrete platforms supported the ships' massive weight. A wet dock completed the layout. Jock's reconnaissance was thorough, laying the groundwork for whatever operation was to come. Each piece of information was a valuable asset in the intricate puzzle they were piecing together against Sheldrake and his operation.

With a new notification from Fabienne. Jock, having settled into his makeshift surveillance centre in his hotel room, juggled his dinner with the unfolding developments in the operation.

The message from Fabienne was concise. "Footage received. Analysing now. Will update ASAP," it read. Jock, with his typical efficiency, had managed to capture vital footage of the yard's activities, zooming in on the faces of the workers and the details of the stolen yachts. This wasn't just any boatyard; it was a den of high-stakes criminal activity, a place where stolen luxury yachts were given new identities.

Jock leaned back, savouring a bite of his steak and the crispness of the beer, his eyes never straying far from the laptop screen. The work of an operative was never done—even as he ate, he remained alert, ready to jump back into action at a moment's notice.

The conversion of Ford's Coca V1 into the elegant, obsidian-hued vessel 'Morning Sun' stood as evidence of the shipyard's remarkable expertise in camouflage. The intricate craftsmanship evident on the LSX 92 Lazzara and the rest of the yachts emphasized the magnitude of the undertaking. These individuals weren't novices; they were seasoned experts in the realms of larceny and deceit.

Jock's GoPro footage was a goldmine of information. Fabienne's analysis of it would provide crucial leads. Every face, every detail captured by the camera could be the key to unravelling Sheldrake's network.

As Jock finished his meal, his mind was already racing ahead, planning his next move. The game was afoot, and he was in the thick of it. With Fabienne's intel and his own skills, they were inching closer to blowing the lid off Sheldrake's operation.

Jock read Fabienne's LATEST message with a sense of accomplishment. 'Confirmed—LSX 92 Lazzara, Coca V1, Ferretti 620—checking others.' It had only been a week, but already three hijacked yachts were confirmed. The operation was gaining momentum.

Jock knew without a doubt that the yard workers were complicit in the fraud. They might not know the full extent of the hijackings' consequences, but they were clearly in deep. Observing the workers, Jock noted discrepancies. Their lifestyles didn't match those of typical blue-collar workers. Flashy cars, upscale homes, luxury toys—these were giveaways.

His evenings were spent at 'The Billabong', the local watering hole frequented by the boatyard crew. It was here that Jock blended in, watching, listening. After a couple of nights, it was clear that

Demi, the Greek Australian, was the odd one out. Demi lingered at the bar until closing, often arguing with his girlfriend on the phone. Jock, ever the shadow, heard it all from his vantage point near Demi's house. The white powder residue around Demi's nose didn't go unnoticed either.

Jock made his move, befriending Demi over shared drinks and casual banter, carefully avoiding any work-related talk. By the eighth night, they were like old mates. Demi opened up about his family troubles, his desire to escape.

"Why not just walk away?" Jock prodded.

Demi's response was telling. "I've got the best job in the world, so it was a no-brainer," he said, unwittingly revealing the allure that kept him tied to the shady operation.

Jock's infiltration was textbook—blend in, gain trust, extract information. Each piece of intel, every conversation, brought them closer to unravelling Sheldrake's criminal web.

Jock's persistence finally paid off on the fifth night when Demi casually mentioned his boss, Sheldrake, would be back the next morning. Seizing the opportunity, Jock switched his base of operations from a comfortable hotel to a more modest motel directly across from the boatyard. He chose a room on the third floor, giving him an unobstructed view of the yard's entrance. This was more than a vantage point; it was his observation post.

Fabienne, working remotely, instructed Jock to set up his video camera for live footage. With no satellites available for her to tap into, Jock's eyes were her only window into the boatyard's activities. She was also digging into Sheldrake's background, waiting on a copy of his passport photo from an immigration contact.

Morning rolled around, and there was no sign of Sheldrake. Jock, ever the professional, remained vigilant, his GoPro primed and ready. When a blue Mustang finally rolled up at 10 am, Jock was on high alert. He captured footage of the man he presumed to be Sheldrake, though the angle only offered a view from behind.

Undeterred by the initial setback and unwilling to miss any detail, Jock stayed glued to his spot, his dedication unyielding. He even resorted to using a vase rather than leaving his post. As the day wore on and the workers dispersed, Sheldrake finally emerged. Jock was ready, filming him with the GoPro, adjusting for a clearer, closer shot. The footage was crisp and detailed, instantly transmitted to Fabienne in Geneva.

Jock meticulously stowed his surveillance gear in his car, ensuring everything was out of sight before making his way to the Billabong pub. The ambiance inside was charged with the energy of the after-work crowd, gathered for what locals dubbed the 'six o'clock swill'—a rapid-fire drinking session to cap off the day. Amid the buzz, Demi spotted Jock by the marble bar and beckoned him over, a casual gesture that belied the significance of the encounter that was about to unfold.

"This is Mr. Sheldrake, the boss. Meet Jock, my new mate. He's considering work options around here," Demi introduced, his tone casual.

Sheldrake extended a firm handshake to Jock, sizing him up with a discerning eye. "And what sort of work are you thinking of diving into?" he enquired, his Australian accent voice betraying nothing.

"Been tinkering with engines most my life. Cars, trucks, reckon I could handle boats too," Jock replied, his accent adding authenticity to his cover story.

Sheldrake's questions followed, probing Jock's background subtly yet deliberately. Jock, playing his part to perfection, spun a tale of an undocumented immigrant looking for under-the-table work, down on his luck and desperate.

Sheldrake's response was noncommittal, yet he invited Jock to see him the next morning, a potential opening for Jock to infiltrate the operation. After Sheldrake departed, Jock lingered for a while with Demi, careful not to arouse suspicion, then made his way back to the hotel via a roundabout route.

Settling into his hotel room, Jock opened his laptop, diving into the details of the cover story that Fabienne had meticulously crafted for him. The file was comprehensive: it listed the crew of 'Auckland's Angel', the hotel he supposedly stayed at in Brisbane, and even the bars he had 'frequented'. Every detail was designed to withstand scrutiny, to make his cover as a trawler worker who had jumped ship in New Zealand and ended up in Brisbane utterly believable.

As he absorbed the information, Jock knew that memorizing this cover was crucial. Sheldrake, a man evidently cautious and thorough, would likely probe into his background. Any inconsistency could blow Jock's cover and endanger the operation.

The warning from Fabienne echoed in his mind. Sheldrake was not just a small-time crook but a dangerous player with extensive connections. The stakes were higher than Jock had initially anticipated, and the danger was real.

Demi, acting as Jock's informal guide, led him through the gates of the boatyard, their conversation light, peppered with the kind of banter common among men accustomed to the rough-and-tumble of yard work. They navigated the busy yard, making their way up the two flights of stairs to Sheldrake's office. Demi's knock on the door was confident, the sound of someone familiar with the territory.

Sheldrake's office was a stark contrast to the activity outside. Behind a simple wooden desk, Sheldrake exuded an aura of authority, the room's sparseness underscoring his no-nonsense approach. The black leather sofa near the door stood out, a lone piece of luxury in an otherwise unadorned space.

"Sit, please. You too, Demi," Sheldrake motioned as he closed the door behind them. Both men complied, taking seats on the sofa, while Sheldrake settled into his chair behind the desk. The physical distance between them was small, yet it felt significant, a clear demarcation of authority in the room.

The meeting was more than just a simple job interview; it was a dance of subtleties and unspoken evaluations. Jock, maintaining his guise, was acutely aware of every gesture, every word, as he navigated this crucial step in his undercover operation.

As Jock and Demi settled into Sheldrake's office, the atmosphere was tense but controlled. Sheldrake, with a calculating gaze, addressed Demi in a tone that hinted at past transgressions. "Demi, when you came to me, you were in a bad way. Now, look at you—comfortable, living a good life. I just asked for your discretion about our operations here."

Demi started to protest his innocence, but Sheldrake cut him off with a dismissive wave. "Enough, Demi. Sit down."

"Jock, you can drop the act. I've been around enough to recognize an ex-military man. You reek of it. And I'm sure you've got a well-crafted cover story to go with it," Sheldrake said, his tone laced with certainty.

Jock, tried to maintain his facade. "You've got the wrong idea, Mr. Sheldrake. I'm just here for a job, nothing more," he responded, attempting to sound as convincing as possible under the circumstances.

Sheldrake chuckled dryly, not buying it for a second. "We do our homework too, Jock," he said as he tossed an old photo onto the desk. It showed Jock and Tuck in their military days, a snapshot from a distant desert operation. The picture was a stark reminder of Jock's past, now laid bare in front of his adversary.

Sheldrake's expression was one of smug satisfaction as he eyed Jock and Demi. "I was tipped off about MIDAS snooping around. Wasn't hard to connect the dots once you showed up," he declared.

Jock weighed his options. His cover was blown, but he needed to keep his wits about him. "MIDAS? Never heard of them," he said, trying to feign ignorance despite knowing full well that Sheldrake had seen through his ruse.

Sheldrake leaned forward, a predator sensing the vulnerability of its prey. "Let's not play games, Jock. I know who you are, and I know who sent you. But you walking into my yard? That was a mistake."

Demi, caught between the two men, looked like he wanted to be anywhere but there. The tension in the room was palpable, a deadly standoff between a seasoned operator and a formidable adversary. Demi, visibly shaken by the turn of events, stammered, "I didn't know, Mr. Sheldrake." His fear was palpable, a stark contrast to Sheldrake's cold composure.

Jock, sensing an opening, made a split-second decision to confront Sheldrake. But before he could fully act on his impulse, Sheldrake revealed a Heckler and Koch 9mm semi-automatic, equipped with a silencer. A quick shot rang out, and Jock was hit in the knee, collapsing to the floor in agony.

Demi, shocked and disoriented, barely had time to react before Sheldrake turned the weapon on him. The room was suddenly filled with the gruesome aftermath of Sheldrake's swift and deadly action.

Lying on the floor, Jock, through gritted teeth and seething with pain, managed to spit out a curse in Scottish, his training and experience coming to the fore even in this dire situation.

Sheldrake, unfazed by the carnage he had just inflicted, coldly instructed Jock to return to the sofa. Jock, drawing on reserves of strength he didn't know he had, dragged himself back to the couch, leaving a trail of blood and debris from his shattered knee.

Sheldrake's eyes narrowed as he posed his questions, each one sharp and pointed. "How much does MIDAS know? What have you reported back? And have you been taking surveillance photos of me?" His tone was calm, but the underlying threat was unmistakable.

Jock, despite the pain throbbing through his knee, kept his expression neutral. He knew any information he gave up could compromise the entire operation. "MIDAS? Look, you've got the wrong guy. I'm just a mechanic looking for work," he reiterated, sticking to his cover story despite the evidence laid out before him.

Sheldrake wasn't convinced. He leaned back in his chair, his gaze never leaving Jock. "You expect me to believe that? After I find a photo of you with Tuck in military gear? I'm not a fool, Jock."

"I can see you fumbling with your phone in your pocket, no doubt sending a compromised signal. Won't make any difference as I will be out of the country before any of you friends can react," Sheldrake said.

"Cheerio the noo, and fuck you," Jock replied.

"You Celts are tough old bastards. Business is business. But I do hope you have a God to go to," Sheldrake said, as he shot Jock twice in the head.

Fabienne's world came crashing down as the ominous beeps from Jock's phone echoed through her workspace. Adhering to protocol, but with a heavy heart, she immediately severed the connection. Her fingers moved swiftly across her keyboard, erasing every digital footprint that linked Jock's phone to MIDAS's network. The task was mechanical, but her mind was elsewhere, grappling with the grim reality of what those beeps likely signified.

Once the digital cleanup was complete, Fabienne sat motionless, surrounded by her array of screens and computers. She bowed her head, fighting back tears, the weight of the situation bearing down on her. She understood the risks, the perilous nature of their work, but the human cost never got easier to bear.

Sheldrake, with a cold and methodical precision, concluded his dark deed in the quiet of the office. He then turned his attention to Jock's phone, extracting it from the lifeless grip. Utilizing Jock's thumbprint, he unlocked the screen, only to be met with an empty blue screen. "Very clever," he muttered under his breath, a begrudging respect for the security measures that had been put in place by MIDAS.

Despite the gravity of what had just transpired, Sheldrake's composure remained unshaken. His expression gave away nothing as he prepared to rejoin the hustle of the boatyard. He carefully composed himself, erasing any traces of the events that had just unfolded in the secluded office.

As he descended the stairs back to the workshop, the contrast between the weighty stillness of the office and the lively activity below was stark. The workers, engrossed in their tasks, remained completely unaware of the violent turn of events that had just taken place mere floors above them.

As Sheldrake navigated through the boatyard, he approached the four workers busy with the hull of a yacht. His stance was that of a typical yard boss, but his intentions were far from ordinary. "Boys, you're needed in the engine room. They could use some extra muscle down there," he called out casually.

"Aye aye, gaffer," the workers responded in unison, setting aside their tools and heading towards the Lassara yacht. They were used to shifting tasks on the fly, a common occurrence in the dynamic environment of the boatyard.

However, as soon as they descended into the bowels of the yacht, Sheldrake quietly followed, his steps muted amidst the sounds of the yard. With a swift, surreptitious move, he closed the hatch leading to the engine room and secured it firmly, trapping the workers inside.

The oxyacetylene bottles, heavy and cumbersome, were no match for his physical fitness and determination. Within ten minutes, he had manoeuvred seven of them into the main cabin of the hull, directly above the engine compartment where the English workers were unknowingly sealed in.

Returning to his car, he retrieved a small detonator equipped with a time delay switch. Equipped with a half-mask respirator for protection, Sheldrake re-entered the cabin. He methodically opened each bottle valve halfway, releasing the gas, then strategically positioned the detonator amongst the cylinders.

His task completed, Sheldrake exited the yacht and swiftly made his way back to his Mustang, where he stowed his emergency pack in the trunk. The drive to Perth Airport was a quiet one, punctuated only by the distant, muffled thud of the explosion echoing from miles behind. Sheldrake, a man with many aliases and a history shrouded in secrecy, was no stranger to hard choices. However, the killing of these men, though a calculated move to erase any links to his operation, was a necessary action to conclude his operation cleanly, leaving no loose ends.

As he drove, Sheldrake reflected on the day's events. It was a day he could have done without, a day that added another dark chapter to his already complex life. But in the world, he navigated, such decisions, however grim, were part and parcel of the trade—a trade where survival often meant making the toughest of choices.

Jock's ultimate sacrifice had not been in vain. The photographs he had managed to send back to Fabienne before his untimely demise were critical pieces of intelligence. As Sheldrake made his way onto his flight, a world away, Fabienne was deep in analysis, running the images through advanced facial recognition software. The data Jock had collected was about to bear fruit, potentially exposing the depths of Sheldrake's operations.

Fabienne, well aware of the significance of Jock's contributions, faced the grim task of dealing with the aftermath. MIDAS had been operating incognito in Australia, and their presence was not known to the local authorities. This added a layer of complexity to the situation, particularly with the need to repatriate Jock's body. It was a delicate situation that required careful handling and a few favours called in from her extensive network.

In the midst of this, Fabienne made a tough call. She decided not to inform Cutler, who, alongside Tuck, was prepping for a critical operation on the Reef Explorer. She knew that the news of Jock's death could potentially impact their focus and effectiveness.

Fabienne found herself tasked with the intricate challenge of managing the intricate logistics and navigating the emotional aftermath of Jock's passing, all while ensuring that the ongoing operation maintained its momentum.

chapter twenty-one
Promises and Vendettas

The USS Lincoln's deck was a hive of activity as the HH 60G Pave Hawk, a combat search and rescue helicopter derived from the venerable Black Hawk, was prepped for action. This particular Pave Hawk had been upgraded in 2012, boasting improved hold and hover stabilization, crucial for the precision required in Cutler's plan. With a service ceiling of 14,000 feet, it was perfectly suited for the mission at hand.

President Shelby, via Admiral Collinson's directive, had given Captain Robert Granton Reynolds III clear instructions to provide Cutler with any necessary resources and assistance. The helicopter's emergence from its hangar storage was a spectacle, signalling the start of a critical operation.

To Cutler's surprise, instead of a standard Zodiac dinghy, a state-of-the-art Spectre-class super stealth attack boat was brought onto the flight deck. This four-meter-long marvel of military engineering was the latest in stealth, undergoing sea trials aboard the USS Lincoln. The deck crew efficiently rigged the stealth boat to the Pave Hawk's cargo hook, preparing for an unprecedented field test.

The Spectre's cutting-edge design featured state-of-the-art super-cavitating surface craft technology, drastically decreasing hull friction by a staggering 900 times when compared to traditional watercraft. Its hull incorporated specially engineered cells aimed at minimizing radar reflection and emissions, rendering it nearly invisible to detection. Thus far, the USS Lincoln's surveillance systems had been unsuccessful in registering any trace of the boat's presence, showcasing its remarkable stealth capabilities.

Captain Reynolds, fully aware of the significance of Cutler's mission, saw this as an opportunity to test the boat under real battle conditions. The ongoing trials were critical in determining the boat's operational viability before committing to extensive production, a decision hinging on vast public funds.

The operation's success hinged on skilled navigation and technical expertise. To this end, two engineers from Stealth Information Systems, the brains behind the boat's design, were carrying out the trials for the US Navy Based out of the historic Cammell Laird shipyard in Birkenhead, United Kingdom, these engineers were not only pivotal in the boat's development but also served as directors of the company.

Their expertise would be invaluable in guiding the Spectre stealthily to the Reef Explorer. The mission's nature and the technical challenges it presented required their unique skill set. As the preparations continued, the air was electric with anticipation. This mission was not just a crucial operation for Cutler and his team, but also a live field test for one of the most advanced pieces of naval stealth technology.

Donny Evans, despite his advancing years and an array of health issues including angina, a hip replacement, and troublesome knees, was a mechanical and electrical maestro who refused to consider retirement. His so-called 'apprentice', Adam Jones, a spry 50-year-old, was the mastermind behind the sophisticated software that powered their latest creation.

Together, they formed a formidable team, each complementing the other's skills.

Adam took the helm of the stealth craft, his eyes keenly monitoring the heads-up display and control units, while Donny made sure all the mechanical components functioned flawlessly. Captain Reynolds had cleverly coerced them into participating in this mission, subtly hinting that any refusal would lead to the project being deemed a failure.

The financial crash of 2008 had been a turning point for Evans and Jones. They had climbed the ranks of the company and, during those tumultuous times, had invested heavily in it, buying up bonus shares Their commitment wasn't just professional; it was personal and financial. This contract with the navy, therefore, represented a pivotal moment—it was a make-or-break situation for their company.

As evening approached, the USS Lincoln's deck was the scene of intense preparation. At 1900 hours, eight SAS troopers assembled for the mission briefing. The operation commander, a figure of authority and experience, led the briefing, ensuring that every detail of the plan was crystal clear. Cutler, along with his strike teams and the engineering duo of Evans and Jones, were also present, absorbing every aspect of the mission.

The briefing was meticulous, with the commander outlining each stage of the operation. As he concluded, he emphasized the importance of synchronization—a crucial element in ensuring the mission's success. Each man present, from the seasoned SAS troopers to Cutler and his team, to the unlikely pair of Evans and Jones, understood the gravity of the task ahead. As watches were synced, a silent acknowledgment passed among them—they were ready for whatever lay ahead on the Reef Explorer.

As Cutler was making the final preparations for the mission, his communication device buzzed to life. It was Fabienne, reaching out with last-minute information.

"Hi, Cutler. There's something you need to know before you go in," Fabienne's voice was urgent, cutting through the pre-mission tension.

Cutler's focus sharpened. "What's up, Fabienne? We're about to move out."

Fabienne hesitated, measuring her words with precision. "This concerns Sheldrake. After receiving his photo from Jock, I ran it through facial recognition software. It seems someone attempted to scrub his digital existence, but the program can unearth such attempts and restore the data. What we've discovered is monumental. Sheldrake isn't merely a criminal strategist—according to our intelligence, he's a key Al-Qaeda operative, masquerading as Kasim Asfour."

Cutler processed the information, his mind racing with the implications. "Al-Qaeda? That's a game-changer."

Fabienne delved deeper. "There's more to it. He's entangled with the CIA too. His actual name is Carl Bridge, and he's been operating under numerous aliases. I've been tracking him: he entered the US as Bridge, surfaced in Australia and Bali as Sheldrake, and appeared on the M15 watchlist as Kasim Asfour. I've even got images of him across various Middle Eastern countries, and in Miami just days ago. Plus, I've spotted him entering a Miami residence shortly after the deputy chief of the CIA and Vice President Treisman."

Cutler let out a low whistle, his voice tinged with a mix of scepticism and the gravity of Fabienne's disclosure. "A CIA agent deep in a yacht scheme, committing murders, and entwined with Al-Qaeda? That stretches credibility. Are you absolutely sure about this intelligence, Fabienne? Could it be a red herring, someone laying a false trail?"

Fabienne's response was measured, yet firm. "I know it sounds absurd, Cutler, but the evidence is solid. The facial recognition match is conclusive, and there are multiple data points that confirm his identity as Carl Bridge. It appears he's been operating deep undercover, possibly gone rogue. His motivations are still unclear, but his involvement is undeniable."

"And there's the connection with this WCU and Conrad Ford. Asfour, it seems, killed Ford's son over it," Cutler said, his thoughts racing. "He must have been buying it for Al-Qaeda. And Ford, driven by greed, got his lad killed for more money. But the CIA's involvement, that's puzzling. Fabienne, you have CIA links—can you find out more?"

"He's also been spotted alongside Umar Aziz, using his Asfour alias. His dealings, particularly those involving weapons, are linked to the hijacking of the Reef Explorer," Fabienne emphasized, highlighting the seriousness of the situation.

"We can't ignore this, Fabienne. Aziz's connection points to a sprawling Al-Qaeda network. The CIA's role in this is unclear, but it's essential we find out. From what you say, the trail leads as high as the vice president, but does it end there? I'm concerned we might be unwitting pawns in a larger scheme. We must act swiftly and collect all the intelligence available," Cutler replied, his mind racing with the implications.

"I will use my contacts; I will see what I can dig up" Fabienne confirmed.

Fabienne's voice was a blade of ice cutting through the static. "Presidential order just in, Max. Green light from the top brass."

Cutler's reply cut through the static, sharp and urgent. "Finally. Get President Shelby on the line. He needs to hear every sordid detail we've dug up. His reaction will be our litmus test—if he's complicit, it'll show."

Fabienne, understanding the gravity of the situation, acknowledged with a determined edge in her voice. "Consider it done. We'll have answers soon enough."

Cutler realised this move placed them on a knife-edge, balancing between exposing a potential conspiracy and the risk of tipping off someone at the highest level of power. The weight of their discovery loomed over them, as they prepared to confront possibly one of the most powerful men in the world. Would President Shelby prove an ally or an adversary? The answer to that question could change everything."

"I'm on it. But there's more—Bridge, Asfour, Sheldrake, whatever his name, we've pinned him in Pashtunistan, Pakistan. Another alias. Give me the word, and I'll go after him."

"And then?" Cutler's tone was steely.

Cutler's face hardened as he absorbed the full extent of Asfour's carnage. "He's a one-man army of destruction. The Trench kids, Robert Ford, Samantha, his entire security detail… and now Jock,

Old Joe. He tried to kill you, Tuck and Colton. This man needs putting down, CIA or not." Muttered Fabienne.

A wave of shock passed over him. "Old Joe and Jock, gone?" The names hit him like physical blows.

Fabienne's voice was heavy with regret. "I should have told you sooner. Jock was killed in Fremantle, and Old Joe's boat explosion… it's all connected, all trails leading back to Asfour."

Cutler's jaw clenched. "Old Joe had a son. And Jock… get Cheryl on it. Whatever they need."

Cutler's next command was a cold directive, fuelled by a mix of duty and vengeance. "Fabienne, find Asfour. End this. Nothing to lead back to MIDAS."

"Has it ever?" Fabienne shot back."

Colton's attention to detail was relentless, a trait that had served him well in a career defined by precision and calculated risks. With methodical movements, he surveyed the Spectre's anchorage, ensuring every strap and buckle was tightened to perfection. The Spectre, a sleek embodiment of stealth, had to be delivered to the operation zone without fail. It was a critical component of their strategy.

Evans and Jones stood ready, their gear checked and rechecked under Colton's vigilant eye. They formed the core of Strike Team Two, a unit that was an ad hoc unit rather than a finely tuned machine like the Spectre itself. Their role was pivotal, second only to the lead team in the order of engagement, and Colton was determined to have every element under his command in flawless readiness.

The two SAS units, representing the pinnacle of military prowess, stood as the third and fourth strike teams. These soldiers were more than just men; they were the sum total of countless hours of gruelling training and hardened resolve. As they conducted their final gear their silence was not a lack of things to say but focus on the gravity of the task ahead.

Each member was a paragon of their craft, carrying the kind of poised readiness that only comes from having faced the reality of mortality and walked away, not always unscathed. They communicated through concise gestures and brief nods, a silent language that ensured stealth and understanding.

Their gear was a mix of standard issue and specialized equipment, each piece selected for its reliability and efficiency. The muted clinks and clatters of magazines being seated into HK416: semi-automatics., the soft rustling of maps, and the quiet hum of communication devices being tested formed the backdrop to their preparations.

For these men, the operation was a culmination of their training and everything they stood for. The stakes were life itself, and their silent nods were vows to each other that they would not falter when called upon.

The hangar was a hive of focused activity as the strike teams prepared. There was a palpable sense of anticipation, the kind that comes before the storm of action. Each member of the teams checked their equipment, their weapons, and most importantly, their resolve. They all knew the plan, the risks, and the importance of their roles. Every second of preparation now could mean the difference between success and failure, life, and death.

In the midst of the quiet bustle, Captain Reynolds oversaw the preparation. His experienced eyes missed nothing, assessing the readiness of his troops and the reliability of their gear. This was the calm before the storm, the deep breath before the plunge. And for Colton, Evans, Jones, and the SAS teams, it was another day at the office, albeit one that carried the weight of international security on its shoulders.

Captain Reynolds demanded real-time visuals of their approach and strike. The American helmets, adorned with the US flag, were rejected by Cutler in favour of their own advanced gear. The drone operator and technician synced their equipment, readying for the operation.

In the hangar, Cutler and Tuck faced two large crates. "Fabienne and the Air Force pulled through," Cutler noted.

"Don't celebrate yet," Tuck countered cynically. "For all we know, the suits are in shreds."

"Ever the pessimist," Cutler chided.

Together, they unveiled two black Taslan combat suits, laying them out meticulously. Stripping down, they ignored the raucous whistles from the sailors, their focus laser-sharp on the mission ahead.

As Cutler and Tuck donned the combat suits, the fabric clung to them, a second skin designed to slice through air with minimal resistance. Next, they assembled the components of their remarkable gear: the Typhoon stealth wingsuits, a marvel of engineering in unassuming brown camouflage.

The suits, the brainchild of ex-Navy Seal John White, had attracted a rapt audience in the hangar. White, a long-time ally of Cutler, had defied military scepticism with these next-gen wingsuits, funded by Cutler's own investment. They were more than equipment; they were a leap forward in all sense of the words.

The wingsuits were masterpieces of military engineering, blending cutting-edge technology with the principles of aerodynamics. Made from a lightweight yet incredibly strong carbon composite, they were designed to withstand the extremes of high-altitude jumps and rapid, agile manoeuvres in the air.

At the core of each suit was the central body attachment, resembling a turtle shell in its shape. This component was not just a structural element; it was the suit's operational heart. It housed the intricate mechanisms and systems that made these wingsuits more than just gliding apparatuses. This central piece was the hub from which all other functionalities branched.

The tail wings, small but crucial, provided stability and control during flight. Located at the rear of the suit, they were engineered to be both effective in steering and minimal in creating drag. The parachute void nestled among these tail wings was a subtle yet vital feature, ensuring that in the event of an emergency, the suit's occupant could deploy a parachute without entanglement or delay. This operation called for the use of the parachute.

The most striking features were the angular wings, seamlessly integrated into the turtle shell. These wings were the essence of the suit's aerodynamic prowess. Their swept-back design allowed for an optimized glide ratio, minimizing air resistance while maximizing lift and control. This design enabled the wearer to pilot themselves with precision, vital for the complex operations these suits were intended for.

Every inch of the wingsuit was a validation to the meticulous attention to detail and understanding of flight dynamics. These suits weren't just equipment; they were a fusion of science and artistry, enabling their wearers to soar through the skies with the grace of a bird and the precision of a fighter jet. In the hands of skilled operatives like Cutler and Tuck, they transformed from mere tools to extensions of their own bodies, integral to the success of their dangerous mission.

Cutler was unaware that Captain Reynolds had been observing from the hangar's stairs, drawn by the allure of the high-tech gear. As Reynolds approached, his curiosity was palpable.

"These are no ordinary wingsuits, Captain," Cutler explained, pride evident in his voice. "Their stealth capabilities are unparalleled, they're practically invisible on radar. The in-built guidance system, synced with your drone's software, gives us real-time visuals.

Reynolds, both impressed and guarded, pointed out the gap in their plan. "You're launching from 80 miles out, still short of your target."

Cutler unveiled an unexpected element of their gear, pushing the boundaries of their operation's audacity. "We've got an ace up our sleeve," he said, his voice tinged with a blend of confidence and anticipation. "Rocket thrusters."

He gestured towards the sleek attachments, futuristic in their design and promise. "These aren't just for show. They're the key to covering that critical distance. The suits are tried and tested, but these thrusters," he paused, allowing a moment for the significance to sink in, "they're uncharted territory for us. Their first real test."

Reynolds shook his head, a mix of admiration and disbelief. "You're walking a tightrope between bravery and folly."

Cutler's reply was tinged with grim humour. "If we succeed, it's a triumph. If we fail… well, John White's going to lose his prized inventions to the depths of the Mediterranean."

Reynolds, puzzled, asked for clarification, unaware of the high-stakes gamble Cutler and Tuck were about to undertake.

Cutler's assessment of the landing zone underscored the high-stakes nature of their operation. "The poop deck on the Reef Explorer is tight, really tight. It's the only spot Stahmer and his team can't lock down. We've got to make this work despite the odds."

Reynolds, concern etched on his face, questioned their landing strategy. "Is there even enough room for both of you? Two six-foot wingspans on such a confined space—it sounds like a recipe for disaster."

Cutler nodded, acknowledging the risk. "Precisely why we can't land with the wingsuits. White's designs are groundbreaking, but they aren't made for precision landings. So the plan is to shed them at the last 120 feet and switch to conventional parachutes. It's a risky transition, but it's our best shot."

Captain Reynolds' remark carried a depth of meaning, reflecting the fine margins, upon which the entire operation balanced. "Either very brave men or fools," he mused aloud. "The outcome of this operation will be the ultimate judge."

Reynolds' musings gave way to action. He ordered his crew to prepare the gear for transport, but Cutler interjected. "We'll handle the loading, Captain. We need to ensure everything is perfect. Any error, no matter how small, falls on us."

As Reynolds offered a solemn salute to Cutler and Tuck, a moment of levity broke the tension. "You don't salute a fool," Tuck murmured to Cutler, "so I guess we're brave."

After Reynolds left, Cutler and Tuck meticulously inspected the wingsuits. They scrutinized every inch for potential flaws—a fracture, a tear, anything that could jeopardize the mission. Satisfied, they carefully loaded the turtle-shaped bodies onto the Bell Boeing Osprey.

Captain Reynolds' brief appearance, poking his head into the Osprey, brought a moment of levity with his caution against any 'Charlie Foxtrots'—military slang for chaotic situations. Tuck's retort, a jab at the perceived Navy penchant for mishaps, was met with a chorus of good-natured expletives from the SAS team, reinforcing the inter-service rivalry in jest.

The Bell Boeing Osprey, an aircraft that defied conventional aviation norms, rose gracefully into the sky, its rotors shifting seamlessly from a vertical to a horizontal position. For Cutler, this flight in the Osprey was not just a physical journey but a metaphorical leap into the unknown. The aircraft's unique tiltrotor design allowed it to take off and land like a helicopter yet fly with the speed and range of a fixed-wing plane. Its versatility was a fitting parallel to the adaptability and ingenuity required for their mission.

As the Osprey ascended, Cutler peered out of the window, his gaze following the Sikorsky MH-60S Knighthawk chopper carrying the Spectre. The USS Lincoln, a symbol of naval power and precision, grew smaller below them, a reminder of the vast scale of their operation. The Osprey, with its sleek lines and formidable presence, was a marvel of engineering, a blend of rotorcraft flexibility and airplane efficiency.

The hum of the engines and the rhythmic whir of the rotors were a soundtrack to Cutler's mixed emotions. The anticipation of the challenge ahead was palpable, a feeling shared by everyone on board, except Tuck. Yet there was also a thread of apprehension, a natural response to the unknown variables and potential dangers that lay ahead.

In the crammed space of the Osprey, the atmosphere was thick with the tension of anticipation. Cutler, ever the informant, tried to shed light on the unique capabilities of the Osprey to Tuck, whose pragmatic concerns boiled down to "Is the fucker safe to fly?" Cutler's response, comparing the relative safety of the Osprey to their experimental wingsuits, was a stark reminder of the perilous nature of their mission.

Around them, the interior of the Osprey was a strategic jigsaw puzzle. The two Zodiac dinghies, essential for the SAS maritime approach, were stashed securely, their outboards silent but ready. The SAS teams, four men each, exuded a quiet intensity as they meticulously checked their gear.

Guarding the precious wingsuits, two ratings stood watch, aware of the invaluable role the suits played in the operation. As Cutler and Tuck donned the wingsuits, they did so with the practiced ease of men accustomed to operating in confined spaces under pressure.

Tuck adjusted his headset, the static crackle giving way to clarity. "Cutler, I had a call with Falser's wife. He's in a real bad place. Also heard Cheryl and Esme came out of it okay. But there's something else. Once we're back, Bull and I are going to settle the score with Conrad Ford."

Cutler's voice came through, steady as ever. "I've got news, and it's not good. We lost Old Joe and Jock."

A heavy sigh filled Cutler's ears. "Fuck it. Ford or Sheldrake?"

"Best bet? Ford for Old Joe. But Jock… that was Sheldrake's doing."

Tuck's voice was tinged with a mix of anger and regret. "Old Joe had his days, sure. But Jock… he dodged more bullets than I can count. This one's on me. I pulled him into this mess."

The hum of the Osprey's engines provided a steady backdrop to the weighty conversation even piecing the headsets, Cutler's voice, always a grounding force, broke through the din.

"You don't have to worry about Sheldrake," he said, his tone resolute. The words carried the kind of assurance that only came from years in the field, from knowing when to hold a grudge and when to let it go. "Fabienne's got a score to settle with him too. The guy tried to burn us, tied to kill her family, us, and she was right there in essence when Jock went down."

Tuck, usually the more impulsive of the two, absorbed this. His hand instinctively went to the scar on his left wrist, a reminder of past battles, of losses endured. He knew the stakes, knew the kind of ruthless vendetta Fabienne could unleash. Sheldrake was as good as hunted.

Cutler continued, "You'll get back, Tuck. But if you don't…" He paused, a rare hesitation in his otherwise steady voice. "I'll take care of Ford with Bull. That's a promise."

The words hung in the air, a solemn pact between warriors. In their line of work, promises were more than words; they were bonds forged in fire, unbreakable and sacred.

As the aircraft banked southwest, towards danger, their resolve solidified. They were ready for what was to come, armed with skills, wits, and the unyielding will to set things right.

chapter twenty-two
Final Descent

The story of Ivan Mikhailov read like a grim fable. Sixteen years in the unforgiving cold of a Siberian gulag, a casualty of the state's ruthless whims. His crime? The kind of dissent that only made sense in a regime that feared freedom. And now, in a twist that could only be described as bitterly ironic, his son, Vitaly, commanded a warship. A warship bearing the name of one of the loneliest places on earth—Siberia.

This wasn't just any ship. The Siberia was a Slava-class missile cruiser, a behemoth of steel and firepower. Over six hundred feet of sovereign Russian might, cutting through the ocean with the grace of a predator. No prefixes adorned her name, a Russian tradition that lent a certain starkness to their vessels. Siberia, as cold and formidable as the place it was named after.

At the helm was Captain Vitaly Mikhailov, a young lion at just 31, already one of the youngest captains in the Russian fleet. He wasn't just commanding a ship; he was steering his family's legacy out of disgrace. His father, labelled a traitor, was a ghost that Vitaly had worked tirelessly to exorcise. To him, the resurgence of Russia as a global power wasn't just political; it was personal redemption.

Vitaly stood for the new Russia, a nation shaking off the vestiges of a siege mentality that had long confined its maritime strength to regional waters. The Black Sea, the Baltic, the Pacific, the Caspian—these had been Russia's aquatic bastions. But the world was changing, and Russia with it. Under leaders who envisioned a Russia unbound, the navy was stretching its limbs, reaching for a global presence.

Vitaly Mikhailov was more than a captain; he was a symbol of this new era. He and his peers were not just trained for blue water operations; they were born for it. The old constraints, the tentacles cast by American dominance in key global theatres, were receding. Russia was stepping onto the world stage, no longer content with being a shadow in the Black Sea.

The Russian navy, once a sleeping bear, was now awake, hungry for a presence that matched the country's growing geopolitical ambitions. And men like Vitaly Mikhailov, ambitious, skilled, and fiercely patriotic, were at the forefront of this charge. They were the vanguard of a navy not just seeking to make waves, but to command them.

As the Siberia emerged from the Black Sea, the sun cast its glow against the backdrop of an unblemished blue sky. The mighty vessel had waited patiently for the perfect conditions to navigate the treacherous and bustling waters of the Bosporus Strait. The passage through this narrow chokepoint was always a delicate operation, requiring precision and timing, especially for a warship of her size.

Once into the Sea of Marmara, the Siberia set her course towards the Dardanelles Strait, another critical and challenging navigational route. This 38-mile winding waterway was notorious for its tight bends and busy traffic, a true test of a captain's skill and a ship's handling. Emerging into the open waters of the Aegean Sea felt like a release from a tense bottleneck, the ship now free to flex her maritime muscles.

Navigating through the Greek archipelago, the Siberia sailed with a poised confidence. The islands of Lesvos and Naxos slipped by. Dimmed lights on the port and starboard sides. Even the historic castle of Kos, a relic from the Knights of St. John, was visible, a fleeting glimpse of history for the sailors on deck.

As they reached latitude 35.5, adjacent to Karpathos and south of Rhodes, the Siberia's purpose and capability came sharply into focus. She was a vessel built for battle, carrying a formidable array of SS-N 12 Sandbox surface-to-surface cruise missiles. With a range of 340 miles and a top speed that belied her size, she was a formidable adversary on the open sea.

In the dark depths of the Mediterranean, a silent custodian of Israeli naval power glided with lethal purpose. The Dolphin-class 2 submarine, an engineering marvel birthed in German shipyards, was the embodiment of stealth and destructive capability. At the helm was Captain Boaz Levy, a commander whose reputation was as deep and enigmatic as the waters he patrolled.

This submarine was not just a vessel; it was a statement of Israel's strategic prowess, equipped with an arsenal that could shift the balance of power in the region. Its torpedoes, both nuclear and conventional, were instruments of war that Levy had mastered, though he had never unleashed their fury in actual combat.

As the submarine cut through the water, its destination was the Reef Explorer, a vessel that had unwittingly found itself a pawn in a larger game of international chess. The orders were clear yet weighty with consequence. If the Reef Explorer was deemed a significant threat to the security of Israel, Levy's mission was to neutralize it, regardless of the collateral cost.

The reality of this mission weighed heavily on Levy. He was a man who had envisaged his career pitting him against more familiar regional foes. Yet here he was, prepared to engage a target that, until recently, had not been on his radar. The gravity of potentially firing on a ship with passengers was not lost on him, but duty and the defence of his homeland were principles that guided his every decision.

In the vast, open expanse of the sea, these three entities—the Lincoln, the Siberia, and the Dolphin-class submarine—moved with precision and intent. Unseen beneath the waves, Captain Levy's submarine was a hidden dagger, its blade poised and ready to strike should the order be given. The quiet tension of this underwater pursuit added another layer of danger and risk to the intricate tapestry of military strategy playing out across the world's oceans.

As the day waned over the Mediterranean, the Reef Explorer's bridge was a hive of quiet activity. Saddar, the Libyan navigator, was the epitome of focus as he peered at the radar screen. His colleagues, wrapped in prayer behind him, provided a religious backdrop to the tense vigilance up front.

His eyes narrowed as he discerned the blips on the screen. "Aziz," he called out, "we've got two aerial contacts, about 70 miles south. They just lifted off from a big vessel. Looks military."

Aziz, standing a few paces away, turned sharply. "What's their heading?"

"Southbound, but they're holding parallel. Not closing in on us yet," Saddar replied, his gaze not leaving the screen.

Aziz's instructions were crisp and clear. "Keep an eye on them. They're too far for an aerial strike for now, but if they change course towards us, I want to know immediately."

As he spoke, his men rose from their prayers, their faces set in solemn determination. "Prayers are done. Everyone, back to your posts. Radios on at all times," Aziz commanded. Turning to Abdul, he added, "Put the WCU in lifeboat one. Get it off the top deck discreetly. And use our guys for it, not the Somalis. We can't afford their curiosity."

Back in the Sikorsky MH-60S Knighthawk chopper carrying the Spectre boat, Colton, Jones, and Evans, the pilot skilfully adjusted the rotors' pitch. "1,000 yards to drop," announced the co-pilot.

"Roger," the pilot responded, expertly lowering the chopper until it was a mere 30 feet above the waves.

"Winchman, go stealth," ordered the co-pilot, a signal that set-in motion the next phase of their meticulously planned operation. The tension was high, every crew member acutely aware of the gravity of the mission that lay ahead in the darkening waters below.

The winchman on the chopper gave the Spectre just enough slack to let it kiss the Mediterranean gently. He knew his job; the boat needed clear water for the team's leap. Colton, the first to jump, was a picture of combat-hardened experience, his thumbs-up signal belying the danger of the manoeuvre. Over fifty times he'd done this, and it showed.

He hit the water in his dry suit, resurfacing quickly, saltwater stinging his nostrils. Efficiently, he covered the 30 feet to the Spectre, scrambling aboard. The boat, caught in the sea's sway, tested Colton's grit as he worked to detach the cargo line. Jones had briefed him on the controls—a crash course to keep the Spectre steady. They couldn't risk it drifting into the drop zone for the next jumpers.

Jones and Evans, donned in bulky red survival suits, awaited their turn. These neoprene encasements, complete with sealed feet and wrists, made their movements cumbersome. Captain Reynolds had insisted, half-jokingly, about not drowning civilians, "even the English ones," he had quipped.

Jones faced the chopper door, his body rigid with hesitation. He'd never done anything like this in his fifty years. The jump master, sensing his fear, gave him a firm, encouraging push. Jones plummeted, landing awkwardly, butt-first into the sea. Surfacing, he gasped for air, treading water until his lungs settled, then began the swim to the Spectre.

Evans, no younger but evidently braver, approached the exit with surprising calm. He stepped out into the dark abyss without a second glance, plunging into surprisingly warm waters. Colton had underestimated him; the chief engineer was a seasoned swimmer, a fact unknown to most.

Once aboard and out of their survival suits, Jones and Evans assumed their roles. Jones, the software expert, took the pilot's seat. Evans, the engineer, stood by the control panels, vigilant.

Jones hit the stealth switch, cloaking the Spectre's signature. With a press of the ignition, the engines hummed to life, silent but potent. The boat edged forward, then picked up speed. Colton, caught off guard, gripped a handrail. Evans, a rock in the storm, adjusted his stance, his experience showing as he monitored the lit-up control panel, ensuring everything was operating within limits.

The stealth mode of the Spectre engaged with a flick of a switch, rendering the boat almost invisible against the vast backdrop of the sea. Jones with a practiced hand, ignited the powerful yet silent engines. The boat began its journey cautiously, picking up speed gradually. Colton, caught off guard by the sudden acceleration, instinctively reached for a handrail. In contrast, Evans, a seasoned mariner, adjusted his stance effortlessly to the boat's movement, his attention fixed on the glowing control panel.

Colton's adaptation to the sea's rhythm was quick. He shifted his focus to the .300 Win Mag sniper rifle, handling it with the utmost care and precision. Past experiences, particularly a tragic incident in the DEA where a jammed weapon had fatal consequences, had taught him the importance of meticulous preparation. His choice of the heavier .300 rifle was strategic, preferring stability when shooting from the moving Spectre. Moreover, Colton's familiarity with the rifle meant he could make rapid, accurate adjustments for targets within a 700-yard range without the need for minute calibrations.

Jones communicated with Cutler, aboard the Bell Boeing V-22 Osprey, confirming their ETA. The Osprey, powered by two Rolls-Royce AE 1107C engines and cruising at an altitude of twelve thousand feet, maintained its position, hovering sixty miles parallel to the Spectre. Cutler and Tuck, aboard the Osprey, were in sync with the Spectre's movements, poised for the critical phases of their mission that lay ahead.

Meanwhile, the setting sun cast a fiery glow on the Bell Boeing Osprey, transforming the aircraft into a silhouette against the fading light. The Osprey, part plane, part chopper, was approaching the drop zone just as dusk swallowed the last of the daylight. Inside, Cutler's hand moved with practiced ease as he flicked on his microphone, tuning into the frequency of the USS Lincoln for a critical update.

Inside the Osprey, every inch of space was vital. Cutler and the jump master carefully hoisted the tortoise-shaped shell, aligning it with Tuck's back. Tuck meticulously checked the release mechanism while a rating and the jump master held the shell, cautious not to let it crash onto the aircraft's floor. After ensuring a smooth release, they repeated the procedure for Cutler, attaching his shell with equal precision.

The next step was securing the thruster rockets onto the bracket of the shells. The jump master, wielding a spanner, made sure they were firmly mounted. The final addition, the fixed swept-back wings, had to wait until the last moment due to space constraints. They would be locked into position only when they stood at the open cargo door, ready to jump.

The inability to sit, with their gear attached, drew a humorous comment from the jump master about their resemblance to a mix of futuristic and comic book characters. Despite the joke, the mood was tense as they began their final checks.

Cutler and Tuck tested their communications and video head-up displays. Cutler meticulously checked the connections between his and Tuck's equipment. "Tuck, you're first on the platform. I'm right behind you, 30 seconds later. Follow my lead when I move forward."

"Roger, safety off," Tuck responded, his voice steady as he disengaged the safety on his weapon. The response told Cutler all he needed to know: Tuck was laser-focused, ready for whatever lay ahead.

Cutler then confirmed the comms with Colton and made a final check with Stahmer's satellite phone. Satisfied, he gave Tuck the thumbs up. Tuck, in turn, went through his communication checks, ensuring he was fully synced and operational.

The Osprey's amber light flickered on, signalling the minute warning. Cutler tapped Tuck's helmet twice, their customary good-luck ritual practiced over countless missions. As they prepared for the jump, the late addition of hydrogen peroxide rockets to their gear loomed in their minds. This was uncharted territory—a wingsuit jump with the added thrust of a rocket. White had been reluctant to sanction their use without rigorous testing, but Cutler had been persuasive.

These rockets were no small enhancement. They promised a force of 100 kilograms and speeds up to 160 miles per hour. Cutler and Tuck had poured over the operating procedures, calculating their extraordinary potential—a 20-minute sustained flight, covering 60 miles, a feat that would smash existing records.

Cutler quipped about their impending Guinness World Record, a light moment in the midst of gravity. Tuck, ever the pragmatist, only yearned for the liquid variety of Guinness.

As the jump master secured their wings, Cutler and Tuck ran through their final checks. Their semi-automatics were safely holstered inside the suits. The Osprey's pilot adjusted the aircraft's speed and rotor pitch, optimizing conditions for their exit.

The jump master, tethered to the ramp, prepared to launch the drone first, its feed crucial for their head-up displays.

Tuck leaped first, diving into the open sky, the weight of the rocket now a part of him. Thirty seconds later, Cutler followed, eyes fixed on Tuck's rapidly receding form. He adjusted his posture, angling his legs to catch up, the thrill of the chase electrifying.

Meanwhile, the Pave Hawk that had dropped Colton veered towards Cyprus, followed by the Osprey. Captain Reynolds had ordered both away from the USS Lincoln to avoid arousing suspicion.

Cutler was acutely aware of the risks of wingsuit flying. The statistics were sobering—high injury rates, an all-too-familiar brush with mortality. Yet here they were, pushing the boundaries further than ever. As he activated his rocket, surging past Tuck, the rush was incomparable.

The moment Tuck's rocket booster ignited; it marked a transformation. The raw power of the hydrogen peroxide thrusters was not just a mechanical enhancement; it was an electrifying surge that propelled him into an adrenaline-fueled realm few had ever experienced. The force of the booster was immediate and overwhelming, catapulting him forward with a velocity that defied his wildest expectations.

"Fucking awesome!" Tuck's voice, laced with a mix of thrill and disbelief, crackled through the comms. The sensation was more than speed; it was like being thrust into another dimension, where the rules of gravity and inertia were rewritten. He was a bullet slicing through the sky, the roar of the wind now a distant whisper against the thunderous rush of the booster.

The exhilarating sense of acceleration was akin to a roller coaster's drop, but magnified a hundredfold, unrelenting and pure. It was as if he had tapped into some primal force, a raw, unbridled power that connected him to the very essence of flight.

As he soared through the air, the landscape below becoming a blur, Tuck found himself lost in the moment, the thrill of the booster eclipsing everything else. For those seconds, nothing else existed but the sheer exhilaration of speed, the euphoria of defying the limits of human capability.

This was more than a jump; it was an ascent into the annals of the extreme, a dance with the very edge of daring and danger. In that breathtaking rush, Tuck understood the true allure of pushing boundaries, of stepping into the realm of the extraordinary.

Cutler's voice, tinged with a mix of awe and freedom, crackled through the headset. "This is it, Tuck. This is the freest you'll ever feel. Forget about your car repayments, politics, all that stress. It's just you and the heavens now. With this rocket, I feel like a fighter jet, but it's peaceful, too. The connection with the elements, it's something else."

Tuck, ever the straight shooter, responded with his characteristic bluntness. "You lost me at blah blah blah. Like I said, fucking awesome."

Cutler adjusted his trajectory slightly, aligning himself with the Reef Explorer. Tuck followed suit, finding a sweet spot twenty feet behind in Cutler's slipstream.

"46 miles out. Check," Cutler called out.

"Check," came Tuck's response, his voice steady despite the buffeting from a warm thermal rising from the sea below.

Colton, on the other end of the comms, chimed in. "Strike One to Strike Two, how far out are you?"

"Twelve nautical miles and closing. You two sound like you're having the time of your lives," Colton replied, his voice tinged with a mix of envy and excitement.

Cutler, weaving through the stratus clouds, caught his first glimpse of the Mediterranean Sea rushing beneath him. "All in a day's work, Tuck. You know me, no fun allowed," he joked, his heart racing with the thrill of the flight.

Meanwhile, aboard the Reef Explorer, pressure was mounting. Stahmer, armed and alert, edged towards the poop deck, his semi-automatic at the ready. Ghislaine and Shultz, armed with just knives, moved stealthily, each step calculated and silent.

Shultz, embodying the skill and ruthlessness of an elite operative, took the guard by complete surprise. His movements were swift and lethal, a well-orchestrated ambush that left no room for error or resistance. With the efficiency of a seasoned predator, he applied a chokehold to immobilize the guard and followed it with a decisive, fatal stab to the base of the skull.

The guard's demise was almost instantaneous; his body rendered lifeless in mere seconds under Shultz's expert hand. With no time to waste and with methodical coldness, Shultz undressed the guard and quickly disposed of the body over the railings, into the dark, unforgiving waters below. This action was a grim but necessary part of their mission, executed with a chilling detachment.

Ghislaine, ever efficient, assisted Shultz in dressing in the guard's clothes, a disguise to blend in. Together, they prepared for the next phase of their mission, their movements as fluid and lethal as the waters they sailed upon.

The stage was set, the players in motion. Above, Cutler and Tuck soared like celestial predators, while aboard the Reef Explorer, a deadly game of stealth and strategy played out. The convergence of these two forces was imminent.

Jones piloted the Spectre silently through the water. They were a mere 2,000 yards from the Reef Explorer, the current aiding their approach. Jones had killed the engines, not willing to risk even the slightest sound that might betray them to the terrorists on board. The Spectre's hull, equipped with light cells sensors, blended seamlessly into the night, rendering it virtually invisible.

Evans, with focused intent, activated the thermal detector, sweeping the ship for heat signatures. "Stahmer, give us a wave," Colton commanded tersely. Stahmer, Shultz, and Ghislaine moved into view, each motion calculated.

Evans's voice was low but clear. "Two shadows starboard side, one on the poop deck. There's a guard up top, his gun's hot— must've been fired recently. Heat's clustered on decks four and five, likely the theatre. Two more on the bridge."

Colton relayed the intel to Stahmer and Cutler, his voice a whisper in the night.

On the Reef Explorer, tension hung thick in the air. "Updates on those radar blips?" Aziz asked, his voice steady.

Sadar replied, "Headed towards Cyprus. Caught a small blip from the west, but it's gone. Maybe birds."

"And the nearest vessels?"

"That warship is still hanging south. Nothing else within 100 miles."

Aziz, ever the strategist, pulled out his smartphone, his fingers flying over the Snapchat app. The message was brief, 'In position. What's the word on the Russians?'

Asfour's reply was prompt, 'Siberia's in play, carrying Sandbox missiles. 150 miles north of you. Stay the course, Aziz. Don't pull any stunts.'

Aziz typed back, 'Equipment set in Lifeboat eight. Launching in ten. All's going to plan.'

'Godspeed, Aziz,' came Asfour's final message.

Back on the Spectre, Colton peered through his scope, the guard's cigarette glowing like a beacon in the night. The sea's gentle swell toyed with his aim, the guard's silhouette dancing in and out of the crosshairs.

This was the calm before the storm, a moment of eerie stillness where every player was set, every plan in motion. The night was about to erupt into a maelstrom of action, each side poised for a confrontation that would shatter the silence of the Mediterranean night.

Colton's voice was steady, focused. "Can you steady her?" he called out to Donny Evans, who was manning the engineering console below.

Evans, a picture of calm efficiency, replied without hesitation, "Not a problem." With a deft flick of a switch, he activated the boat's stabilizers. Silently, they emerged from the Spectre's sides, instantly steadying the craft. Colton felt the difference immediately, the gentle rocking of the boat coming to a halt.

"Three minutes," Colton announced crisply into his transmitter, his eyes never leaving the scope.

Up front, Jones was glued to the infrared camera, his attention caught by a sudden movement. "Lifeboat launching," he reported quickly.

"Strike Team One. They're launching a boat from port side. Make your approach from starboard," Colton relayed the update.

"Copy," came Cutler's response, a note of readiness in his voice.

"Copy," Tuck's voice echoed in the headset, laced with determination. As they both recalibrated their course, the task demanded absolute precision. Their head-up display lasers guided them, but even the slightest adjustment at their breakneck speed required a finesse that only seasoned professionals like themselves could manage.

The shift from port to starboard, though minor in distance, was a challenging manoeuvre at the velocity they were traveling. The air around them was a tempest of their own making, a whirlwind stirred by the combination of their speed and the rocket boosters' power.

Cutler, leading the way, was acutely aware of the delicacy required. Each subtle tilt of his body, every minute shift in his weight, had significant implications at these speeds. The stakes were high—a miscalculation didn't just mean missing the target; it could spell disaster.

Behind him, Tuck mirrored Cutler's movements, his body cutting through the air with equal agility and precision. They were like two shadows darting through the sky, their movements synchronized to perfection. The thrill of the flight was matched only by the gravity of their mission, each aware that any error could be costly.

As they continued their swift, calculated descent, the Reef Explorer loomed larger in their vision, a hulking silhouette against the backdrop of the sea. Their training, instincts, and the advanced technology guiding them coalesced into a single, focused objective: execute the mission flawlessly.

"Ten seconds," Cutler intoned, a signal for Tuck to cut the power to their rocket propulsion systems.

Stahmer, on the Reef Explorer, heard the lifeboat being lowered one deck below. He caught a glimpse of it hitting the water, steering away from the ship. He didn't have time to wonder why. His focus was on the task at hand.

As Cutler and Tuck descended, they fine-tuned their flight paths. Their wingtip distance was meticulously maintained—a gap of just six feet. Cutler gave a prearranged signal, a subtle rock of his wings.

At 400 feet above the sea, in perfect synchrony, they hit the pressure pads on their gloves. The turtle suits disengaged, flying backwards, caught by the wind and plummeting into the sea's depths. The drone, monitoring their descent from the USS Lincoln, narrowly avoided one of the jettisoned suits, diving sharply to maintain its visual on the duo.

Tuck deployed his parachute at 230 feet, Cutler followed at 200, ensuring he hit the deck first. The chutes billowed open, their descent slowing to a controlled drop. Expertly manipulating their lines and toggles, they performed a break turn, aligning themselves with the poop deck.

With practiced ease, both men flicked off the safety on their chest-strapped guns, ready for whatever awaited them on the Reef Explorer.

Overhead, the drone, a silent overseer in the night sky, buzzed above the Reef Explorer. Back on the USS Lincoln, the operator focused, engaging the red laser guidance beam. It painted a small but unmistakable red dot on the deck of the Reef Explorer, marking the drop zone amidst the rolling swell.

Cutler, eyes narrowed and focused, zeroed in on that glowing target. The sea's undulating rhythm made the landing spot a moving target, a challenge he was ready to meet.

Imran, standing guard on the top deck, was a loyal follower of Aziz, but tonight, his role took an unexpected turn. The moon, having waned from its full glory days before, left the sky dark, dotted with stars. One in particular caught his eye, a bright satellite cruising across the heavens. But suddenly, it blinked out, obscured by something in its path.

The realization of danger dawned on him slowly, a chilling sensation creeping up his spine. His trained eyes scanned the sky, but the obscuring cloud moved on, revealing once again the bright North Star.

But then, the light revealed more than just celestial bodies. The silhouette of a black parachute, descending rapidly, caught Imran's attention. In a reflexive motion, he flicked off the safety of his weapon and swung it towards the approaching threat.

Meanwhile, Colton, prone atop the Spectre, had his target in sight. His breath steady, his hand sure, he squeezed the trigger. The sniper rifle's report was muffled by the sea's hush, and Imran's head burst apart in a grisly display.

"Strike teams, sentry disabled. Out." Colton's voice was calm, the deed done.

Shultz, positioned at the edge of the poop deck, watched as Cutler made his approach. The deck's swaying was more pronounced from his vantage point, a warning to the sea's unpredictable nature.

Cutler, in an acrobatic display, tucked his knees and cleared the railing by mere feet. His landing was precise, but the displaced air from the ship's motion filled his chute, lifting him momentarily. He wrestled with the canopy, fighting to stay on deck and not be swept back over the railing by the unforgiving breeze.

This was more than just a physical battle; it was a struggle with death, a play of precision and peril played out on the high seas.

Shultz, quick to react, leaped onto Cutler's billowing chute, trying desperately to deflate it. Cutler, pinned under the weight of both Shultz and the chute, could only brace as the momentum slid him violently across the slick deck into the steel bulkhead. The impact left him winded, gasping for air, but there was no time to recover. The chute, still filled with air, threatened to drag him back towards the stern.

Shultz, grappling with the canopy, finally managed to gather it in, freeing Cutler. But they were now right in Tuck's landing path.

Tuck, hurtling towards the deck, realized the perilous situation. His only choice was to brake hard, risking injury to all three of them. He yanked the brake lines, the chute responding instantly, but the manoeuvre was risky.

Shultz, dragging Cutler, scrambled clear of the landing zone just in time. Stahmer, watching from a distance, gauged Tuck's perilous descent. It was a critical moment, with Tuck's landing now a dangerous gamble.

As Tuck neared the deck, he swung his legs, aiming to vault over the railing. His calculations were precise, but fate intervened. Mouhamed, on the bridge, unexpectedly altered the Reef Explorer's course, throwing Tuck's trajectory off.

Suddenly, two armed Somalians burst onto the scene, alerted by the lack of response from the top deck guard. Colton, watching through his sniper scope, momentarily had them in his sights before they disappeared behind the bulkhead.

The Somalians, instantly on high alert at the sight of Shultz and Cutler with the parachute, raised their weapons. A burst of gunfire rang out, bullets tearing through the fabric of the chute, narrowly missing Shultz and Cutler.

Stahmer, realizing he was too far to intervene, could only watch as the scene unfolded. The first Somalian kept firing, rounds whizzing perilously close to Cutler and Shultz. Then, as abruptly as it had started, the gunfire ceased.

In this moment, the deck of the Reef Explorer had become a crucible of chaos and danger. Every second counted, every decision could mean the difference between life and death. The tension was palpable, the air charged with the imminent threat of more violence. The fate of Cutler, Shultz, and Tuck hung in the balance, precariously teetering on the edge of disaster.

The Somalians changed magazines ready for a second volley of gunfire. The standoff on the deck of the Reef Explorer was a maelstrom of violence and split-second decisions. The first Somalian barely squeezed the trigger before Colton's sniper round found its mark. The man crumpled to the deck, his lifeblood pulsing out in diminishing spurts as he faded into death.

Ghislaine, her knife a glint of deadly intent, charged the second assailant. He swung his weapon in a wide arc, not fast enough to shoot, but sufficient to knock Ghislaine off her trajectory, sending her skidding across the deck. Her intervention, however brief, bought Stahmer the precious seconds he needed.

Stahmer, weapon-less and desperate, lunged at the Somalian, forcing him against the rail. The gun clattered overboard, leaving the two men locked in a fierce struggle. The Somalian, younger and stronger, began to overpower Stahmer, his hands tightening relentlessly around Stahmer's throat.

Above them, Tuck was in his own battle, swinging his legs to gain momentum for the landing. He paused, a fatal delay, but necessary for a clear shot. With a deep breath, he took aim. Below, Stahmer was on the brink, the Somalian's grip unyielding. Then, abruptly, the pressure vanished. Tuck's bullet had found its mark, the impact shattering the Somalian's head.

Stahmer collapsed, gasping for air, comprehending in those ragged breaths that Tuck had just made the ultimate sacrifice for him.

Tuck's struggle was not just against physical forces but against the very essence of defeat. He had Cheryl, his adopted daughter Esme, and a life worth fighting for. His body swung with desperate vigor, his legs clearing the rail by mere inches. It was a battle against gravity, a fight for survival.

But physics had the final say. Tuck's lower body crashed against the metal barrier, the sickening sound of snapping bone echoing over the deck. On the poop deck, those close enough heard the gruesome snap of Tuck's femur. Cutler and Colton, through the comms, caught the grunt of pain, the expletive that followed, and then silence as Tuck disappeared overboard, dragged by his parachute into the sea.

In the water, Tuck's world was one of blinding pain and fading consciousness. His instincts screamed for survival, even as waves of darkness clawed at the edges of his mind. He fought to fill the parachute canopy, to use its drag to keep him away from the lethal churn of the ship's propellers. The wind, an accomplice in his plight, pulled him first right, then left, drawing him away from the Reef Explorer.

Each touch of the waves was a jolt of agony, shooting from his shattered leg through his entire body. Tuck released his chute, plunging into a swell that engulfed him in pain. The suit and helmet, meant to protect, now felt like weights dragging him down.

Beneath the water's surface, Tuck's struggle became a solitary battle. He saw visions of Cheryl and Esme, so vivid against the backdrop of his darkening vision. He fought to kick, to swim, but only one leg responded, the other a source of relentless pain.

chapter twenty-three
Downfall

President Shelby had witnessed it all. His decades in Washington had provided him with an intimate understanding of the political landscape, a terrain marked by covert agreements and concealed operations. He was well-versed in the historical intricacies—the clandestine files of the CIA. The rumours of CIA involvement with drug money in the jungles of Vietnam, the Iran-Contra affair, and Operation Condor assassinations of South American right-wing politicians. These were the shadowy chapters of governance, the concealed aspects of American politics, hidden beneath the surface.

But President Shelby had clung to the belief that those days were behind them, that the government and its agencies had matured, evolved. Yet, as he hung up the phone with Fabienne and Ryan Welt, a bitter rage took hold. The dots connected into a grim picture—the sordid past hadn't passed; it had merely donned a new disguise.

With steely resolve, Shelby summoned the joint chiefs of staff into the Oval Office. The air was thick with the gravity of the moment as he had them swear on both the Bible and the Tanakh, insisting on truth.

"Collusion, black ops, Conrad Ford, Sheldrake aka Kasim Asfour—swear to me, on these sacred texts, you've had no part in it," he demanded, his voice cutting through the room's hush.

Each chief, one after the other, placed their hand upon the holy books and swore their innocence, their ignorance. Welt made it crystal clear—this was to stay within these walls.

Shelby, with a steely edge in his voice, laid down an ultimatum to ex-president Nash. He threatened to bring the full weight of the Senate down on him, to push for an unprecedented impeachment if he didn't divulge the whole truth. It was a high-stakes gamble, a move that could either bring about justice or backfire spectacularly. But Shelby was willing to roll the dice.

Cornered and concerned about the legacy he would leave behind, faced President Shelby with a resigned candour. His reputation, once untarnished, now hung precariously in the balance. Without outright denial, he began to unravel the threads of a black ops that had been set in motion years before.

The plan, audacious in its scope, was originally pitched to him by his then-Chief of Staff Treisman, now Shelby's vice president. Its objective was clear: to curtail Russian expansion in the Mediterranean. The unwitting architect of this scheme was none other than Conrad Ford, a man driven by the desire to reclaim lucrative government contracts. Ford had come forward with an offer that promised to be a game-changer: the WCU, a weapon of unparalleled potential.

The plot thickened with the involvement of Deputy Director Allen, who had an asset deeply embedded within Al-Qaeda, crucial for ensuring the success of the operation. After much deliberation, the ex-president Nash had given the green light to Treisman and Allen, with one critical stipulation—no government funds were to be used. He had wanted to distance the official channels from this operation, wary of potential blowback.

However, the ex-president's carefully laid plans unravelled as Shelby disclosed the grim realities of how the operation had been financed. The revelation that Conrad Ford had been given carte blanche to peddle arms indiscriminately on the global stage, and Asfour's role in pilfering and flipping yachts, hit him like a physical blow. The consequences of these decisions were dire, leading to loss of life, including American citizens.

Nash's reaction to Shelby's revelations was one of disbelief and horror. The operation he had sanctioned, under the guise of national security, had spiralled into a dark saga of illegal arms deals and deadly consequences. This was a far cry from the controlled, strategic manoeuvre he thought he had set in motion. Now, facing the consequences, he grappled with the realization that his actions had unleashed a chain of events far beyond his original intent, staining his legacy with the blood of innocents.

Two years had passed since Shelby's last cigar—a vice relinquished at the behest of the first lady. But tonight, Welt presented him with a box of Montecristo whites. Shelby retreated to the Rose Garden; the privacy of the night air preferable to the risk of leaving evidence of his lapse in the Oval Office.

Out in the garden, Secret Service agents shadowed him, their presence a silent vigil. He paused by the flower bed, a small bird catching his eye. With a flick of the lighter, he ignited the cigar, the aroma mingling with the earthy scent of thyme planted in meticulous patterns around the trees.

The flame's glow, the cigar's smoke, the night's quiet—the scene was a solitary man's contemplation, a leader burdened with the weight of knowledge, enveloped in the fragrance of secrets and smoke.

The smoke from President Treisman's cigar twisted and curled into the night air, a visual manifestation of his simmering anger. He exhaled forcefully, each puff a release of his pent-up frustration. Halfway through the cigar, Welt approached him, the timing as precise as everything in Welt's world.

"What next, Mr. President?" Welt asked, his voice steady despite the unfolding storm.

Shelby's reply was tinged with a mix of bitterness and resolve. "I am the president of the United States, and yet I'm treated like a mushroom by those in power—kept in the dark, fed crap. That includes the vice president."

"Orders, sir?" Welt was all business, ready to act.

"Get the vice president. I don't care what he's doing or who he's with. I want him here within the hour." Shelby's command was unequivocal.

Welt handed Shelby a mint Tic Tac before departing, a small gesture amid the grander scheme of things. Shelby seeking a semblance of normalcy, moved to the Nevada roses, plucking one and tucking it into his lapel, hoping its fragrance would mask the cigar's scent.

President Shelby's mind was preoccupied with the complex layers of the unfolding conspiracy, but it was Fabienne Asper's parting words that truly unsettled him. Her assertion that the situation might be more convoluted than initially reported hinted at a deeper, possibly more perilous web of deceit.

"I don't think it's as clear cut as what I've reported, I have threads leading elsewhere. Do you want me to keep digging?" Fabienne had asked, her tone indicating she was ready to delve deeper into the murky waters.

"Yes, I want you to continue," the president responded decisively, understanding the gravity of granting such authorization. "You'll have access to any file required. I'm granting you SAP clearance."

He was referring to Special Access Programs, the most secretive echelons of classified information. SAPs were the vaults of the nation's most closely guarded secrets, accessible only to a select few with stringent security clearances. Even among those with Top Secret clearance, access to an SAP was limited to individuals with a specific need to know the sensitive information contained within.

He paused, a thought crossing his mind. "But from what I've heard, you might already have had access to these files." There was a hint of wry acknowledgment in his voice, a nod to Fabienne's reputation for being always one step ahead in the intelligence game.

For President Shelby, granting SAP clearance to Fabienne was not just a decision; it was a leap of faith, one that could unravel the threads of a conspiracy that reached deeper than he had ever imagined.

Meanwhile, Special Agent Rick Alderman interrupted the Vice President, Treisman, amidst his dinner with senators at Hampson Restaurant. Treisman's initial dismissal turned into reluctant compliance when he learned the president had sent for him.

"Excuse me, gentlemen, duty calls," Treisman quipped to his company, disguising his irritation with a veneer of humour. He took the phone from Alderman and retreated to a quieter spot.

"Welt, what's so urgent?" Treisman's tone was a mix of annoyance and curiosity, unaware of the storm brewing on the other end of the line.

Vice President Treisman's s request to reschedule was met with a firm denial from Welt. "Afraid not," Welt stated, as a special agent approached with Treisman's overcoat, a subtle indication that the Secret Service was already in on the plan.

Welt led the vice president to the Situation Room, located in the basement of the West Wing of the White House. This room, often referred to as the nerve centre, was where critical decisions were made, especially in times of crisis. It was a hub bustling with activity and tension, housing intelligence analysts, duty officers, communication specialists, and the national security advisor. They were all there, waiting in anticipation.

The atmosphere in the room was charged. The black leather chairs around the long rectangular conference table were filled with the joint chiefs of staff, their expressions grave, their focus sharp. President Shelby sat at the head of the table, his presence one of controlled urgency.

As Vice President Treisman entered, the sensors in the ceiling detected a breach of protocol—he hadn't left his cell phone outside as required. A duty officer promptly took his phone, an action that didn't escape Treisman's notice. His gaze then fell on the screens displaying live feeds of Max Cutler and the SAS teams aboard the

Osprey. He moved to take his usual front row seat but was stopped in his tracks as President Shelby stood up.

"I need a word, Richard," the president said, his tone serious. He led the vice president into an adjoining conference room, with Ryan Welt following closely behind. The joint chiefs of staff exchanged glances, the tension palpable, as they realized that the day's interviews had unearthed something significant.

"I gather we're here over the hijacking in the Mediterranean?" Treisman ventured, trying to gauge the situation.

"You know we are, Richard," the president replied, cutting straight to the chase.

"On the screen, those look like SAS teams. Are the Brits sending them onto the Reef Explorer?" Treisman's asked, trying to piece together the unfolding scenario.

"In conjunction with ourselves and a private contractor, MIDAS," the president confirmed.

"Is that wise, Mr. President?" In the high stakes, charged atmosphere, the confrontation in the side conference room was laced with tension and veiled accusations. President Shelby, with Ryan Welt by his side, faced Vice President Treisman in a moment fraught with implications.

Welt, unflinching, chimed in, challenging Treisman. "As a former CIA director, surely you understand the strategic implications here?"

Treisman, feeling cornered, shifted his focus. "Why is Welt here, Mr. President, questioning me like I'm a suspect rather than the vice president?"

Shelby's response was firm. "Welt stays, Richard. Remember, I chose you for this position."

Treisman expressed his gratitude, but Shelby cut to the chase, confronting him with allegations of undermining the administration. Treisman feigned ignorance, but the President pressed on, revealing that Deputy Director Allen was currently under intense interrogation.

Treisman, visibly uncomfortable, denied knowledge of any operation. But Shelby was relentless, citing Fabienne Asper's findings from GCHQ, linking Treisman to a meeting about the operation and its connection to Carl Bridge, now known as the terrorist Kasim Asfour.

The vice president attempted to deflect, advising the president to let the matter go. But Shelby was resolute, questioning Treisman's role and the operation's true target.

President Shelby laid down his ultimatum with unflinching authority. The air in the room seemed to thicken as he spoke, his words cutting through the tension like a knife.

"Let me be absolutely clear," Shelby began, his voice a blend of resolve and cold determination. "The public will be informed later tonight that you've had a heart attack. You'll be moved to a dark site and interrogated until we get the truth."

Treisman, the vice president, recoiled at the president's words, his voice a mix of disbelief and indignation. "You can't do that, I'm the vice president of the United States."

Shelby's reply was swift and decisive, a verbal knockout blow. "I can, because I am the president." His words resonated with the power vested in his office, underscoring the gravity of the situation.

The room, already heavy with the weight of revelations and accusations, seemed to close in around them. The exchange was more than a mere conversation; it was a showdown of political power, a clash of wills between two men who had navigated the treacherous waters of Washington's elite. For Treisman, the threat was clear and imminent, a stark reminder of the perilous game of power and secrecy in which they were all players. Shelby's move was bold, a gambit that spoke of his readiness to push boundaries to uncover the truth, no matter how high the cost or how deep the fall.

Treisman, now with his back against the wall, made a final, desperate attempt to regain control of the situation. His voice, a mix of defiance and calculation, echoed in the tense room. "These operations don't come with written presidential orders, but I assure you, it was a presidential decree. I have proof."

His claim, bold and audacious, was a last-ditch effort to shift the narrative in his favour. The room, already charged with the electricity of high political drama, seemed to pause at his assertion. It was a move that smacked of desperation yet carried the weight of potential truth. The room was a battleground where veiled threats were weapons, and words were both shields and swords.

Treisman's revelation, whether true or a bluff, added another layer of complexity to the already dense web of intrigue.

President Shelby, with a tone that cut through the tension like a blade, brought the conversation to a pivotal point. "Fabienne Asper has hinted at hidden depths and unseen forces at play," he said. "She's suggesting that this operation, shrouded in secrecy and crafted for deniability, might not have been sanctioned by the highest office, but by someone else."

Treisman's response, was a mix of admission and deflection, his voice tinged with a flustered urgency. "I will admit to my part in this," he began, the words of a man cornered. "I did it for my country, to prevent the Russians from gaining more ground. But let's be clear, it was sanctioned by the president, and the president alone."

His statement, while partly an admission of guilt, was also an attempt to shift the ultimate responsibility upwards to the highest level of power. It was a desperate move, one that reeked of self-preservation under the guise of national interest.

President Shelby, a seasoned player in the game of political nuance, watched Treisman closely. He read the nuances in Treisman's body language—the slight stammer, the evasive gaze, the too-quick defensiveness. All these signs spoke louder than Treisman's words, painting a picture of a man scrambling to save himself.

President Shelby's tone was firm and unyielding, his words laced with a finality that brooked no argument. He leaned in, his gaze fixed intently on Treisman. "What's the target, Richard? Think carefully," he cautioned, his voice a blend of stern warning and a sliver of opportunity. "You see those three men in suits? They're here to take you for interrogation. Tell me the target, and maybe we can resolve this without dragging your name, and mine, through the mud."

The three men in suits stood ominously in the background, an unspoken threat to Treisman, a reminder of the gravity of his situation. They were the embodiment of the consequences awaiting him, should he choose to continue his charade.

Treisman, now visibly sweating under the intense scrutiny, realized the precariousness of his position. The president's offer, while not a guarantee of clemency, was a lifeline in a sea of uncertainty. It was a chance to mitigate the damage, to possibly save some semblance of his reputation and dignity or was it.

This was a pivotal moment, a crossroads where Treisman's next words could seal his fate. The path he chose now—to confess or to continue his deception—would determine the course of events to follow.

Vice President Treisman, his back against the wall, finally revealed the true scope of the operation in a tone laced with both justification and a hint of desperation. "The Russians have been pushing to establish a port in our operational theatre for years. We can't let them gain a stranglehold over such a crucial region. The oil, the access to the Suez Canal, the security of Israel… it's all at stake."

President Shelby's response was measured yet revealing. "So it's the nuclear barge in Tartus?"

Treisman's facade cracked. "Yes, it's the barge. Destroy it, and they can't build there for centuries."

"And the fallout?" the president pressed, his tone implying more than just the literal repercussions.

Treisman's reply was chillingly pragmatic. "You can't make an omelette without cracking eggs."

Welt, unable to contain his contempt, interjected, "You're a complete asshole."

Treisman dismissed him with a wave. "You're not high enough up the food chain for your opinion to matter, Welt."

President Shelby , his disgust palpable, compared Treisman to some of history's most notorious dictators. "Hitler, Mussolini, Stalin… all driven by massive egos and sociopathic tendencies. I see that in you now, Richard."

Treisman's defence was coldly logical. "Someone has to make the hard decisions to keep our country safe. Diplomacy has its limits."

President Shelby's response was laced with a mix of disbelief and moral outrage, his voice rising in intensity. "You're talking about poisoning the Mediterranean for generations, Richard! Think of the innocent lives at risk in the region. This isn't just a strategic move; it's a humanitarian disaster."

Vice President Treisman, undeterred and resolute in his stance, replied with a chilling rationalization. "We've done it before. Take the Marshall Islands, remember Bikini and Eniwetok atolls for instance. Granted, it was on a much smaller scale, but the principle remains the same."

His words hung heavily in the air, a stark reminder of past actions taken in the name of national security that had left indelible scars. Treisman's comparison to the nuclear testing in the Marshall Islands, where the repercussions are still felt to this day.

Welt, seizing a moment of clarity amid the heated exchange, asked the critical question. "Can the attack be stopped?"

Treisman's answer was evasive, pointing to Carl Bridge, now Kasim Asfour, watching from afar. "Work it out, man. He's probably holed up with the Al-Qaeda leadership, watching all this unfold."

The president, weighing the gravity of the situation, pointed out the legal and moral implications. "What you're planning could constitute a war crime. It violates the Geneva Convention, not to mention our own laws."

Treisman remained defiant, seeing himself as a patriot rather than a villain. "We've undertaken one of the most complex and necessary operations in our nation's history. It's an operation that deserves commendation, not condemnation."

In the charged atmosphere of the situation room, Vice President Treisman remained unflinchingly committed to his course of action. "The Russians are about to lose their sole base in the Mediterranean; we're pushing them back to the Black Sea," he declared, his voice carrying a tone of triumph. "Al-Qaeda will take the credit, but we'll know the truth. They're unwittingly serving our interests. It's a perfect outcome. Stand down, Mr. President, and let events unfold."

President Shelby, however, countered with a cautionary tale, his voice laced with a warning. "You know the story of the frog and the scorpion, Richard? It's a tale of inherent nature and inevitable outcomes. Are you not seeing the parallels here?"

Treisman brushed off the analogy. "We've meticulously planned this for years, Mr. President. We don't leave anything to chance."

Shelby's response was a pointed reminder of the importance of comprehensive intelligence and oversight. "You're in the situation room, Richard, a place born from the lessons of the Bay of Pigs, where lack of intelligence led to disaster. You, Allen, and Bridge—or Asfour, as you call him—have been operating in isolation. I'm still assessing Conrad Ford's role in this. But look around you, at these analysts gathering real-time intelligence. You're operating without this critical input. What you can't measure, you can't manage. Don't claim to have everything under control."

Vice President Treisman's response was steeped in the hardened, sometimes ruthless logic typical of high-stakes international espionage narratives. "We have Bridge deep within Al-Qaeda's leadership. He's been our eyes and ears for years. This operation is an affirmation to American intelligence capability," he asserted with a tone of pride.

President Shelby, while acknowledging the significance of the operation, expressed his reservations. "I'm not questioning the tool, Richard. It's how you're using it that concerns me."

"History will be our judge," Treisman retorted, justifying his actions as necessary for national security.

Welt, attempting to steer the conversation towards specifics, pressed Treisman about the mysterious WCU. "What is this weapon that Ford developed? No one at the Pentagon seems to know about it."

Treisman, evasive, admitted Ford's involvement was limited to his expertise with the WCU. But when pressed further by President Treisman about its capabilities, Treisman was cryptic. "You'll find out soon enough. I thought we were just sweeping leaves here, Mr. President. Turns out, we're in the eye of a hurricane."

President Shelby undeterred, noted Treisman's uncooperative stance and informed him of Allen's and Ford's ongoing interrogation by the FBI.

The tension in the situation room was palpable as President Shelby flanked by Welt, returned to the heart of the action, leaving Vice President Treisman behind under the watchful eyes of Secret

Service agents. The room was abuzz with activity, eyes fixed on the screens displaying the high-stakes operation unfolding in real time.

President Shelby, his stance reflecting the gravity of the situation, addressed Vice President Treisman's Secret Service detail with a firm and authoritative tone. "Take the vice president home, but understand this—he's effectively under house arrest," he ordered.

The three Secret Service operatives, accustomed to following directives without question, nodded in acknowledgement. Shelby's command was unequivocal, and the seriousness of his tone left no room for doubt.

He continued, ensuring there was no misunderstanding. "FBI agents will be stationed outside his residence. They are to ensure that no visitors are allowed. This is a matter of national security, and it's imperative that these instructions are followed to the letter." His gaze lingered on each of the operatives, reinforcing the seriousness of his directive. "Is that clear?" he asked, his eyes scanning the faces of the surprised agents.

The agents responded with a unanimous and resolute "Yes, Mr. President." They understood the magnitude of the task assigned to them—to guard the vice president, a key figure in a rapidly unfolding political drama.

As they escorted Vice President Treisman from the room, a tangible sense of tension and urgency filled the air. For President Shelby, this was a decisive move, a necessary step to contain the situation and prevent any further escalation of the crisis. The room, still buzzing with the activity of the ongoing operation, now also bore the weight of a political decision that would undoubtedly have far-reaching consequences.

The main screen offered a split view of the drama. On the left, the drone's aerial footage showed Cutler, leading the operation, a mile ahead of Tuck in their descent toward the Reef Explorer. The right displayed Cutler's perspective from his headgear, giving an up-close view of the mission. A separate screen to the side broadcasted footage from the bodycam of the SAS strike team leader, lying in wait on the Zodiacs, ready to move on Cutler's signal.

"Cutler's team has secured the poop deck, and the Spectre's guards are neutralized, Mr. President," the duty officer reported.

Phase one of the operation was a success, but President Shelby knew the hardest part was yet to come. "Phase two is more complicated," he acknowledged, his voice steady despite the mounting tension.

The national security advisor likened the next phase to "Trying to land a parachute on a bouncy castle in the middle of the sea," a comment that underscored the daunting challenge ahead.

The room watched in awe as Cutler expertly landed on the poop deck, a confirmation to his skill and experience. The situation grew tense as terrorists emerged and exchanged fire with Cutler's team. A collective sigh of relief washed over the room as the threat was neutralized. "Cutler's got a good team around him," the national security advisor remarked, admiration evident in his voice.

The focus then shifted to Tuck. The rocking camera on his headgear and his frantic leg movements signalled trouble. The drone adjusted its angle, capturing Tuck's struggle. The joint chief of staff from the Navy muttered, "He's done for," as they watched the ship change direction, complicating Tuck's approach.

In a scene that could have been lifted straight from a *Mission Impossible* movie, the situation room was gripped by a palpable, chilling silence as Tuck's ordeal unfolded in excruciating detail. The clarity of the audio from Tuck's headset was hauntingly vivid. Each person in the room flinched as the gruesome sound of Tuck's femur snapping and the profanities reverberated through the speakers.

The infrared camera in Tuck's helmet transmitted a stark, high-definition image that held everyone in rapt attention. The screen showed Tuck's desperate struggle against the relentless pull of his parachute. His body, a plaything to the merciless winds, was dragged backwards over the choppy sea.

The room watched in shocked horror, the tension escalating with every passing second. Tuck's struggle was visceral, his pain almost tangible through the screen. His futile attempts to release the parachute were met with failure, and the room collectively held its breath as he plummeted into the unforgiving sea.

As Tuck hit the water, a collective gasp echoed through the room. The camera continued to broadcast, showing Tuck's increasingly desperate battle to stay afloat. His grunts and groans of agony were as clear as if he were in the room with them, each sound a stark reminder of the harsh reality of their profession.

The situation room, usually a hub of controlled chaos and strategy, was now a theatre of stark human drama. The people, seasoned in the art of war and intelligence, found themselves confronting the brutal reality of their choices and actions.

As Tuck sank deeper, his struggles grew weaker, his efforts to fight the inevitable waning. The room watched, helpless and horrified, as the audio from his headset gradually faded into an eerie silence, the finality of which was a heavy weight in the air.

In that moment, the room was united in a shared experience of shock and helplessness, a stark reminder of the perilous nature of their work. The silence that followed was a harrowing reminder to the gravity of their operations, where every decision, every action, could have life-or-death consequences. This was the brutal reality of their world, unvarnished and unapologetic, a world where death was a consequence of bravery.

"Change the image. Let the man die in peace," President Shelby ordered solemnly, a gesture of respect for the fallen operative.

Attention quickly returned to the ongoing operation as the national security advisor announced, "Mr. President, Cutler has given the 'go' signal to the SAS leader."

The screen now focused on the SAS strike team leader's bodycam, filling the screen with their tactical approach. The room, still reeling from Tuck's demise, watched intently as the next phase of the operation unfolded.

chapter twenty-four
Wings on a Prayer

In the situation room, President Shelby's order to switch the feed from Tuck's tragic end shifted the focus back to the ongoing operation. The SAS strike team leader's bodycam feed filled the screen, drawing everyone's attention to the next critical phase.

Meanwhile, far away in Geneva, Fabienne Asper, an integral part of MIDAS, was overcome with grief. The news of Tuck's demise struck a deep chord, disentangling the stoic composure she had maintained throughout her career. Her isolation as a child had made her find refuge in books and knowledge, leading her to a life of solitary dedication to her work. Her move to MIDAS had brought a semblance of family she never had, with Tuck becoming like a brother to her. His loss was not just a professional blow; it was deeply personal.

On the Spectre, Colton received the same devastating news. "Copy that," he responded tersely, immediately shifting gears. "Forget the lifeboat for now; we've got a man in the water." His voice was a blend of command and urgency as he directed the drone operator to search for Tuck. Every second was crucial, and Colton knew it.

The drone pilot, under strict orders, conducted a brief but thorough search. The drone's camera located Tuck's parachute floating ominously on the surface and a faint blinking light below—a grim indicator of Tuck's position. The drone relayed these images back to the Spectre, guiding Colton, and his team to the site.

"Parachute 160 yards west from your position," the drone operator conveyed, his voice laced with a mix of professionalism and sympathy. "Probably body recovery."

Colton, maintaining a calm yet commanding presence, kept his focus on the dual aspects of the mission. While Jones adeptly redirected the Spectre towards the distress signal, Colton shifted his position to maintain a strategic view of the poop deck. His eyes scanned the area with vigilance, ready to respond at a moment's notice if another threat emerged.

The Spectre cut through the waves; its course set towards the location where Tuck had disappeared into the sea. The urgency of the rescue was palpable, but Colton's experience in handling high-stakes situations was evident. He knew the importance of not losing sight of the primary objective—securing the Reef Explorer—while attending to the immediate crisis.

Simultaneously, the drone operator, adhering to the orders received, deftly guided the drone back towards its original task. The drone's camera once again focused on the lifeboat, ensuring continuous coverage of the crucial aspects of the operation. This swift reorientation of the drone's focus was essential for maintaining situational awareness over the broader scope of the mission.

Back on the Reef Explorer, Cutler coordinated the next move with Stahmer and Ghislaine. "Ghislaine, stay here with Shultz to secure the poop deck for the SAS boarding parties," he instructed, detailing the tactical approach for the imminent SAS assault. He emphasized the need for vigilance and readiness, preparing them for the worst-case scenarios.

Ghislaine's question about identifying friend from foe was met with a pragmatic response from Cutler. "Remember, they're not human beings; they're targets. Aim centre mass, double tap to conserve ammunition."

Ghislaine's concern for Tuck, tinged with fear for Cutler's own safety, highlighted the close bonds formed in the crucible of such high-stakes operations. Cutler, with a reassuring yet realistic touch, tried to offer some hope about Tuck's chances, but the grim reality of their situation hung heavily in the air.

"Focus on your part of the mission, Ghislaine," Cutler said firmly, his directive a reminder of the task at hand. "Your safety is paramount. Go, get ready."

Cutler then turned to Stahmer, laying out the plan to disarm the explosives on deck six. His instructions were clear and concise. "If I'm out of the picture, continue the mission. Inform Colton once the explosives are secured."

Stahmer's question about Tuck's survival prospects received a grim but honest response from Cutler. "No," he admitted, his voice betraying a hint of sorrow for his comrade.

Aboard the Spectre, the tension was almost tangible as Jones and Evans kept a vigilant eye on the unfolding situation. As they approached the floating parachute, Colton's commanding voice broke through the heavy air. "Jones, come up here," he ordered, with an urgency that demanded immediate compliance.

Jones quickly made his way to the top of the boat, his movements sharp and attentive, reflecting the seriousness of the moment. Colton, wasting no time, instructed him to lie down. In his hands, he placed a rifle, swiftly instructing Jones on its operation. The situation was critical, and there was no room for error.

"Don't shoot one of ours or the SAS," Colton commanded, his voice carrying the weight of the grave responsibility he was entrusting to Jones. The instruction was clear, but the gravity of it was not lost on Jones.

Jones, lying prone with the rifle in his hands, was visibly uncomfortable with the sudden responsibility thrust upon him. His hesitance was evident, a clear indicator of the high-stress environment they were operating in. The stakes were incredibly high, and the margin for error was virtually zero.

Colton, driven by a mix of duty and desperation, prepared for a daring dive into the sea to search for Tuck.

Stripping down to his shorts, Colton dived into the dark, churning waters with a sense of urgency. His strong strokes took him deep, fighting against the suffocating pressure in his chest and the entangling lines of the parachute. He surfaced twice, each time gasping for air before diving again, driven by a relentless determination.

Navigating through the murky depths, Colton finally spotted the emergency light's faint blinking. With every fibre of his being focused on the task, he followed the suspension lines, hoping against hope to find Tuck still attached to the parachute. The visibility was poor, adding to the challenge of the rescue, but Colton pushed on, propelled by a combination of skill, experience, and sheer will.

In the turbid waters, Colton was plunged into a dire scenario, where every second was a battle against the relentless pull of the sea. As he descended into the abyss, the darkness enveloped him, turning the rescue into a blind, desperate search. He could barely make out Tuck's form, obscured by the gloom of the deep. Colton's lungs began to burn.

The situation was fraught with danger. The parachute's canopy loomed like a dark giant jelly fish in the water, its tentacles a potential trap that could ensnare him just as it had Tuck. But Colton's training and instincts took over in this life-and-death struggle. He navigated through the water with a desperation, his movements swift and purposeful despite the encroaching panic of asphyxiation.

Upon reaching Tuck, Colton's hands moved with practiced efficiency. He couldn't see much in the dark conditions, but he could feel the outline of Tuck's body, still tragically attached to the parachute that had become his anchor to the ocean's depths. In a rapid sequence of actions, Colton located and activated the jettison mechanism on Tuck's webbing. The parachute, now a deadly weight, was released, and Colton grasped Tuck's helmet firmly.

With his own breath running critically low, Colton made a powerful upward thrust. He was fighting against not just the weight of Tuck's body but also the drag of the water and the tangled lines that threatened to pull them both into the abyss. His muscles burned with the effort, his lungs screamed for air, but Colton's determination was unyielding. He propelled them both towards the surface, each kick a defiance against the lethal grip of the sea.

Breaking the surface was a relief and a torment simultaneously. Colton gasped for air, his lungs burning from the exertion and lack of oxygen. He was painfully aware that Tuck had been underwater far too long. Fifteen minutes submerged was way beyond the threshold of survival.

Evans put the Spectre on auto pilot and worked quickly to pull Tuck's lifeless body onto the diving platform. They he assisted the exhausted Colton back onto the boat. His ebony skin was streaked with salt, his breaths coming in laboured pants as he tried to recover from the ordeal. The realization that his efforts were likely in vain weighed heavily on him.

Jones, seeing Colton back on deck, relayed Cutler's instructions for him to return to his lookout position. "If you can take over, I would much appreciate it," Jones added.

"Two minutes," Colton shot back breathless.

Colton, still catching his breath, acknowledged the grim reality of Tuck's fate. "He's dead," he said, instructing Evans to remove Tuck's headgear and cover him. There was a solemnity in his voice, a recognition of the loss they had just endured.

After regaining some of his strength, Colton climbed back to his position atop the Spectre's canopy. "Back on station," he transmitted to the team aboard the Reef Explorer.

Ghislaine's voice came through, filled with concern. "What about Tuck?"

Cutler's response was curt, a reflection of the mission's urgency. "We'll discuss after the mission. Stay focused."

Cutler, moving stealthily through the ship, was a picture of focused determination. His communication with each MIDAS agent was crisp and to the point, his every move calculated. Reaching deck six, he quickly assessed the situation. The sight of the explosives rigged along the railing sent a jolt of urgency through him.

Spotting the Arab guard, Cutler knew he was in a precarious position. The realization that using his weapon would attract unwanted attention forced him to retreat and reassess. His whispered communication with Stahmer indicated the delicacy of their situation. "Standby," he instructed, knowing any rash move could jeopardize their mission.

The situation called for a sniper's precision, and Colton was up to the task, despite the challenging conditions. Aboard the Spectre, he lined up his shot, the Spectre's movement making the guard's head a difficult target. Colton's first shot missed, startling the guard, but his quick reflexes and sharpshooting skills ensured the second shot found its mark. The guard was down.

Cutler's acknowledgment of Colton's success was tinged with relief and a hint of dry humour. The removal of the detonator from the explosives was a critical step in securing the deck. The operation was progressing, but the risks remained high.

Cutler's next order to Stahmer was bold and risky, reflecting the do-or-die nature of their operation. Stahmer's response, half-joking but underscored with genuine concern, showed the trust and reliance each member of the team placed in one another." Put your weapon down and go out with your hands held high."

Cutler's directive to Stahmer was a risky gambit, a move that could tip the scales either way, but time was of the essence. Stahmer's response, tinged with apprehension yet laced with trust, underscored the high stakes they were playing with. "What's this, a 50-50 gambit?" Stahmer remarked.

"More 60-40," Cutler said.

As Stahmer complied, walking onto the deck with his hands raised, a scene fraught with tension unfolded. Cutler, with the stealth and agility of a seasoned operative, moved into position. His keen observation had already revealed the presence of another terrorist, a mirror to the one he had just neutralized.

The situation reached a critical point as Stahmer knelt, hands behind his head, drawing the guard's attention. This diversion created the opening Cutler needed. With the guard's focus split between Stahmer and deciding his next move, Cutler saw his chance.

Moving with precision and speed, Cutler closed the distance to the guard. His boots, silent on the deck, did not betray his approach. In one fluid, lethal motion, he drew his switchblade and struck. The blade found its mark at the base of the guard's skull, a swift and decisive action that left no room for a counterattack. Cutler's manoeuvre was clinical, the kind of ruthless efficiency necessary in such life-or-death scenarios.

Stahmer's reply to Cutler's earlier estimation of the odds was dry, a moment of dark humour in the midst of danger. Cutler's response was equally pragmatic, focused on the task ahead. "Maybe," he conceded about playing the bait next time. But for now, their mission was clear—to disarm the explosives.

"Start from aft and remove the detonators," Cutler commanded, his tone leaving no room for debate. He would handle the starboard side, ensuring they systematically neutralized the threat. Their plan was to meet at the forward end of the deck once they had completed their task.

Stahmer and Cutler executed their task with a precision that spoke of their extensive training and experience. Their mission to disarm the detonators was critical, a task that required a combination of technical skill and tactical acumen.

Stahmer, displaying both a skilled touch and unshakable composure, methodically advanced towards each explosive device. His actions were marked by a graceful precision, combining caution and purpose to minimize the risk of setting off a lethal chain reaction. The detonators, ingeniously set up along the safety railing, served as a testament to the terrorists' painstaking preparation. Drawing upon his extensive knowledge of explosives, Stahmer relied on a combination of wire cutters and electronic jammers, the tools of his trade, to render each device harmless. The intricate process of disarming these explosives paralleled the high-stakes task of defusing a ticking time bomb, where a single misstep could result in catastrophic consequences.

As Cutler and Stahmer moved with the precision and silence of seasoned operatives. The duo's task was compounded by Stahmer's handicap—he was operating with only one eye. This added challenge meant Cutler had to compensate, simultaneously assisting in the disarmament process while maintaining a heightened level of vigilance.

Cutler, with one eye on the task and the other scanning their surroundings, was the epitome of a multi-faceted operator. His situational awareness was acute, a necessary adaptation given Stahmer's visual limitation. Every shadow, every sound was a potential threat, and Cutler's heightened senses were tuned to detect the slightest hint of danger.

Their chosen path beneath the bridge was a tactically sound decision, offering them cover and keeping them out of sight from any terrorists that might be patrolling above. The area was dimly lit, casting deep shadows that played to their advantage. They moved through this semi-darkness like ghosts, their steps barely making a sound on the metal deck.

The tension in the air was almost tangible, as each movement they made carried with it the risk of detection. Cutler's hand hovered near his weapon, a constant reminder of the ever-present danger they faced. He was prepared to switch from the role of technician to combatant in an instant if the need arose.

This careful, methodical progress under the bridge was a dance with danger, each step a choreographed move in a deadly ballet. The operation required not just technical expertise in disarming the explosives but also an exceptional level of tactical skill and mental fortitude.

Together, they worked in unspoken harmony, attuned to the dangers of their environment. The clink of the disarmed detonators being carefully placed in a secure bag was the only sound in the otherwise silent operation.

Throughout, they conversed through silent signals, a non-verbal language Cutler had taught all his operatives, particularly those from civilian backgrounds, in contrast to military training. Their next step was to regroup with the team, navigating back through the ship's maze-like hallways, where every turn could hide an ambush.

Reaching the poop deck, Cutler initiated communication with the supporting SAS teams. His concise message, "Detonators secure," was a signal for the next phase of the operation. The response from the SAS team leader was swift, indicating their impending approach.

Three teams of four SAS operatives, highly trained and equipped for stealth and combat, approached the Reef Explorer aboard Zodiac boats. These small, manoeuvrable crafts glided silently through the water, ideal for special services missions. Each team was a display of precision and readiness.

The first team, clad in dark, water-resistant gear, blended into the night. Their faces obscured by night-vision goggles and black balaclavas, only their focused eyes visible. They carried compact, suppressed firearms, ready for quick, quiet engagement. This team moved with a practiced, fluid coordination, communicating through subtle hand signals.

The second and third teams equally equipped, showed a similar level of discipline and preparedness. Their gear laden with tactical equipment—knives, ropes, and explosives for breaching. They scanned their surroundings with acute awareness, prepared to react to any threat.

Cutler's orders were quick and clear. "Stahmer, when they get here secure the SAS grapple lines. Watch for surprises, Ghislaine." He handed her a semi-automatic. The nod from both Ghislaine and Stahmer was a silent acknowledgment of their readiness and trust in Cutler's leadership.

Shultz, Ghislaine, and Stahmer experienced a sudden surge of adrenaline as the first missile erupted into the sky. Launched from a rocket launcher stationed on the top deck, it tore through the air, its presence announced by a roaring sound and a trail of thin, ghostly vapor. The first missile, with its roaring ascent and trailing vapor, had been a shock, but the second, with its deadly accuracy, brought a stark, brutal reality to the fore. The top deck of the Reef Explorer had transformed into a battleground, the rocket launcher's presence indicating a higher level of enemy preparedness than they had anticipated.

The terrorists, having been alerted to the approach of the boats, had strategically positioned themselves on the port side of the ship. This placement fortuitously kept them hidden from Colton, who was stationed on the Spectre with a vantage point that only covered the starboard side. Cutler had previously cautioned that their surveillance was limited to the starboard side, but despite this, the SAS commander had decided against an attack from that direction, considering it too risky.

Cutler's team, designated as Strike Team One, was just one component of a larger operation involving three other SAS strike teams—Two, Three, and Four. Each team had its specific role, working in tandem to ensure the mission's success. However, a vital piece of tactical information had been withheld from Cutler and his team. The SAS commander, for reasons unknown, had decided not to inform Cutler of a critical decision affecting the operation's scope.

This lapse in communication meant that Cutler and Strike Team One were operating without full knowledge of the overwatch limitations. They were under the impression that they had comprehensive surveillance and support, especially from the Spectre's position. However, the reality was starkly different. Their overwatch was restricted to just the starboard side, leaving the port side—where the terrorists were now strategically positioned and waiting—outside their field of vision and control.

This gap in their situational awareness posed a significant risk. Without knowledge of the enemy's exact location and movements on the port side, Strike Team One was at a disadvantage, potentially walking into an ambush. The terrorists, aware of their blind spots and taking full advantage of the situation, were well-prepared and positioned for a confrontation. This oversight in intelligence sharing not only heightened the danger for Cutler and his team but also added an element of unpredictability to the operation, complicating their mission objectives.

Meanwhile, the three SAS Zodiac boats, attacking form the port side and agile in the water, reacted with swift precision. The operatives, aware of the imminent danger, manoeuvred the boats to evade the deadly projectiles. As the first missile screamed past, missing the lead Zodiac by mere feet, it was a narrow escape that spoke volumes of the SAS's training and reflexes. The operatives in the other two boats had reacted with almost supernatural speed, But the second missile's success was a grim reminder of the ever-present danger in such missions. Strike Team Three was no longer. The third missile landed behind the third Zodiac.

The explosion that claimed the lives of four of their comrades was not just a loss of skilled operators; it was a personal blow to each member of the team. In the tight-knit world of special forces, these were not just colleagues but brothers-in-arms. The sight of the Zodiac, now just debris and fire on the water's surface, was a poignant moment, filled with a mix of grief, rage, and a renewed sense of purpose.

In the wake of the explosion and the ensuing fire that had engulfed the first boat, illuminating the night with its fierce blaze, the remaining SAS operatives were forced to quickly recalibrate their strategy. What had begun as a mission shrouded in stealth had now escalated into a dire struggle for survival and immediate retaliation. Each team member, though reeling from the shock and grief of witnessing their comrades' demise, knew the critical need to stay focused. Drawing upon their rigorous training, they adapted to the rapidly changing and now glaringly illuminated situation. With the urgency heightened by the fiery backdrop, they increased their speed, no longer concerned with maintaining silence, and began executing sharp, zigzag manoeuvres across the water, moving away from the light of the flames and into the safety of the darkness.

Responding with swift decisiveness, Cutler gestured to Shultz to prepare for action. Both were equipped with semi-automatics cradled in their left hands, their right fingers ready on the hair-trigger. In unison, they raised their weapons to align with their line of sight. Taking point, Cutler started up the stairwell, with Shultz closely following just a step behind.

As they ascended, Cutler subtly transferred the weight of his weapon to his left hand and raised his right fist—a silent command for Shultz to pause and maintain silence. With careful precision, Cutler leaned forward to stealthily peek over the crest of the top stair, vigilant for any signs of danger or movement ahead.

After a quick scan, Cutler gestured to Shultz to step back and then joined him, whispering their next move. "This deck is clear.

There's a maintenance stairway leading to the funnels. Can't see the exact number of terrorists, but they're on the platform above. The smoke is a dead giveaway. We'll adopt a crouch position—you move left, and I'll go right. Stick to the perimeters where the light is dimmest; we'll be harder to spot. Let's rendezvous at the stairway's base."

"Understood," Shultz responded, his voice low and steady.

Their progress was smooth, except for the need to navigate around the clutter of deckchairs strewn across the deck. As they neared the stairwell, the pungent smell of cordite grew stronger. Reaching the stairs, Cutler once again raised his fist, instructing Shultz to stay put.

Handing his gun to Shultz to avoid any accidental clanging against the stairs, Cutler drew his trusted Fairbairn–Sykes fighting knife, a double-edged blade. He placed it between his teeth and began a cautious, quadrupedal ascent. Upon reaching the top, Cutler turned away from the platform, took the knife from his mouth, and held it above the top stair. He moved it from side to side, using its reflective surface to discreetly survey the area ahead. Satisfied, he placed the knife back between his teeth and quietly descended to rejoin Shultz.

Cutler gestured towards the back of the metal stairway, signalling Shultz to position themselves out of the direct line of sight from the platform. He then raised three fingers—index, middle, and ring—and mimed a choking gesture, followed by crossing his hands as if they were bound. Shultz, understanding the message, raised his left fist in acknowledgment: three hostages were tied up.

Next, Cutler indicated the presence of two hostiles by raising his index and ring fingers, then touching his left forearm with his right hand. He then motioned his right arm downwards and behind him, a signal for Shultz to veer right when they reached the top of the stairwell.

On the platform, the situation was tense as the two terrorists hurriedly reloaded their missile launchers, ready to unleash another volley. In their haste, they had overlooked a crucial detail: the halogen lights remained active, starkly outlining their figures against the backdrop of the ship's red funnel. This error made them distinctly visible and vulnerable.

One of the terrorists, with ruthless focus, had his sights set on the Zodiac speeding towards them, carrying the last of the SAS strike teams. This team, knowing the dangers awaiting them, continued their steady approach, aware of the hostile reception planned for them.

Near the terrorists, the situation for the two hostages was dire. Bound and forced into a kneeling position, their restraints were secured tightly to a balustrade. This strategic placement by the terrorists was sinister, putting the hostages in immediate danger and significantly complicating any rescue efforts by Cutler and Shultz. The close proximity of the hostages to the terrorists was a deliberate move to use them as human shields, adding a grave complication to an already tense situation. This required Cutler and Shultz to execute their rescue with extreme precision and tactical acumen, balancing the need to neutralize the threat while ensuring the hostages' safety.

Aziz's voice crackled through the terrorist's headset with a new directive, "New target, 25 degrees east of true north from the Reef Explorer's location." The terrorist quickly shifted his focus, abandoning the standard rocket launcher for a more sophisticated piece of hardware. He grasped the Armitech-developed launcher, a cutting-edge weapon boasting a formidable range of ninety nautical miles, a vast improvement over the eight-kilometre range of the missile launchers aimed at the SAS boats.

With practiced precision, the terrorist inputted the coordinates for the new target, aligning the launcher to the specified 25 degrees east of true north. His fingers danced over the controls, setting the range with meticulous care.

Upon pulling the trigger, not a single missile but two erupted from the launcher in swift succession, blazing a trail across the sky. This simultaneous dual launch underscored the exceptional prowess of Armitech's cutting-edge engineering, marking a groundbreaking advancement in missile technology. The capacity to fire multiple missiles in rapid sequence substantially heightened the level of threat posed by this innovative weaponry.

The acquisition of such a weapon was a sinister development, made possible by Conrad Ford's dealings. Ford's collaboration had ensured that Asfour, and in turn, Aziz, received this advanced Armitech rocket launcher, drastically escalating the terrorists' firepower and posing a grave new threat to the mission and forces involved.

The second terrorist, with cold efficiency, followed suit and changed missile launcher and let off one missile towards the port of Tartus. The launch was a calculated move, aiming at the nuclear barge in the port. The launch of the missile not only heightened the stakes of the situation but also added an urgent timer to the unfolding events, as the consequences of its impact could be catastrophic. Cutler and Shultz, now dealing with multiple critical threats, needed to act with speed and decisiveness to prevent a tragedy.

In a moment thick with tension and anticipation, Cutler and Shultz, their senses heightened, waited just below the top step. These two minutes were crucial, allowing their eyes to acclimate to the glaring brightness above. Then, with a burst of adrenaline-fueled energy, they sprang into action, weapons primed and ready.

Cutler, with the precision of a seasoned operative, swiftly eliminated the terrorist on the port side before fully stepping onto the platform. Shultz, mirroring his partner's efficiency, turned his focus to the terrorist on the starboard side. His shot was precise, instantly fatal, but it set off an unintended chain reaction. As the terrorist's body spun from the force, his finger reflexively clenched on the trigger, launching a rocket that screeched through the air to violently collide with the Reef Explorer's funnel. The impact was catastrophic, igniting an explosion that sent a storm of metal shards hurtling into the air, fortunately away from the hostages and the operatives.

The explosion's shockwave was like an invisible, forceful hand, violently pushing back against everything in its path. Cutler and Shultz, caught in this maelstrom, were flung backwards with ferocious intensity. Shultz was sent hurtling down the stairwell, a whirlwind of motion that somehow, almost impossibly, missed every step, culminating in a jarring crash onto his back at the base. Cutler, on the other hand, was launched upwards and over the railing in a trajectory that defied gravity, only to come crashing down harshly onto the deck below, landing heavily on his side.

On board the USS Lincoln, Captain Reynolds observed the explosion in the distance, judging that either the ship was hit by a missile, or Cutler had not deactivated all the rigged explosives.

The four members elite of the SAS unit swarmed over the poop deck rails on the grapple lines Stahmer had secured as the explosion occurred. The strike leader stopped for a second and pushed his transmitter.

"Strike Team One, this is Strike Team Three. Strike Team Two down. We have just heard an explosion, can you confirm?"

Cutler was the first to recover, his right shoulder dislocated, and he had some blood on his face from a small piece of shrapnel. The transmitter was on a band around his neck, and he clicked it on with his left hand.

"Strike Team Three, Strike Team One. Stray missile when taking out two combatants, damage to the funnel but not critical," Cutler reported.

"Roger, Strike Team One." Shultz shook off the pain of the fall and staggered towards Cutler.

"You, okay?" Shultz asked, on seeing Cutler's dangling arm.

"Pop my arm back in and go check on the hostages," Cutler replied.

Shultz gave the thumbs up to confirm the hostages had only received minor injuries as SAS Strike Team Four surged onto the deck. The squad leader said nothing but nodded his respect at Cutler and Shultz, and then they were gone, their mission to retake the bridge.

The tension in the air was palpable as the Russian guided-missile cruiser, now just 130 miles from the Reef Explorer, loomed ominously on the radar. Captain Mikhailov didn't need the drama of glaring lights or blaring alarms; the quiet blips on the radar and the soft buzz of low-level alerts were enough to set his nerves on edge.

"Three missiles launched from the Reef Explorer, captain. One's heading for Tartus, two are on our course," the tactical officer reported, his voice steady but urgent.

"How far out?" Captain Mikhailov's voice cut through the tense atmosphere.

"Eighteen nautical miles and closing fast," came the reply, laced with the implicit urgency of the situation. The tactical officer was already lining up the ship's short-range surface-to-air defence system, targeting the incoming missiles.

"Are they locked?" Mikhailov barked at his weapons officer, his tone sharp.

"We've got a lock on the two targeting us, but the third is bound for Tartus. It'll hit before we can intercept," the officer replied, the gravity of the situation evident in his voice.

"Launch!" Mikhailov's command was curt, decisive.

As he ordered his communications officer to warn Tartus, Mikhailov relayed the dire situation to Admiral Sokolov. His expression grew graver with each word exchanged, tension etching deeper lines into his brow.

"Missiles one and two destroyed, Captain," came the update, a brief respite in the mounting pressure.

"Good. Now target the Reef Explorer," Admiral Sokolov commanded without hesitation.

The SS-N 12 Sandbox, a formidable surface-to-surface cruise missile, momentarily faltered as it broke free from its vertical housing, a brief pause that was almost imperceptible. But this hesitation lasted only a fraction of a second before the missile's powerful engines roared to life, propelling it forward with ferocious speed and determination.

As it raced towards its target, the Reef Explorer, the missile maintained a harrowingly low trajectory, skimming just feet above the undulating surface of the ocean. This low-altitude flight pattern was strategic, designed to evade radar detection and make interception more difficult. The missile's path, a blend of precision engineering and ruthless efficiency, was a chilling display of military prowess.

Equipped with a highly destructive payload, the SS-N 12 was more than just a weapon; it was a symbol of impending doom. Its design, optimized for maximum damage upon impact, ensured that it would unleash a devastating blow to its target. The sleek, menacing form of the missile cut through the air, leaving a trail of condensed air and sea spray in its wake, as it unerringly homed in on the Reef Explorer.

Aboard the USS Lincoln, the atmosphere shifted dramatically as Captain Reynolds received the startling update. The radar operator's report, delivered in a tense, clipped tone, detailed the sudden emergence of three missiles from the Reef Explorer, followed swiftly by a Russian counterstrike. This information sent a ripple of shock through the vessel's control room, instantly heightening the sense of urgency.

The room, usually a hub of disciplined activity, transformed into a whirlwind of intense action and sharp focus. The crew, well-trained for such emergencies, sprang into action, their movements swift and purposeful. Captain Reynolds, with a grave expression, issued the command for action stations. The sound of alarms, loud and insistent, reverberated throughout the ship, cutting through the air and signalling the severity of the threat.

Officers and sailors alike responded with a mixture of professionalism and underlying tension. The energy in the control room was palpable, a tangible manifestation of the crew's readiness to confront the imminent danger. Each person, from seasoned officers to the youngest sailors, understood the gravity of the situation. They were not just facing a potential military confrontation, but also the very real possibility of a missile strike.

Captain Reynolds, standing firmly at the helm, issued orders with a calm yet commanding presence, directing his crew in the preparations to defend the ship and potentially engage the enemy. The USS Lincoln, a symbol of naval power, was now bracing for a confrontation that could escalate into a full-blown maritime conflict.

On a lifeboat a fair distance from the unfolding chaos, Aziz's attention was glued to a computer screen, which displayed the alarming image of the SS-N 12 Sandbox surface-to-surface cruise missile hurtling through the air. With a sense of urgency, he whipped out his encrypted satellite secure phone and quickly sent a Snapchat message to Asfour: 'Russian missile launched.'

Asfour's response came rapidly, within twenty seconds, using the same modern, inconspicuous medium of communication. 'They will fire a second, make sure you have everything in order before that,' he advised, indicating the critical need for readiness in the face of escalating danger.

Meanwhile, aboard the USS Lincoln, Captain Reynolds was intensely focused on the radar screen. The missile was represented as a small, rapidly advancing blip, with data message boxes popping up to provide detailed information on its trajectory and speed. Without hesitation, he issued a decisive command. "Gunner's mate quad six, seek and destroy missile heading towards Tartus." In response, four Evolved Sea Sparrow missiles were launched with precision from the quad rocket launcher on the port side of the ship.

Captain Reynolds, not taking any chances, quickly followed with another command through his binoculars. "Gunners mate quad seven, seek and destroy Russian cruise missile heading towards Reef Explorer." Another set of four Evolved Sea Sparrow missiles was promptly dispatched from the starboard side quad launcher.

The crew on the USS Lincoln, ranging from seasoned officers to young sailors, instantly recognized the distinctive sound of their missile launchers in action. They turned towards the spectacle, watching as the missiles blazed a trail into the evening sky, disappearing over the horizon within seconds.

The strategy was to position the Evolved Sea Sparrow missiles above the incoming Russian cruise missile and then knock it down from above. The advanced rear guidance system of these missiles afforded them exceptional manoeuvrability, though this feature also meant they expended their energy more rapidly. This was a calculated risk, considering the high stakes of intercepting the incoming threat before it could reach its target.

Aboard the Israeli Dolphin-class submarine, Captain Levy was in a critical position, just two miles west of the USS Lincoln. In a move marked by both strategic caution and the necessity to avoid friendly fire, his radio operator promptly informed the Lincoln of their position, ensuring clear lines of communication in the increasingly complex theatre of operations.

Captain Levy's gaze was fixed on the radar, observing the sequence of events unfolding with rapid intensity. He tracked the missiles launched first from the Reef Explorer, then the Russian ship Serbia, and finally the counter-response from the USS Lincoln. With the situation escalating rapidly, he ordered his crew to action stations, readying them for any required engagement or defensive manoeuvres.

Meanwhile, the Russian cruise missile was rapidly closing in on the Reef Explorer, now only ten miles away and mere seconds from its target. Above, the Sea Sparrow missiles from the USS Lincoln locked onto their target, descending with lethal intent. The first two Sea Sparrows, however, fell short, missing the cruise missile by about sixty feet. It was a tense moment, but the third and fourth missiles did not miss their mark. The resulting explosion was deafening, the shockwave reverberating through the air and across the decks of the Reef Explorer. The passengers on the ship were engulfed in a wave of fear and panic, their terrified screams echoing in the aftermath of the explosion.

Captain Mikhailov, aboard the Russian ship, observed the destruction of his missiles with a mixture of frustration and resolve. "The Americans are protecting the ship," he muttered, more to himself than his crew. He knew well the challenge of intercepting a single missile, but multiple strikes presented a far greater challenge. Determined, he ordered the launch of missiles two through four, ready to test the Americans' defensive capabilities to their limits. In his mind, the destruction of the Reef Explorer seemed inevitable in this endgame scenario.

However, the situation took another turn as the Russian radar operator reported a new development. "Captain Mikhailov, we are picking up a signature for a Dolphin-class submarine, two miles west of the American position," he announced. This revelation added yet another layer of complexity to the already tense situation, introducing a new and potentially game-changing element into the equation.

Captain Mikhailov, upon hearing about the Israeli Dolphin-class submarine, remained composed and focused. "Track its position and inform me immediately if they open their torpedo tubes," he instructed. In this complex situation, even the smallest detail could tip the scales, and the presence of an Israeli submarine added a significant variable to his calculations.

Elsewhere, the intricacies of the terrorists' plan were known only to Aziz and Khalid, a decision driven more by operational necessity than trust. As Khalid piloted the lifeboat, Aziz worked intently at a portable computer terminal. He extracted a hexagonal wolfram cylinder from a container and connected it to the laptop via USB. After a brief pause, he sent another message to Asfour: 'WCU operational, securing.' Their communication method, modern and seemingly casual, belied the gravity of their actions.

Meanwhile, Mouhamed, in charge of the bridge on the Reef Explorer was not fully aware of the complete plan. He watched from the CCTV as gunfire erupted and masked special forces, relentless and efficient, advanced towards the bridge and the theatre. The images on the screen showed a brutal and swift confrontation, with the attacking forces making significant headway against both Arab and Somali terrorists. Mouhamed saw a SAS operative take a bullet in the shoulder but continue to fight—a warning of their determination and training. It was clear to Mouhamed that they were rapidly losing ground.

With the realization that the bridge would soon be stormed, Mouhamed prepared himself, wiping his hands and face with a wet wipe. The thought of capture and the horrors he had heard about Guantanamo Bay filled him with dread. Surrender was not an option he or his comrades could consider. He had been surprised when Aziz and Khalid abruptly left the bridge in the lifeboat, the purpose of their departure unclear to him.

The CCTV feed then showed billowing smoke from the ship's funnel, a sign of the impact from the explosion above. Alarms blared on the bridge, indicating they had sustained damage. The original plan, Mouhamed knew, had always been to blow the ship in case of an attack, and that moment, it seemed, had arrived. With a quiet prayer, Mouhamed resignedly pressed the detonation switch for the explosives, setting off a chain of events that would have irreversible consequences.

No explosion. No blinding light, then paradise. Just the background noise of gunfire. With an overwhelming feeling of failure, Mouhamed pushed the detonator a second, then a third time. Still no blast. Mouhamed gripped his gun, ready for the final onslaught, unaware the SAS team was less than ten seconds away.

Two Somali terrorists decided to escape and with skill bypassed the SAS units, hoping to hide in the stern of the ship or chance their arm by jumping into the sea. They had not reckoned on Stahmer and Ghislaine protecting the starboard side of the poop deck. They crawled on the deck as the next round of bullets from the MIDAS agents whipped over their heads, pinging off metal structures and ricocheting. Suddenly, they threw their weapons forward, and one of the Somalis raised a white serviette he had been using as a tissue. Stahmer beckoned them forward indicating for them to place their hands behind their head. They did not reach Stahmer, Cutler and Shultz on the starboard side opened up with their semi-automatics on the two men, their corpses lay at the feet of Ghislaine.

"Very much the English gentleman, Stahmer. We don't take terrorist prisoners, high chance of suicide bombers, they are expert at it," Cutler said, quietly.

Aboard the USS Lincoln, it was a hive of activity as officers and ratings concentrated on their duties.

"Captain Reynolds, three more Russian cruise missiles inbound and lined up on the Reef Explorer, four minutes before impact," the officer of the deck reported.

The tactical action officer intervened. "Captain, we have a problem. The Russian field base at Tartus have destroyed the missile launched from the Reef Explorer towards the port. I am trying to abort our tracking missile, but it's not responding."

"Not responding, use self-destruct. Ready quads three and eight," the captain ordered.

"Captain, our tracking missile has turned left five degrees, it's like someone else is controlling it."

"Impossible, must be a software problem. Try self-destruct again. Keep at high alert and be ready for anything," Captain Reynolds ordered.

Aziz's message to Asfour carried a chilling revelation: 'I have control of one American missile, trying to get control over the Russian cruise missiles.' This news, upon reaching the Al-Qaeda leadership in their hideout, was met with a murmur of approval, a sinister acknowledgement of the escalating chaos they were orchestrating.

On the Reef Explorer, Cutler couldn't believe the situation as he observed three cruise missiles, low and fast, cutting through the air towards them. He, along with Stahmer, Ghislaine, and Shultz, watched almost helplessly, transfixed by the impending doom. These missiles, like deadly phantoms, skimmed the surface of the Mediterranean, their approach a grim reminder of the fragility of life in the face of such overwhelming force. The realization that there was little they could do against this onslaught was a bitter pill to swallow.

In a desperate attempt to mitigate the disaster, Cutler grabbed his radio. "Evans, cruise missiles incoming, fast! Get the Spectre out of here, now!" he barked, hoping to save at least some of the those on board the Reef Explorer from the impending catastrophe.

Meanwhile, back in Geneva, Fabienne witnessed the unfolding horror in real-time, thanks to her privy access to satellite feeds—a backdoor she had created during her tenure at GCHQ. The enormity of the situation overwhelmed her, inducing her first-ever panic attack. Trembling uncontrollably, her eyes, red from tears shed for Tuck, were fixed on the screen. The cruise missiles, captured in chilling detail by the satellite imagery, loomed larger with each passing second.

As the missiles closed in, now just 500 feet and less than two seconds from impact, the fate of many hung precariously in the balance. Cutler, with years of experience in high-stakes situations, noticed a subtle change—the warheads' nose cones adjusted slightly. This minute detail, almost imperceptible to most, hinted at a last-moment alteration in their deadly trajectory. The tension was at a breaking point, as everyone braced for the impact, hoping against hope for a miracle in these final, critical moments.

Cutler's voice, steady and reassuring, broke through the tense silence. "You can open them," he said gently to Ghislaine, who had instinctively shut her eyes and pressed herself against Cutler's chest, seeking comfort, knowing these were her last seconds.

The cruise missiles, with their deafening roar, soared perilously close to the Reef Explorer. The sound was so intense, so deeply resonating, that it caused physical pain to those on board. The missiles, flying just twenty feet above the top deck, were so close that the crew could discern a message scrawled in Russian on their sides. The displaced seawater from their rapid passage sprayed up, drenching everyone on the deck.

On the USS Lincoln, the atmosphere was a contrast of controlled urgency. "Captain, Captain, all three warheads missed the Reef Explorer; they were never the target… We were, sir," the navigation officer reported, his voice calm despite the gravity of the revelation.

Meanwhile, Aziz, with a sense of triumph, messaged Asfour: 'I have control of all three Russian missiles. I have locked in the targets.' Asfour's immediate reply came with a clear directive: 'You have your instructions, one target, not targets, Aziz.'

Captain Reynolds, aboard the USS Lincoln, reacted with rapid command. "Quads two, three, four and five target the missiles.

Use the cannons as a last resort!" His voice carried the weight of command and urgency.

"Cannons activated," the tactical action officer reported, his tone detached and professional as he followed the captain's orders.

"Launch an AGM-158C LRASM at the Siberia," Captain Reynolds commanded, his voice resolute and firm over the communications system of the USS Lincoln. The order set into motion a crucial offensive action against the hostile vessel, employing one of the most advanced weapons in the Navy's arsenal.

The AGM-158C LRASM (Long Range Anti-Ship Missile) represents a significant evolution in naval warfare technology. Designed for superior performance in contested environments, the LRASM boasts enhanced range capabilities, allowing it to strike targets from a much greater distance than traditional anti-ship missiles like the Harpoon. This extended range provides the USS Lincoln with the ability to engage the Siberia while remaining at a safer distance, reducing the risk of counterattack.

Additionally, the LRASM is equipped with state-of-the-art survivability features. Its stealthy design and advanced materials make it more difficult for enemy radar systems to detect and intercept. The missile also possesses sophisticated onboard sensors and targeting systems, allowing it to accurately identify and home in on its target amid a complex array of enemy ships.

Aziz, however, was not swayed by Asfour's instructions. The Weapon Control Unit (WCU) and its software had taken longer than expected to acquire the missile codes, which explained his initial failure to control the first missile. Now, the radar and sonar display showed the positions of the Reef Explorer, Siberia, the USS Lincoln, and a nearby submarine. The WCU was working more efficiently, having acquired all three Russian cruise missiles. Aziz mused over Asfour's foresight—his intuition about a second Russian launch was spot-on.

Aboard the Siberia, Captain Mikhailov faced an unprecedented situation. His tactical operations officer reported a loss of control over the missiles. Known for his composure, Mikhailov, for the first time, raised his voice in alarm, "Who has control of my missiles and what's their heading?" The response was unsettling. "No data on who is controlling them, but their course is directly towards the USS Lincoln." This unexpected turn of events signalled a dramatic and dangerous shift in the high-stakes confrontation unfolding on the Mediterranean waters.

Captain Mikhailov looked stunned; he was about to start at best a major international incident, at worst, World War Three. That would mean death and destruction on a global scale. Personally, he knew there would be hell to pay, the end of his career. Like his father before him, spending the rest of his days in a prison in the area of Russia that his ship was named after, Siberia.

The Russians were some months away from completing their base in Tartus, so having a full weaponised unit there had not seemed practical to the generals. Radar had picked up the American missile heading towards the port. They had placed one active system named A-135. The unit had three Gorgon and Gazelle missiles with nuclear warheads to intercept incoming ICBMs. The Russian captain in charge was twenty-three years old, and this was his first assignment, and he panicked. He fired all three missiles at the incoming threat, successfully bringing it down, but the port had no other defences against a further attack.

As the cruise missiles neared the USS Lincoln, its cannons fired. The Evolved Sea Sparrow missiles struggled to acquire their targets. Captain Reynolds realised they were on the brink; he was not ready to give up without a fight. The guns spat out thousands of rounds, cordite and smoke filled the air. Many of the sailors crossed themselves or said a silent prayer ready to meet their God; others ran to the sides of the ship prepared to jump after impact, others just watched.

With less than two miles from the USS Lincoln, two rockets dramatically changed course veering 80 degrees to port. The third remained on course for the USS Lincoln.

Alarms sounded on the Israeli submarine as the new heading was directed towards them, too late to do anything. It was over in a flash, the missiles did not descend into the sea, one passed overhead heading east, and one tracking south, locked onto two separate targets.

In a desperate bid to neutralize the imminent threat, the USS Lincoln deployed two Evolved Sea Sparrow missiles, targeting the Russian cruise missile that was barrelling straight towards them. The situation was critical, every second counting as the two American missiles raced through the sky with a singular purpose.

The Sea Sparrows, designed for such high-stakes interceptions, closed in on the Russian missile. The interception occurred breathtakingly close to the USS Lincoln, the Sea Sparrows kissing the projectile less than a hundred yards off the ship's starboard side. The collision was not just a meeting of metal and explosives; it was a moment of tragedy.

The impact of the missiles triggered a catastrophic explosion. The force of the blast was immense, and the unspent fuel from the Russian missile ignited upon contact, unleashing a fiery inferno that swept across the starboard side of the USS Lincoln. The explosion and subsequent firestorm were devastating. Five American sailors, caught in the blast, perished instantly, victims of the missile's lethal payload and the resultant conflagration.

The tragedy was compounded as other sailors were injured by shrapnel, the metal fragments acting as lethal projectiles in the wake of the explosion. The scene on the USS Lincoln was one of chaos and destruction, the ship now bearing the physical scars of the encounter—blackened, damaged, and ablaze.

Efforts to contain the fire and tend to the injured began immediately, the crew working with urgency amid the smouldering wreckage. The air was filled with the sounds of alarms, shouts of coordination, and the intense crackling of flames, as the USS Lincoln, a proud symbol of naval might, faced one of its darkest moments. The shock of the incident was profound, not just for the physical damage inflicted but also for the loss of life, a grim reminder of the dangers inherent in such high-stakes maritime conflicts.

"That's why they used a computer expert. Fabienne said something was wrong and she was right," Cutler said to himself.

Special Air Service units secured the theatre and bridge; all the terrorists apart from the two on the lifeboat and Awaale who hid in the engine room had been killed. The drone pilot saw the upsurge of energy in far more detail, as did the president of the United States back in the situation room. There was a sense of shock amongst the military chiefs.

The AGM-158C LRASM, launched from the USS Lincoln with a lethal precision and deadly intent, took less than two minutes to reach the Siberia. In those fleeting moments, the missile, a pinnacle of modern military technology, homed in on its target with an unerring focus.

As the LRASM approached the Siberia, the Russian vessel's anti-missile defences, though advanced and formidable, proved insufficient against the sophisticated capabilities of the American missile. The LRASM, equipped with stealth technology and advanced evasion capabilities, slipped through the defensive net, evading radar detection and intercept countermeasures with chilling efficiency.

The moment of impact was both instantaneous and catastrophic. The missile struck the bridge of the Siberia with devastating force. The explosion that ensued was monumental, a concussive blast that ripped through the structure of the ship with unbridled ferocity. The bridge, the nerve centre of the vessel, was obliterated in an instant.

Captain Mikhailov, along with thirty other officers and ratings who were on the bridge at that moment, met their demise instantly. The sheer force of the explosion left the bridge in ruins, with twisted metal and shattered equipment serving as a stark testament to the devastating power of the attack.

The aftermath of the attack was a scene of chaos and destruction. Fire and smoke billowed from the devastated area, spreading rapidly through the adjoining compartments. Shrapnel and debris, propelled by the force of the explosion, caused further damage and injuries to the crew in the vicinity.

The ship, now without its command centre and key personnel, was plunged into disarray. Surviving crew members, reeling from the shock, and grappling with the sudden loss of leadership, scrambled to contain the fires and assess the extent of the damage. The Siberia, once a symbol of naval prowess, was now a crippled giant, its capabilities severely compromised and its fate uncertain.

In the tense, charged atmosphere, Captain Levy aboard the Dolphin submarine executed his secondary orders with precision. Adjusting the submarine's position by 30 degrees, he opened all the torpedo tubes, a decisive move that did not go unnoticed. Tactical officers aboard both the Siberia and the USS Lincoln immediately reported the Dolphin's preparations for a potential strike.

Captain Reynolds of the USS Lincoln, despite the heightened alert, remained confident that they were not the target, paralleling his earlier assumption about the Russian cruise missile.

Two cruise missiles remained in play. One targeted Tartus, the other headed south.

The atmosphere at the Tartus port, a Russian naval facility, was charged with a mix of excitement and trepidation. The young and relatively inexperienced Russian officer in charge of the missile team had just expended their limited missile supply to intercept a rocket launched from the Reef Explorer. The initial triumph of downing the missile quickly turned to anxiety as a new, unexpected threat emerged.

A cruise missile, this one from the Russian ship Siberia, followed the same trajectory, only minutes behind the first. The realization that they were now tracking a missile from their own nation added a layer of complexity and dread to the situation.

The Russian defence unit in Tartus, having exhausted their missile defences, was left with no option but to trigger the evacuation alarm, sending a reverberating warning throughout the base, now buzzing with activity and rising panic.

Secondary sirens wailed from the nuclear barge stationed at the port. Crew members scrambled to secure the vessel, hastily closing watertight doors in a bid for safety. Yet the urgency of the moment was overshadowed by a grim reality: it was impossible to take the reactor offline quickly. Shutting down a nuclear reactor was a process that could take days, if not weeks, leaving them in a precarious position.

In a last-ditch effort, the Russian weapons officer employed an unconventional defence tactic. He ordered the operators of two Uran-9 tracked unmanned combat ground vehicles, originally designed for land-based insurgency conflicts, to turn their weapons seaward. The vehicles, armed with 7.62 mm machine guns and four 9M120 Atika anti-tank missiles each, opened fire on the incoming missiles, a desperate move to intercept the threat.

Cutler's actions were swift and determined as he navigated through the chaos on the top deck of the Reef Explorer. Amidst the destruction wrought by the explosion, his mission was clear: to find a missile launcher for a crucial counterstrike. The sophisticated launcher used against the Siberia was now a mangled heap of metal, destroyed in the explosion, forcing Cutler to opt for a more traditional rocket launcher, limited to an eight-kilometre range but still potent.

Racing against time, Cutler contacted Jones via radio, his voice urgent but clear. "Jones, do you have the lifeboat position?" he called out, amidst the noise and confusion around him.

Jones' response was prompt, offering precise coordinates. "The location is at 34.9 degrees North latitude and 35.863 degrees East longitude." Cutler quickly oriented himself in the direction of these coordinates, a calculated gaze across the darkened sea.

Next, Cutler reached out to the drone operator, adapting to the situation with resourcefulness. "Drone Operator, laser light Bearing at 34.9 degrees North, 35.863 degrees East and highlight," he instructed, seeking to pinpoint the lifeboat's exact location in the vast expanse of the sea.

"Copy," came the concise reply from the drone operator. Within seconds, a laser dot pierced through the night's darkness, marking the lifeboat's position. The dot, a beacon in the dark, was visible to Cutler, providing him with the precise targeting he needed.

As he prepared to use the rocket launcher, Cutler's resolve was palpable. "Get this right," he muttered to himself, a mix of determination and pressure evident in his tone. The weight of the moment was not lost on him; the success of his next action could significantly alter the course of the ongoing confrontation, a responsibility he bore with a grim sense of purpose.

Aziz's journey, from his troubled childhood in Birmingham to his final moments on the lifeboat, was marked by a transformation fuelled by radicalization and a commitment to a cause he believed in, albeit one that led him down a path of destruction. The small, bullied boy he once was had become a distant memory, replaced by a figure who played a pivotal role in a large-scale, devastating operation.

Aziz's final moments were steeped in a complex mix of resignation, determination, and a skewed sense of purpose. As he knelt in prayer on the lifeboat, there was a deep awareness within him of the inevitable end that awaited. His participation in this mission was never about coming back; it was about the impact he believed he could make—an impact he saw as significant and far-reaching for his cause.

His thoughts were not just on the destruction of the nuclear barge, which was substantial in itself, but also on the broader, more ambitious targets he had unilaterally decided to pursue. In deviating from Asfour's original plan, which focused solely on the nuclear barge, Aziz had expanded the scope of the mission to include striking the Suez Canal and the Knesset in Israel. In his mind, these additional targets held symbolic value, representing a direct attack on what he perceived as the heart of his adversaries' power and influence.

For Aziz, hitting these targets was about more than causing physical and economic disruption; it was about sending a message, striking fear and uncertainty in the hearts of those he considered enemies. He envisioned the blockade of the Suez Canal as a significant blow to Western interests, while an attack on the Knesset, the seat of the Israeli government, was symbolic of a direct challenge to Israel's authority.

In these final moments, Aziz imagined the aftermath of his actions, believing that they would elevate him to a status of veneration within his cause. He saw himself not just as a participant in the mission but as a key architect of a larger strategy, one that would resonate far beyond the immediate scope of the attack.

But he made a mistake, while he had set the coordinates for Israel and the Suez, he had control of the missile to the much nearer target the nuclear barge.

Khalid, his accomplice, was also caught in the moment, his attention fixed on the distant fireball on the horizon—a stark reminder of the chaos and destruction that had unfolded. Their focus, however, was abruptly shattered as a Sea Sparrow missile, with ruthless precision, targeted their lifeboat.

The missile strike was swift and absolute. In an instant, the lifeboat, along with Aziz and Khalid, was obliterated, leaving no trace of their existence. The explosion erased them from the physical world, ending their part in the unfolding drama.

The moment the explosion occurred, the situation aboard the nuclear barge rapidly spiralled out of control. The loss of command over the nuclear missile was instantaneous and catastrophic. In a split second, the missile, now unguided and unpredictable, veered off course with a lethal autonomy. It struck the battery on the port side of the barge, resulting in a secondary explosion that further escalated the already dire situation.

Thick, billowing smoke enveloped the barge, obscuring much of its structure. However, from the vantage point of the Reef Explorer, the barge was still tragically visible, illuminated by the intense, raging fireball that had erupted. The scene was one of utter devastation, a stark visual testament to the chaos and destruction that had unfolded.

Amidst this turmoil, the drone operator aboard the Reef Explorer relayed a critical observation. "Nuclear barge intact," he reported, his voice cutting through the tense atmosphere. This update, indicating that the nuclear reactor itself had not been breached, was a profound relief to Cutler. The implications of a compromised nuclear reactor would have been catastrophic, not only for those in the immediate vicinity but also for the wider region.

The significance of this news extended far beyond the decks of the Reef Explorer. In Washington, Moscow, and capitals across the Mediterranean, the confirmation that the nuclear barge's reactor remained intact would be received with a collective sigh of relief. The potential for a nuclear disaster had loomed large over the incident, a threat that would have had far-reaching environmental, political, and humanitarian repercussions.

Upon learning of the dire situation on the Siberia, Captain Reynolds acted swiftly. The destruction on the Siberia's bridge had left a void in command, and he knew he had to step in to help avert further catastrophe. After establishing contact with the ship, he was connected with a second engineer who was among the few surviving officers. Captain Reynolds conveyed the critical information that an unknown third party had commandeered their missile systems.

The engineer, in a state of shock and desperation, needed convincing, but the urgency in Captain Reynolds' voice and the gravity of the situation left little room for hesitation. With some persuasion, the engineer agreed to reach out to a weapons controller who was stationed in the secondary bridge—often referred to as the 'battle bridge'—a secure command centre designed to function independently of the main bridge.

Deep within the hull of the ship, protected and fortified, the battle bridge stood as a last bastion of control, equipped with full navigation and combat systems. When the weapons controller at the battle bridge was reached, he was initially hesitant; he had received no orders from Moscow and was understandably reluctant to take any unilateral action.

However, Captain Reynolds, understanding the geopolitical ramifications of the missiles reaching their targets, especially if they were to strike Israel, impressed upon the weapons controller the severe consequences that could ensue. The urgency was clear: it was not just a matter of military protocol but of international peace and the potential for a significant crisis.

In those stretched, nail-biting seconds that felt like hours, the weapons officer's hands hovered over the control panel, his mind racing through the gravity of their dire predicament. The air was thick with the unspoken understanding of the imminent danger, each heartbeat echoing against the silent tension that blanketed the room. With a resolve that was both terrifying and awe-inspiring, he recognized the critical need for swift, decisive action—a choice that bore the heavy burden of consequence and the stark realization of the stakes involved.

Without a moment's hesitation, yet carrying the full weight of the decision on his shoulders, he initiated the self-detonation sequence for the missiles still slicing through the air toward their target. It was a move that demanded courage and a deep understanding of sacrifice, knowing well the potential repercussions of his actions. This wasn't just about strategy or tactics; it was about making a call that could alter the course of events, a choice where failure meant unthinkable loss.

As the command was executed, a palpable sense of resolve settled over him. The decision to neutralize the threat mid-flight was more than a tactical manoeuvre, it was a testament to the burdens that come with command, the kind of decision that defines leadership in moments of crisis. It was a stark reminder of the delicate balance between action and consequence, a balance that he, in his role as the guardian of lives and the instrument of peace, had to navigate with unwavering determination and an acute awareness of the cost. The weapons officer, grasping the magnitude of the situation and recognizing the need for immediate action, made the decision to self-detonate the missiles while they were still en route. It was a decision that carried the weight of responsibility and the sobering knowledge of what was at stake.

With the press of a button, the weapons controller sent the commands to the rogue missiles. In a matter of seconds, the missiles were neutralized, exploding harmlessly in the sky before they could reach their intended targets. The detonations were bright flares in the sky, signalling the aversion of further tragedy.

The actions taken by the weapons officer, guided by Captain Reynolds' intervention, not only prevented a potential international incident but also likely saved countless lives. In those critical moments, the secondary bridge of the Siberia had become the unexpected command centre that held the fate of nations in its hands.

The relief that followed was felt not just on the Siberia or the USS Lincoln, but across the globe, as a looming disaster was narrowly averted. As the rescue boats from the USS Lincoln arrived, a sense of relief finally began to permeate through the tension that had gripped the Reef Explorer. The surviving hostages and crew members were swiftly offloaded, and a skeleton crew was set up to maintain the ship. Cutler gathered his team. The Spectre, their extraction vessel, was already pulling up alongside.

They opened the starboard hatch, secured it methodically, and prepared to board. As they did, the rush of adrenaline from the intense battle began to ebb away, replaced by the sombre reality of their loss—their comrade and friend, Tuck.

But as they boarded the Spectre, a shock awaited them. Tuck's familiar, gruff voice cut through the air. "Left it a bit late to take that lifeboat out, would have blown the fuckers to smithereens at least ten minutes before you did," he shouted, his tone laced with his characteristic bravado.

Shultz was in a state of confusion. Visibly stunned, he managed to respond, "He was a bit busy, Tuck. How the hell did you survive that long in the water?"

Ghislaine's confusion mirrored that of the team. "But how? Tuck was under water for over fifteen minutes?"

Cutler, piecing the puzzle together, added, "The headgear White supplied had an oxygen cylinder, good for twenty minutes. Kicks in above twelve thousand feet and I guess below water."

Ghislaine, her relief mixed with a touch of anger, demanded, "You knew?"

"I wasn't sure it worked under the water; there was a good chance he was dead, and I didn't want to get your hopes up," Cutler replied, his voice tinged with the complexity of command decisions.

Tuck, ever the tough character, cut through the tension. "I need fucking morphine, and a beer to keep my head party going," he shouted, bringing a wave of laughter from the team, a much-needed release after the relentless stress and uncertainty they had endured.

In that moment, aboard the Spectre, the team's relief was palpable. The unexpected survival of Tuck was not just a personal victory but a rare moment of light in the darkness of the harrowing events they had just lived through.

chapter twenty-five
The Final Countdown

Fabienne Asper operated as a linchpin in a network of international intelligence. Her dealings weren't just with GCHQ and the Americans, but extended into the surreptitious corridors of Mossad, Israel's intelligence agency.

Over the years, Fabienne had built a relationship of mutual respect and utility with a Mossad senior commander, a connection that had grown only more valuable as he ascended to the position of prime minister of Israel. Information was the currency, and trust was a rare commodity, earned through a history of reliable intelligence.

Fabienne's world was one where revenge was a cold, calculated act, devoid of emotion—a necessary response in the game of global security. When she provided the Israeli prime minister with intelligence on Ebi Bouzidi involvement in the unsuccessful attack on the Knesset, it was more than just sharing information; it was a move in a complex strategic dance. The link to Ebi Bouzidi, a key target of Mossad's pursuit for years, made the intelligence even more compelling.

Bouzidi was a master of evasion, always slipping through Mossad's grasp just as they closed in. But now, with precise coordinates for an Al-Qaeda meeting in Razmak and confirmation of Bouzidi's attendance, the Israelis had a critical opportunity. It was the kind of chance that the prime minister, seasoned in the art of intelligence warfare, couldn't afford to ignore.

Fabienne's intelligence had always been top-notch, and the Israeli prime minister knew the value of her information. But Fabienne had her conditions. This stipulation wasn't just professional; it was personal, a reflection of her deep involvement and investment in the outcome.

The Israeli prime minister was acutely aware of the dangerous undercurrents shaping the geopolitical landscape. At the heart of this brewing storm was Ebi Bouzidi, an Al-Qaeda strategist notorious for his grand and destructive ambitions. For eight long years, Bouzidi had been meticulously fanning the flames of potential conflict, with an audacious endgame in mind: to provoke a war between Israel and Iran. His strategy went further, aiming to embroil Saudi Arabia in the conflict, casting it as an ally of the Americans and Israelis. Bouzidi's calculations were clear—such a scenario would create deep rifts among Sunni Muslims in the region, playing directly into the hands of Al-Qaeda.

Bouzidi, with his cunning mind and ruthless tactics, saw the escalating tensions between Israel and Iran as a fertile ground for recruitment, fuelling the fire of global Islamic jihad. His vision extended beyond regional conflict; Bouzidi also relished the prospect of America and Russia clashing in the Mediterranean. This added layer of international tension would not only distract global powers but also potentially weaken their influence in the region, creating more openings for Al-Qaeda to exploit. In Bouzidi's strategic calculus, the resurgence of Al-Qaeda was paramount. He recognized the prominence that ISIS had gained over the past decade, dominating headlines and recruitment. For him, it was time to bring Al-Qaeda back to the forefront of the global jihadist movement. His aim was to capitalise on international conflict and regional instability.

Bouzidi saw a path to reinstate Al-Qaeda's dominance in the realm of global terrorism. The plan to bomb the nuclear barge in the Mediterranean Sea was a chilling prospect, not just for the immediate devastation but for the long-term geopolitical repercussions. Bouzidi, the mastermind behind this nefarious plot, wasn't just aiming for a one-time act of terror; he was orchestrating a move that would resonate across the globe, changing the balance of power and forcing the West into a precarious position.

The Mediterranean Sea, a vibrant hub of biodiversity and a lifeline for millions, stood on the brink of an ecological catastrophe. A nuclear explosion in these waters would unleash a radioactive nightmare, irreversibly contaminating marine ecosystems, crippling the fishing industry, and decimating the bustling tourism sector that countries like Spain, Italy, Greece, and Croatia relied upon. The pristine beaches of Monaco, the historic coasts of Turkey, the idyllic shores of Cyprus—all would become ghostly remnants of their former glory.

Bouzidi's plan was cold and calculating. He was well aware that the radioactive fallout would not discriminate, impacting Arab nations as well. Yet, in his twisted logic, the long-term gain outweighed the immediate harm. He envisioned a scenario where the West, reeling from the economic blow and the public outcry over a contaminated Mediterranean, would be more inclined to make concessions, even if it meant the establishment of a Caliphate, to prevent another disaster.

This was more than terrorism; it was a strategic move in a larger game of global politics. Bouzidi was playing a high-stakes chess game, where nations were pawns, and the endgame was a reshaped world order. In his mind, the West, already weary from prolonged conflicts and political strife, might find the cost of opposing the establishment of a Caliphate too high in the face of another potential catastrophe.

The Israeli prime minister, fully cognizant of Bouzidi's dangerous game, was navigating a precarious path. The threat of a wider conflict, which could engulf not just the Middle East but also draw in global superpowers, loomed large. Bouzidi, from the shadows, was attempting to orchestrate a conflict of immense proportions, and countering his dark designs was a challenge that required not just military might but also strategic acumen and diplomatic finesse.

Meanwhile, Kasim Asfour, Ebi Bouzidi, and four other top-tier Al-Qaeda leaders were ensconced in their stronghold: a fortified stone complex nestled in Razmak, a mountain village in Pakistan's tribal areas. The Razmak plateau, with its harsh, imposing mountains, had been a crucible of insurgencies and rebellions throughout history. The village, steeped in a legacy of conflict, was home to two cemeteries of British soldiers—silent witnesses to the bloody encounters that had unfolded between the British forces and local insurgents over the years.

The meeting of these Al-Qaeda leaders was shrouded in secrecy, known only to a trusted few. Ingeniously, the satellite dishes used for their communications were camouflaged higher up on the plateau, while fibre optic cables, laid under the guise of water mains replacement, snaked their way to the town, ensuring a secure and undetected line to the outside world. In this remote, historical bastion of rebellion, plans that could alter the geopolitical landscape were being quietly woven, far from prying eyes and ears.

In a world where the lines between nations and their intelligence agencies blur, a secret relationship had formed between two unlikely allies: Pakistan's Inter-Services Intelligence (ISI) and Israel's Mossad. This alliance, fostered in secret corridors and undisclosed meetings, was an embodiment to the adage that in the world of espionage, there are no permanent friends or enemies, only permanent interests.

Their communication channel, established discreetly through officers stationed in their respective embassies in Washington, D.C., allowed for the exchange of critical intelligence and operational collaboration. Mossad, known for its relentless pursuit of Israel's security interests, had successfully positioned a Kidon unit within Pakistan. Kidon, a name that resonated with a sense of awe and fear across the intelligence community, represented Mossad's elite assassination squad, known for their precision and lethality.

The Kidon unit, often whispered about in the corridors of intelligence agencies worldwide, is the embodiment of Mossad's lethal arm. This elite assassination squad is shrouded in mystery, and its very name, Kidon, which means "bayonet" or "tip of the spear" in Hebrew, evokes a mix of awe and apprehension. Known for their exceptional and deft skills, the members of Kidon are specialists in targeted eliminations, trained to carry out their missions with chilling precision.

The unit's base of operations was a nondescript farm near Peshawar, strategically located hundreds of miles from Razmak but close enough for operational reach. In this secluded location, they had ingeniously concealed a Super Heron drone in a barn. The drone, a marvel of surveillance and offensive capabilities, was capable of carrying a significant payload, a 500-kg warhead, making it a formidable tool in targeted operations.

Over the past two years, the Kidon unit had utilized six of the eight warheads they had smuggled into the country, executing high-value targets within Afghanistan. Their presence in Pakistan, a closely guarded secret, was a bold move, emblematic of Mossad's commitment to neutralizing threats to Israel's security, wherever they may be.

When the unit received the coordinates from Fabienne Asper, relayed by the Israeli premier, they sprang into action. The meticulous preparation of the drone operation began with the uploading of the satellite link to control the drone. Each step was executed with clinical precision, the coordinates entered with the assurance that came from years of training and experience.

The meeting of Al-Qaeda's top brass unfolded in a cold stone room, deep within a secluded complex. The juxtaposition of the room's ancient architecture and the modern technology of three large screens created an anachronistic atmosphere, thick with tension.

On these screens, the consequences of their recent actions played out in real-time. CNN broadcasted live images of the USS Lincoln, shrouded in smoke and chaos. On BBC World News, analysts delved into the potential fallout from the unsuccessful attack on the nuclear barge, their words painting a grim picture of the luck. Al Jazeera showed a live feed of the Siberia, its Bridge a mass of metal and flesh.

Despite the late hour, the room buzzed with a tense energy. It was 3 am, but sleep was the last thing on the minds of those gathered. They were well aware that in just a few hours, they would each depart to different locations, continuing their operations in isolation.

The rich aroma of gahwa, the traditional Arabic coffee, filled the room, offering a momentary distraction from the weighty atmosphere. Asfour, the mastermind behind the operations, expected accolades from his peers. Yet the plaudits he anticipated did not materialize. Instead, there was a palpable sense of unease that permeated the air, the failure to blow up the nuclear barge had infuriated the Al-Qaeda members.

The compound was isolated, the nearest dwelling over a mile away, ensuring their planned celebrations, or lack thereof, remained confined within their walls. But Asfour, felt a nagging unease. Something was amiss, and it went beyond Aziz's deviation from the plan, which involved targeting three locations instead of focusing solely on the nuclear barge as instructed. Asfour's instincts, honed through years of living on the edge, were rarely wrong. This disquiet he felt was a signal, an alert to a deeper, perhaps more sinister, undercurrent that he couldn't yet discern.

In this moment, Asfour stood at the precipice of a revelation, his senses attuned to the subtle shifts in the dangerous world he navigated.

The tension in the room escalated dramatically. Asfour, suddenly found himself at the centre of a treacherous betrayal. His confusion over Aziz's actions gave way to a shocking revelation as Ebi Bouzidi, a key figure in the room, coldly unveiled his true intentions.

"I still don't understand why Aziz went off-plan and targeted the USS Lincoln, Israel, and the Suez Canal," Asfour voiced his perplexity, his words filled with a mix of frustration and suspicion.

Bouzidi's response was chillingly calm, betraying none of the tension that electrified the air. "Because I gave him orders to do so before he left," he said, his voice steady and devoid of emotion. The revelation struck Asfour like a physical blow, the realization of betrayal dawning upon him.

As Bouzidi continued, the room seemed to shrink, the walls closing in on Asfour. "Kasim, you have been key to this operation, and for that, we are grateful. For that and that alone, we will make your death quick. I would like to say painless, but a public beheading on the internet cannot be without pain, I am afraid."

Asfour's reaction was instinctive, born of years of survival in the most dangerous of circumstances. He stood up abruptly, his trained eyes scanning for any weapon, any means of escape. But he was not quick enough, or perhaps it was already too late. Strong arms on either side of him forced him back into his chair, an unspoken yet clear message that resistance was futile. Semi-automatics were trained on him, their barrels a stark reminder of his dire situation.

In a scenario that could have been lifted from a tense espionage thriller, Asfour found himself cornered, his carefully constructed world unravelling before his eyes.

"I don't understand, I have served you well," Asfour protested, his voice a mix of confusion and desperation. His plea echoed in the cold stone room, a stark contrast to the confidence he once exuded.

"You served your masters well. The Americans," Bouzidi retorted coldly. The evidence he presented next was damning—a series of photographs dropped onto the desk, each one a nail in the coffin of Asfour's cover story. The images depicted Asfour entering a villa in Miami, in the company of the vice president and the CIA's deputy chief. Another showed him in combat gear in Iraq, alongside the same CIA official. There was also a photo of him shadowing Vice President Treisman, known to have been a CIA base head in Shanghai.

"Photoshopped, to discredit me. These are not genuine," Asfour asserted, a hint of panic seeping into his voice. But his denial was weak, almost feeble against the mounting evidence.

Bouzidi, unmoved by Asfour's protest, explained the depth of their investigation. "Yes, we thought of that when we received the photographs, delivered by email two days ago to one of our agents in Pakistan. We have sources in Iraq and Shanghai who have verified these photographs. You should have grown a beard at least; that might have confused them, but it did not. Our digital and forensic experts have also verified the photographs as authentic."

Asfour's attempts to rise were swiftly quelled by a guard who used the butt of his semi-automatic to force him back down. Bouzidi's next revelation was a crushing blow. "We should have done this earlier, but we looked further back and discovered that Kasim Asfour died aged ten in Saudi Arabia. Despite your Arabic appearance, you are an American named Carl Bridge." Bouzidi then laid down several photographs of a young Carl Bridge in school and college.

The room was thick with tension as the truth of Asfour's identity was laid bare. His years of deception, his carefully crafted persona, all unravelled in a matter of moments. The guards, weapons at the ready, watched Asfour intently, aware that the man they had known as an ally was, in fact, an enemy—a spy planted in their midst. Bouzidi's revelation was not just a statement of fact; it was a sentence, the final verdict in the trial of Asfour's loyalty.

Asfour, cornered and desperate, scrambled for any sliver of hope. "You could trade me. I am valuable. Why waste it on a two-minute snuff movie?" he pleaded, his voice tinged with a mix of fear and bargaining.

Bouzidi's response was cold and calculated, reflecting the ruthless logic of their brutal world. "After today, do you think the CIA will acknowledge you ever existed? That two-minute movie will be played thousands and thousands of times. You're going to be an internet star," he said with a grim finality. His words were a stark reminder of the expendability of spies once their covers are blown.

As the tension in the room reached its peak, an unexpected interruption occurred. The screen that was showing CNN flickered momentarily, drawing the attention of everyone in the room. The familiar face of the newsreader vanished, replaced by the image of Fabienne.

Her sudden appearance on the screen was startling, a jarring intrusion into the grim scene unfolding in the stone room. Fabienne, known for her intelligence and resourcefulness, was now broadcasted live, her presence on the screen a mystery that momentarily shifted the focus away from Asfour's dire situation.

"Good day, well maybe not. I hoped you like the photographs. Asfour, Bridge, whatever you are calling yourself today," Fabienne began, her voice laced with a cold, calculated disdain. "You have killed many, including people in my organization, and you have tried to kill many more. This is MIDAS's revenge," she declared with an icy finality.

Asfour, looked dumbfounded, his composure crumbling under the weight of this unexpected confrontation. His eyes flickered with a mix of fear and disbelief, as he realized the extent of his predicament.

Bouzidi, ever the opportunist, seized the moment. "Thank you for your assistance, MIDAS woman," he said with a sardonic smile, relishing the turn of events that had his enemy, Asfour, at the brink of his downfall.

In the dimly lit stone room, Fabienne's image on the screen held everyone captive. Her words, delivered with a steely calmness, were a stark contrast to the chaos that had unfolded earlier. "You, Sir, are responsible for attempting to pollute a good portion of the planet," she began, her voice cutting through the tense air like a knife. "You think you have been controlling this attack, but I am afraid someone else has been pulling your strings. However, it would take too long to explain, and you don't have time."

The mention of someone else controlling the events added a new edge to the conversation The revelation that Bouzidi might not be the mastermind he believed himself to be was a psychological blow, one that visibly shook him.

"You also tried to bomb the Knesset, and I am afraid the Israeli prime minister does not take kindly to that," Fabienne continued. Her next words were a countdown, each number echoing ominously in the room. "In fact, in ten… nine… eight…" she intoned, with a cold precision that sent shivers down the spines of all present.

With every count, the sense of impending doom grew. The room was frozen in a moment of intense anticipation, as each participant braced themselves for the unknown, yet undoubtedly grave, consequences. The finality of Fabienne's countdown was palpable, a foreboding promise of retribution from powers beyond the room's stone walls.

Where fear is as tangible as the bullets that fly, Fabienne's face on the screen became the harbinger of imminent doom. "My face will be the last you all see," she declared, her voice cold, devoid of any emotion but filled with a deadly promise.

At her words, Bouzidi and his entourage, men who had navigated the dangerous waters of global terrorism, suddenly found themselves in uncharted territory. They jumped up, instinctively knowing that their time was up, their usual composure shattered by the stark realization of their vulnerability. Asfour, however, remained an island of calm in this storm. Seated amidst the pandemonium, he was the picture of resignation.

Unlike his counterparts who scrambled to flee, Asfour seemed to have accepted his fate. His manner was passive, almost eerily so, in stark contrast to the frenetic activity around him. He understood, perhaps better than anyone else in the room, the ruthlessness of the world in which they operated. In this realm, where life and death were decided by the pull of a trigger or the press of a button, there were moments when escape was not an option.

Fabienne's countdown reached its climax, her voice a chilling blend of menace and promise. "The Israelis and MIDAS have a present for you. Three… two… one…" The finality of her words hung in the air, heavy with impending catastrophe.

Then, in less than a heartbeat, the world as they knew it ended. There was no sound to warn them, no time to react. The 500 kg warhead, a silent angel of death, tore through the roof of the complex with devastating precision. In an instant, the stone room and the men within were engulfed in a maelstrom of fire and force, obliterating everything in its path.

The explosion that sealed the fate of Bouzidi and his cadre did more than just extinguish their lives; it obliterated the trace of their existence and the ideological legacy they sought to imprint on the world through their alignment with ISIS's radical mission. This moment of destruction not only negated their physical presence but also effaced any potential influence or recognition they might have garnered within the extremist landscape. Their hopes to be remembered as glorious leaders, to be heralded for their actions and to further the group's notorious objectives, were instantly nullified. The aftermath left no room for tales of valour or martyrdom amongst their ranks or in the wider narrative of global jihadism they aimed to influence.

In the broader context of their mission, which was to propagate the reach and impact of ISIS's ideology through acts of violence and terror, the loss was twofold. Not only did it represent a tactical defeat in the immediate sense, but it also underscored the ephemeral nature of their claimed victories. Any progress they believed they had made towards establishing a dominion of fear and extending the shadow of ISIS was, in an instant, reduced to ashes. The legacy they envisioned, marked by a trail of dominance and influence, was instead swallowed by the annals of history as a mere blip in the ongoing saga of humanity's struggle against the forces of extremism.

Furthermore, this erasure served as a grim reminder of the ultimate futility that underpins the extremist quest for legacy through violence. The aspirations and actions of Bouzidi and his followers, once perhaps seen by them as a path to glory and a step towards the realization of their caliphate dreams, were rendered mute. Their narrative, intended to inspire fear and loyalty, became instead a cautionary epitaph of the inevitable downfall that follows such a path of destruction.

In the aftermath, the world was left to reflect on the costs of radical extremism—not just in lives lost, but in the cycles of violence perpetuated by ideologies that seek to divide and destroy. The story of Bouzidi and his men, rather than elevating their cause, became a stark testament to the resilience of those who stand against such ideologies.

chapter twenty-six
The Fallout

International leaders grappled with the fallout of a rapidly escalating crisis. The Israeli prime minister, after a terse and unsatisfactory call with the Russian premier, was adamant in his demand for immediate action to remove the nuclear barge from the region. His tone was one of urgency, underscoring the potential catastrophic consequences if the barge was not dealt with promptly.

Simultaneously, the Syrian president, caught in a whirlwind of confusion and anger, was desperately trying to get through to his Russian counterpart. The unexplained attacks on Syrian soil had sent shockwaves through his administration, demanding explanations, and accountability. The urgency in his voice and the rapid succession of calls illustrated the high stakes and the delicate balance of international relations.

Meanwhile, aboard the USS Lincoln, a mournful duty was being carried out. An impromptu mortuary had been established for the sailors who had bravely given their lives in service, their sacrifice standing as a poignant reminder of the perils encountered by those in uniform. Among them lay the fallen members of the SAS Strike Team Three and the terrorists, bearing witness to the intensity of the conflict that had unfolded.

The tragedy extended to the Reef Explorer, where twenty-three hostages had tragically lost their lives amidst the attack. The grim count of casualties painted a harrowing picture of the cost of the thwarted attacks. Each of these developments contributed to a complex and volatile situation, where decisions had far-reaching implications. In the halls of power and on the decks of warships.

In the war room, the air was thick with tension, like a dense London fog, as President Shelby and Ryan Welt remained after clearing the room.

"I'm going to hang Treisman out to dry after this fiasco," President Shelby said.

"With respect, Mr. President, you can't. This will drag an ex-US president into the storm, not to mention the CIA. The political fallout for the country would be devastating. Let Treisman retire, get him out of the picture," Welt said.

President Shelby was interrupted when his secretary knocked and entered. "Fabienne Asper on the video link, do you want me to put her through?" she asked.

"Yes," Shelby replied, his voice carrying a mix of anticipation and gravity.

Fabienne's image appeared on the screen, composed and professional as ever.

"We would like to thank you personally, and all of Cutler's team, for a job well done," Shelby began, acknowledging the critical role they had played.

"Thank you, Mr. President. I need to discuss something with you, not over the screen but in person, along with Max Cutler," Fabienne responded, her tone indicating the seriousness of her request.

"That can be arranged," President Shelby agreed, sensing the importance of what Fabienne was proposing.

"Can I just confirm that Vice President Treisman and Deputy Chief Allen are secure?" Fabienne asked, her expression serious.

"I can confirm that," Shelby replied.

At that moment, Ryan Welt interrupted with troubling news. "Sir, I was informed ten minutes ago that Allen hung himself."

Shelby looked shocked, his face reflecting the shock. Fabienne raised her eyebrows in surprise and concern. "How the hell does that happen in a secure unit?" an incredulous President Shelby asked.

"We don't know all the details yet, but it seems he hung himself with his prison coveralls," Welt explained.

"Jesus," muttered the president, the weight of the news evident in his voice.

"Mr. President, we need the meeting sooner rather than later," Fabienne pressed on, understanding the urgency of the situation. "We need the meeting to be private, just the three of us."

"I should be there," Welt interjected, concerned about the implications of such a confidential gathering.

President Shelby, recognizing the magnitude of MIDAS's contribution and the sensitivity of the forthcoming discussion, made a decision. "For what MIDAS has done, I think a private meeting is the least I can do. Granted," he said, overriding Welt's objections.

"Thank you, Mr. President, may we request that the meeting be held outside the Oval Office? I don't think you want this conversation recorded."

President Treisman sat in deep thought, the weight of the unfolding events evident on his face. "Allen's dead. That does tie up a loose end, though the FBI believed he had more to reveal. He failed the polygraph on questions about the extent of involvement in this black operation," he mused, his voice tinged with a mix of frustration and resignation.

Welt chimed in, bringing a stark perspective to the table. "It seems everything points to Vice President Treisman and ex-president Nash. But you can't just lock up and interrogate a vice president. If this gets out, your leadership, Mr. President, could be jeopardized. It would be a political frenzy, eclipsing even the Nixon scandal. Imagine the global reaction if it's revealed that an American sitting vice president and ex-president orchestrated the attack on the Reef Explorer and planned to detonate a nuclear barge."

The president shook his head, still grappling with the enormity of the situation. "I still can't fathom the rationale. Yes, it would put the Russians on the back foot, possibly even drive them from the Mediterranean. But the potential environmental catastrophe, far worse than Chernobyl… it's incomprehensible."

Welt, ever the strategist, outlined a plan. "It failed, and we control the narrative now. We'll release selective footage to frame it as a terrorist attack on the barge, coupled with a miscommunication involving the USS Lincoln and Russian forces. There will be fallout, but it's manageable and won't jeopardize your Presidency."

The president then shifted focus to another critical aspect. "What about Conrad Ford? Have we secured the designs for the WCU?"

"FBI raided his headquarters here, and the Malaysian Special Branch raided the factory in Kuala Lumpur. They've seized all computers and designs, but so far, there's no evidence of WCU production or design. Ford is denying any knowledge of a WCU," Welt reported. "We can't arrest him either; his connections to Vice President Treisman and the former president make it complicated."

President Shelby visited Vice President Treisman at his luxurious residence. Ensuring complete privacy, Shelby made sure all Secret Service agents remained outside the room.

"Richard," President Shelby began with a stern tone, "let me be absolutely clear. Your career in politics is finished. You know, as well as I do, that if any connection between you and the Mediterranean crisis comes to light, not only will my Presidency be jeopardized, but you will face imprisonment. And the former president could very well be the first in history to face impeachment." Treisman attempted to interject, but Shelby cut him off. "Shut up and sit down, Richard. Think about the damage your actions have caused to the United States' standing in the world. You have two options, and only one offers you a semblance of a normal life."

Shelby laid out the plan. "For now, we issue a press statement saying you are unwell. Once this crisis settles down in a month or so, you will announce your retirement and fade away from the public eye."

Treisman responded defiantly, "Not going to happen."

Shelby, unfazed, continued, using Deputy Chief Allen's death as leverage. "Allen is dead, apparently by suicide, but we both know that's not the case. I'm not above issuing such orders, Richard."

"If someone must fall on their sword, so be it," Treisman conceded, with a hint of resignation. "But I want my Secret Service detail to remain post-retirement."

Shelby was firm in his response. "The American people won't fund your security after what you've done, Richard. Not under my administration. You have enough wealth; hire private security."

"Better hire the best," Treisman shot back. "Max Cutler is going to come for me, I have no doubt about that."

****

President Shelby's day began with a diplomatic lunch with the American ambassador, a gesture of cordiality and formal relationship maintenance. After the lunch, he was swiftly escorted in a bulletproof Mercedes SUV to the Carl Jung Medical Centre, a private healthcare facility nestled on the Rue des Alpes, Switzerland.

Meanwhile, at the clinic, Cutler, Colton, Stahmer, Ghislaine, and Shultz underwent their routine post-mission medical check-up. The team was now in the process of recuperating and debriefing after their intense mission.

The first to welcome Tuck, who had been flown in by the American military, was Fabienne. The medical staff at the USS Lincoln were reluctant to let him go so early, but their Geneva counterparts were soon to understand why—Tuck was not an easy patient. Between his constant cussing and cursing, the nurses found their hands full. After further examinations in Geneva, Tuck was scheduled for a second surgery to adjust some screws in his injury, with a projected recovery time of at least three months.

Tuck, restless and eager for news, requested Fabienne to arrange a secure line to Bull. "Hi Bull, guess you know who it is and why I'm calling?" he began.

"Tuck, heard you got yourself messed up?" Bull's voice came through, laced with concern and a tinge of admiration.

"Just a bit. I'll be back in action in a few months," Tuck reassured him.

Bull responded with a hint of vengeance in his tone, "Good, we have some hunting to do."

Tuck, seeking details, enquired about the Everglades incident and expressed his condolences for the loss of Bull's brother-in-law, the sheriff. Bull's reply was laden with raw emotion and a sense of justice served. He had taken down the perpetrators with the help of Cortez, a trusted ally.

"I'll handle Ford when I'm back on my feet," Tuck declared, his voice carrying a promise of retribution.

"I want in on that action, Tuck. My sister's been in tears since the sheriff was killed," Bull said firmly, his voice hardening with the resolve of a man who had lost too much.

"Wouldn't have it any other way," Tuck replied.

In the private hospital room, a sense of camaraderie filled the air as Cheryl, Cutler, Fabienne, Colton, Stahmer, Ghislaine, Cortez, Shultz and the recovering Basmati gathered around Tuck's bed. The mood was lightened by Tuck's jovial spirit despite his injury. As they exchanged stories and updates, the president made his entrance, greeting each member with a handshake before closing the door, leaving his security detail outside.

Shelby's words of appreciation were heartfelt. "I would like to express gratitude to all of you. Your actions have not gone unnoticed, and we owe you a great deal." However, Shelby's expression turned more serious as he requested a private word with Cutler and Fabienne.

Tuck, never one to miss a beat, humorously demanded his due recognition. "Where the fuck is my purple heart for this?" he quipped. Cheryl chided him for his language, but Shelby waved it off with a smile, acknowledging the informal nature of their meeting. He, however, clarified that there would be no official recognition due to the classified nature of their operation.

Cutler, Fabienne and Shelby then excused themselves to a separate room reserved for relatives. The secret service y detail maintained a vigilant watch outside, ensuring their conversation remained private.

"You requested an urgent meeting with me. You have something to tell me, no doubt. I could tell from Fabienne's voice the other day," Shelby said.

Culer turned to Fabienne. "This is your baby. You tell him."

"Tell me what, Fabienne?" the president asked.

Fabienne opened her computer, an image of a ship filled the screen. She leaned forward, her gaze fixed on President Shelby as she began to describe the vessel. "Mr. President, let me introduce you to the Hǎi Lóng Tiān Yǎn, or as we call it in the field, the Sea Dragon Eye. It's not just a ship; it's a game changer."

Her voice was calm, but there was an underlying tone of urgency. "Imagine a vessel around 180 meters long, sleek and painted deep ocean blue. It blends into the sea, sir, like a shadow. But it's what's inside that really counts."

She paused, ensuring she had the president's full attention. "This ship is a paradox, Mr. President. It's designed for nuclear spill containment, equipped with state-of-the-art robotics for handling radioactive material, but that's just the cover. The real purpose is intelligence gathering. Its supercomputers and arrays of antennas are hidden under a retractable dome – they can intercept and process vast amounts of data, including military intelligence from our bases and ships."

President Shelby leaned in, intrigued. "Go on," he urged.

"The Hǎi Lóng Tiān Yǎn, sir, is practically invisible. Not just visually, but electronically too. Its stealth technology masks its electronic footprint, making it a ghost on the radar. And it's not just about collecting data; it can tap into underwater cables, breach communication networks – you name it."

Fabienne noticed the president's frown deepening. "And defensively," she continued, "it's no sitting duck. The ship can defend itself with a range of anti-aircraft and missile systems. Plus, it's nuclear-electric hybrid propulsion means it can remain at sea for months, silently."

She paused, letting the information sink in. "In essence, Mr. President, we're looking at a vessel that's a guardian of the environment on the surface and a predator of information beneath. It's a significant strategic asset… or threat, depending on its use."

In the tense atmosphere of the room, President Shelby leaned back, a thoughtful expression on his face. "Two questions, Fabienne. First, how did you come to know about this ship? And second, do you believe it's connected to the incident with the nuclear barge at Tartus?"

Fabienne nodded. "Yes, Mr. President, I believe there's a connection. Back when I worked for GCHQ, we debriefed a

Chinese defector. One of the subjects that came up was the Hǎi Lóng Tiān Yǎn. At that time, it was just in the planning stages. It's a leap ahead of anything we've seen in the West."

Cutler, who had been listening intently, added his insights. "Imagine, Mr. President, a ship equipped to clean up nuclear waste in the Mediterranean, escorted by Chinese warships. It would be a beacon of hope for the countries around the Mediterranean, desperate for help. This would give China an unprecedented leverage in the region, along with their sophisticated data-gathering capabilities."

Fabienne continued, "They could even strike a deal with Syria. If Russia were expelled from Tartus following a nuclear disaster, China could easily step in to establish a port. Overnight, it wouldn't be Russia with a major base in the region, but China."

Shelby, visibly intrigued, leaned forward. "But how does this tie back to the attack in the Mediterranean?"

Fabienne explained, "After connecting the dots, which I will detail shortly, the trail led back to China. I started monitoring their naval movements and discovered satellite images of a fleet off Taiwan. Among them was a ship I hadn't seen before, but I recognized it from the defector's description—the Hǎi Lóng Tiān Yǎn. It had been launched about a month earlier and was undergoing sea trials."

"And the connection?" Shelby pressed.

"Two weeks before the attack, it changed course, sailing through the Taiwan Strait into the South China Sea, and then through the Malacca Strait into the Arabian Sea, heading for the Red Sea. It was on a direct course for Tartus, only days away when the attack failed. After the failure, it turned back towards China," Fabienne concluded, allowing the gravity of her statement to sink in.

Shelby, with a furrowed brow, questioned, "Is it too far-fetched to think the ex-president knew about this, if China's involved?"

Cutler responded, his voice steady, "Unlikely. He was vehemently anti-Russian, probably duped by a scheme that played to his ego."

Shelby pondered, "So you are saying Treisman could be the key player?"

Fabienne brought up an old photo on her tablet, showing a much younger Treisman in a compromising position with a young Chinese man. "This was back when he was stationed in Shanghai. We suspect he fell for a classic honey trap. His career would've been ruined had this come out."

Cutler chimed in, "Treisman's been sloppy. He stored encrypted files of his past indiscretions on his personal computer, he has a whole file with boys' photos on, which we've managed to hack."

Shelby leaned in, studying the photo. "But this isn't concrete evidence. What else?"

Fabienne elaborated, "We traced his financial ascent. No family wealth, but he set up as a banker after leaving government service. He had a large influx of massive during his early business career, mostly from China."

Cutler added, "It's a complex web of finance and influence. Treisman's rise was too meteoric to be clean."

"He was a financier, a banker for several years after he left government service," Shelby said.

"I've gone back twenty years, most of his dealings were with China and Hong Kong, and you can't trace the money over there. In short, he made millions, with most of it coming out of China. China ensured he had the funds to launch his political career."

"What about Allen?" Shelby asked.

"Allen was in over his head financially in Shanghai, where he likely fell into a recruitment trap," Fabienne began, her voice steady but laden with the weight of her findings.

Shelby leaned forward, intrigued. "So if Treisman didn't bring Allen into the fold, who did?"

On cue, Fabienne displayed two revealing photographs on the screen. The first, a dated image showing a younger Treisman in Beijing in the 1980s, with a man she identified as the recruiter. "Beijing wasn't as developed back then, which helps us pinpoint the timeframe of this photo," she explained.

Fabienne's question hung in the air, charged with implication. President Shelby, usually unshakeable, was visibly unsettled by the revelation.

"What time did we speak by video the other day?"

"I don't know, 11 am?" Shelby said.

"It was 11.32 am precisely. Allen's death was reported at 11.35 am by Welt, I've been into the FBI records, he was found at 11.55 am, how could Welt report him before he had been found?" Fabienne asked.

"Shelby absorbed Fabienne's question, a mix of disbelief and concern etched on his face. "That's… that's impossible," he stammered, the weight of the implications dawning on him. "Welt reporting Allen's death before it was officially discovered. That suggests he knew… He was involved."

Fabienne's expression remained grave, her tone firm. "Exactly, Mr. President. It suggests premeditation, that Allen's death was more than just a suicide. It points to a deeper, darker manipulation within your administration.

Fabienne nodded, her eyes fixed on the president. "It's more than just a discrepancy in time. It suggests that Allen's death wasn't a suicide as reported, but rather a calculated move to silence him permanently."

Shelby's gaze hardened. The implications were clear and deeply troubling. "Welt, someone I've entrusted with the highest level of national security, might be orchestrating a cover-up? If you are right this goes beyond conjecture. It's a potential breach right at the heart of my administration. But I am still not convinced."

He returned back to Cutler and Fabienne.

"Ok, you've given me a lot to think about. I don't want a word of this going beyond this room," Shelby said, his voice steady but carrying an undercurrent of unease.

Cutler nodded, understanding the gravity of the situation. "You can't afford to let this come out, can you, Mr. President?"

The Secret Service agent walked in and whispered in the president's ear. Shelby's expression turned grave.

"Welt took a flight to Hong Kong last night, soon after you left," Cutler stated matter-of-factly.

Shelby's frustration was palpable. "He'll have a surprise when he lands. I've drained his accounts and set up a welfare fund for all those killed or injured, including American and Russian military. He's in the wind."

Shelby interjected, "Why did you let him go?"

Cutler responded, "Because you would have covered it up. You couldn't afford to have your chief of staff exposed. That's why Fabienne insisted on a private meeting, knowing Welt would know his cover was blown. The Chinese aren't about to replace the money for a blown asset. Try living in Hong Kong on a small Chinese pension."

"So what is it you want, Cutler? I can feel it in the air," Shelby enquired, his tone indicating he already knew the answer.

"I want Treisman, and I want Conrad Ford," he declared, his voice a low growl of determination. "They've crossed a line—maiming, killing. They attacked us in the Everglades, almost killed Tuck's fiancée, and took out the Sheriff. I'm not here to make threats; you've seen what Fabienne can do. I want both men, Mr. President. No arguments."

President Shelby, his face a mask of contemplation, nodded slowly. "So this is why you insisted on a private meeting, away from the prying ears of the White House," he mused, understanding the gravity of Cutler's request.

"Exactly," Cutler affirmed, his gaze unwavering.

The president leaned forward; the weight of his decision palpable in the air. "Vice President Treisman is retiring due to ill health soon. His Secret Service detail will be gone, but he'll have private security. Make it look like an accident, Cutler. The same goes for Ford. And I assure you, there will be no investigations. But the ex-president is off-limits."

"Cutler's expression didn't change. "We have no interest in him. He's just a pawn, a fool led by Welt and Treisman."

Cutler, his expression unchanging, watched the president closely as Fabienne revealed the fate of Carl Bridge, or Asfour as he was known. The video on the screen showed a remote stone house in Pakistan being obliterated, leaving nothing but dust and debris. "Courtesy of the Israelis," Fabienne stated matter-of-factly, her tone betraying no emotion.

President Shelby, his face reflecting the stark reality of the situation, turned to Cutler. "MIDAS seems to have its fingers in many pies, Cutler. You have connections and capabilities that are… impressive," he said, his voice trailing off slightly.

"I hope we never find ourselves on opposite sides in the future," Shelby added, a hint of warning underlying his words. It was a subtle acknowledgment of the power and reach that Cutler and his team wielded—a power that even the president of the United States respected and, perhaps, feared.

Cutler's response was calm and assured, "Mr. President, let's hope it stays that way. MIDAS operates with a clear code. We're here to protect and serve, in our own way. Our paths align more often than not."

In the muted light of the shipyard's reception building in Birkenhead, the atmosphere was a blend of anticipation and solemnity as President Shelby, accompanied by his security detail and eighteen UK police officers and special branch, made his way to a particular building. This place, at the far end of the yard, was home to the privately-owned company responsible for the development of the Spectre, a vessel that had garnered significant attention from the US Navy.

Upon arrival, the managing director of the company greeted the presidential entourage. With the efficiency and precision typical of the Secret Service, Shelby's detail swiftly communicated the president's intention to meet exclusively with two of the company's directors, Jones and Evans.

The large boardroom, offering a magnificent view of Liverpool's skyline across the River Mersey, seemed almost regal with the iconic Liver Buildings and the impressive cathedrals dotting the horizon. The ambiance of the room shifted as Evans and Jones stood to greet President Shelby, their faces a mix of curiosity and respect. The other directors, present in the room, were discreetly ushered out by the managing director, leaving the president with his chosen audience.

Jones, with an air of concern, was the first to break the silence. "Do you know how the guy from MIDAS who hit the rail and fell into the sea is doing?" he enquired.

Shelby, with a hint of a smile, replied, "Saw him earlier today, swearing like a trooper." His response brought a sense of relief, evident in Jones's expression.

Before delving into business matters, Shelby's secretary presented a crucial prerequisite. "Before we discuss business, I need you both to sign the American Official Secrets Declaration," she stated firmly.

Evans, cutting straight to the point, interjected, "Do we get the contract to develop and produce more Spectres for the US Navy if we sign?"

President Shelby, placing a leather-bound file on the table, affirmed, "Yes, this contract is dependent upon it."

The revelation prompted Evans to whistle in astonishment, while Jones, gazing directly at Welt, remarked, "Four Spectres, that's 300 million dollars. Where do we sign?"

Shelby elaborated, "Three for the Navy and one for the Seals in the next financial year. If you deliver on time, there will be more orders." He then added with a note of genuine respect, "I might add you deserve it. From what I've been told, you are both very brave men."

The room was filled with a sense of accomplishment and pride. The signing of this declaration was not just a formality but a recognition of their bravery and the pivotal role their creation, the Spectre, had played. It was a momentous occasion, marking a significant milestone in the collaboration between a private company and the US Navy, fostered under extraordinary circumstances.

chapter twenty-seven
Retribution

In the rugged, unforgiving terrain of the Rocky Mountains, just outside Breckenridge, Colorado, Conrad Ford, the former magnate of Armitech, found himself in an enforced retirement. The American government had kept its side of the bargain by not prosecuting him for his dirty dealings, but the cost to Ford was more than financial. His once-powerful company, the brain behind the controversial WCU, was sold off for a fraction of its worth, leaving him isolated and powerless, a drastic fall from his days of influence and backdoor political games.

The sprawling ranch, encompassing a vast 30,000 acres, was Ford's retreat from the world he could no longer control. His wife, Emilia, trapped in a haze of alcohol and sedatives, was a constant reminder of the personal tragedies that had accompanied their precipitous decline. Haunted by the loss of their son and the tarnished legacy they bore, the couple lived in a sorry echo of their former lives.

Ford, ever the restless soul, found retirement an ill-fitting suit. His plans for the ranch, including converting thousands of acres into cropland and managing a herd of 200 Quarter Horses, did little to quell his restlessness or temper. Security details, essential given the swirling rumours of his involvement in military fatalities, were a revolving door due to his irascibility. His tarnished reputation made hiring ex-Special Forces personnel impossible, leaving him with a ragtag team of local cowboys for security.

Unbeknownst to Ford, the net was closing in. Fabienne, with her unparalleled skills in intelligence gathering, had already sent satellite images of the ranch to Tuck and Bull. These images were the genesis of a meticulously crafted plan, one born from a thirst for justice and a need to balance the scales.

Tuck, pushing his recovery with a determination born of a deep-seated need for retribution, was gearing up for the operation. His training was intense, running eleven miles daily and honing his skills in the swamps of the Everglades. His resolve was mirrored by Bull, whose reservation had become the staging ground for their meticulous planning.

The sprawling size of Ford's ranch presented a challenge in itself. Its sheer scale made it a fortress of sorts, with security concentrated around the main house and a network of CCTV cameras keeping watch. However, for Tuck and Bull, this was not an insurmountable obstacle. They pored over the satellite images, plotting a route that would bypass cameras.

In the unforgiving wilds surrounding Conrad Ford's sprawling ranch, Tuck and Bull had embarked on a mission that was as much about strategy as it was about stealth. Their preparation was meticulous, their approach methodical.

Tuck, despite his initial jest about Bull's choice of weaponry, was genuinely impressed by the Bowtech Diamond Deploy that Bull had brought. It was a far cry from traditional weaponry, its modern engineering a symbol of precision and power. The compound bow, complete with cam wheels and a scope, was a perfect blend of traditional skill and modern technology.

Bull, ever the craftsman, had complemented his high-tech bow with a more primitive yet no less deadly arrow. He had fashioned it from wood sourced from the Everglades, but the crowning touch was the shark tooth he had sharpened into a lethal point. The tooth, filed to a blunted tip, was a nod to his heritage, a blend of the old and the new.

Their sniper hides, meticulously constructed and camouflaged with local foliage, were virtually undetectable. They had thought of everything—from clingfilm for self-sanitation to self-heating food packs and water for sustenance. Bluetooth earphones were a small luxury, providing a distraction from the long hours of vigilance.

The vantage point they had chosen was strategic, offering an expansive view of Ford's ranch—the house, the paddocks, the croplands, and the river winding through the southern crags. Armed with powerful binoculars, they settled in for a long haul, their eyes never straying far from their target.

Ford's routine was predictable, almost to a fault. Each morning, like clockwork, he would mount his American paint horse and ride out across the ranch, his movements shadowed at a distance by a security guard in a rugged Chevrolet Silverado. Tuck and Bull observed as Ford followed the same route each day, riding east past the old rodeo corral, then south to the riverbank, before following the river for three miles.

It was during these morning rides that Tuck and Bull gathered the intelligence they needed, mapping out Ford's habits and routines. They watched and waited, the two men lying in wait in their hides, their eyes and ears attuned to every move Ford made.

The plan they were crafting was one of patience and precision. They knew the importance of understanding their target, of getting into his rhythm and routine. It was a waiting game, a game of cat and mouse, and they were more than ready to play.

Tuck and Bull identified a raised bank area out of view from the driver in the Chevrolet, who parallel tracked Ford down the riverbank. Tuck noted the time that Ford was out of sight; the average was four minutes. It was the only location and time that gave them a window to launch an attack. The area was down by a small creek, nestled between two small hills. The rocks were ragged and sharp and would rip the SUV tyres to shreds. Conrad Ford would follow a narrow earthen track, barely wide enough for his horse to traverse.

Tuck and Bull left their hides at 4 am, smelling like the damp earth that had been home. There was one camera in the area; they took a two-mile detour to remain outside the cameras range. By the time they reached the creek bed, dawn was an hour away. Tuck climbed up behind an outcrop of rock, entirely hidden by the creek bed. Bull went higher up, behind a substantial boulder that had been dislodged by an avalanche a decade before.

Before selling the ranch to Conrad Ford, the elderly owners who had lived on it for 60 years had done their best to maintain it. Age and mobility had worked against them, and parts of the ranch were poorly maintained, scrub brush and a tangle of weeds had to be circumnavigated as Conrad Ford headed down towards the creek. Ford enjoyed the coolness of the dawn; it would be scorching by midday and uncomfortable to ride. Conrad Ford passed within twenty feet of Bull, oblivious to the danger. The spotted American paint horse sauntered past the rock, turning its head a fraction, its nostrils flaring, sensing a presence. Ford scolded the horse and dug his heels into the side of the animal and continued down to the creek.

In the deep quiet of the early morning, Conrad Ford's routine unfolded predictably, unaware that he was being observed. He stopped by the creek, allowing his horse to drink. Unhurried, he took out his breakfast—biscuits and gravy—from his saddle sack, savouring the first bite in solitude. His guard, parked a distance away in the Chevrolet Silverado, remained a passive observer, trusting in the apparent safety of the vast ranch.

This routine was precisely what Bull and Tuck had been waiting for. Hidden in their carefully crafted hide, they counted down the minutes, knowing the guard's patience would only last so long. Bull stood up, his stature imposing against the backdrop of dense foliage. His movements were calculated and deliberate as he took the arrow from its sheath and loaded his Bowtech Diamond Deploy.

Bull's eyes narrowed in focus, a silent intensity radiating from him as he pulled back the drawstring to its maximum tension. In that moment, he murmured a phrase coined by Muhammad Ali, a tribute to the precision and deadliness of his upcoming action. "Float like a butterfly, sting like a bee." The words were a quiet declaration of his intent, a blend of grace and lethal force.

With a steady hand, Bull aimed the arrow with the blunted shark's tooth precisely at the base of Ford's skull. In a fluid motion, he released the arrow, watching as it sliced through the air with unerring accuracy. The impact was sudden and brutal; the blunted tooth fractured the occipitocervical junction. Ford's body crumpled, falling off his horse, rendered unconscious in an instant.

Tuck, who had been waiting for Bull's signal, burst out of his hide. His movements were swift and efficient as he reached Ford's fallen body. He quickly retrieved the arrow and checked Ford's condition, ensuring their mission's success without crossing the line they had promised not to cross. They weren't there to kill Conrad Ford, but to deliver a message, a reckoning for his actions.

In the shadowy dawn, the aftermath of their precise strike against Conrad Ford was stark and grim. Tuck, his hands steady and his movements methodical, manoeuvred Ford's limp body, positioning it to mimic a fall from the horse. He ensured every detail was just right, his expression hard and unyielding. This was more than a mission; it was personal retribution.

"It's a clean break, this motherfucker won't be able to ever take a piss again by himself," Tuck spat, his voice laced with disdain as he arranged Ford's body. "A clear spinal break. He's going to spend the rest of his miserable life depending on others for every little thing. Let's see how he likes being utterly helpless." His hands worked with a mix of precision and anger, ensuring Ford's position looked natural, like a tragic accident.

Tuck then carefully positioned a large stone under Ford's neck, adding to the illusion of a severe fall. It was a deliberate touch, one that would ensure no questions about the nature of the incident. This was their art—leaving a scene that told the story they wanted it to tell.

Bull, standing a few feet away, watched Tuck's actions with a mixture of satisfaction and reflection. His voice, when he spoke, was low but filled with intense emotion. "That's for my sister's husband," he murmured, the words tinged with both sorrow and satisfaction. In this desolate landscape, they had delivered their own form of justice, far removed from courts and laws.

Bull's gaze lingered on Ford's motionless form. This was more than revenge; it was a statement. They had infiltrated the fortress-like ranch, bypassed high-tech security, and struck down one of the former most powerful men in the defence industry. They had turned Ford from a predator to prey, leaving him a broken man in the dust of his own empire.

As the security guard finally became suspicious and began his approach, Bull and Tuck disappeared into the landscape. They were like ghosts, leaving no trace of their presence. Conrad Ford, once a man of power and influence, lay unconscious on the ground, his world forever altered by the actions of two men driven by a quest for justice.

Later that afternoon, Shelby's new chief of staff informed the president, "Just got news through that Conrad Ford has been hurt in a horse-riding accident. Spinal cord injuries. The doctor says he will be paralysed from the neck down. He can't remember how he fell."

President Shelby's voice carried a mix of resignation and a hard-earned wisdom as he reflected on the situation. "Well, I suppose if you dance with the devil, you are bound to get somewhat burnt," he said, his tone tinged with satisfaction.

* * * *

In the faint twilight, as the sun dipped below the horizon, casting a soft, reflective glow over the waters, Cutler and Colton remained vigilant aboard their discreetly moored yacht. They were just off the Rhode Island coast, their attention fixed on the larger, more luxurious yacht that bobbed gently in the distance. This vessel, lavish and imposing, belonged to the ex-Vice President Treisman, who was enjoying his customary birthday week vacation.

As the former vice president, Richard Treisman, embraced his annual birthday tradition with a week-long sojourn on his luxurious yacht, the circumstances surrounding him had undergone a seismic shift. Gone were the days of the protective cocoon provided by the Secret Service, now replaced by a makeshift security apparatus cobbled together from the private sector. Cutler and Colton had meticulously adhered to their agreement of silence about the Mediterranean operation. Yet they had strategically scattered breadcrumbs of information, subtly implicating Treisman in the deaths of Special Forces personnel. This information warfare had effectively turned Treisman into a pariah among ex-special ops circles.

Treisman's fall from grace within the military community had left him with limited options for his personal security. Unlike Conrad Ford, who had managed to hire cowboys for his security, Treisman found himself relying on personnel whose experience was more aligned with managing unruly patrons in bars than protecting a high-profile political figure. This shift in Treisman's security detail provided Cutler and Colton with a unique window of opportunity. They observed the yacht and its new guards with a seasoned eye, identifying weaknesses and potential vulnerabilities.

The change in Treisman's circumstances was not just a matter of security personnel. His once-untouchable status had eroded, leaving him vulnerable to the very forces he had once commanded.

This vulnerability was not lost on Cutler and Colton, who saw in Treisman's diminished stature an opportunity to level a playing field that had been skewed for far too long.

As the yacht bobbed gently on the waves, its occupants oblivious to the watchful eyes observing them from a distance, the stage was set for a reckoning. The pieces were moving, the players were in place. For Treisman, the isolation of his yacht had become a double-edged sword—a sanctuary turned into a potential trap, all under the watchful gaze of those who sought to settle old scores.

Colton, stationed on the upper deck of their covert vessel, kept a vigilant watch. His infra-red scope, detached from its usual place on his rifle, served as his eyes, scanning the yacht's crew and security. He noted the captain's presence on the bridge, shadowed by a crew member. The atmosphere was tense, the stakes high. Cutler, Colton, and Shultz had agreed—the mission would be aborted if it meant endangering innocent lives. Their quarrel was solely with Treisman.

The yacht's deck was quiet, save for the gentle lapping of the waves against its hull. Treisman's personal assistant, Maria Sysco, was busy taking notes. Cutler knew the operation hinged on her movements—they needed her out of the way.

Shultz, meanwhile, was ready with the fireworks they had acquired from a local store. His role was crucial: to orchestrate a grand display from the rocky outcrop south of Treisman's yacht. The chosen spot was perfect for distracting Maria Sysco, the crew and security, offering them a front-row seat to the spectacle. Shultz waited patiently for the signal—three distinct clicks in his headset—the cue to commence the fireworks.

Cutler's operation was a masterclass in precision and ruthlessness. The darkness of the ocean depths was his ally as he stealthily approached the yacht, hidden beneath the water's surface. His rebreather, a crucial piece of equipment, ensured his presence remained a secret, eliminating the telltale trail of bubbles that could betray his position.

Colton, vigilant from their strategically positioned yacht, initiated the diversion. A series of clicks on the transmitter and the night sky was suddenly ablaze with fireworks. The display was mesmerizing, drawing the attention of the yacht's crew and security away from the rear deck where Treisman was enjoying his solitary ritual. It was the moment Cutler had been waiting for.

The yacht, a symbol of power and luxury, floated unsuspectingly above him. Cutler's target, former Vice President Treisman, was mere feet away, yet entirely oblivious to the impending danger. As the country music blared, masking his movements, Cutler emerged from the water in silence, ascending onto the yacht's diving platform with the grace and silence of a predator.

Springing into action, Cutler lunged at Treisman from behind. The surprise was total, the execution flawless. His right arm locked around Treisman's neck in a vice-like grip, while his left hand stifled any potential outcry. The neoprene suit provided Cutler some insulation against the burn of Treisman's cigar, which the former vice president desperately pressed against his assailant in a futile attempt to fight back.

The music and fireworks continued to provide a sonic backdrop to the deadly dance unfolding on the yacht. Cutler's whispered words in Treisman's ear were a mix of cold retribution and finality. Treisman's struggle was brief and futile against the overwhelming force of Cutler's trained physique.

With the timing of an expert, Cutler waited for the crescendo of another rocket burst before dragging Treisman into the water with him. The sudden submersion was a shock to Treisman, but while Cutler was in his element, Treisman was gripped by panic. The struggle was intense but brief. Cutler, his training and determination evident, maintained his hold as they descended into the depths.

Forty feet down, where the water was a cold, unyielding shroud, Treisman's struggles ceased. His eyes, once filled with a mix of defiance and disbelief, now mirrored only the emptiness of defeat. In a silent, hauntingly poignant moment, the life faded from them, leaving a void that the ocean depths would keep.

Methodically, Cutler replaced his mouthpiece, drawing a much-needed breath of air. He then removed it again, placing his lips close to Treisman's, giving one deliberate breath. It was a calculated move, designed to ensure Treisman's body had buoyancy and would rise to the surface, adding a semblance of natural demise to the orchestrated encounter.

Cutler, with a practised ease, made his way back to the yacht. The surface world remained oblivious to the drama that had just concluded beneath the waves. Colton, ever vigilant, kept watch through his scope, narrating the futile rescue attempts aboard the yacht.

"They've recovered him. CPR… defibrillator… but it's no use," Colton reported, his voice betraying no emotion.

"He's gone. I made sure of it," Cutler replied, his tone even, yet carrying the weight of finality.

"Yeah, they've stopped trying. He's not coming back," Colton confirmed, as the yacht's crew ceased their efforts.

In those final moments, as Cutler absorbed the reality of what he had done, a sense of grim satisfaction settled over him. It was a feeling not of joy, but of a mission accomplished, a retribution exacted. The night sky, with its stars obscured by the light of the yacht, bore silent witness to the events.

Justice, in Cutler's world, had been meted out with a calculated precision, leaving no trace, no clue, no sound—just the silent depths and the secrets they would forever hold.

Cutler and his team found themselves once again in the comforting embrace of Cheryl's dining room, the air filled with the aroma of a robust lunch spread before them. It was a stark contrast to the solemnity broadcast on television, where Treisman was being honoured with a state funeral, a spectacle of mourning attended by President Shelby, surrounded by a cadre of former presidents, all except for Nash. The commentator's voice, sombre and respectful, briefly mentioned Nash's absence due to a recent stroke.

"Stroke my arse," Colton muttered under his breath, scepticism lacing his tone.

Cutler nodded in agreement, his eyes still on the screen. "Shelby's just playing it safe. Can't have Nash, a loose cannon with eyes on the global stage, stealing the spotlight. Especially not one with a penchant for danger."

Tuck, leaning back with a plate of pot roast, grimaced at the eulogies praising Treisman. "If Shelby lays it on any thicker, I swear I'm going to redecorate this table with my lunch."

"It's tempting to call this just another day at the office," Cutler mused, his voice tinged with a rare hint of contemplation. "But let's be honest, this one hit too close for comfort."

"And yet, here we are, no fucking medals, no fanfare," Tuck added, his gaze sweeping over the team, a wry smile touching his lips.

Days like these were scarce—a flurry of events tumbling one after the other, each pivotal and tumultuous. As they lingered in the early evening glow, on a bright Cypriot morning, Guano secured his citizenship, neatly slotting the last piece into their complex scheme. Meanwhile, Asfour the gravity of his situation.

In a move marked by chilling precision, Fabienne had handed over undeniable proof of Asfour's duplicity to the Al Qaeda leaders—evidence of his double life as an American agent. It was a betrayal met with stony silence rather than ceremony. Now exposed and forsaken, he found himself at the harsh mercy of the Afghan wilderness, staked out under the relentless sun. Ants began to crowd over his still-breathing form—a stark depiction of the grim fate reserved for traitors.